I0612386

THE HALLOWED

JON DOBBIN

THE HALLOWED

JON DOBBIN

ENGEN
BOOKS

Published in Canada by Engen Books, Chapel Arm, NL.

Library and Archives Canada Cataloguing in Publication information is available on the publisher's website.

Copyright © 2025 Jon Dobbin

Originally published as *The Ghosts of Crimson Hollow* (2022), *The Devil's Work* (2022), and *The Stone of the Under God* (2022).

NO PART OF THIS BOOK MAY BE REPRODUCED OR TRANSMITTED IN ANY FORM OR BY ANY MEANS, ELECTRONIC OR MECHANICAL, INCLUDING PHOTOCOPYING AND RECORDING, OR BY ANY INFORMATION STORAGE OR RETRIEVAL SYSTEM WITHOUT WRITTEN PERMISSION FROM THE AUTHOR, EXCEPT FOR BRIEF PASSAGES QUOTED IN A REVIEW.

This book is a work of fiction. Names, characters, places and incidents are products of the author's imagination or are used fictitiously. Any resemblance to actual events or locales or persons living or dead is entirely coincidental.

Distributed by:
Engen Books
www.engenbooks.com
submissions@engenbooks.com

First mass market paperback printing: June 2025

Cover Image: Matthew LeDrew

CONTENTS

CONTENTS

THE GHOSTS OF CRIMSON HOLLOW

For Hayward and Willie Jim.
Thank you. Rest Easy.

CHAPTER ONE

I

The shot echoed across the plain, and Jim Colton watched his prey waver and die. A puff of dust rose around the deer, and a strangled bleat cracked the air. Colton parked his wide-brimmed hat on top of his forehead and nodded to himself.

"Dinner is served," he said and slung his rifle over his shoulder beside his aged, leather rucksack and moved to his kill. Colton's boots scrabbled over the rocky ground, the welcome sound of isolation that had pervaded his existence these past three years. Colton's daddy always taught him that a certain strength came from being alone, a wisdom that townsfolk would never understand. Colton had been on both sides of the argument, but he had to agree with his daddy; there was a peace to being alone that the conveniences of city life could never hope to mimic. A life lived without obligation to others was a life worth living.

Of course, he thought, allowing yourself to think on things like that with such concrete surety was bound to invite trouble to dinner. It just so happened that it came a little earlier than expected.

A gunshot sounded in the distance. Colton looked up with a sigh and pulled his gore-encrusted hands out of the deer in search of his old field glasses. Shadows danced under the sinking orange sun, effigies of what might be a wagon and several horses riding erratically over the hard-packed ground. More shots sounded, followed by a high-pitched wail with some excited yowling for dessert. Highwaymen were on the prowl, and the wagon was their quarry.

Colton let out a sharp whistle and packed away as much as he could before his horse, Bill, pulled up along-side him. The old, black Morgan snuffed loudly and went back to grazing for something to munch on.

"Yeah, I know you're here," Colton said with a grum-ble and did his best to clean his hands. Another shot rang out, nearer now, that brought an annoyed whinny from Bill.

"Ain't so friendly, are they?" Colton said and swung into his saddle, satisfied he'd packed everything of im-port in Bill's saddlebags. "I suppose we could leave well enough alone. It isn't our fight after all, and Crimson Hol-low ain't that far."

Bill stomped one hoof and shook his head.

"You're right," Colton said and urged the horse on-wards. "Besides, if we don't stop them, they'll be making that racket all night." Colton's face split into a humourless smile, snapped the reins and pushed Bill into a run.

II

Five brigands assailed the lone wagon, firing their guns randomly, more to stir up fear than do damage. Two people sat at the front of the wagon, an older gentleman with a shock of bright red hair and a pair of spectacles perched on the end of his nose, and a younger woman dressed in pants and a shirt, her curly blonde hair bounc-ing free in the pursuit. Colton couldn't tell if there were more people in the wagon, but if there were, they weren't doing much to help the situation.

The wagon itself wasn't much to look at. Dragged by two stallions that had seen their heyday years ago, its old, burlap covering slowly filled with holes. The bandits were as ramshackle as the old wagon, dust clinging to their flesh and clothes from too many days on a hard ride. Colton sighed. The bandits were synonymous with one another, each man no better than a mongrel frothing at the mouth; a pack of rabid, wild dogs looking for something to sink their teeth into. These mutts had the wagon on their scent and were looking to tear it to shreds.

Colton pulled his rifle from Bill's saddle and fired twice; the gun bucked against his shoulder—a familiar hurt. One of the bandits fell from his horse, a scream dying in his throat. Colton watched another bandit stare about confused and put a bullet in him for his trouble. Three to go.

The remaining highwaymen fell back, taking stock of their missing members. Colton swung his rifle towards them and kept them in his sights. One of them, a fella in a black coat and red bandanna pulled up around his nose, cast a quick glance in Colton's direction and pointed one gloved finger.

The two others, equally masked, stared him down, their hands twitching around their six-shooters. Colton raised his rifle, a Winchester repeater, giving them a choice—a chance.

With a high-pitched yip, the bandits turned their horses and headed back over the horizon, leaving their hard stares to keep him company.

The wagon wasn't far off. The woman leaned over the driver lying on the ground. "Shit," Colton said and swung off Bill. "You folks all right?"

"Don't mind this old windbag," the woman said, brushing straw-coloured hair out of her blue eyes. "It's barely a flesh wound." She was a fine-looking woman, her cheeks flushed with excitement.

Colton knelt next to them, his eyes on the trickle of

blood that smeared the old man's white shirt. "Let's have a look, just to be sure." He'd seen his fair share of wounds and knew that some of the worst didn't look like much at all. Those were the type that killed you from the inside out.

The old man rose to meet him, his skin just as white as bone. "Thank you, sir," he said in a quavering voice. "I'm not sure what would've become of us if you hadn't chased those bastards off."

"Wasn't a problem," Colton said, the image of the deer carcass crossed his mind fleetingly. "Mind opening your shirt?"

The old man obliged. "My name is Dr. Basil Forsythe, and this," he gestured to the blonde, "is my assistant, Ms. Alice Green."

Colton nodded to each in turn, distracted by the thin line of blood that ran over the doctor's shoulder. "Looks like Ms. Green was right. They only winged you." He stood and wiped his hands with Forsythe's discarded shirt. "You'll need to clean that and wrap it, but it won't give you much trouble."

"Thank you," Alice said. "I think we have some spare cloth on the wagon. I'll fetch some."

"Check the horses again, Alice, will you?" Forsythe called out as she moved off. Colton could hear a short bark of a response.

"What are the pair of you doing out this way?" Colton asked, striking a match to light his cigarette. "You don't seem the type to travel this far away from civilization without some help."

"That obvious, eh?" Forsythe chuckled. "Well, you're not wrong. I'm a dentist by trade. I plied my services on the road some years ago now but never this far and not for a long time. I have a small shop set up back east, cozy. Regular patients and all." He glanced at his shoulder and studied the damage. "What brings me back to the saddle is more of a personal interest than anything else. A hobby."

"Getting shot at and robbed by highwaymen. Mister, that's some hobby."

"You aren't kiddin'," Forsythe laughed. "No, my hobby is archaeology. Heard of it?"

Colton shook his head.

"Well, let me enlighten you," the doctor said with a wry smile. "Archaeology is the study of our past. Of the times gone by, you understand. We use material remains to understand what previous cultures from bygone eras might have done and why. For instance, did you know that the Egyptian kings of yore, the pharaohs, would often be buried with all their riches and, sometimes, their servants?"

"No, sir. Why would these kings want to do something like that? Seems a waste to me."

"Status, of course. They maintained their kingly status even in the afterlife, complete with a fortune and a full service of servants at their disposal."

"Not sure that's how things play out after you're gone, Doc. As for you, I don't mean to disappoint you, but there ain't no pharaohs or kings buried around here."

"No, but just outside of Crimson Hollow, you'll find something much more valuable."

CHAPTER TWO

I

Crimson Hollow wasn't much of a town, not anymore. It was little more than an afterthought, a forgotten settlement that fell more on the side of Colorado than New Mexico at the state border. The town started its life as Fort Carmine, an isolated camp that did little more than make the Union feel better about itself. After the war, when its futility became well known, the military abandoned it.

It stayed that way until a few ambitious frontiersmen and settlers from back east used the walls for shelter. More buildings sprouted up, and the town began anew. They took on the new name, Crimson Hollow, after a nearby cavern made up of red stone and clay—the Crimson Hollow. The new town was far enough away from anyone and anywhere else that it was a comfort to the people who lived there. No intruders, no outsiders, just the rare appearance of a traveller in search of food and shelter, and the local recluse—Colton—who lived on the outskirts. The town remained small but thrived, and life was good. For a while.

Colton didn't know much about it, but from what he could gather, people just up and left. No explanation, no note, just gone. In some cases, whole families disappeared overnight, leaving all their belongings behind. Colton had seen it with his own eyes: a house filled with everything from food to family pictures—abandoned. Rumour had it that those who hightailed it during the night heard odd things, that they had voices in their heads besides their own. Whether that was true or not, and the consensus it was not, those who remained gave the empty houses a wide berth. There was fear brewing in the heart of Crimson Hollow.

Night was groping at their heels by the time Colton led the old wagon into town. Forsythe's horses hadn't been harmed, but the excitement had pushed them hard, and they were tired and weak. Colton rallied them, and Bill's calm confidence led the small team onward when they might have given up on their own. Colton made a note to give Bill an extra carrot when all was said and done.

Crimson Hollow was quiet, the houses dark. Colton led the wagon to Baker's Saloon, the only place in the town that might be willing to deal with the newcomers. Baker's wasn't much of a saloon. It was a small wooden structure, house-like, with a flat roof and no sign adorning its façade. If you weren't from Crimson Hollow, you might pass right by it and not give it a second thought. Tonight was another story.

Another wagon sat outside Baker's. A half dozen people crowded there, standing around looking confused and a little worried.

"Dr. Forsythe?" A middle-aged man stepped away from the crowd and made for Colton and the other wagon. He was a broad man, his stomach leading him where he hoped to go. His suit, though obviously well made, was tight on him and looked to have some wear on the shoulders.

"Desmond!" Forsythe called out. "I told you we'd make it." The doctor's long face drew tight around the curve of his smile.

Wearing a crooked grin of his own, Desmond stepped up to the wagon and took the reins from the doctor and

Ms. Green. "I doubted you for only the scantiest of minutes," the broad man said with a braying laugh.

"You were right to," Ms. Green said and stepped out of the wagon. "If it hadn't been for this good man here," she gestured towards Colton, "why, who knows what those brigands may have done to us."

"Well, my thanks to you, sir. Desmond Channing," he said and reached forward to shake Colton's hand. Desmond was a wholly unattractive man. His cheeks were pockmarked and red, his nose was bulbous, and his eyes, a striking golden brown, protruded from his head as though they were looking for a way to escape his other features. Even his handshake was weak.

"Weren't a problem," Colton said and tipped his hat to those gathered. "But now that I've seen you safely to your friends, I'll be taking my leave. Safe travels."

"Mr. Colton," Forsythe said. "Please don't leave so hastily. Why not let us buy you a drink?"

"I doubt ole Joe is up for visitors tonight." Colton motioned toward the nondescript saloon. "Not much activity in this town after dark."

"Stick around anyway," Alice said. "I'm sure Desmond has made arrangements with this Joe fella. You never know unless you try."

II

Baker's drab outside gave no indication that beyond its unremarkable door was an honest-to-goodness saloon. Sure, Colton mused, it was no New York City attraction, but for a town the size of Crimson Hollow, it was something.

Five tables were scattered around the room, an eight-foot bar stood opposite the door, and there was a kitchen out back, the scent of the stew they'd cooked for supper still hanging heavy in the air. To the side, a piano sat idly by, its housing covered in a thin layer of dust and its yellowed keys anxious to be tinkled once more.

Colton was surprised to see three of the townsfolk sitting at the bar, Baker behind it, now staring at the newcomers as if they were a sign of the second coming.

"Jim," Baker said, wiping down a scratched-up tumbler. "Didn't expect to see you around...with all these friends."

"Just here for a drink," Colton said.

Forsythe and his company spread themselves out, some sitting at tables, others sidling up to the bar. Soon, Baker's was filled with the sound of conversation and laughter. Colton, after receiving his whiskey as promised, sat off to the side by himself. He could feel every curious gaze, every cursory glance in his direction. Truth was, Colton didn't come to town often, only when his supplies were low. He'd set himself up on the outskirts, a small lean-to close to a creek and some wilderness. He lived as his daddy taught him: off the land and at one with nature. John Colton, his father, had been what the big city folks might call a mountain man. He was a big, bear of a man who covered himself head to toe in the skins of animals he'd caught. He'd taught Colton how to trap, how to skin, how to hunt. It didn't matter what was caught, Big John Colton preached that everything had a purpose, from a moose's molar to a squirrel's belly fat. If it was part of your hunt, part of your kill, you found a use. Next to his upbringing with his father, Colton found living on his own easy.

"You're a quiet one," Alice said and sat across the table from Colton, drawing him out of his thoughts.

"Daydreaming, I suppose," he flashed her a smile and sipped his whiskey.

"I wanted to thank you again," Alice said, her eyes heavy-lidded, her gaze distracted. "I'm not sure what we would've done if you hadn't arrived when you did."

"You weren't far from town." Colton pointed at her to emphasize this statement. "You would've made it."

"It's kind of you to say so, but I don't lie to myself about the little things in my life, let alone having been nearly killed...or worse."

"Fair enough." Colton nodded and took another swig of his drink. "Travelling east to west by wagon isn't the safest bet. Why not take the train?"

"It may not seem like we have all our ducks in a row, Mr. Colton, but we did think this through," Alice huffed, her face red.

"No offence meant. Just a question." Colton raised his two hands in surrender, though a sly grin broke through his stony face.

Alice smiled and sighed. "No, no. I must admit, I'm a little flustered. You hit close to home, sir. I had suggested the train, but Desmond suggested wagons. I think it was the Doctor's romantic notions of wagon travel, kindled from flowery stories of vagabonds, newspaper articles, and the tales of his patients, that swayed him in Desmond's favour. Still, it was hotly debated up until the day before we left."

"Not sure who'd be filling the good doctor's noggin with that malarkey, but now you all know for yourselves. An expensive endeavour as well."

"We had some fundraising, and many of us pinched pennies for the opportunity to work alongside Dr. Forsythe. But we had to cut some corners. No hired guides or guards, just ourselves, our equipment, and two wagons."

"Well, there's six other men, aside from the doctor. If any one of them were halfway decent with a gun, that should've been enough to keep the bandits at bay."

"Let me assure you, Mr. Colton, I need no man to take care of me," Alice gave him a devilish smile, "but you're right. Highwaymen might have been deterred but look at who's in our company." She gestured broadly to the rest of the room. "Two Chinamen, too small to be intimidating, Desmond and Dr. Forsythe, too old to bully anyone away, and Mr. Wright." She pointed to a man in the corner flanked by two others. He was a thick man, though his inset, piggish eyes didn't betray any sign of intelligence beyond the most basic sort. He had jowls that shook when he talked like some great hound whose lips slavered over a discarded bone. "Mr. Wright may look the part, but he's as yellow as a whipped dog. He doesn't like to deal with people much, barely speaks a word. That's why he spends so much time underground digging. To get away from the rest of us."

"Smart man," Colton smiled, but there was no good nature in it.

"I suppose one could say that, but smart or not, he wasn't going to keep any bandits away. We were doomed to begin with, but, lucky for us, you were in the right place at the right time."

Colton raised his glass and took another swig of his whiskey.

"Mr. Colton, I hope you don't mind me asking, but after today, I'm…we're…desperate. Would you consider being our guide and bandit deterrent for the remainder of our trip?" Alice laid both of her hands on Colton's free hand. They were freezing cold, as though she'd dunked her hands in a bucket of icy water, and while they were small and pale, they were callused and strong.

The door of the saloon opened, and a waft of sweating horses and dust filled the room. Sheriff Young and his deputy, Reg, stalked in, their hats pulled low and faces grim. That wasn't unusual, the whole damn town wore a grimace on their face, the kind that comes with long, hard hours of work with nothing to show for it, or that comes from fear and stress and anger. Crimson Hollow had both in spades.

"Joe," the sheriff nodded to the bartender and studied the room, "a fine crowd you have here tonight." Baker shrugged and poured up two glasses of whiskey. The sheriff's face was long and severe, his narrow chin sharp enough to cut a man. Tall and lanky, Colton couldn't help but picture the sheriff's long arms wrapping around some fugitive who was foolish enough to try and get away from him.

The sheriff's eyes came to rest on Colton, and he visibly sighed. "This your doing, Jim? They your friends?"

"No, sir," Colton said, aware that Alice had moved her hands from his arm and placed them in her lap. "I helped a couple of them out of a tight spot on the road. We're here for a celebratory drink." Colton lifted his drink and finished it off.

"That's good, Jim. Why don't you get on back to your place? Don't look like there'll be much room around here for you once your friends are sorted for the night." The sheriff took another look around the room and tried on a smile that almost fit.

"My thoughts exactly, sheriff." Colton stood and made his way toward the door. Reg returned to the sheriff's side and handed him a drink. Reg was a young man, and his thick, doughy face and broad, rounded shoulders were more suited to farm work than the law, but you did what you could around Crimson Hollow.

"See you next week for your supply run. I'll have Ms. Moore put your things together for you. Quick and easy, in and out."

"Much obliged, sheriff," Colton said and pushed past him.

"Next time," Sheriff Young called after him, "put up your guns before you enter my town."

III

Colton was just on his horse when Alice spilled out of the saloon, her head swivelling about looking for something.

"Ms. Green?"

"Mr. Colton," she said with a start and then moved to him. "You never answered my question."

"Ms. Green, I appreciate your concerns, but…"

Alice cut him off. "We have no one else to turn to. Our days are numbered here, and we don't have time to get to know the locals or ask for their help. We know you."

"No, you don't."

"Fine, we don't really know you, but we know you more than anyone else around here. Besides, you've already saved us once. That tends to bring folks closer together."

"Shouldn't you consult with Dr. Forsythe?" Colton said with a sigh.

"This is for Basil. He's a good man, an intelligent and dedicated man, but his romanticized notions make him painfully unaware of the real world. The world you and I know so well, Mr. Colton." She moved closer and put one hand on Bill's neck. "Please, we'll pay you. If for nothing else, to put this woman's heart at ease."

Colton sighed. "Where are you doing this archaeology?"

Alice smiled. "The real Crimson Hollow."

CHAPTER THREE

I

The town was quiet, dark. Dr. Basil Forsythe's archaeological gathering had finally, mercifully, gone to rest in the bed laid by their overflowing cups. The bartender had been kind enough to put up the old men and the woman; the others made a place for themselves in the wagons.

All of them, except him. He had no taste for the inn's straw-stuffed mattresses and little taste for sleeping on bloated sacks of digging instruments and scientific doodads. Not, at least, when there were fully stocked homes empty, their beds waiting for use.

He had overheard the bartender and Sheriff tell Channing that the houses were off limits. That they wouldn't be lent or rented for any sort of money. His dull-witted deputy stood behind him and nodded his head viciously. Superstitious as old maids around a fire and as full of gossip.

Not him. He wouldn't spend another night without a proper bed.

With the big hero left for his own home, the rest of the group soon passed out. When the two Chinese had given up their sentinel watch, he snuck out and headed for the closest house he could find. A small, pale house, its windows had their curtains drawn; its eyes closed. Even better for him—better not to be seen by anything or anyone. Still, the hairs stood up on the back of his neck as he pushed the door open, and a chill ran down his spine.

Nerves, he thought and continued into the home. Like the outside, the inside was small. Just a kitchen, a living area, and a bedroom. He made for the bedroom. A large bed sat in the middle of the room, still made with fresh linens. He ran his hand over the sheets, felt the softness of the mattress under his weight and was caught between a sigh of relief and a jump for joy.

As he lowered himself onto the bed, the creak of the aged wooden frame echoed through the small house. It was an echo that spoke of a place unlived in, of abandonment. He was alone for the first time in weeks and not huddled up against anyone else for warmth or comfort. He shut his eyes, a smile fixed on his face. He was alone.

Something shifted in the other room, and his eyes shot open.

Strange house, he thought, strange noises. But something nagged at him. Why was the house empty? Why did the people leave here in such a hurry? Why did he have that tingle at the back of his neck?

He sat up, his heart thudding out of his chest, his eyes panning around in the darkness. Nothing.

With a chuckle, he lay back in bed. Strange house, strange noises.

A breath roused him. A gust of warm air on his ear, his neck. He jumped to his feet. "Who's there?" But his voice fell flat. Dead on the air.

He moved to the bedroom door and stared out into the kitchen. A table, two chairs, a wash basin, a water bucket, and a rocking chair in front of a small fireplace.

"I thought this house was empty," he said to the room, to its shadows. "I'll take my leave now. Sorry if I..." his final words died in his throat. Something in the shadows moved.

II

Colton had been to the Crimson Hollow; nearly everyone who had passed through town took the short trek out into the flat lands to see it. It wasn't much out of the ordinary, just a large hole surrounded by rock and dust. The interest was in the depth and the consistency. No one really knew how far down the hollow went. Some of the townsfolk said that it was bottomless. Others said that it led straight to China. The more religious sort said it was a gateway to hell.

To hell or China, it didn't matter, people were obliged to test it. Colton had heard tales of the exploration down there. The first was a private within the Union army stationed at Fort Carmine and bored out of his mind. He wrangled together a couple of his buddies, and they made the day trek out there with a length of rope and a few bottles of liquor. The story goes that when the three boys stood over the hollow, their youthful urge to put themselves in danger shrivelled faster than a slug under salt. The private who thought up the idea mustered up the courage, though, and with the aid of his friends, was lowered into the earth. They had a thirty-foot rope with them, and the most the private could do was dangle his legs over the abyss and tell his buddies it was no good.

A local trapper tried it a few years after that. He had some ill-conceived notion that there might be a vein of gold or silver that he could lay claim to. So, with his three sons, he brought a sixty-foot rope and tried the same thing the private had done just a few years earlier – it ended with the same result. The trapper had a modicum of success, however, and was able to find a small outcropping of rock solid enough to lay his feet on. "Even if all the gold in the world had been down there, I wouldn't have dug. Too dark, too much work," he said when he returned to town.

Most people believed that, too.

Aside from the depth, the other strange thing about the Crimson Hollow was the red rock. Red rock is no stranger to Colorado, but it usually comes in bunches or is relegated to certain areas of like-minded rock. The Crimson Hollow was the only red rock for miles. Colton had heard the townsfolk refer to the hollow as a drop of God's blood or the Devil's tongue, but most times, they stuck with the Crimson Hollow.

Colton had detailed to Alice where his lodgings were and agreed that he'd meet them there at noon the following day. They set off after that, two wagons and Colton leading the way. Most of Forsythe's party were in hard shape, their eyes puffed with purple bags and crisscrossed with red veins, all except the two Chinese men, who were charged with driving the wagons. Forsythe disappeared into one of the wagons shortly after they set off, while Desmond and Alice stirred up the energy to sit with their Chinese companions to help guide the wagons.

"Long night," Colton said, urging Bill to slow so he could ride next to Alice and her wagon.

"Too long," Alice said, one hand shading her eyes from the sun. "When the doctor gets into his drink, he rarely cares to stop, and he expects company. I'm not about to let Desmond have his ear any more than he already does."

Colton nodded. It made sense—Alice wasn't in an enviable position. Most men considered women less intelligent, too emotional, and less able to make the hard choices. Colton knew that wasn't true, but he couldn't change the minds of the many. Besides, he figured that Alice could handle these situations on her own. Strong people do that.

"So, what is this archaeology to you people? The doctor told me he was a dentist, but how does that relate to digging up dirt in search of a king's treasure?"

Alice chuckled. "I suppose it seems pretty silly to you, and rest assured, you're not the only one. At worst, it might be called a hobby; at best, it would be referred to as a calling. Dr. Forsythe, Desmond, and I are all members of the American Antiquarian Society, and we all have a belief that the future is firmly planted in the past. To understand where we are going, we must know where we came from. It's fascinating, really."

"I see." Colton pushed his hat up on his forehead. It was a hot day, the sun bearing down in the cloudless sky. "So, what does your calling expect to find in the hollow?"

"Did you know, hundreds of years ago, before America was ever discovered by Christopher Columbus, other travellers roamed the seas looking for new places to live?" Colton shook his head. He'd never really thought much about it. "Well, there were a people known as the Vikings. Scandinavians and Norwegians, mostly, who took to the sea even before our European ancestors. Dr. Forsythe believes they might have landed on the American shores and developed settlements that have since been lost to time — unless we can uncover them again."

"What does this have to do with the hollow?"

"Well, there were rumours that a trapper by the name of Matthew Curtis delved into the hollow in search of gold and silver."

"I heard that story," Colton interrupted. "The man came up empty-handed and feeling like a fool."

"On the contrary, Mr. Curtis was reported to have had some trouble returning to the surface, and in his flailing to find purchase, he managed to lay his hand on a little piece of history — the blade of a Viking sword."

Colton whistled through his teeth. "An honest-to-goodness sword?"

"Well, no, not exactly. He grabbed a piece of the

sword's blade." Alice saw the skepticism on Colton's face, and her words hurried out of her. "But all the experts who have looked at the blade agree that it is an ancient piece and could be related to the Vikings."

"Could be," Colton shrugged.

"Well, that's half the fun, Mr. Colton. You see, we've read the books by Atwater and Priest, and we've visited the Smithsonian Institution, but the presence of Vikings has only been rumoured. We will be able to prove or disprove this by searching further into the hollow. If we find more artifacts, then we'll be able to prove that Vikings were on American soil even before Columbus!"

"Let's hope that's all you do."

"What do you mean?"

"Perhaps you'll dig up ghosts that don't want to be disturbed," Colton said and urged Bill to the front once more.

III

After a few days at the Hollow, Colton found he didn't have much to do. He was hired to keep any ruffians out of the archaeologists' hair and scare off any would-be thieves. Trouble was, out here in the plains, there wasn't much to guard from. Any real threat would be sighted coming a long way out, but there hadn't been any sign out of the ordinary since they arrived.

Colton tried to help in other ways, asking if he could take part in any of the planning or digging, but he was only met with half-hearted smiles and "We'll let you know." It certainly didn't help that another baker's dozen worth of folks showed up on the second day. Hardier folks these, not city-bred intellectuals from the East like Forsythe or Channing, no. This group were the workers. Alice had told him they'd arranged some extra help before they'd left, local boys who had done this sort of thing before. They looked the type, all grim and calloused. With nothing else to occupy him, Colton fell back on what he knew: hunting.

Rattle Snakes were plentiful on the prairie, some foxes, coyotes, cougar if you weren't lucky, prairie dogs if you were. His hunts never gained him anything substantial, he'd been lucky to run across the deer just days before. Instead, he brought back enough to keep himself fed and give him some materials to play with. Snakeskin could help with sores, abscesses, and boils. Have enough of it and you could craft a wallet, boots, even a hat, maybe a vest. Same could be said of any animal skin, really. Colton had no intention of doing any of that. He just wanted to keep busy.

Forsythe's company, on the other hand, didn't seem to know how to do the same. They spent a lot of time talking and planning, but no one really did anything. He saw the massive Tobias Wright and his pair of diggers sit around drinking, kicking dirt they should be shovelling, just waiting for someone to tell them where to start. Forsythe, Alice, and Channing spent their time talking by the wagons, some rough map drawn up and laid between them. Sometimes, he'd catch Forsythe staring longingly into the hollow.

The two Chinese fellows usually kept themselves busy. Colton learned their names, Li Qiang Chen and Liu Wei Zhao, or Lee and Lou, respectively. Lee, his dark black hair plagued with streaks of white or grey, was the elder of the two. He spoke the better English of the two and would often help Lou translate. Lou was younger, an inch or two taller, and broader at the shoulder. He kept his long hair in a braid and had a long mustache. He smiled easily and was anxious to learn about the animals and plants around these parts that were not only edible but tasty, too. That's what they said they did: cook. Colton knew they

did much more. He saw them cook up breakfast and supper for the rest of the group, take care of the horses, and
do any small repairs that needed to be done. From speaking with them, Colton discovered that they were part of
the dig team too and had some experience in mining and
building the train lines. When they weren't keeping themselves busy, they liked to play a game of dice that Colton
couldn't quite catch on to.

The days went by like that: Colton hunting, preparing
his materials, and maybe getting hustled by the two Chinese men. It wasn't a bad way to earn a wage, but it did
little for his wandering heart. It wasn't until the third day
that everything changed.

"We're going into the hollow," Forsythe said from atop
a small wooden crate. He stood in front of the hole and
drew everyone's attention to him, arms out, voice raised.
Alice and Desmond stood on either side of him. "We've
been trying to ascertain the best place to dig, and we just
don't have enough information." He looked at everyone
in turn. "We were looking for someone to volunteer to go
into the hollow."

A silence came over the group. Colton could feel the
tension as they began to look at one another. By now, everyone had heard the tales of the Crimson Hollow, some
had likely made up their own, he imagined. Colton nearly
volunteered himself, but heights didn't agree with him. It
didn't stop Alice from giving him a pleading look, which
he chose to ignore.

A young digger stepped around Tobias. "I'll do it."
The tension lifted with a shared release of breath as Colton and the rest of the group watched the young man step
forward. His name was Colm Tanner. He'd been with Tobias for a few years now, and Colton gathered that they
might have been related. If they were, it wasn't a close
relation. Where Tobias was big and thick, Colm was slight

and thin. He had a pointed, weasel-like face and the buck-teeth to enhance the illusion. Up until now, Colton hadn't been sure if he had heard the boy talk outside of a harsh whisper.

"Good man," Forsythe said and moved to greet him. Desmond and Alice did the same, all of them shaking his hand, patting him on the shoulder. Colton noticed that Tobias did neither and just returned to his place around the fire.

IV

"Now, we're going to lower you down," Forsythe's voice echoed into the hollow. They had managed to rig up a pulley system. Lou and Lee, the foremost engineers on that, stood by ready to help lower Colm. Colton, Desmond, and Tobias also joined in to help. "We don't need you to be down there for long, son," Forsythe said and placed his hand on Colm's shoulder. "All we need you to do is swing the lantern around and tell us if the walls along the edges of the hollow are solid rock or packed dirt. We just need to know where to start and how to do it. It's a matter of shovels or dynamite."

Colm nodded to the old man, took the lantern, and gave Colton and the other men on the rope the thumbs up. Colm wasn't big, but moving a man of any size at a controlled rate would play on your strength and endurance. In only a few minutes, Colton felt the strain on his arms, back, and legs. The worst, however, was his hands. He had rawhide gloves on, but the friction of the rope on his gloves was intense. If he had chosen to do this with bare flesh, his hands would've been torn to shreds.

They continued to lower the young man, breathy grunts coming from each of the men on the rope. "You see anything yet?" Forsythe called out and stared down after Colm.

There was no answer save for Forsythe's own words echoing back at him.

"Colm!" Forsythe tried, louder this time. "Talk to me, boy!" He looked around at Alice. Colton saw his eyes; they were frantic.

"Colm!" Alice yelled and joined Forsythe at the edge of the Hollow. "Colm!"

"Why isn't he answering?" Tobias's rough voice whispered from behind Colton.

"Bring him up," Colton said and started to pull back on the rope. Desmond and Tobias followed suit.

"I'm okay," a distant echo rose out of the Hollow. "I'm okay, it's just..."

"What is it, boy?" Forsythe called down.

"There's stairs."

That's when the screaming started.

CHAPTER FOUR

I

The rope slid across Colton's hands, the friction and heat too much to bear. He let go; they all did. Lee and Lou had fallen away from the pulley, confused, the handle spinning out of control. Tobias made to grab for the rope, but his lumbering stature was unsuited for the momentum he threw himself into, and he fell flat on his face. Desmond looked as dumbfounded as Colton felt, but he attempted to step on the violently falling rope only to be tripped up and tossed on his ass. The archaeological party held their collective breath as Colm's screams echoed out of the cavern.

Colton threw himself on the rope, his hands struggling to wrap around the flailing piece of hemp. Even so, the rope managed to pull him forward towards the edge of the Crimson Hollow.

"Jim!" Alice's voice cut through the air, and with a grunt, Colton pushed himself off the rope and rolled out of its path. A cool wind rushed over his face. His eyes fluttered open, and he peered over the precipice of Crimson Hollow.

"Jesus," Colton said and pushed himself away from the edge, his breath coming in gulps. A second longer, his screaming would have joined Colm's. But there was no screaming, not anymore. Just silence.

Colton scurried over to the edge once more, slowly

and carefully, and peered down. It had felt like the boy had fallen for minutes, hours, but it must've been only seconds. He lay on an outcropping of rock, his body broken with a bloody halo outlining his head.

A scrabbling sound came up from behind as Tobias settled in beside him. The bigger man, his face coated in dust and dirt, stared with his mouth agape at the prone body of his dead relative. Tobias's eyes hardened beneath a thin sheen of tears, and he thumped a ham-sized hand down on the ground. Perhaps they had been closer than Colton had thought.

A cacophony of muttering erupted behind them. Everyone wanted to know what had happened but feared what they'd see if they had to look for themselves. Colton let out a heavy sigh and clapped Tobias on the back. Alice was the bravest of the lot. She came within a few feet of the opening, her eyes pleading for the answer that her mouth couldn't ask. Colton shook his head.

"Okay, everyone," Alice said, turning back to the rest of the group. "Let's give Tobias some space. Lee, Lou, how about you check on that pulley system and get it fixed. We'll need to send someone down to get poor Colm."

"And to start our excavation," Forsythe said from his place overlooking the hollow. "The boy found something. No digging needed. Just some strong ropes and strong backs." The old man laughed. His face lit up with a rapturous smile, and he let out his glee. "Stairs! Imagine," the old man mumbled and started back towards his wagon.

Colton took stock of Tobias. The big man was still on his hands and knees, his eyes peering down at Colm's body. If there had been any sign of grief or anger on Tobias's face, Colton couldn't see it.

He approached Alice, who joined everyone else in watching Forsythe walk away from the scene. She had a handkerchief to her mouth, her eyes wide and uncertain as Forsythe made his exit.

"What was that about?" Colton asked and ran a hand over his face, trying to clear off the dust and grime.

"Jim," Alice said with a start. "What happened to your face?" She took her handkerchief and ran it over his cheek, the silk cool and smooth over his day-old growth of stubble. When she pulled it away, it was smeared with blood.

Colton looked down at his hands. Two long slices across his rawhide gloves exposed the shallow wounds that crossed his palms. They wept blood.

II

With Colm's body buried in a shallow grave, Forsythe pushed his people onward. Thick ropes dangled into the Crimson Hollow from every angle, knotted upon themselves for easier purchase when Forsythe's workers dared to descend. It was a temporary measure, Alice had assured Colton, and pointed to the lumber that was being brought into the hallow.

"Scaffolding?" Colton asked and watched Tobias cinch a pile of boards together and lower them into the hole.

"Scaffolding of sorts. Basil modified the design to include stairs rather than ladders, but essentially the same thing, yes."

"Don't you think it's strange," Colton said, leaning back, "that of all the years this hole has been around, no one has had the same success as us? Not only is there an outcropping safe enough to stand on and explore, but there's stairs! How did we succeed where others haven't?"

Alice held Colton in her gaze for a moment, and he could tell she was working through something. She almost said it, the corners of her mouth quivering around the words that she held onto like rocks rolling over her teeth. "I suppose we knew what we were looking for. We weren't looking for gold or some sort of thrill, we were looking for history."

"Maybe." Colton tried on a smile that didn't quite fit. History, artifacts, ghosts.

"Ms. Green!" Forsythe's voice called over the commotion of his workers' comings and goings. His marble blue eyes, wide and fierce, rested for a moment on Colton before they crawled their way over Alice. Colton thought he saw a shiver cross Alice's shoulders, but he couldn't be sure.

"Alice," Desmond said as he bounced into view. "Come now, something's been found, and Basil wants us to be the first to see it." Forsythe nodded along with this, a jagged smile cracking his pale lips.

Whatever hesitation Alice may have had disappeared, disguised behind a mask of joy as she made for the scaffolding. Desmond laughed as she passed and limped after her. Forsythe followed suit, but not before he gave Colton a curt nod.

III

Forsythe's workers swarmed the Crimson Hollow, ants milling about their hill. Colton had attempted to follow Alice through the throng of people, but he'd lost her when she descended into the hollow. He looked over the edge. Fear tinged by the lingering last image of Colm thickened his breath and scraped at his throat. Alice moved through the scaffolding, her arm intertwined with Desmond's as he directed her onward. Forsythe followed.

The scaffolding did more than serve as an easy entrance into the chasm before them, it also acted as a marker for the ledge that had claimed one of their own. From here, with the scaffolding in place, Colton wondered how no one had seen the outcropping before—it seemed so obvious. And the stairs, the last thing Colm had said before he fell to his death, were as evident as the sun in the sky. Colton's mind wandered back to his brief discussion with Alice. How did they find what dozens, hundreds, of others never had? Or maybe the question shouldn't be how but why.

Tobias pushed passed him with a grunt, his two arms loaded down with more boards.

"I hear they found something," Colton said to the big man.

Tobias shrugged and went to work tying the boards into more manageable piles to deliver to the builders via rope.

"You think that'll be it?" Colton pressed. "Now that they found something, we'll be packing up and heading for home?"

Tobias tied the hemp rope tight; the creak of its submission to him hissed audibly. "No, we shan't be going home," he said and started the slow process of dropping the bundle of boards into the hallow. "Where there's one thing, there'll be another and another."

Colton nodded. In for a penny, in for a pound. Forsythe and his crew were desperate to prove themselves. He spared a thought for Alice, on her need to be recognized alongside Desmond and Forsythe. To stand out. He shook his head; she already did.

"I didn't think you'd stick around," Colton said. "After what happened to Colm and all." The big man had remained quiet for a day or two after Colm's death. He'd kept to himself, moved his belongings further from the rest of the camp, and had his own small fire each night. "I figured you might have been preparing to leave us." Colton had seen that sort of thing happen in the past. Deserters from the war.

Tobias paused for a moment, his broad shoulders tensing before he eased himself back into the work. "I'd planned on cutting out," he said. "Dr. Forsythe turned me around. Swayed me a different way."

"Yeah, Forsythe seems to be able to do that. I'm sorry about Colm, by the way. I didn't know him well, but he seemed like a good kid."

Tobias shrugged and tied another pile of boards together. His oversized head rolled towards the scaffolding with his inset, brown eyes staring at the walkway. "Here it comes," he said in a whisper.

Colton followed the bigger man's gaze and saw Alice. She was the leader of the pack this time, her blonde hair blazing in the midday sun. The smile on her face was wide, defiant, triumphant. Her eyes were wild with excitement. In her arms, she held something the size of a log, a cloth draped over it to conceal it from view.

"Yes, but what is it?" Colton said and turned back to camp.

IV

They burned their fires bright that night, Forsythe distributing booze from crates out of the back of his wagon. Tobias had heard their drunken singing even from Colm's grave. He sipped from his own bottle of whiskey and sat down next to the makeshift cross.

The shootist, Colton, had it almost right. Tobias had been planning on making a quick exit, putting some dust and distance between him and Forsythe's crew of degenerates. Difference was Tobias wasn't about to leave without a little blood on his hands. Eye for an eye, the good book said. If it was good enough for the Bible, it was good enough for Tobias. Colm hadn't needed to die that way. He was a part of Tobias's crew, diggers. They had one job: digging into the earth, not hanging above it.

Tobias chuckled around another drop of whiskey. "That fall really brought you back down to earth, didn't it?" He laughed again, so hard that it brought tears to his eyes. So hard that soon it was only tears.

Wiping his eyes with the heel of his hand, Tobias took another swig from his bottle. He hadn't thought much about whose blood would sully his hands; he just knew the job had to be done. Forsythe was a name that came to mind; after all, he'd brought them all together for this endeavour. Promised them fame, notoriety, money. He promised them the world. Where'd it get them? Then he called Tobias to his side. Forsythe, the mourning, the understanding. The same man who nearly danced a jig at Colm's death was dabbing his eyes with a satin handkerchief and bemoaning the loss of someone so young and so full of life. Tobias had a half-mind to murder the man right there, in front of his lackey, Desmond.

"I couldn't," Tobias said through fresh tears. "I'm a coward." He looked at his hands, thick and caked with dust and dirt. "What good are these if not to choke the life out of men who treat the world as if they are owed something, men like Basil Forsythe?"

For digging.

"Yes," Tobias said. That's what it came down to, his only skill, used in aid of Forsythe's purposes. He wanted Tobias to dig. Knew that Tobias was the man for the job. Offered him more money than he'd ever heard of before. "What was I supposed to do, turn down that kind of money?" Tobias drained the remainder of his bottle and crawled towards Colm's still fresh grave. The musky scent of the dirt, moist in the evening coolness, slithered around him as he plunged his two hands into the grave. "Believe me, Colm. Say you believe me."

Tobias stayed like that for some time, letting the tears come. When he pulled himself away, the night was darker still, and the fire the rest of the camp had been enjoying was only a touch of orange in the distance. He wiped his eyes, feeling the slick dirt and mud streak across his face. "I'm sorry, Colm."

He managed to get to his feet, the bottle of whiskey in his belly working against him the whole way and looked out over the plains. It was a clear night, the moon bright enough to light Tobias's surroundings in a dim, pale light. Everything was still, the world quiet. The morning would come soon, and he'd have to go to work. Busy work until the diggers were needed, hoisting boards, moving rocks, but work was work. Anything to keep him busy out here until he had his money in his hand. Maybe then, with money in them, would his hands find the courage to teach Forsythe the power of the people below him. Maybe then he could get his revenge.

Tobias stumbled toward his lonely tent, not too far from Colm's grave, little more than a shadow in the moonlight. He had only taken a few steps when he heard it. Rustling behind him, the slight movement of earth. Tobias turned, the dim light casting a ghostly reflection on his discarded whiskey bottle but nothing else. Animals, he thought, lizards or snakes that cut through the dirt in search of warmth.

He only took another couple of steps before he heard it again, louder this time, more fervent. Tobias rested his hand on his knife, tucked in its leather holster at his belt. He rarely carried a gun, his size and demeanour often scared off anyone who wanted to make his life difficult, though it was times like this that made him wish he had a six-shooter handy.

There was nothing there the second time he turned but the same pale light reflecting off the liquor bottle. "Y'all better be a snake or something," he said to the night. "I ain't got time for this. Go to bed, it's what I'm aiming to do. No more funny business." His answer was the moonlight, the darkness it barely held at bay. Tobias grunted and carried on toward his tent.

He refused to turn around the third and fourth time he heard the noise, a scrabbling of earth on earth, rock on rock. By the fifth instance, the hair on the back of Tobias's thick neck stood on end. His broad shoulders quaked as a shiver ran down his back. Once more, the frenzied sounds returned, but he refused to give them any more attention. Though really, he didn't know if he could face whatever was making the noise. Animal, creature, whatever it was, it wasn't pleasant. Tobias could feel the evil sloughing off what was back there, a harsh, shallow breathing filled with hate and anger and desperation. He could feel hungry eyes boring into his neck and back, and he quickened his pace.

Wobbling, laden down with a belly full of drink, Tobias moved away from his solitary tent, his eyes now focused on the smouldering remains of the main campfire, safety in numbers. There was a different sound behind him now—footsteps. Tobias could hear the crunch of dust and dirt under boot and the slither of something being dragged. His breath caught in his throat. Sweat rolled down his face, into his eyes.

At every footstep behind him, Tobias wanted to look. He wanted to see what was coming after him, wanted to stand his ground, but he couldn't. His brain said to fight, his body screamed to run. Whatever was back there wasn't normal. Wasn't of this world. He gripped his knife tightly.

The footsteps were slow, slower than Tobias even on his drink. Even so, they were close. They got closer and closer; no matter how fast Tobias pushed himself, he couldn't escape them. He moved into a patch of thin grass, where the camp's horses sometimes grazed under the hot sun. There was movement at his back, a hand on his shoulder, pushing.

Tobias fell in a pile, his knife lost in the shadows of the grass. The musky, dirt scent crept around him, soon replaced by the sour stench of rot and death. He shook his head at the ground. No, he wouldn't turn. No, he wouldn't look. His brain, once the fighter, now told him that if he looked, it wouldn't just be in his imagination anymore. If he saw what was standing over him, it would be made real. When the hand grabbed his shoulder and twisted him around, he closed his eyes tightly.

"Nonononononononono," Tobias whispered and tightened his eyes until pain spread to his temples down his nose. A hand clamped around his throat, its strong fingers digging into the fatty flesh that draped around his neck. Air cut off, the life draining from him, Tobias's eyes shot open as he gasped for oxygen.

Colm stared down at him, his cracked and misshapen skull, chunks of gore dried into his hair. Colm with his grey skin and vacant, white eyes. Colm, with a lopsided smile on his dead face.

Tobias tried to call his name, tried to tell Colm how relieved he was that he was alive and okay. The words died in his throat; Colm's hand squeezed.

Tobias flailed, his meaty hands slapping at Colm's arm and head. Colm didn't budge. His cloudy, opaque eyes stared down upon Tobias, but they were unfocused, vacant. Tobias grabbed at Colm's face, his thick, sausage fingers clawing at the dead man's eyes and cheeks. Colm still didn't move, didn't acknowledge any of Tobias's efforts at all.

A darkness crowded around Tobias's vision, and he felt himself weaken, his brain slow. The last thing he saw was Colm's mouth, curled into a snarl, teeth chomping, ready to bite.

CHAPTER FIVE

I

"Tobias is dead," was the first thing Colton heard when he woke.

From what he could piece together, that morning, just as the sun cracked the horizon, Lee and Lou were up exploring the campgrounds, taking a walk and enjoying the brisk, cool air. They noticed some blood here and there, but that wasn't unusual after a celebratory night of drinking. There was bound to be a fight or two, but more likely, it was just drunken buffoonery gone awry.

Still, there had been an obvious patch of blood in the grass just outside of camp, some signs of a struggle, too. Lee and Lou took note but didn't think much of it. It wasn't until they had made their way to the Crimson Hollow that they noticed anything strange. The scaffolding, freshly built, was leaning forward, its body pulled into the chasm. It was by some engineering miracle that the whole thing didn't collapse into the bottom of the damned hole, if there was such a thing.

Lee sent Lou to wake up Forsythe and the others while he took a look at the tipping structure. Tobias hung from the scaffolding, the braided hemp cord cutting deep into his thick neck. Lee told Colton later that Tobias's tongue lolled from purple and black lips, a smattering of blood drops scattered around his face, and his eyes were wide open as though he were caught mid-scream.

Lou had found Desmond smoking idly outside his tent, and together, they roused the camp. By the time Colton was awoken, Tobias had been removed from the scaffolding, his body resting on the edge of the hollow.

II

No one spoke much after that. Some had trepidations about continuing the work, but Forsythe eased them on, saying all the right things. "Tobias was a beloved brother," Forsythe's voice, rough from barking instructions, rose above the crowd. "He was an essential part of our team and, as lead digger, integral to the work effort. After Desmond and Ms. Green, Tobias was the first person I approached about all of this." Forsythe waved his hand at the Crimson Hollow. "He was a quiet man, meek despite his size, but a professional. He'll be sorely missed." Forsythe let his chin fall to his chest and clasped his hands together at his waist. Everyone was silent, waiting.

"Tobias's death is going to be hard for us all," Forsythe continued. "But let's not forget that he was a troubled man. It wasn't but a couple of days ago that many of you reported to me your fears that Tobias had been distancing himself from the camp. That he had been upset about Colm's death and seemed ready to cut and run. Well, I took it upon myself to talk to the man," Forsythe said and rocked back on his heels, hands now intertwined behind his back. "And I can tell you, he wasn't well. He fell into a stupor once we were alone in my tent, bawling and crying about poor, poor Colm. I comforted him as best I could, but the man had lost his mind with grief. He admitted that he had thought about leaving, about putting all of this behind him. Still, I couldn't have foreseen this as his method of escape," Forsythe said and paused.

Colton looked out at the rest of the camp, all scattered about, most of them with their heads down in reverence.

Alice was standing behind Forsythe, dabbing her eyes with a handkerchief. Desmond did his best to look stoic, but all he could manage was confusion.

"In memory of our lost friends, let's push through. We've already found a significant artifact, but we'll find more. We are discovering history, people. History!" Forsythe turned on his heel and went back towards his wagon and tent. The others scattered, moving back to their designated jobs.

Colton didn't believe that Tobias had taken his own life. Sure, the man had been terribly hurt by the death of Colm, and he freely admitted that he was thinking about leaving camp, but when Colton had talked to him the day before, the man had been turned around on that. Had said that Forsythe had helped to change his mind. Tobias had been a bit moody, maybe even sad, but Colton thought he'd been renewed. Certainly, nothing pointed to suicide.

He scanned the dispersing crowd for Alice, catching a glimpse of her blonde hair bouncing off after Forsythe and Desmond. Colton made the effort to push through the throng of folks. Alice might know what Forsythe had said to Tobias to keep him on or push him over the edge, so to speak.

"Mr. Colton," a hoarse voice called out to him. Colton turned to see the young Mack King, the only remaining digger left of Tobias's crew of three. He was a strapping lad, still not grown into his size, but had the grey haze of a needed shave on his chin and long dark hair.

"Yes, Mr. King." Colton looked over his shoulder in time to see Alice disappear into Forsythe's tent.

"Mr. Forsythe said you might be able to give us a hand moving Tobias," King said and jabbed his thumb in the direction of the body.

"Yeah," Colton said and ran a rough hand over his forehead, "I can do that." Alice had disappeared, busying herself with her tasks for the day. He sighed. "It may not be the most dignified for ole Tobias, but let's grab a wheelbarrow. None of us wants our backs thrown out with the work ahead."

King nodded and scurried off, motioning to a young carpenter, Clay Brooks, to follow him and get things sorted.

"Don't forget the shovels," Colton called after them and took another look at the people milling around. Forsythe had a way with words and with people. Tobias was brought around by him one day then killed himself the next night. Colton shook his head; something didn't feel right. He didn't like the idea of Forsythe volunteering him for things either. It was something he'd have done anyway, but it felt too purposeful. It was like Forsythe was trying to keep him away from something. Colton didn't like it. He'd talk to Alice about it later, learn what he could from her about Basil Forsythe.

III

It was a long, hard trek over the rocky, uneven terrain as Colton helped the young men drag Tobias's corpse to Colm's grave. Might as well keep the bodies close. To their credit, the two lads were more than eager to push through their shallow wheezing breaths and sweaty brows to get Tobias to his resting place. Colton wouldn't let them.

"Know your limits, gentlemen," he had said when they halted about halfway through the journey. "You'll be no good to anyone wore out from the first leg of this journey, and I'll still need you to help me shovel through this dirt." Colton kicked at the ground and lit a cigarette.

King and Brooks steadied the wheelbarrow where it was and collapsed into heaps on either side of it, their huffing and puffing loud enough to scare any game animals away. Colton frowned at the thought. He'd been meaning to go hunting, get Lee and Lou some more meat for their stew.

"You boys must've pissed someone off to get put on gravedigger duty," Colton said as he blew out some smoke.

"No, sir, we volunteered," King said. "Isn't that right, Clay?" The other man nodded.

"Needed a break from the dregs of the earth?"

"That cave ain't right," Brooks said. "Scares the piss out of me."

"That's right," King picked up. "Feels like someone is watching you the whole time you're in there. Then, when you finally get to leave, old Forsythe is staring at you with his bugged-out eyes."

Colton nodded. Forsythe had become more and more obsessed with the goings-on of the cavern. Most days, he'd spend glowering down on his workers, waiting and watching. "Sounds like you fellas are spooked, is all. Can't say I blame you with all the goings on."

"All due respect, sir," King said, "but you haven't been in that cave. You don't know." Colton frowned, but the young man was right; he'd never set foot in the caves—not yet. He'd have to remedy that.

They were close enough now that Colton could make out Tobias's tent and his small fire-pit. Didn't look like it was disturbed, but Colton would still take a quick look. He let the youngsters catch their breath and wandered over to a small patch of sparse grass. The camp horses had come up here a few times, Bill amongst them, to graze. Might be a good place to set a snare for a prairie dog or rabbit.

The ground was soaked in blood, a deep red that reminded Colton of good wine. Looked like something had already met its end there. He ran a hand over the sparse grass, feeling it prickle against his palm. There were no signs of coyotes, though he didn't expect any. Coyotes wouldn't have gotten that close to camp anyway. An eagle or hawk could have taken something big enough to cause this mess, but they wouldn't leave blood behind. Not this much, anyway. Colton could see the signs of the horses being around, maybe some mouse or rat tracks, but nothing too recent. What stood out were the boot prints. They were recent, he could tell from the definition around the edges, and because of that, he could see two different kinds of boots—different sizes, shapes, and tread. Who else had been up this way besides Tobias?

"Colton!" King called out. "Come check this out." Colton took one last look at the tracks and shook his head.

"What is it, King? Need some help to get up off your ass?" Colton tried to keep his voice light, jovial, but he wasn't quite feeling it. There was something strange about the blood, the boot prints.

"Take a look at this." King's face was drawn, pale. He gave a quick look over his shoulder at Brooks, and Colton could tell both were out of sorts. King had his hand on Tobias's chest, his thumb and forefinger gripping one side of the old button-down. Colton nodded to the young man.

The raw wound from the rope stood out as King moved the shirt, but it wasn't what caught Colton's eyes; it was the nasty bite mark on Tobias's breast. It had gone deep. Colton could pick out muscle and bone under the jagged edges of the wound. He got closer, pushing King's hand away and flinging open Tobias's shirt. The wound was raised and sore-looking, blackened veins crawled out of it like some sort of root seeking purchase, and it wasn't the only wound. Colton counted three more bites on Tobias's chest and stomach, but none as bad as the first. He'd seen something like this before, but he couldn't place it.

"How'd you find this?" Colton turned on the other two men.

"I thought I saw something out of sorts," Brooks spoke up. "Thought it might have been a snake bite, it looked so ugly. Thought it might bring some peace of mind to some knowing that Tobias here up and killed himself because he ran into a rattler, and not anything to do with the dig or camp."

"Does that look anything like a snakebite to you?" Colton pointed at Tobias's chest.

"Not now that it's out in the open." Brooks hung his head. King followed suit.

Colton covered Tobias's chest again then leaned on the wheelbarrow. "Snake would have to be as big as a god-damned horse to make that kind of mark." He pinched the bridge of his nose. He'd seen that sort of bite before, but from where? Was it a story his father had told him? Then it clicked.

"So, what is it?" King asked, taking his eyes off his boots.

"Coyote or something, right?" Brooks added.

"No, son," Colton said and turned to face them once more. "Those bites are man-made."

IV

Colton left the two young men to take care of Tobias's burial and hurried back to camp. They weren't too pleased with the prospect of doing it on their own but got to it after Colton flashed the six-shooter at his hip. With that out of the way, he made them promise not to say anything about the bites to anyone until he gave the go-ahead. They were more than happy to oblige.

The camp was milling about, everyone in their places doing their jobs. He saw some of the workers bringing piles of dirt up in wooden trays, pouring them out onto other trays with a wire mesh fixed to the bottom. Others would then work the dirt around, sifting through it to look for anything that might have been missed. Once these workers were done, they'd throw what was left over the side of the Hollow and start again. Ashes to ashes, dust to dust. Colton had seen that sort of work before, had seen many a gold fiend panning through icy waters up in the mountains, hoping to find some gold. His father would always point them out to him on their daily search for food and materials. They were so quiet and knew their mountain home so well that the would-be prospectors never suspected that they were being watched. According to Colton's father, that was just as well. Those searching for riches were bound to be jealous of others poking around in the same area. Jealous, greedy, whatever you wanted to call it, Colton's father wasn't wrong. Colton had seen what happened when a man jumped another's claim. Most times, it ended up with a man broken and bloody; other times, they ended up dead. A shiver crossed Colton's shoulders, he hoped this archaeology was saner than the gold hunt.

Forsythe was at the lip of the hollow, barking orders and overlooking everyone's work. Desmond stood just behind him, nodding along to everything Forsythe said. There was no sign of Alice with them. Good, Colton thought, and headed to Forsythe's tent in search of Ms. Green.

V

Alice jumped when he threw open the burlap flap that doubled as a door to Forsythe's tent. She turned on him with a gasp, her blue eyes wide, one hand grasping a pencil tightly.

"Mr. Colton," she let out a breath and chuckled. "What are you doing here?"

Colton watched her turn back to her work. She was a good-looking woman, her blonde hair shining even out of the sun. She wore green trousers, almost as green as the burlap tent they stood in, and a white button-down blouse tucked in at the waist. Colton hadn't seen many women in that style of dress before, but Alice could pull it off. He let his eyes hang on the curve of her hip and waist a moment before he spoke.

"We need to talk. And I'd rather not do it with Basil Forsythe or Desmond Channing in earshot." Colton moved into the tent and peered over Alice's shoulder. Forsythe's tent was large, like something a general would issue orders from in the war. To one side, there was a cot, a trunk, and a chair overflowing with books and pieces of paper. On the other side sat a small table with its own set of chairs. In front of Colton and Alice, there was a longer table with even more books spilling off it. To the side of that table, a grey and mottled piece of wood peered out from beneath a cloth. A face was hewn in it, nothing that Colton could make out; it was too aged, too damaged. Still, the shape of its eyes remained, staring out at him.

"And why would you care if Basil or Desmond were in attendance?" Alice asked, her voice low but light, distracted by the task at hand.

"What are you doing?" Colton asked and stepped even closer, standing at her shoulder, avoiding the wooden artifact's gaze. Alice smelled of perfume and something else he couldn't immediately place—chalk dust.

"I'm sketching a rough map of the cavern we've explored so far," Alice said, her hand moving quickly over the sheet of paper in front of her. The paper itself was leaning on a lectern, something he'd seen some teachers use in the towns he'd passed through. It wasn't anything fancy, just a wooden structure with a small, angled desktop for reading from or, in Alice's case, drawing upon. He didn't have to think much about what a lectern was doing in Forsythe's tent. The man likely practiced his speeches from there every night before he shut his eyes.

The sketch itself was something else; Alice had a real talent for it. Colton could see a singular opening that stretched out into several different directions, creating a strange star-like formation. In the center of the star was a large circular room, and each arm reached out from that point with its own hallways and rooms along the way. It was huge.

"Looks like a snowflake," Colton said with an unsure chuckle.

"It's more likely some runic formation related to the Norse people." She gave Colton a small smile and clarified: "Vikings. We believe it to be in the image of something they had called the Helm of Awe."

Alice folded the paper and tucked it into her pants. "Mr. Colton, this cavern itself is an archaeological marvel. We could have discovered something that might rival the findings made in Egypt. This is not only an amazing but an important find."

Alice pushed passed him and made for the tent door, but Colton stepped in her way, his hands up in front of him. "Please, Ms. Green. I need you to hear this."

"Fine," she said with a roll of her eyes. "But Basil is expecting this in short order."

Colton detailed what he had found on Tobias, not sparing the gory details, despite his urge to do so. Alice took a step back and sat hard on Forsythe's cot then covered her mouth with her hand.

"And you're sure it wasn't some...some animal that bit into him?" she asked after some time. Colton sat down next to her.

"I was born and raised in the mountains by my father. I'm sure you've heard some of the strange tales that come down from there." Colton looked to Alice, saw her nod. "I can tell you most of them are bull, but that doesn't mean all of them are. I lived there; I should know. My father told me once about a group of prospectors, probably about four, who heard that there was a cave filled with gold near where we lived. My father saw them once or twice, but he paid them no mind, and they gave him the same courtesy. They had come up in the early fall, when it was still warm, even that high on the mountain and worked through their days toiling, every day finding nothing more than more rock. This went on until winter hit proper. My father told me it was a bad winter that year, told me that he could feel it coming long before the snow started to fall. He hadn't heard much from the prospectors, so he decided to head over there and let them know about the coming weather."

"That was nice of him," Alice said, wringing her hands together.

"My father was decent enough. Didn't really cater to city dwellers, but he valued life of all shapes and sizes. Anyway, they laughed him out of their cave. Turns out, they had managed to find some gold after all, and they were going to be damned if they didn't stick it out. My father just shrugged and left—he gave them fair warning, but he wasn't about to force grown men to do something they didn't want to do."

"And then the winter came on."

"And then the winter came on," Colton nodded. "My father was too busy taking care of his family to pay much attention to the prospectors, but he did say that snow came down heavy and that we were stuck in our little shack for a couple of weeks before he could make a real dent in the snow and go out scrounging for food."

"What about the prospectors?" Alice said.

"Well, my father didn't have time or the desire to check on them, not until the thaw started to come on again. Once that happened, my father took to hunting further and for longer, and one day, he heard something. It was a strange sound, not quite animal, but certainly not human. He thought it might have been the death throes of something sucking on its last breath. My father followed the sounds, and it led him back to the cave. He remembered the prospectors then and went in to check on them, afraid a bear or a pack of wolves had descended on them. What he found was worse.

"There was only one man in the cave when my father walked in, his rifle at his side. The man was rake-thin, not much more than a skeleton with a thin layer of flesh covering it. My father ran to him, checked on him, but he noticed something was off. It was the smell, the smell of rot and death and flesh and blood. He looked around the cave, and there were bones everywhere, but they weren't animal bones."

Alice began to wring her hands again.

"All at once, out of nowhere, this skinny, skeleton of a man attacks my father. He doesn't have a weapon on him, but he is scratching and clawing and biting. My father had no choice but to put a bullet in him."

"That is a horrible tale, Mr. Colton, it truly is. I'm sorry your father had to live through that, and you had to live it vicariously through him. However, how does this have anything to do with poor Tobias's wounds?"

"My father was a quick shot, but not that quick. The man managed to sink his teeth into my father's arm, took a chunk of flesh with him, too. I know those bites are from a man, Ms. Green, because I saw it my whole life, a scar on my father's arm."

CHAPTER SIX

I

Colton squatted over the patch of grass once more while Bill nickered behind him, stomping his hooves. Alice said she'd let Forsythe and Desmond know about what he'd found. She said she thought that it might be best coming from her, and Colton agreed. The last thing he wanted to do was get involved in the camp politics. Alice knew those boys better and was good at that sort of thing anyway. Still, something rankled him. He trusted Alice, saw the belief and fear in her eyes, the seriousness of the matter, but she was almost as enraptured by the goddamn dig as Forsythe. He'd seen her face when she was escorting that artifact up the scaffolding. Colton didn't think he'd be pushing it if he said she'd been in ecstasy, near to a damn religious experience.

He went to Bill and patted the horse's strong neck. "Not going to have a bite?" Colton asked and waved a hand toward the grass. Bill shook his head with a sigh. "No, I wouldn't either in that mess." Colton couldn't be idle while he waited for the aftermath of Alice's conversation with Forsythe. Couldn't let his head fill with doubts about what she was going to say or not say. Instead, he made his way out to look around again while the sun was still in the sky. There was nothing new. Still just the pool of blood and two sets of boot tracks. Nothing that might tell him more of the story about what happened or how

Tobias got those bite marks.

"Come on, fella. Let's go pay our last respects," Colton said and swung himself into the saddle. He'd seen King and Brooks coming back into the camp, faces red and sweat staining their shirts, but with an empty wheelbarrow. He figured they got the job done well enough, but he might as well take a look anyway.

The grave looked all right. Could have been dug a little deeper—a mound of dirt about the size of Tobias's stomach still stood above the ground—but it wasn't bad. The two of them had managed to line him up pretty good with Colm's grave; the camp looked to be setting up their own little Boot Hill. Colton frowned and dismounted. Bill, for his part, took a few wide steps away from the graves, gave a little nicker and snorted his annoyance.

"It's good you have reverence for the dead, Bill. I'm proud of you," Colton said. The hair on his neck and arms squirmed, and he could feel a pair of eyes lingering over his back; he wanted to take his own long steps away from the graves. "Damn it, Bill, you got me all spooked now, too." The horse snorted.

Both graves were marked with a makeshift cross, put together from some leftover supplies in camp. Looked like the young fellas decided to carve Tobias's name into his with a buck knife. Colm's remained blank. There was something else about Colm's grave that gave Colton pause: the dirt was still fresh.

Colm had died a few days ago now, and though that wasn't a long time, Colton expected to see some signs of settling. Instead, the dirt was as brown and moist as Tobias's. He knelt to put his hand in the dirt. His first thought was that King and Brooks dug like dogs trying to hide a bone and tossed the earth everywhere, but that didn't seem to be the case. Unlike Tobias's grave, Colm's was in line with the ground, he was buried deep—deep enough, anyway. Coyotes was his second thought, but he didn't think it fit. Sure, the graves were far enough away from camp that the coyotes wouldn't be scared off by human noises, but coyotes didn't need to dig in the dirt for food around here; there was plenty for them to hunt and eat. Fresh, too. Besides, camp was far enough away, but Tobias's tent wasn't.

Colton was surprised by how close Tobias had gotten to Colm's grave. Not more than a few yards away, the tent's entrance faced Colm's feet. "Since we're here, hey boy?" Colton said and guided Bill to the tent.

It was a nice little setup, something Colton himself might put together if he were looking to pack light and cut out quick. A small fire pit, a small tent, and a few belongings left around. Easy to pack up and go. Inside the tent was a sleeping roll, an extra blanket, some jerky, and a tin of coffee. The only thing Tobias had that Colton might not have included was a shovel and a pick. Tools of his trade, Colton supposed.

The only boot marks around here were what he'd assume were Tobias's—big and wide with a thick tread. He'd seen them in the bloody grassy patch. "Wait here, fella," Colton said and walked back to the graves. Bill snorted in his wake. The graves had more than a few boot prints, animal prints too, but Tobias's were easy to find all around Colm's grave, stepping on top of other prints, making them his own. But there was something else. Another print that was on top of Tobias's. It was smaller, not as heavy set, but it was there all the same and fresher. They matched the other boot prints he'd seen in the grass.

II

Colton rode into camp a few minutes later to find it in another uproar. From Bill's back, he spotted Alice's golden hair near the entrance to the Hollow. He let Bill graze and pushed his way towards her, fearing that this might all be because of what he had told her, that she might have brought some sort of trouble on herself for telling his story. If Forsythe was as obsessed with the dig as Colton thought he was, the old dentist wouldn't take too kindly to someone throwing a kink into his plans to become famous.

"Let me through," Colton said and elbowed his way into the group. The entire camp stood dumbfounded and quiet, circling around something, Alice included. "What the hell happened?" he asked. Alice didn't take her eyes off the centre of the circle, like she were entranced by it. Forsythe stood next to her, equally mesmerized.

It was Desmond Channing, the rotund right-hand man of Forsythe, writhing on the ground as though he were wrestling with invisible snakes.

"Give him some space," Colton said, and the crowd took a step back. He grabbed a hammer from someone nearby—he didn't know who—cracked off the head and moved in on Desmond. He'd seen a piece of wood shoved into someone's mouth before when they were convulsing, crossways, to block the tongue from retreating into the throat. He'd never done it personally, but it didn't look like anyone else was about to take it on.

As Colton made to move in on Desmond, the convulsing man screamed. It was like nothing Colton had ever heard before. A high-pitched whine that was more akin to a coyote's howl than any sound a man could make. As it went higher and louder, people around Colton had put their hands over their ears, their faces pinched with pain. When the scream stopped, Desmond groaned, and with a sickening crunch, he arched his back so only the heels of his feet and the back of his head touched the ground. Prayers and mumbled oaths surrounded Colton as he got closer to Desmond. Unsure if he could do anything at all, Colton carefully reached out to the afflicted man. Desmond collapsed, and a small figure rolled out of his hand.

III

"What is it?" Colton peered down at the small figure, the setting sun catching on its silver surface. Desmond had been moved off to his tent, his breathing coming in harsh barks like a man drowning. There were no wounds on his person, but Colton had heard that sound on the battlefield, coming from someone with a gut shot; he didn't like Desmond's odds.

Forsythe had ordered everyone back to work, but he remained behind with Alice and Colton, each of them looking upon the small likeness of a person long dead. No one had the desire to touch the thing.

"Not all Viking artifacts are swords and helmets," Alice said. "They were people with different interests and hobbies. They were artists as well as fighters."

Colton nodded. There was some art about the figure. He could see the eyes, nose, and mouth of it, the arms and hands. The lower half of the body was broken in a jagged diagonal, but what remained had intricate patterns carved into it. In one hand, the figure held a sword, the other held a shield.

Colton turned to Forsythe. "What was Desmond doing with it?"

"Desmond forgot one of the first rules of archaeology," Forsythe said with a shake of his head. "Never touch the artifact directly. Always use gloves or some cloth to transport the artifact. Leather would be preferable."

"And because he didn't follow that rule, he had a fit?"

"Mr. Colton, do you know how many diseases and ailments may be within the depths of this earth? Because I do not. I certainly cannot say what caused the men and women who created this cave system to die off and leave their belongings behind, but I cannot rule out disease. Perhaps, by touching that artifact, poor Desmond has contracted whatever killed our Viking friends."

"And you suspected something like this might happen?" Colton pushed his hat up on his forehead and ran a hand over his brow.

"There are rules for a reason, Mr. Colton. I knew the possibility, but so did we all." Forsythe looked at Alice. "Desmond failed to follow the rules, and, unfortunately, he'll have to pay the consequences."

"There are three men dead or dying from your archaeology, Mr. Forsythe. Don't you think that's enough death on your hands? Why not pull up and leave, take the artifacts you have and go?"

"There's more down there. If we leave now, we may miss out on a bigger, more profound find. We are making history here, Mr. Colton. We have found the remains of a Viking settlement in the Western United States in the middle of a state with no ocean for a thousand miles. How did they get here? What brought them to this exact spot? The more we look, the more we uncover."

"Is it worth more lives?" Colton asked and made to grab Forsythe by the collar. If he couldn't talk some sense into him, then he would shake it into him.

"Mr. Colton," Alice blocked his path, her hand resting on his chest. "Jim, we feel terrible about what has happened here, but I have to agree with Basil; it is worth the risk. We all knew that when we signed on to this mission. Desmond, certainly, would understand our continuation of the dig."

Colton looked down at Alice, her golden hair not so shiny in the dying sunlight. He stammered, unable to find words to respond. He couldn't believe that she was siding with Forsythe in this.

"Think of it this way," Alice continued. "Colm was an unfortunate accident before we even started digging. Tobias was likely the result of his grief over Colm's death, and Desmond is not dead..."

"Yet," Colton said.

"Yet. They are all tragic and upsetting, and no one feels worse than Basil or I. But Desmond is the only casualty of the actual dig, and he isn't dead," she held up her hand. "Yet."

"And what if there are more deaths?" Colton asked, his fists clenched at his sides. "Whose fault will it be then?"

"It depends on how they die, of course," Forsythe said. He sounded bored, impatient. He fidgeted with his shirt seams and looked over his shoulder at the Hollow.

"And what about the bites I found on Tobias?"

"I've discussed that with Ms. Green," Forsythe said with a sigh. "While it is disconcerting, we have no way of knowing what impact that played on his death. Ultimately, it appears that his hanging is what caused it, whether he had those bites or not. Perhaps an intruder did that while he was up by Colm's grave and away from the safety of the camp. Then again, isn't that something that we are paying you to ensure, Mr. Colton? Perhaps you could focus your worry on ruffians from without, and we'll worry about what happens within, hm?" With that, Forsythe turned on his heel and returned to his place at the edge of the hollow.

"And what of the strange feelings your workers get down there in those caves?" Colton asked Forsythe's back. The older man gave him a cursory glance over his shoulder and continued toward the hollow, shaking his head.

"Please," Alice said, her hand still firm on Colton's chest. "Please, Jim. Trust us, trust this process. We don't want anyone to die, but our work is..."

"Important. So, I've been told. I best follow orders,"

Colton said and turned away from Alice, Forsythe, and the hollow. "Make sure nothing disturbs your precious, valuable work."

Colton walked away, letting his anger and frustration leak out of him with every step. He didn't like being ordered around. Forsythe wanted him to keep an eye on things outside the camp, but Colton had other ideas. It was time for him to visit the hollow.

CHAPTER SEVEN

I

Night fell quickly. Lee and Lou went about the daily business of feeding the camp and cooked up another stew. Those coming out of the hollow were smacked in the face with the aroma, which set their stomachs to growling. Before long there was a crowd surrounding the fire, stuffing their faces with stew and rye whiskey and shooting the shit. Colton didn't join them.

He was accustomed to biding his time. Any kind of hunter will build up patience in the stretches between when they last saw their prey and when they saw it again. Fishermen did it, too, did it in spades. Colton sat in the opening of his tent, an untouched bowl of stew in his hands and his eyes on the camp.

They weren't a raucous bunch; a few drinks in them and they'd start petering off towards their beds, eager to sleep off the work of the day, only to start anew with the morning light. Forsythe and Alice hadn't joined them, and Colton was hard-pressed to remember any time they had. They might be checking up on Desmond; then again, they might not.

A couple of hours, that's all it took, and the last of the workers were off to their tents, the fire already dying in its pit. Colton went to work. He made sure his six-shooter was strapped to his waist, shook a box of matches in his coat pocket, picked up his oil lamp, and made for the hollow.

II

The scaffolding wasn't as steady as he'd like. It swayed with each step he took, but Colton went slow, pausing when the steps creaked, his ears cocked.

He stepped foot on the stone outcropping where Colm had lost his life, the stony stairs before him, and had another thought. He lit his lantern as he moved forward, the map he'd seen over Alice's shoulder clear in his mind. The hollow made him nervous. Not that it was a giant hole in the ground. No, he'd seen others like it before, maybe not this treacherous, but similar enough. The Crimson Hollow, though, had a presence. A personality. It was like a mean dog who's been poked with a sharp stick once too often. More likely to bite you as it was to let you pet it. There were all kinds of stories surrounding the place, about the number of people who tried to explore it, measure it, understand it. Maybe too many people poked it for its liking, and now it was going to have a go at biting.

Alice had a talent for mapmaking, as it turned out. Colton followed the cavern opening into a hallway, just as he had seen Alice draw earlier. It was truly dark in the cave. As black as ink spilled from an inkwell. The orange light of his lantern cut through the haze, but it was a battle, and not one that he thought his lantern would win. Rooms broke off from the hallway, three on either side. They had no doors, and the rooms looked as though they had caved in on themselves a long time ago. If Alice's map was as accurate as it appeared to be, at the end of the hallway would be a large central room that would lead to seven other hallways, each similar to the first with six rooms.

The atmosphere was thick, the air filled with dust and a foul smell of earth and dirt. Colton could see no evidence of digging or recent tool work, but the walls surrounding him must have been done by a true craftsman, each smooth and rounded. More than Colton had thought possible. Markings lined the upper half of the walls, some faded with time, the grey stone reclaiming it some, but others stood out, shadowed by his swinging lantern.

The main room was just up ahead, the lantern's weak light just reaching the room's threshold. Colton paused. Something moved behind him, the whisper of a foot-step. He contemplated snuffing out the light, hiding in the darkness, but decided against it. He had a map in his mind, but he'd never been in these tunnels before. He'd be more likely to trip, fall, and break his neck as he would to safely guide himself through. Instead, he held the lantern up high. He hoped that it might increase his view and that if whoever was following him chose to shoot, they might aim at the lantern, not him. It wasn't his best idea. He moved back the way he came, swinging his lantern in the rooms he passed, but there was nothing there aside from rocks and destruction. He moved on.

The main room was larger than he had expected. Equally as precise as the walls in the hallway Colton had just exited, this large circular room had smoothly chiselled walls. Though the room was so large his lantern couldn't breach the entire darkness that concealed it, he could see enough to know it was bigger than any house he'd ever been in. It was no wonder that Forsythe and Alice had become so obsessed.

Colton wondered at the architecture. This massive room had been dug through the rock and sediment and still hadn't caused any sinkholes above, no cave-ins either. There were columns of stone in place around the room, each carved with more markings and symbols, but Colton wasn't sure that they alone would take all the weight of the world above. Then again, perhaps that was what formed the Crimson Hollow in the first place—a cave-in that broke through the earth and flung another chamber like this one to hell.

Just on the edge of the lantern's light, in the center of the main chamber, Colton saw a stone table. He found some papers strewn across it, notes and the like, and an old, leather-bound notebook. The paper wasn't ancient, though, and the writing appeared to be English. He placed his lantern on the table and shuffled through. Cat scratches, words written hastily and with an idle hand. Colton could make out only a few words: altar, idol, death.

Something shifted behind him. He distanced himself from the table, hoping to hide in the shadow. There was no one. The chamber stayed eerily silent, engorged with secrets of the dead. Colton fought back a shiver that threatened to run the length of his spine and stared into the darkness around him. He wanted to call out, to announce it was only him. After all, everyone in camp knew him and had no reason to be suspicious of him. His mind told him that, but his gut told him different. Told him to keep his mouth shut and hurry the hell out of there.

Colton's mind and body came to a compromise, and he went back to the table, picked up the lantern and moved on. The other side of the large room was much the same as the last. In the beam of light from his lantern, Colton could pick out broken glass or clay shattered across the floor. Might have been from some old pottery, maybe an urn.

Just like Alice's map had said, there were seven openings besides the entranceway, each marked with an arch of stone covered in the same writing he'd seen on the columns and walls. He studied the floor around him. Footprints crisscrossed through the soil and dust, too many to pick out one specific set but an easy guide to where Forsythe's workers had concentrated. Most of the traffic headed into the hallway directly across from the doorway Colton had used to enter the room. There were tool marks on the floor, wheelbarrows that led in the same direction. Colton followed along, hoping to find answers to a question he didn't know how to ask.

This hallway was less cramped than the last one; the air was more open, and Colton didn't feel as though the walls were closing in on him. The rooms he passed were open and free of any sign of cave-ins or debris. They were small, not much larger than the size of a bedroom. Furniture and shelves, both rotten and collapsed, lined the insides. Colton stepped into the first room on his right. Wheel marks lined the floor at various angles, likely from loading up the bits and bobs they could find there. Perhaps loading up some dirt to bring to the sifters he'd seen the day before. Whatever the case, the room was empty of anything that might be an artifact or any information about the cavern or the people who made it.

The next two rooms Colton checked were much the same. Empty except for the debris that was unrepairable or useless. The third room was a different story. There was another stone table in this room, still adorned with plates and cups and books, and the chairs that surrounded the table were occupied, by the looks of it, with their original inhabitants. Four skeletons sat around the table, their bones yellowed with time, propped up against the back of their chair, their skinless mandibles hanging open in a silent scream.

Colton panned the light around the room. Cobwebs as thick as rope hung throughout, draping the dead and everything else in the room. Forsythe hadn't let anyone disturb the room yet, but Colton knew it was only a matter of time. A treasure hunter like Forsythe wouldn't be content until he had ripped this place apart, stealing whatever he could in the process.

Another noise turned Colton around. He held his lantern against the gloom, but those ancient shadows wouldn't be deterred. He dropped his free hand to his revolver, felt the comfort of its grip, the cool comfort of the steel on his trigger finger.

"Hello," he called out. His voice echoed in the cavern, bouncing around every room until it came back to him in a cacophony of his voice. Colton waited, standing in the dark, hand on his gun, eyes squinted to see whatever was around him, but he saw nothing. He shivered. Had it been this cold before? he wondered and pulled his jacket closed over his chest.

After a minute of standing there, looking, waiting, Colton moved on to the next room. It went on this way for the next little while, with Colton finding a new passageway and exploring the rooms present. He had to give it to Alice and Forsythe, and Desmond too, they were doing their thing as efficiently as he could imagine. Taking a room, emptying it, and moving on to the next. At least, that's what he figured they were doing.

A shadow passed in front of him, the echoes of footsteps cracking like gunshots in the empty main chamber. Colton jumped back, pulled his shooter and nearly dropped the lantern in the process. The footsteps stopped, and the silence roared back into place, only to be held at bay by Colton's rapid breathing.

"Jesus Christ," Colton said to himself and cocked the hammer of his gun. No more games, he thought and swung himself into the chamber, the lantern held high. There, at the table he'd passed before, someone sat facing away from him. They were skinny and lanky, their stick figure arms resting on the table in front of them, and they had a shock of red hair that stood up on the back of their head.

"Mr. Colton," Forsythe's voice echoed through the room. "What brings you down here when the rest of us are in bed?"

"You're not," Colton said and moved closer, keeping the gun trained on Forsythe's back.

"No, I'm not," he turned in his chair, one arm draped over the back of it. In the dim lantern light, Forsythe's face was drawn and sunken. His eyes were lined with red veins, but they were vacant. The dentist looked directly at Colton as if he were one of his artifacts or a bug he was about to crush. Colton tightened his grip on the gun. "This is when I do my work, Mr. Colton. My real work. You see, I can't get anything done with all that noise. I prefer the quiet, the alone time with my thoughts," he shuffled a few papers on the desk, "and my notes."

"Is that so?" Colton edged his way towards the exit, Forsythe's eyes following him as he did. "Must be hard to navigate these tunnels without a light," Colton said and gave his lantern a little shake.

"You're wrong, Mr. Colton. I know these halls as though I'd spent years exploring them, as if they were my own home."

"Still, must be hard to read and write in the dark, wouldn't you say?" Colton had made it to the first hall-way he'd entered. Behind him was the path to the outside world. A fresh breeze blew over his neck and shoulders.

Forsythe didn't answer, just stared at Colton from the edge of the lantern's light, his eyes shining in the darkness.

Then came the screaming.

Colton looked over his shoulder and then back at Forsythe. The dentist's eyes had snapped onto Colton, the full force of his attention finally locked. Colton couldn't help but feel like a fox in the sights of a wolf.

"Sounds like you're falling down on your job, Mr. Colton. Best attend to that," Forsythe said and stepped into the darkness and out of view.

CHAPTER EIGHT

I

Colton bolted out of the cavern, took the scaffold steps two at a time, and emerged into chaos. The small camp was roiling with people falling over one another, some still drunk and incoherent, others just plain terrified. Colton couldn't see what was causing the ruckus; lanterns were lit, but they were few and far between. Shots sounded to his right. Gun in his hand, he made his way towards the sound.

"We buried him, we buried him," Mack King shouted and took another shot with his six-shooter. His free hand was tangled in Clay Brooks' sleeve, trying to drag him backwards and away from the edge of the camp. Limp in Mack's arms, blood oozed from Brooks's neck.

"What the hell happened?" Colton demanded and moved for Brooks. Mack turned the gun on Colton and pulled the trigger, only to have it click over on an empty cylinder. Colton slapped Mack's gun out of his hand and helped to ease Brooks to the ground. He tore Brooks's shirt and wiped his wound. "What's going on?"

"We buried him, Mr. Colton. I know we did. I was there."

"Who?" Brooks' neck had been bitten. It was similar to the bite that he'd seen on Tobias.

"We buried him, but he was such a big man, maybe we didn't bury him deep enough. But that doesn't matter when you're dead. Right? It doesn't matter when you're dead."

"Tobias?" Colton meant to keep pressure on Brooks' wound, but it had stopped bleeding.

"He came back," Mack cried. "He's back, and he's mad that we didn't bury him right. But we buried him. We buried him."

Colton was tempted to backhand Mack and snap him out of his stupor. Before he could, another round of screams rose from the interior of the camp. Colton pulled his gun and ran towards it, swinging the lantern before him.

Alice ran up to meet him, her hair down, messy, her eyes streaming tears. "Jim, thank God."

"What the hell's happening?" Colton swung the lantern around to see more people scurrying around him, each with a fear-painted expression on their face.

"It's Desmond," Alice said and pointed behind her. "He's, he's..."

Colton pushed past Alice and towards Desmond's tent. Alice was right behind him, stifled sobs rising above the chaos from time to time. Desmond's tent was fairly large, big enough for a family to sleep in, but nothing compared to Forsythe's in sheer size and quality. Colton hadn't checked on the man since he was taken to rest from his fit earlier in the day. He didn't think he would've survived the night.

The tent had fallen inward and was torn apart from the center out, like a large animal got trapped in there and tore its way free. Colton turned to Alice and raised his eyebrows. "Where is he?"

She pointed past the tent. In the darkness on that side of the camp, a figure moved towards them. Desmond walked with a limp, his whole body lurching forward with each step like a man in pain. His dress shirt and coat were missing, the former in tatters around his waist, and his grey, dappled flesh bounced with his jittering movements. Desmond's face was a mask of confusion, anger, and dread. A young man ran past the tottering archaeologist, who made a swipe at him, missing the man by inches. An eager groan spewed from his mouth above the din.

Colton felt metal bite into his sore palm and tore his eyes away from the scene before him. He was gripping his gun like a vise, his fingers white with pressure. He cursed and forced his hand to relax then raised his lantern and his eyes back to Desmond.

"He had been resting," Alice said. "Resting in his tent, but his breathing was hard, coming in quick, short breaths like he was hyperventilating. I was with him, applying a damp cloth to his forehead when he released one last, long gasp that died as he did. I cried over him." She was crying again now, her arms locked around Colton, who watched Desmond stumble around, sniffing at the air like a dog.

"Then he came back," Alice said with a sniff. "Not his breathing. My head was on his chest, I didn't even hear a heartbeat. Nothing. But he moved. His hand clasped around my arm, squeezing. My shriek brought some of the men who managed to free me. I ran, and then this." She waved a hand at the camp. "This all happened."

Desmond stumbled forward, his head frozen in midsniff. Colton had seen hunting dogs do this, but seeing a man mimic the movement made him feel sick to the stomach. Desmond's head snapped forward; his eyes, glowing in the dark, had settled on Colton and Alice. Colton couldn't be sure in the darkness, but he could've sworn he saw Desmond's slack features twist into a jagged smile as he took another step towards them.

"Get behind me," Colton said and pushed Alice to his back. He lifted his gun. "Mr. Channing, that's far enough."

If Desmond heard him, he showed no sign of it. Instead, his broad shoulders hunched, his arms twitching at his sides, hands reaching, and he took two more steps.

"Damn it, Channing," Colton said and fired. A piece of dry earth flew from before Desmond's feet, and a puff of dust followed it. "That's a warning shot. Don't make me kill you."

Another crooked smile, another two steps.

Colton cursed, aimed his gun, and fired. Desmond took the shot on the shoulder, his thick frame twisting with the impact, a spatter of blood misting the air. He didn't fall down, he didn't cry out; he recovered and moved forward again, faster.

Colton fired two more rounds, each hit Desmond in his torso. Colton knew he'd hit the man in the heart, but he kept coming. He didn't even flinch.

Desmond ran, his hands flexing as he moved, saliva draining from his open mouth. Colton pushed Alice back and holstered his gun.

"What..." Alice said from behind him, but Colton ignored her. Had to time it right.

Desmond closed the distance between them fast, his eyes manic. Just as he was about to step within arm's reach, Colton swung his lantern. It caught Desmond on the head, pushing him off course and smashing the lantern in the process. Fiery oil sprayed in the air, most of it landing on the falling Desmond. With a whoosh, he was alight. No sound of pain or panic came from him; he just stood and ran off, the flames bright against the encroaching night.

Colton gripped his gun and guided Alice alongside him further into the camp. "What the hell is happening here?"

"Was...was he dead?" Alice asked at his side. "Was he alive?"

"I can't say." Colton pulled her in the direction of the horses. "I do know that we need to get out of here."

Alice wrenched herself out of his grip. "We can't leave. What about the artifacts, the ruins?"

"We can come back in the daylight, scrounge up what is left over, if you like."

"Not good enough. I should go talk to Basil, he'll know what to do."

"You want to go search for him in the hollow, you're more than welcome. I'm getting the hell out of here."

"What do you mean?" Alice grabbed his arm and turned him around.

Colton sighed, gripped Alice by both shoulders. "He's holed up in the caves down there, doing his work."

"That doesn't sound right," Alice said.

"No, it doesn't. But that's where he is. You want to find him, you do it on your own."

A scream turned them both toward the other end of camp. Silhouettes in the moonlight scattered, running in different directions. A large figure remained, its head cocked at a weird angle, the rumble of a growl on the air. Colton pulled his gun.

They moved quickly, as silently as the haste would allow. There weren't any people milling about here, and that was a good sign. When he saw the outline of a couple of horses ahead of him, he could've almost cried.

The panicked snorting and squealing of the horses erupted as they got closer. Only two remained; the others looked to have broken free from their bindings, likely scared out of their wits and running as far away as they could. Colton hoped they made it without stumbling upon some half-starved coyotes or stepping in a rattler's nest. Bill was close by, where he'd left him, but he wasn't pleased.

"I know, fella. I know." Colton patted Bill's solid neck

and untied his leads. "It's been a strange night." He pulled Bill around the other horse, a tall, grey draught horse that had driven the wagons. It didn't have a saddle. "Bill will take us both, unless you don't mind riding bareback."

Alice made to answer, but she was drowned out by a high-pitched squeal from Bill and the other horse. Bill pulled against his leads and reared back, his eyes wild with fright.

"Easy, boy. Easy," Colton said, trying to soothe the big horse, but his eyes caught movement over in his periphery: a shadow moving within the shadows.

"What is it?" Alice said at his shoulder.

"I don't know. Here, get on Bill. He'll take you to town. Just keep riding, don't look back. Bill will take care of you."

"What about you?"

"I got this big fella to keep me company." Colton pointed a thumb over his shoulder. "I've been known to ride bareback from time to time. Now, go!" He slapped Bill's rear and sent him running toward town. Bill didn't seem to mind too much. Colton smiled at that.

A scrabbling sound, like nails over rocks, came from his right. Colton cocked the hammer on his six-shooter. It came all at once, running on all fours like some poor excuse for a wolf or deer. It moved fast, and before Colton could get his bearings, it was on top of him. Colton rolled with it, tried to toss it off. Its grip was too strong, it held on. He'd lost his gun, his hands now occupied with the strength of his attacker's wiry muscles.

Colton kicked and pushed, but nothing worked. His wounded hands began to hurt, and his arms weakened. He shoved his legs between himself and the creature. With a final exertion, he pushed off with his legs and flung the thing away from him. It landed on its back, a thud that would have driven the breath out of any living thing's lungs. The creature ignored it and jumped back to all fours, like some otherworldly spider.

Rolling to his knees, Colton felt around the ground for his revolver but came up with nothing. As the creature pounced again, Colton pulled his knife. The pointy end pierced the stomach of the beast, and it weakened some. Its arms flailed about, but without the strength it had before. Holding the handle of his knife in both hands, Colton hefted the creature to his side and scurried back from it.

The knife stood out of Colm's stomach, a horrible sundial on a bleak night. Colm's head was still smashed in from his fall, otherwise, he appeared as fresh as if he had died yesterday. Blood and gore stained his mouth and chin, the front of his shirt. His teeth continued to gnash and bite in the air.

"What the hell happened to you?" Colton knelt next to Colm. "You're supposed to be dead, boy."

Colm reached for him, his hands opening and closing to grab at Colton's face. His legs had given up on him, though. They were as lifeless as the rest of Colm was supposed to be. Colton wondered about how deep his Bowie had gone in Colm's stomach.

"What is this, eh?" Colton pulled his knife free. "Some Biblical, end-of-the-world, shit? Are you the new Lazarus, Colm?"

Colm didn't answer, his eyes glowing like Desmond's earlier, just fixed on Colton while his arms flailed at his sides.

Something about his chomping mouth made Colton pause. He remembered the bite marks found on Tobias' chest and stomach, remembered the two sets of boot prints in the grassy patch, remembered the blood. Tobias.

Colton fumbled around on the ground for a few more minutes, burning matches to his fingertips to find his shooter, but he'd found it not too far from where he'd started tussling with Colm. It was still cocked and loaded.

"Apologies, Colm, but I hope you've had your fill," he said and put a bullet into Colm's brain.

An inhuman scream rose out of the camp, a high-pitched squeal that drove Colton to his knees, the heels of his hands digging into his ears. Colton wasn't sure how long it had lasted, just that at one point he stopped holding his ears and blinked open watery eyes, and the sound was gone.

The camp around him was quiet. Nothing moved. There wasn't even a breath on the wind. In the sporadic light of the stars and the ghostly embers of fire, he could see the camp in ruins. Any tents left standing were torn and askew, the wagons had been overturned; it hadn't been wiped from the plains, but the attempt had been made. In the ruins, Colton ignored anything that had a rough human shape, he chose to hope that most of the camp made their way to town. He'd seen too much of the opposite in the war.

The horse was gone, broken free when Colm attacked or when the unholy scream howled—it didn't matter. Colton looked out on the plains and back at the destroyed camp. He could use some extra supplies, but he didn't want to face that kind of damage alone. He reloaded his gun, sheathed his knife, and pulled his jacket tight around him. He'd walk his way to town or until something came and took him.

CHAPTER NINE

I

The sun had nearly reached high noon, the fiery oranges and yellows of its rays lapping down on the land, when Colton fell into his makeshift home. He lay on the floor, happy to be out of the sun, his coat unfurled at his sides, his hat resting just above his head. After a moment's rest and a chance to delight in it, Colton stripped his clothes, found his water supply and drank deeply. Nothing had ever felt so good as that cool water on his dry throat and parched mouth. He could feel it coat his innards, and it gave him a pleasant chill all the way to his stomach.

Colton made his way to his bed and eased himself into it. He'd become so accustomed to his bedroll and blankets on the hard ground that even his old, thin mattress felt downright luxurious.

Images of the camp flashed across his vision: Desmond's twisted smile set aflame, Colm's bashed-in skull that still lived, Forsythe's haunted eyes in the caverns. And what of Alice, Mack, and any other survivors? Had they made it to town, or did something happen to them? The dangers in the plains were numerous: snake bites, wolves, maybe even bandits if they stuck close enough to the roads. Or perhaps they were accosted by one of their dead friends, fresh from the grave and hungry for meat. Perhaps that's what it was, Colton thought, hunger. The bite marks on Tobias, the eager look in Desmond's eyes,

Colm's biting and chomping jaw. They were hungry, and not for animals, but for human flesh. Or perhaps they were too slow, too obvious in their hunger for animals? It didn't matter. Colton had killed two of them, Desmond and Colm. That might have been it. Colton's mind brought him back to what Mack had said when he was dragging Brooks's body into camp.

"We buried him, we buried him." Did he mean Colm or Tobias? Maybe both. It wasn't of consequence. Bill had taken Alice back to the town, he was more than sure of that. He believed others would have made it, too. Lee and Lou, Mack. He hoped for more but didn't want to set himself up for disappointment. If they made it to town, they made it to safety. Sheriff Young was there with enough men to defend the town if Tobias came calling. They were safe; they didn't need him.

He sighed, but he couldn't settle. Something twisted in his stomach, a muscle that just wouldn't unclench. He'd forgotten about something important, something that danced on the tip of his tongue. It was gone as quickly as it had come. Still, Colton felt wrong. He wanted to get up, go see the town, and make sure the sheriff knew what was really going on.

Colton thought all this through heavy eyelids that stayed closed longer and longer with each blink. Finally, and without warning, he passed into sleep, dreaming of what he'd forgotten.

II

"Rest easy, Ms. Green," Sheriff Young said as he swung up onto his horse. "I'm sure it weren't nothing but a few ne'er-do-wells trying to rob you all. We'll take care of it."

Alice stood next to the sheriff's horse, a tall, gray quarter horse that snuffed and grunted as the sheriff adjusted himself in his saddle. "I wish you would let me come with you," Alice said. "If these…ne'er-do-wells…really did try to rob us, I need to appraise what was stolen. I need to see if Dr. Forsythe is there." Alice felt childish and foolish. Just the day before, she was the head of a major archaeological camp (one of anyway), ordering men to dig here or there, to sift dirt, to build something. She was equal to her peers, Basil and Desmond. And now, she was practically begging for this sheriff to just listen to her.

"As I told you before, Ms. Green. There could've been bandits or any manner of bad hombres out there causing a fuss. I'll take my men and have a look. If we deem it safe, or once we clear them boys out, I'll send someone back for you."

"But…" Alice didn't like the look of the sheriff's men. She'd already met his deputy, Reg, but the rest of the six men he had gathered to him looked either too sick, too old, or too drunk to do much against any bandits.

"No buts about it. We'll see you soon." The sheriff let out a whistle and a loud yip, and his horse bolted forward, followed by his poor attempt at a posse. Alice didn't feel good about the sheriff's plans, not at all.

She headed back towards the little inn, her head a bee-hive of thoughts, fears, and memories. Alice hadn't been the first to arrive in town seeking asylum, nor was she the last. The town was a small one, but they made the survivors of her little camp feel as best they could, all things considered. The townsfolk had put them in spare rooms throughout the town, never once suggesting the empty and abandoned houses. Alice didn't push too much on that. Basil had tried to sway the sheriff on their previous visit, and the sheriff had been more than emphatic in his answer.

Alice had lucked into the same room she'd had their first night in town, and though it was a nice enough room, clean and well-maintained, it did nothing to comfort her.

She couldn't, wouldn't, sleep. Her thoughts were on Basil Forsythe and Jim Colton.

She'd known Jim for such a short time, days, but she had no doubt in her mind that he'd saved her life at least twice in that time. He was a strange man, rough in his ways, but kind and willing to help. His time spent alone weighed on him, and he wore it like a piece of armour; a hard outer shell to protect him from everything and anyone around him. He'd developed a life for himself as a hermit, and she wondered if it might have been a self-fulfilling prophecy. His father, having been a solitary mountain man, Jim felt he had to do the same. Alice didn't believe he was cut out as a loner. There was too much investment in the people around him. At camp, he volunteered to help with everything from hunting game to burying the dead.

A pang of regret ran an icy finger over Alice's spine, and she hugged herself. She'd tried to listen to Jim's thoughts, to his fears, but she'd been too excited, too lost in her work. After all, there were so many breakthroughs, so many artifacts found, so many markings to decipher. It was exactly what she had hoped the dig would be. Perhaps that should have been her warning, that and Jim's protestations. Life was rarely too good to be true. Alice wanted nothing more than to confess that to Jim, to apologize and thank him. But he hadn't returned with the rest of the survivors. She didn't know if he was alive or dead.

Basil was also unaccounted for. The poor, brilliant man. Jim, she could believe, would live through such a night, even survive the plains alone and without food or water, but Basil? No. He was a tragically intelligent man, dedicated to whatever he put his mind to, and few problems were placed in his way that he couldn't think his way out of, but he was no survivalist, no frontiersman. He was a city boy, accustomed to his comforts. He was also a romantic, a believer in the fantastic. The thought of bandits on their trip from the East had never crossed his mind, just as the disaster of their camp had likely never even been a possibility.

He was a dreamer, and that held its own charm. And, despite the shock of red hair that he couldn't tame, he had a charisma about him. Alice wasn't ashamed that she'd fallen under his spell just by the passion he held in his beliefs. Most of the camp had only been interested in this whole excursion because of Basil's conviction in it. He had a fiery belief in archaeology, in its practice and the good it could do for the world. They all shared his passion, she and Desmond more so than the rest; they were his closest confidantes, his friends. Even still, they both sometimes felt out of depth with Basil, not only with his understanding of the lore, which was substantial, but his utmost belief in it. Such a man, such a genius, was needed in America, in the world. But Alice had no idea if he was alive or dead.

Jim had told her that he was in the caves, the dig site, at the time of the attacks. That had felt strange. Basil had barely set foot in the cave since it was first opened up. He would oversee the workers from his spot on the lip of the hollow and only take the briefest excursions into the tunnels when a potential artifact had been found. Otherwise, he was pleased to hear Alice and Desmond's reports, and he would often lie on his bed at the end of the day and let them regale him with the day's findings. Alice often thought of it like a bedtime story, the man taking it in as if it were dream fuel. What if he had been going into the tunnels? What if he had been there every night after the rest of the camp had gone to sleep? It was an uncomfortable thought but nothing untoward. Still, why didn't he tell her or Desmond? Alice supposed that it didn't matter, not now. What did matter was that he may have been in the tunnels when the attacks took place. That meant he could have hidden away in the dark and could, potentially, be alive. Maybe even down in those tunnels still.

A voice outside her window drew her from her thoughts. "Someone's coming." She'd made it back to her room, so deep in her thoughts that she hadn't realized she had ended up in bed. The light in the sky had darkened some, and it may have been closer to five o'clock than the noon she'd seen the sheriff and his posse off.

"Someone's coming," the voice rang out again. Alice picked herself up, brushed herself off and made for the voice.

Alice was torn. She hoped that the two men would be there, but as she exited to the street, she could only see one head surrounded by the small crowd of townsfolk and survivors. She still didn't know who she had hoped for more, Basil or Jim. She pushed into the crowd and laid her hands on the arm of the newest survivor and pulled him in for a hug.

"Ms. Green," Colton said with a smile. "I told you Bill would keep you safe."

CHAPTER TEN

I

"Didn't think you were much for hysterics, Sheriff," Reg said, his old mare sidling up along Sheriff Young's horse.

"Care to explain that, Deputy?" Young said with a sigh.

"Well, them folks from out East, they got pretty worked up. Probably nothing wrong out here, maybe a couple of assholes being, well, assholes. Right?"

"Reg, I'm a sheriff. You're a deputy. A person in or around our town says they have some trouble, we take a look. It don't matter if they're from some big city out East or some hole in the ground. But, I certainly wouldn't have taken old Joe there," he pointed to the old fella riding off to their right, "or Dan White," he jerked a thumb at another fella to their left, barely able to keep himself straight in the saddle, "if I thought this were serious."

Reg looked back and forth between the other men, and a smile lit upon his face. "Yeah, no serious business at all."

Young tried on his own smile, but the truth was, he was putting on airs. Boasting to his deputy to make him seem in control. Oh, it wasn't the tales Ms. Green had told him that put a niggling air of fear into him, no, that was likely bullshit. It was the Hollow. Young never liked the Crimson Hollow, never cared to go near it or direct explorers to it. He couldn't quite place his finger on what it was that bothered him about it. It was a feeling, like his gut was talking to him, telling him to stay as far away as possible. Up until today, he had done just that. Now, he was riding straight towards it, and something didn't feel right.

"Jesus Christ," came a cry up ahead, and Young kicked his horse into action.

Darrell McClean had stopped his horse not too far ahead. By the hoof prints and grip Darrell still had on his reins, Young thought he might have stopped his horse short and fast. He set his horse next to Darrell and looked out on the carnage.

"What's the deal, Darrel?" Reg pulled up a minute later. The deputy focused his attention on the other men, waiting for an answer.

"Serious business," the sheriff said and urged his horse on at a slow pace.

There had been a camp here, alright, that much he had believed. He hadn't been sure about the details around the late-night flight back into town, but he was starting to become a believer. Tents lay in tatters around the hard ground, and bedrolls, torn to shreds, had their guts capering in the wind. It looked more like a bear attack than any bandit's handiwork. Young's horse stepped lightly through the wreckage, giving him a good look. Blood had been smeared everywhere, some obvious drag marks, but it was a mess of boot prints, signs of a fight, and indications of death. The tracker in him just couldn't put it together. He wasn't sure anyone could.

"Goddamn," Reg said from behind him. "This couldn't have been done by people, right? It had to be a bear, a wolf pack, or something else, right?"

Young ignored him and tried to organize his thoughts. He'd need a bigger posse. Hell, he might even need to reach out to the army. This wasn't done by no small pack of shit heads looking for a bit of fun and some cash, this was...something else.

"I got someone!" Dan Tucker called out and waved his hand. Young ambled over to have a look. A body, he thought, a body was what Tucker meant to say. There was no one left in that bloody mess.

"Who is it?" Reg asked.

"Damned if I know," Dan hiccupped. "I can't tell if that's his head or his asshole."

"Jesus Christ," Darrell said again and drew Young's eyes to him. Darrell pointed behind them, back towards the Crimson Hollow. There at its edge, in silhouette against the bright sun, someone stood watching them.

Young drew his gun without thinking. His posse, such as it was, followed suit. The unified sound of guns being pulled from leather sent his teeth on edge. Guns being pulled like that, something unpleasant was bound to happen.

He held up his hand, hoping the others understood he meant for them to hold their fire. "Greetings," he said, his voice echoing back at him. "I'm Sheriff Young out of the Crimson Hollow township. We heard there was some mess up around here."

The figure took a step forward, it was shaky, unstable. It reminded Young of Dan Tucker stumbling around after he had his liquid lunch.

"Now, you stay right there, mister," Young called. "If you need help, we can come to you. If not, I'd appreciate it if you kept your distance." Young cocked the hammer on his shooter for emphasis. Still, the figure took another shambling step forward.

"What do you want us to do, Sheriff?" Reg said, his hand quaking around his own six-gun.

"Reg, why don't you ride on over there and have a

look. Make sure the fella is okay. If he looks like the one that done this," he waved his hand at the state of the camp, "then you shoot him."

"Me?"

"Get to work, deputy."

Reg looked like he'd swallowed a pinecone. His face was pale, and a thin layer of sweat covered his forehead, but he urged his horse onward. It didn't take him long to reach the man in shadows, and, in true Reg fashion, he began to jaw with him. Young couldn't make out what they were saying, but he could hear them talking. For a moment there, he relaxed. It wasn't the butcher who did this over there, talking to his deputy, just some innocent bystander who'd managed to survive the ordeal. Shocked, to be sure, but alive. He eased his grip on his gun and let out the breath he had been holding since they found the camp in such a state.

Then Reg was on the ground, a gout of blood spouting from his broken neck. In the span of a blink, the survivor reached up, pulled Reg off his horse and ripped his throat out. Reg's mare ran off, screaming.

Young didn't know who had started it, but one gun went off, and then the others followed suit. Bullets sank into Reg's murderer, his body convulsing with their impact, but he didn't fall down. When the bullets had stopped, Young and his men frantic in their reloading, the figure began to run towards them, an inhuman growl piercing the air.

The sheriff managed to reload and fire, but it wasn't before the killer had leapt in the air and dragged old Joe to the ground with him. Darrell and Dan fired in that direction, felling Joe's frightened horse.

"Goddamnit," Young said and pulled his repeating rifle from its holster on his saddle. He took aim and fired two shots before he realized the figure was gone. He'd put two into Joe's corpse.

A shriek turned him around. Dan had been taken down, and another gout of blood flew into the air. It pasted Dan's horse, which took off in a frenzy. Young took aim, but the creature was gone, and all that remained was Dan's corpse, his throat missing and his left eye hanging on his cheek.

With a curse, Darrell made to turn and go, his horse more than willing to oblige. Young scanned the plain through the sight of his rifle, seeing too late a dark flash take to the sky in one moment, and in the next, Darrell was laid out on the ground, his shirt torn, and his chest puckered open.

"Damn, damn, damn," Young said turning the gun quickly to either side. Nothing. "Enough of this," he said and pulled on the reins, driving his horse back toward home. Something darted in front of him. His horse reared, and he tumbled out of the saddle. Young managed to take the fall well enough, rolled as best he could, but the wind was driven out of him, and his rifle was tossed.

The sheriff got to his feet, sucking air in harsh wheezes, and pulled his six-shooter. It was empty, so he gripped it by the barrel like a makeshift sap. There was nothing around him except the dead bodies of his men and their horses and the mess of a body Dan had found. The figure, whatever it was, had disappeared. He ran to Dan's body, pried his gun from his dead fingers and waved it in a wide circle around him.

A hand closed on his ankle, and he screamed. He turned Dan's gun on the source and fired until the gun was empty, then he fired some more. It was the poor, dead bastard they had found, arm outstretched. "I must've bumped into him," Young said quietly to himself, his mind still trying to make sense of what was happening to him.

The hand closed on his ankle again, this time as Young stared at it. Its blood-soaked fingers wiggled to life before clutching his boot. Young screamed again and tried to fire the empty gun, but it did nothing. The dead man's other hand grabbed the gun and pulled itself up, a low and rasping growl rising from its chest. Young smashed at its head with the butt of his gun, deep cuts and dents formed in the bloody tissue, a crack of something breaking, but the dead man didn't stop rising.

It was only when he was dragged to the ground himself, the corpse's teeth tearing at his neck and throat, did the sheriff stop fighting. It was only then that he knew it was pointless.

II

They had expected the sheriff back the previous night sometime before sundown, and the town was on tenterhooks. Colton couldn't say that he blamed them, but he wasn't all that surprised. He had found Bill and was feeding him an apple, the horse snorting at the sight of him. It felt good to see the old horse, and from the head shakes and nose nuzzling, he figured the feeling was mutual.

Colton didn't know what was happening out at the Crimson Hollow, he didn't know if he could even count on his recollections as truthful. What he did know was that the sheriff and his pitiful excuse for a posse were going to come upon a destroyed camp. The fact that the sheriff hadn't yet returned meant one of two things: he was either struck by the damage and meant to stick around to find out what had happened, or he was dead. Colton didn't favour the latter. If that indeed came to be, that would mean that what he had seen, what he had experienced, was real. He felt a cold shiver work its way around his spine.

Bill finished his apple, and Colton gave the horse a final pat on the neck. Still, just because he didn't want to believe in what had happened didn't mean he wouldn't prepare for it. He spoke to Alice, the survivors, and then the townsfolk.

"Look," he'd said, standing on a stone step outside Joe's. "It's simple. Our camp was attacked. Now, I know the good sheriff is out there doing his duty, but I think it would be in our best interest to prepare for the worst."

"What do you mean?" someone shouted. Colton couldn't pick out who.

"I mean that there was more than a handful of highwaymen out there causing trouble. I mean that there was a whole bunch of trouble going on, and if that turns back this way, we should be ready."

"What do you want us to do?" Joe asked from the front, his thin arms crossed over his chest.

"I'm glad you asked."

He'd already worked out the details with Alice beforehand and had some of the other survivors (Mack, Lee, Lou) take charge of directing the townsfolk to finish the jobs they were assigned. They had done as best they could with what they had, and now it was just time to wait. If the sheriff came back, not a scratch on him, he'd have a newly fortified town; if he didn't come back, well, the town was ready for that too.

Colton scoured the streets. Most people were holed up inside, and he saw little eyes peeking at him from behind windows. He could hear some work being done in the distance, hammers and saws working in unison, final preparations being completed. Other than that, the town remained silent. Colton knew how they felt, even felt it himself. It was about the same in the war, the day or night before the fighting started. The apprehension started in your gut and made it go cold. Eating and drinking were hard, sleeping near impossible. All you could do was wait, your strained eyes fixed, your mind numb, ready for the order to fight. Someone had to tell you to do it; Colton suspected it wouldn't happen otherwise.

In the years hence, they called it a war between brothers, and Colton was sure there were some brothers facing off on either side, but the fighting didn't seem all that brotherly. Man, stripped to his baser nature, given no choice but to fight or die, was just another animal. Survival was the only thing that mattered in those minutes, hours, and days. It took better men than he to overcome those baser natures, use their intelligence, and plan an attack that might give the advantage. Generals, not all good men, had that ability, that skill, those who fought anyway. Colton looked around the town, at the preparations he'd help plan out. He wasn't sure his planning was up to snuff; he was no general, but it'd have to do at any rate.

"See anything?" Colton called up to Lee and Lou. The two of them had taken to climbing atop one of the abandoned houses, giving themselves a better view of the plain that separated the town and the real Crimson Hollow.

"Nothing yet, boss," Lee called down with a mock salute.

Colton smiled and moved on. He hadn't seen Lee and Lou in the ruckus at the camp, hadn't thought about them much, really, though he was convinced they'd forgive him if they knew. For their own part, they might have made the quickest escape that night. They'd told him that they'd heard the noises coming from Desmond's tent and had seen Alice run out of there, crying, and two other boys run in to restrain the recently ill man. There were sounds of struggle and muffled screams, and then Desmond emerged, blood spattering his face and bare chest. They were smarter than most, hid out of his sight, made their way to the horses and took off for town. Colton had to give it to Lee and Lou, they were savvy.

He came upon Mack and his group of villagers putting everything in place. Their tools had stopped sounding, and they were finishing up. Colton gave Mack a wave and kept going. Mack refused to tell anyone what he had seen or heard; he refused to talk about how he escaped. All anyone in town knew was that he showed up just after morning hit, covered in blood, riding one of the wagon horses bareback, his sticky, blood-crusted fingers tangled in the horse's mane. The horse, if the townsfolk were right, looked hard ridden, exhausted. There were scratch marks on its ribs and flank. How they got there was as much a mystery as Mack's escape, though Colton was sure he knew how the horse got those marks.

When Colton finished up his short patrol in front of Joe's, Alice was waiting for him. "What do you think?" she asked, crossing her hands in front of her.

"I think that, worse comes to worst, we'll do all right."

"And the town's people?"

"They know their roles. It's up to them now if they play them. If they choose not to, well, that will make things a little more complicated, but I'm not worried."

"How," she whispered, moving in closer to him, her eyes darting back and forth, "how are you not worried? You saw what happened back there."

"Yes, ma'am, I did. I've also seen what we've done here." Colton pointed to a few of their precautions. "As for what I saw, I can't say for certain that is how it played out. I don't think any of us can. Maybe, when the sheriff gets back, he can fill us in on what really happened."

"If he gets back," Alice said.

"I choose not to think like that, Ms. Green. Not if but when."

Alice nodded, but Colton could tell she was unconvinced. "I hope you're right."

Colton made to move past her, but she caught his arm.

"Tell me again, what happened between you and Basil in those dark tunnels?"

Colton gripped the bridge of his nose between his finger and thumb. "Let's focus on something else."

"I just want to know what Basil was doing down there. I want to know if he still might be alive."

"All those things you'll find out when the sheriff gets back. For now, focus on the business at hand."

Alice offered the smallest smile and made for her place in the plan when Lee's voice cried above the wind, "Something's coming!"

Colton took off, ran for the nearest house, and scaled it. He reached the flat roof as quickly as possible, his eyes scanning the horizon for something.

"There," Lee shouted, pointing into the distance. A single shadow appeared, a silhouette, trailing a tail of dust behind it.

"Anyone got some binoculars?" he asked and looked at the town around him.

"Here," said Lou, and he brought them to his eyes. He started to speak in his own language, speaking directly to Lee.

"He says that there is a single horse riding in," Lee explained.

"Does it have a rider?" Colton said.

"Not sure. There is a big dust cloud surrounding him. It's hard to see."

Even without binoculars, Colton could finally see the horse come into view. It was a vague image with no discernible details or features to make out. He held his breath. It could be the sheriff returning—that would be good news. Maybe what they'd all experienced had just been some shared fever dream. That didn't feel right, though. Colton hadn't gotten by for this long without trusting his instincts. His gut told him that he'd seen something strange, something he was lucky to survive. The horse riding in would tell the tale of whether he was going to need to continue experiencing the strange or if he could count himself lucky and be done with it.

"No rider," Lou said, and Colton's hopes crashed around him.

"What kind of horse?" Alice spoke up, her fingers dancing idly at her chin, her neck.

"Tall, gray," Lou said.

"Sheriff's," Colton said with a sigh.

"Maybe it just got spooked. Maybe the others will be right behind it," Alice said. Colton attempted a smile, but he knew the truth of it. The sheriff wouldn't have let his horse get spooked like that, not unless there was real danger. Even so, it would be the sheriff riding back for reinforcements, not his horse all by its lonesome.

Colton climbed down to the street and faced Alice. "That's possible, right?" she asked, eyes protesting the truth that was playing around in her head.

"We'll keep a watch. If any of the others come back, we'll know," Colton said and turned to tell Lee and Lou the same. They nodded, but their faces were grim. Colton couldn't say that he blamed them.

The street had started to fill with villagers, their eyes gradually moving from the dust cloud rising on the outskirts of town to Colton. They'd known him for years, but only as a hermit who made his life outside their town with as little to do with them as possible. To them, he was the odd fellow who they wanted to call harmless but couldn't quite bring themselves to it when they saw the results of his hunting. Now, Colton stood before them, amongst them, and they looked to him for answers.

"What should we do now?" It was Alice who said it, her voice quaking in the reality of what was to come, but it was as though she spoke for everyone gathered there, their ears perking at the question, their eyes pleading for an answer.

"We have our plans," Colton said around a sigh. "Until then, keep to your homes, hug your children." It wasn't what any of them wanted to hear. Most put their heads down, shoulders dropping in disappointment, disbelief. It wasn't what they wanted to hear, but it was what they needed to hear. The townsfolk headed back to their homes.

"What do you intend to do?" Alice had remained; she didn't have a home to go to. Her eyes had hardened some, and her voice was measured. It hadn't been said, but she had put together what was coming next, and she was preparing herself.

"I'm going to grab Bill, and we'll ride out to get the sheriff's horse. Poor thing could use a rest." Alice smiled a little at that and moved off toward the inn.

What Colton hadn't told her was that he wanted to check the horse for any blood, its own or something else's, and make sure it was tidy for its arrival back into town. Alice may have been hardening herself for what was to come, but Colton wasn't sure the townsfolk had that in them. Not yet anyway.

CHAPTER ELEVEN

I

It had been a couple of hours since Colton and Bill had brought in the sheriff's old horse. Mack could tell the beast had been wiped down, cleaned of whatever had been sticking to it. Whatever he had done, Colton hadn't been able to get the look of sheer dread out of the poor creature's bulging eyes. Mack nearly laughed out loud when he saw it. "I feel the same, ol' buddy," he'd wanted to say, but Mack was having a hard time saying much of anything. Somehow, he didn't think words would ever be able to convey the thoughts and memories playing at the back of his mind. So much so that he didn't want to begin speaking for fear that whatever fell out of his mouth would be one insensible word after another, a nonsensical stream of noise that attempted to explain the terror and horror of what he had witnessed. Talking would provide little more than a road to hell.

With the appearance of the sheriff's horse, Mack knew that it was only a matter of time before those things came crawling around town looking to repeat the show they'd made for him just a day earlier. He couldn't go through that again. Words would have to be his ally once more.

"What are we even doing here?" he asked Lee. "This isn't our problem. We escaped our problem back there at camp. If I had anything to say about it, we'd gather up some horses and leave these folks to protect their home."

Lee stroked his chin. "Some might say that it was our actions that caused all of this in the first place. If so, it is our mess to clean up. We need to stay and see that through."

"Damn it, Lee, you saw what those...those things did back there." Mack shuddered and had to work hard to get his shoulders squared up again. "They're monsters. Ain't no way to stop them. They just keep coming and coming."

Lee shrugged and walked away, returning to his place on the abandoned house. He tried to talk some sense into a few of the other survivors, making sure to keep it quiet around Colton and Ms. Green. Most of them had the same kind of answer for Mack, and more than a few of them had some choice words for him. They had all been there, but they hadn't seen. They hadn't seen what Mack had seen.

Mack was in the bar, trying to convince another member of the old crew to take off with him, some thin fella whose name he couldn't quite remember—Jacob, maybe. The bar was open, but they weren't serving anything harder than piss-warm beer, Colton's orders. Mack figured it was to keep the troops alert, but the only sane thing to do with what was coming down on them would be to let them all drink. Force them to it. If any of them knew what they were in for, they wouldn't want to be sober in the face of it. Mack thought he was getting somewhere with Jacob when Colton approached him. Mack could feel the stare on his back, feel the presence at his elbow. Mack didn't want to turn, didn't want to face Colton.

"Mack," Colton said, drawing his attention, regardless of how Mack felt on the matter. "I hear you've been causing a fuss."

"No, no fuss, Mr. Colton," Mack said, barely able to contain his shivering.

"I'm glad to hear you talking again." Colton took a

seat next to him and nodded to Jacob, who pushed away from the table, relieved. "Shows you've got some toughness." They faced each other for a moment, silence passing between them.

Colton spoke first. "I hear you're looking to hop town." Mack cringed at the accusation. It was true, but he hated to hear it out loud.

"Yeah," he mumbled, his chin to his chest and eyes on the table.

"No one knows what you've been through, but the lack of talking for all that time sure told us it wasn't good." Colton's voice was low, just above a whisper. Soothing. "I can understand you wanting to run from this thing, I do, but you're scaring the piss out of everyone. I can't have that."

"I'm sorry, Mr. Colton. I didn't mean to cause a fuss, but...why are we doing this?" Mack screwed up the courage to look Colton in the eye. "We got no connection to these people. Hell, we don't even know if what we saw back there at the camp is even going to come this far. Maybe it'll just stick close to its hole, protect it like a bunch of ants around their hill." It felt good to get the words out, his thoughts and feelings, but even Mack could tell they were feigned. Hell was coming to town, no doubt about it.

Colton nodded along with Mack's argument and let the words hang in the air for a little while before he answered. "You know, you're right on one thing—I don't have any connection to these people. I've lived just on the outskirts of their town for years, but we aren't connected. I did that on purpose, it made it easier to move on, to not care. I was alone in the world, and I thought I was better for it. Let me tell you, son, that ain't true. Funny as it sounds, this whole thing helped me understand that people, other people, are worth something. They can help you as much as you can help them. Thing is, that comes with a responsibility. You depend on others, they start to depend on you. To up and leave when others are depending on you, well, that makes you a sorry excuse for a human being. We have a responsibility to these people, not because of what they have given us, but because of what we have wrought on them. Sure, we could let them face it alone, but that would mean we face it alone as well, and I don't know about you, but I'd rather not face this by myself."

Mack sighed, hot tears streaming down his cheeks. He squeezed his hands together as tightly as he could. "I don't know if I can do it. I don't know if I can face it again."

"I know, son. I know. Instead of running away, maybe you could do one last thing for us, and not worry about facing down them things."

Mack nodded. He'd like that.

II

Colton had loaded him up with a day or two of supplies, enough water for three, and told him to ride to Alamosa. The town wasn't that big, but they might be able to send some help. Watching Mack ride, giving the horse the spurs and taking off quicker than a jackrabbit, Colton knew he wouldn't be back. May not even make it to Alamosa. The boy was damaged. Whatever he'd seen had been more than any of the other survivors could understand. He wasn't willing to share that, and none of them were willing to hear it. It was better that he was gone, better for everyone.

About two hours later, the dead arrived.

Colton had been letting himself doze in the setting sun when Lee and Lou began shouting. He scrambled back to his perch on the house next to them, his eyes scanning the horizon. It was bright enough for him to just make out dark figures in the distance. Still too far off to gauge who they were, but there was little doubt.

"Shout out numbers and distance," Colton told Lee and Lou and climbed from the house. "When they get close enough, keep to your positions. We'll need you."

Colton made his way through the village, shouting orders, getting people into their positions. The first thing they needed to do was close the doors. The fort, as it had been, was no more. The doors hadn't been closed in since settlers had started to take the town over for themselves. He'd set a couple of groups to work on it, but he didn't know if they'd had enough time to repair everything.

"Get those doors closed," Colton said, directing men who were spilling out of their houses to the job. Three men on each started to pull the ill-used doors closed, the rusted hinges groaning against the effort.

"At least a dozen, boss," Lee's voice carried from his perch. "Still pretty far, but they won't be long."

"The doors won't close," another man said at the doors. They were still pushing, but Colton could see the problem. The hinges had seized up. It wasn't just the rust, but the dust of the roads being kicked up by any manner of traveller that did it. Colton cursed.

"Move out the roadblocks," Colton said. The fort doors were partially closed, each hanging about 45 degrees inward; they hadn't closed off the entrance, but they had made it smaller. The roadblocks, essentially logs with sharpened sticks jutting out of them, would help, but it wasn't ideal.

The six men went to work moving the roadblocks in front of the opening. Colton stood back and studied the entrance. The roadblocks might do the trick, but he didn't want to get his hopes up. He remembered how Colm had clambered around in the dark. If all the dead were as agile, they wouldn't need to use the entrance at all.

"How far out?" Colton asked, looking to Lee and Lou.

"'Bout an hour," they said in unison.

"If they keep up the pace they're using," Lou said.

"If they wanted to run," Lee said with a shrug.

Colton nodded. "All right, people, those who can wield a gun, grab one and get ready to use it. Women and children get to Joe's and lock the door. Block it with some furniture. We'll let you know when it's safe to come out."

"Now, wait a minute," Joe the bartender said, sticking a six-shooter into his holster. "Them boys said that only a dozen people were coming our way."

"Could be more," Lee said.

"It's a long distance," Lou said.

"Whatever. The point is, we have twenty good, armed men here. Give some of the ladies a gun or two, and we'll turn these bastards before they even reach the walls." Some of the other townsfolk started to murmur their agreement. None of the camp survivors joined them.

"Joe, if this were a normal situation, I'd agree with you, but you don't know what we're dealing with," Colton said. "Hell, I don't know what we're dealing with, and I saw it with my own damn eyes. All I do know is that the dead, yes, the dead, are rising up from the ground, and they don't seem to like the living too much."

"The dead? You can't be serious."

Colton stepped into Joe's space, his face just a hair's length from the other man's. "Joe, you ask any of the people here from that camp what they saw, and they'll tell you the same. Now, I don't care if you believe the specifics or not; all you need to know is that there are some people out there trying to get in, and you don't want that. You don't want that at all."

"Okay, Jim," Joe said and backed off. "I'll see that the women and children get set up in the bar."

Everyone else went to their positions, some along the

top of the wall, on rooftops like Lee and Lou, others standing behind the roadblocks. Colton would be there. Until he was needed, he wanted to have another look at what was coming and made to climb up once more, when Alice grabbed his arm and turned him to face her.

"I'm not hiding away," she said. Her face was calm, her mouth a thin, white line.

Colton just stared at her, the woman who had gotten him involved in all of this mess. He did his best not to smile.

"I'm going to be out here with the rest of you, facing down whatever is coming."

"You know how to use a gun?" Colton asked and pulled out an extra six-shooter he had slung through his belt.

"Please, I'm not some delicate flower, nor am I some homemaking mother of ten," Alice said and swiped the pistol from his hand.

"Not that there's anything wrong with that kind of thing," Colton said.

Alice gave him a stony glare. "Mr. Colton, my daddy would curse me from heaven if I ever gave up shooting, riding horses, and gambling. Today won't be the day I start." She put the gun in her waistband and gestured toward the house Colton had been about to climb. "Now, help a lady climb up there, would you?"

This time, Colton did laugh, and despite herself, Alice broke into a big, genuine smile. They stared at each other for another moment before Colton put his hands together and helped Alice up to the roof.

III

"Why have they stopped?" Alice squinted as she stared at the dead men that stood just a few minutes outside of town.

There were more than a dozen. Colton counted at least twenty, though he wasn't interested in keeping track at that point. He recognized big Tobias with his crooked neck; Clay Brooks was missing an arm; even old Desmond was there, half of his flesh cooked off his body. Others included Sheriff Young and his deputy, Reg, both missing the flesh around their throats, and Colm, his crushed head sporting a bullet hole that still hadn't stopped him. Colton cursed. This was not good.

"I'm more concerned with how we stop them," Colton said. "They start coming, you aim for the vitals: heart, brain, that sort of thing. They keep coming, you aim for their knees. They won't be able to take a bite out of you if they can't walk."

They drifted back into silence after that, all of them focused on the dead standing just outside the town's walls, not prepared for what was going to happen next.

The town and the dead remained in that cold stand-off as the sun sank out of the sky. Colton wasn't enthusiastic about having to deal with this in the dark, but he wasn't willing to make the first move either. The dead were dead after all, maybe they'd just fall back into their graves.

A sound like a distant rumble set upon the town. The noise, like a thunderstorm ready to roll over the land and toss lightning upon them, chilled Colton to the bone; his muscles bunched, and his back straightened. He ran a hand over his neck, expecting to find the hair there perked up, unable to go down. The sky darkened, but it was more than the sun setting; the world seemed darker as the noise droned on.

"What is that?" he asked and tried to shake off the feeling of coming dread.

"It's words," Alice said, her ear cocked to the sky. "A chant, not in English."

Colton looked at Lee and Lou. "We don't sound like

that," Lee said and pointed towards the gathered dead.

That's when Colton saw it: the dead men's mouths were moving. He pointed it out to the rest of them.

"It's not their voices, though," Alice said. "It's all one voice. It's like they're some sort of phonograph. They're the horn, repeating the message over and over again."

"If they're the horn, who is the wax cylinder?" Colton asked, trying to get a better look at the group standing before them.

"What are they saying?" Lou asked.

"I don't know. It's not a language I'm familiar with." Alice cocked her ear to the sound once more.

The more he heard it, the easier it was for Colton to pick out the different inflections between words, to hear them separately. "It sounds a bit like Swedish."

Alice raised an eyebrow. "And how do you know that?"

"In the war, in my regiment, a Swede had just come to America and joined the fight. Anders Henriksson, that was his name. He joined with his younger brother, Lars. At night, I could hear them talking back and forth in their language. It sounded something like this."

"Swedish," Alice said and let out a mirthless chuckle. "It makes sense, doesn't it? We were digging around for Viking artifacts, and now we have dead men talking to us in some type of ancient Scandinavian. Norse." She looked into the blinking eyes of Colton, Lee, and Lou. "It's the language of the Vikings."

"Well, whatever language it is, we need to figure it out. Maybe we can talk to them, get them to stand down," Colon said.

"I have some references to Old Norse in my books— Basil had even more—but they're all back at the camp." Alice's face hardened around her frown. "Your Swedish friend around anywhere?"

"He's dead," Colton said and stared out at the talking dead men.

IV

The chanting changed as twilight darkened. Colton perked up his ears as English started to fall in for the Norse.

"By the Old Gods, we take this land. By the Old Gods, we take these lives. By the Old Gods, we live again. Fear not death, for the hour of your doom is set. The Draugr walk."

"I don't think they're willing to talk," Lee said and picked up his rifle. Lou followed suit.

"Doesn't appear that way," Colton said and then turned to the rest of the townsfolk. "Ready your weapons, stay at your posts. Don't let anything inside the walls. They're coming."

CHAPTER TWELVE

I

The dead men didn't charge straight at the walls as Colton had predicted. Instead, they scattered, splitting into two groups like they meant to surround the town or come in from behind. Colton watched for a split second, trying to time their speed and movement. Some shambled and were slow; others dropped to all fours and ran quickly like a dog. Colton called out orders and jumped down to take his position at the gateway.

The firing and the screaming had already begun. Five or six dead men threw themselves in through the doors, their faces pocked by decomposition, their eyes vacant and milky white. One had managed to lodge himself on the spikes of a roadblock, a sharp piece of wood piercing his stomach and extending out of his back. Still, he made to swipe at those closest to him. Colton put two bullets in his head, and he stopped moving—for a moment.

Colton had no time to shout a warning. One of the townsfolk moved close to the roadblock to aim his rifle at another corpse when the impaled man grabbed him and tore into his throat. Colton shot the beast twice more for his trouble.

More of the same happened all over the town. The dead tried to push their way through the defences and were pushed back. The townspeople suffered some losses but kept their numbers up, and those they lost didn't come back to life. At least, not yet.

After a few hours, the dead regrouped in front of the walls. They stood where they had been chanting, displaying their newest battle wounds. Colton could make out at least three corpses with no heads, one without legs, and several missing arms.

"We can't keep this up," Colton said to his companions on the roof. "They got enough fight in them to go forever."

"At least we're whittling them down," Alice said and pointed to the maimed dead, still moving. "They can't fight if they're just a bunch of body parts, right?"

"I'm afraid that our dead might bolster their ranks if they need it. Then we'd really be in the shit. How are we doing on ammo? I haven't done a count, but I'd suspect we're getting pretty low."

"So, what do we do, boss?" Lou had a piece of cloth tied around his forearm, blood slowly seeping through it.

"We keep fighting until none of us are left. Take as many of them with us as we can and pray they don't use our bodies in the afterlife."

"That's no way to win," Lou said and shrugged.

"No, sir. It isn't," Colton agreed, mopping sweat from his brow. He wasn't sure why the dead were having a break, but he was glad for it. He'd tasked some men to pile debris in front of the open doors and nail some boards across the opening if they could. It'd give the dead a harder time getting in, but the bastards weren't afraid to climb.

"We need to get back to the camp," Alice said, drawing their attention. "If I could find something in my notes, in Basil's notes, maybe we could end this with a word or two."

"If you're right," Lou said, "the problem there is getting through all those dead people."

"And you don't know if you're right," Lee said. "This is a curse. We're cursed."

"Mr. Colton, please. It's either we die trying to stay alive in here or die trying to stay alive out there. In here, we have no other options. At the camp, well, maybe we'll find something that can help."

"Not much of a choice," Colton said, "dead one way or the other."

"We need to try," Alice said. Colton nodded. A chance, no matter how small or ridiculous, was better than none.

"Okay," he said at length.

"How do you plan to get past the dead folks?" Lou asked, resolved to the choice that was made.

Colton eyed the corpses standing there as if awaiting orders. He sighted Desmond near the front of the lot of them, his skin still charred and melted, but missing more of the rest of his body, an arm gone, half of his face.

"I think I have an idea," Colton said. "We'll leave as soon as I can organize it."

"I'll go with you," Lee said. "I'd like to see this curse lifted in person." He looked at Lou and gave him a pat on the shoulder. They nodded to each other, and they were off, Lou left to guard the roof.

II

The townsfolk weren't pleased that he asked them to open the gates, but they obliged if it meant the end to this nightmare. Colton sat atop Bill, rubbing the horse's thick neck. Alice sat behind him; he could feel her hands gripping his coat tightly. Lee had borrowed a little snowflake Appaloosa and was mounted up next to them.

"When I give the go-ahead, open the doors," Colton said to the crowd that stood in front of him. "When we're out, close it back up as best you can. We might give you some time to get the boards back up, but I can't guarantee it." Colton looked out on the townsfolk and the camp survivors and saw the fear and uncertainty in their eyes. "We'll make a straight line for the camp, look for what we need, and head back."

"What if you don't make it back?" Joe asked, his boot leaning on a box of whiskey.

"Then, we're dead. Just keep fighting. Don't give them anything; make them work for it." The crowd was quiet. He looked towards the roof and saw Lou looking over his shoulder at them. This had better work, he thought. "Let's go."

On his word, the doors were pulled wide, and Bill shot through them. Lee came behind them, the Appaloosa snorting and chomping. They were barely out the doors when they were closed again, and Colton could hear the barricades being moved back in place. Now it was on to step two.

They turned the corner of the town walls and rode into the face of the dead, their cold, white eyes lighting on their movement. Just as one began to stagger towards them, a bottle of booze crashed against its skull, and flames swam over its skin, its clothes. More crashes followed, and Colton chanced a look back at the town. Lou and several others were tossing bottles with flaming rags sticking out of their throats. Some of the corpses reacted as Desmond had when Colton smashed the lantern over his head and ran in the opposite direction. Colton thought, perhaps, this was due to some scrap of self-preservation remaining in their dead heads. Others just fell to the ground with the impact, the flames happily feeding on their flesh.

It had worked better than Colton had thought, but they weren't through yet. The dead, with whatever intelligence they had, launched themselves at Colton and Lee. Thunderclaps sounded, and the end of Colton's gun ignited, pushing the dead back with more bullets in them.

Behind him, Lee did the same, and from the walls of the town, more guns blasted away, their aim now guided by the fire burning the moving corpses.

The dead fell, whether from the fire that was engulfing them or from the bullets that rained down upon them, Colton couldn't say. He did know that it was a brief reprieve for the town, where, unless Alice was able to figure out some sort of magic word to return the dead to their graves, they'd be back and beating on the doors. He kicked Bill into a run and aimed him for the Crimson Hollow.

CHAPTER THIRTEEN

I

The night was quiet, the pale light of the moon and its stars barely revealing the path ahead of them. In the years that Colton had lived there, he'd never heard a night so silent. The yips and howls of coyotes didn't pierce the distant air, the wings of an owl didn't beat against the wind, the scurrying of rodents couldn't be heard scrabbling over stone—it was an unnatural silence that set Colton's teeth on edge. He'd become accustomed to the noises and felt at ease in their presence, felt normal. Their absence put him on guard and off-kilter. He strained to hear them, hoping to find something familiar to let him know that he wasn't alone, but even the critters of the Colorado plains knew something wasn't right. They hid, waiting for it to be over. The only sound that penetrated the deep night was the quickening beats of their horses racing towards the Crimson Hollow.

The wreckage of the camp was how they had left it; the dead had no need for extra clothes, rations, or other supplies. There were no bodies. All that had fallen had taken the trip back to town with their fellow corpses.

"Help me find my tent," Alice said after they'd tied up the horses. Colton and Lee kicked through some of the fallen tents and came upon two lanterns. One had only a little oil left, the other sloshed around at half full. They lit them both.

The orange lamp's glow helped illuminate more of the carnage that had become their camp. Everything had been torn to shreds: tents, bedrolls, clothes, even books. Lee and Colton shared a worried glance at the state of the ripped pages half-stomped into the packed earth and dust. Alice didn't seem to notice or care, and they pushed on.

"This is it," Alice said, picking up a piece of torn burlap. "Hold this open and hand me a lamp." Lee and Colton obliged, handing over the mostly full lamp and did their best to hold the tent up so Alice could get a good look. After a few minutes, she exited, cursing under her breath. "Let's try Basil's tent." Alice stomped off towards the far edge of the camp, her eyes scouring the ground for any sign of Forsythe's former abode.

"Here." Lee got to it first and raised his lantern in the air, guiding Alice and Colton to him.

"Ain't no way we can hold this up while you look, Ms. Green," Colton said, eyeing the oversized tent with more than a little suspicion. He took Alice's lantern and spent a moment feeling around him, finally coming up with a long pole that had been used to keep the tent steady. With the help of Alice and Lee, Colton managed to stick the pole in the middle of the tent to give it some kind of shape and lift the roof so Alice could have a look. Colton and Lee still had to hold the sides to make sure the tent didn't collapse on her while she looked.

Alice was in Forsythe's tent longer than her own, but when she exited, she had two books in her hands. One was a notebook, puffed up with added pages and its leather-bound cover stained with coffee, tea, and wine. The other book looked more educational, like something you'd find in a school or a library. On the spine, it read, *Norse Mythology, Religion, and Language.*

Colton nodded to the books. "Think you'll find what you need in those?"

"Maybe," Alice said with a frown and held up the notebook. "This is one of Basil's notebooks, but it isn't the book he'd been using lately. I'll look through it, but I'm not sure it's what we need." She held up the schoolbook. "If the notebook doesn't work, this might help translate some of the runes in the cave. Might be worth a try."

Colton and Lee managed to dig out a table and chair from Forsythe's tent and set them up for Alice to do her work. It was shaky as hell and far from perfect, but it would have to do.

They'd placed one of the lanterns on the table for a reading light and tried to make themselves busy. Colton let Lee keep the other lantern so he could try and find some supplies from the overturned wagons. If they couldn't find a solution to fix all this, which Colton was losing more hope for the longer he was away from town, they could at least bring back some ammo, guns if they were around, and any food that still looked edible. In the meantime, Colton sought out his own tent, hoping to gather the things he'd left behind, his repeating rifle, for one.

The tent, like the others, wasn't hard to find, even without a lantern to light the way. He just had to kick around in the general area he remembered having it set up. His tent had been trampled, but most everything he had left behind was in its place, more or less. Colton picked through the wreckage, finding his rifle and some extra ammo. Anything outside of that, he left alone; he wouldn't need to worry about that unless the night went the way they'd hoped.

Out of the corner of his eye, a shadow moved. Like a spring, he spun himself around, rifle to his shoulder and eye looking down the sight. The moonlight did little to help him differentiate the shadows that now closed around him, and whatever movement he'd seen had stilled or was gone. Colton chanced a look over his shoulder. The two lanterns were in the distance, the light illuminating small features of his companions. He backed away from his tent, moving as best he could towards Alice.

"How're you doing over there, Ms. Green?" Colton cringed at the echo of his voice in the night.

"I think I may have found something," Alice called back, her face a mask of concentration as she bent over the books.

"That's good," Colton said, faltering some as movement drew the barrel of his gun to his right, closer to the damned Hollow.

This time, there was more substance to the shadows, the vague shape of a man hunched over, his arms dragging towards the ground. Two white eyes stared back at Colton, glowing in the dark. If Colton hadn't been looking for it, they might have disguised themselves as stars in the night sky. As he looked upon them now, seeing the outline of a long, thin face surrounding them, he could tell that they were not burning stars in the sky but burning orbs of anger and hate.

Colton froze and saw the creature do the same. He didn't know if the heavy breathing he heard was his own or that of the beast before him, but it filled his skull. They stood like that for mere moments, looking at one another, trying to read the other's intentions. It felt like they'd be stuck like that forever.

"This isn't good," Alice said and changed everything.

At her voice, the creature pushed forward, a roar surging from its throat. It was met with the bark of Colton's rifle, the muzzle flash igniting the space between them. In those seconds of light, Colton could see Forsythe's face staring back at him, ruined by fury and twisted upon itself. Then he was gone, loping off somewhere in the shadows.

"Lee," Colton kept his eye on the sight of his rifle,

"pull your gun and get back to Ms. Green."

"What's going on?" Alice cried out.

"I've found Dr. Forsythe."

Alice's sobbing filled the silence. Colton mentally implored her to stop, to stay quiet, but he couldn't bring himself to say it aloud. He took another quick glance behind him and saw Lee with his pistol drawn and ready, Alice with her face in her hands.

Movement to his left turned him, and he fired blindly, seeing earth dance up in the dim light. Alice sniffled behind him, her breathing erratic.

"Is...is he dead?" she managed. "Is he one of them?"

Colton panned his gun back and forth, keeping up his slow pace as he moved towards his companions. He thought of what little he had seen of Forsythe, thought of those burning, rage-filled eyes. "No," he said. "No, he's something else entirely."

"Okay, I think I—" Alice's voice was cut off when Forsythe swiped a hand at Colton's barrel, pushing it to the side, a shot going off in the dark. Colton felt the crack of Forsythe's other hand as it landed on the side of his head and sent him falling to the ground.

Dazed, Colton tried to pull his pistol, but Forsythe landed a kick to his guts that sent him sliding backwards, tangling him in the wreckage of tents. Forsythe stood over him, his mouth descending below those glowing eyes, wet teeth, sharper and longer than any man's should be, bared.

It was the crisp snap of a gunshot that saved Colton's life. Forsythe's body rocked with the impact, a snarl of pain escaping his blackened lips. Lee stood close by, lamp lifted in the air, smoke rising from his gun.

Fire again, Colton tried to say, but he was dazed, and his breath hadn't returned. Instead, he mumbled something that even he couldn't understand. Lee stood motionless, his eyes wide as he took in every aspect of the Forsythe that was getting back to his feet.

Forsythe was shirtless, his thin body lined with stringy muscles coated in dust and dirt. His back hunched forward around a bulging spine, and his fingers had developed claws as his mouth had grown fangs. The fingers looked sore, the claws like elongated pieces of bone that burst through the fingertips, leaving a trail of viscera and pus to stain the remaining flesh.

"Dr. Forsythe," Lee said and bowed. "You aren't aware of what you are doing. Please stop."

Forsythe eyed Lee and his gun, his glowing eyes betraying no emotion. Instead, he stood in front of Lee, his hands clenching and unclenching, impatient, needy.

"Basil." Alice was standing behind Lee, her face a conglomeration of sadness, confusion, and terror. "Basil, I know what is happening. I think I can help you."

At these words, Forsythe pounced. Colton tried to get up, tried to shout a warning, but he wasn't in time. Forsythe's hands sank deep into Lee's gut, causing blood to spew from his mouth instantly. Alice, shocked, staggered backward as Lee wilted to the ground, his gun and lantern dropping with him. Forsythe tore himself free of Lee's stomach and, in a blink, had Alice in his arms, and in another, he was at the scaffolding leading to the cavern. He took a moment to look back at Colton struggling to free himself from his burlap restraints before he disappeared into the hollow, Alice over his shoulder screaming for help.

II

"It's bad," Lee said around some words in his own language.

Colton knelt over him. He'd wrapped him up as best he could in what he could find around. Clothes, mostly, and some of the burlap material of the tents. The wound was already oozing through the makeshift bandages.

"It ain't good, but I've seen worse," Colton lied. Lee forced a smile that ended in a grimace.

"What will you do?" he asked, frothy blood leaking from the corners of his mouth.

"Go get her, die trying." Colton stood, lantern in hand. "She said she'd figured something out. That's the best I've heard in a while." Lee nodded.

"I'll keep everything in order up here," he lifted his gun, leaned it on his shoulder. "See you soon." Colton clapped the man on the shoulder and headed for the hollow.

III

Nothing had changed since he'd been in the cavern last. He had expected a small army of dead men waiting for him, their slack-jawed expressions staring daggers into his healthy flesh. Instead, he was met with nothing and no one. The cavern stood dark and open, with hardly any sign that it had ever been visited by man or animal.

Colton pushed ahead, his lantern leading the way, six-gun poised in his other hand. A surreal sensation fell over him like a sheet, and his stomach twisted. He'd been in these tunnels just days before, doing the same thing; it was as if he were walking through a bad dream.

His lantern cut through the thick atmosphere, dust motes scattering within the orange light. He laid the heel of his gun hand on one smooth, rounded stone wall, then pulled his hand away with a fright. It was warm and clammy like living flesh. He made it to the main chamber, the air heavy with the foul smell of earth, and swung his lantern towards Forsythe's table. No one there.

He aimed his gun, expecting the whispered fall of a footstep, but found only his ragged breathing to betray the silence.

The craftsmanship and design were still something wondrous, and Colton forced himself to take in what little surroundings he could see in the barely lit room. Again, he expected a small movement, something from behind him, and again there was nothing there but rock and shadow. Colton cursed.

The rest of the cave played out the same way, with Colton cautiously pointing his lamp and gun in each room and hallway, only to find nothing but shadow and bad memories. Colton emerged into the main chamber once again, still cautious, still bearing his revolver in one hand, his lantern in the other. This chamber was different, lighter, brighter, too. Colton peered into the room, looking for candles or lamps, anything that might make a difference, but to no avail.

"Welcome back, Mr. Colton," Forsythe said, the flare of a match exposed him as he sat at the stone table, smoking a cigarette. "I'm surprised to see you here, after your run-in with that creature."

"The creature was you, Doc," Colton said and knocked back the hammer of his six-shooter. Forsythe looked back to normal; his shock of red hair wavy over his face, which was free of fangs or blackened lips.

"In a sense, perhaps. I merely forfeited my body for a while, let her take over." A crash sounded to the side that made Colton jump, and a crow joined them, knocking over an urn in its arrival, zooming in from the entrance.

"The bird?" Colton demanded, his face unable to contain his confusion.

"No mere bird, Mr. Colton. This is a high priestess, maybe shaman is a better term for it." Forsythe called the bird to him with some small clucking noises, and it landed on his sleeve. It turned its head quizzically to Colton, its eyes the same burning white that he had seen in the creature that had captured Alice. "She's been stuck here for some time. Here and her followers, that is."

"The Vikings?"

"Not really. Oh, they had been Vikings; even the shaman was a Viking in her day. It was the trek to this place, America, that made the change." Forsythe let the bird hop from his arm to the desk, where its onyx talons scratched along the cover of a leather notebook. "You see, their commander wanted them to take over this place, pillage and wreck things as they had done throughout their entire history. The shaman, well, she had other plans. She'd been drawn to this place the moment she stepped foot on the shores of America, a place of power and magic that became irresistible. She marched the troops across this land, losing many in the process, until she finally came to the Crimson Hollow. I suspect it was death that made the power surge. It wasn't just poor Colm that died while trying to search out this cave system. Untold numbers of people, explorers, Natives, and settlers all lie at the bottom of this chasm. Death, as I'm sure you know, has a power all its own.

"More men lost their lives when she tasked them to begin digging into the hole to make the caverns as you see them now. Beautiful work, isn't it? It took them many years to finish the task. By the time it was complete, many had died, and others were too old to enjoy the spoils of the dig."

"And what spoils do you mean?" Colton asked, gun still pointed in Forsythe's direction.

"The magic in this place. The ability to use it at will. Life after death. However, as a shaman," he nodded to the crow, "she was able to lengthen her life, such as it is, in another form. She couldn't do the same for her warriors. Instead, she promised them the ability to return from the dead once she could regain some of her power. Once the cave had been opened once more."

"The dead, those attacking the town, are the spirits of dead Vikings?"

Forsythe lit a candle on his table, illuminating Alice's face. "Why don't you tell him, Alice? You certainly seem to be on the right track about all of this." he reached across and removed a gag from her mouth.

"Yes, and he knew all along," Alice said, squirming against the restraints around her arms and legs that kept her in place in her chair. The crow snapped at her. "He'd interviewed that man who had taken the sword from here, heard a rumour that a ghost thirsted for blood in the caves. Then he delved into his research, and..."

"And I found a reference to a Viking band that went missing in this place long before Columbus set foot on these shores. I must admit, I had been curious, but I want you to know, Alice, that I didn't come into this with any aspirations of taking this on. It seemed altogether foolish. Superstitions of a primitive culture, just like those buried pharaohs in Egypt," he chuckled. "It was that first night in town, a night spent in one of those abandoned houses, when the shaman came to me. Possessed me. Showed me that all of this was real. That I could have the power to converse with the dead, to control them. I had no idea about any of this brutish stuff. Though that has been fun as well." Forsythe tipped a wink towards Colton.

"Basil, please," Alice said. "Put a stop to this, it's not too late."

"I have power, strength, and an army of unstoppable Viking warriors to command. Why would I want to stop? Think of it, Alice, think of the knowledge we could gain, of what we could take with the shaman's help. I will know all the secrets of the world, of existence itself. Isn't that what you've wanted as well, knowledge?"

"Knowledge of the past to improve the present, Basil.

It's what we've always agreed to."

"Who's to say my reign wouldn't bring about a better world? One world ruled by one ruler. Everyone the same, everyone equal. It would be paradise."

"One man's paradise is another man's hell," Colton said and fired.

The shaman flew into action, and in a blink, it was in the bullet's path. It hit her, driving the crow backwards towards Forsythe, who stood, mouth agape. The crow shifted from black feathers to a black, oily liquid. The liquid crashed into Forsythe, who took a step back at the impact. Instead of splashing, the liquid that had been a crow clasped onto Forsythe stuck to him and began to sink in. Colton could see it slither into the older man's skin, black veins that then crisscrossed his person. Forsythe shook then grunted, and in the flame light, he shimmered. It was like his body was at odds with the space around him. Whether it was trying to fold in on him or push him out, Colton couldn't be sure. When the shimmering was at an end, Forsythe the beast had returned.

"Shit," Colton said and fired again. The gun was thunderous in the cavern, echoing around the chamber like something on a slingshot. Still, the bullet found its home in Forsythe's chest. It did nothing.

Forsythe charged.

With nothing else to do, Colton ran towards the cave entrance and back to the edge of the hollow. His legs took him most of the way, but it was a push from Forsythe that launched him through the air, finally skidding to a stop at the precipice. Gasping, he rolled away from the edge, unsure of where his gun or lantern had fallen.

He was on his knees, about to get to his feet, when Forsythe latched a hand onto the back of his neck. He hoisted Colton into the air, his toes just scraping the floor, until there was no more floor to scrape. Colton hung over the dark abyss that was the Crimson Hollow, panic rising in his throat.

"Fear not death." Forsythe's voice was unrecognizable. A hideous buzzing encompassed it, like two voices speaking at once, neither overpowering the other, neither gaining the advantage, so they settled for a truce and spoke in a third voice. "You cannot run from it. Your time is simply your time."

Colton gripped Forsythe's forearm with one hand while his other slid his knife from its sheath and slashed at Forsythe's eyes. The beast released Colton, and for an instant, he fell into the pit, and he figured he'd finally get to see hell. Instead, he kept hold of Forsythe's arm and stabbed his knife into his chest to keep purchase.

Forsythe reeled, falling away from the edge, free hand covering its eyes that bled a black ooze. Colton's extra weight on the beast's off-balance frame pulled it towards the edge. The creature twisted and attempted to fall to the ground, but Colton twisted with it. Forsythe lay on the edge of the precipice, Colton closer to the cave's entrance.

The creature screamed in its jumbled voice, and this time, Colton could hear both the shaman and Forsythe clearly. He curled himself into a ball, placed his boots on Forsythe's chest, and pushed off. He sent himself skidding along the red, rocky floor just as he pushed the creature into the oblivion of the Crimson Hollow.

IV

"Please tell me you know how to end this," Colton panted as he stumbled into the main chamber once more. He hadn't given himself a chance to recover, instead, he ran to find Alice. Along the way, he found his lantern, still lit despite lying on its side. There was no sign of his six-shooter.

"Jim," Alice said, "you're alive!" A quake took over her voice, and she managed a jittery smile. Colton went to work on her ropes. He'd lost his knife in the pit with Forsythe and the shaman, so he went to work untying the tight, coarse knots.

"I'm alive for now, but I don't know for how long. You figure out that magic word?"

"Not necessarily," Alice squirmed against her bindings, "but I might be able to disrupt the shaman's hold on this place."

"Sounds like a magic word to me," Colton said after freeing Alice's arms and moving to her legs.

"I just need the books I had before Basil abducted me. Have you seen them?"

"I've been a little busy," Colton said and finished untying the knots.

"Help me look."

They scoured the chamber. Colton gave up his lantern to Alice and took the candle that had been left on the table by Forsythe. The floors were barren save for layers of dust and scattered pebbles that had fallen loose from the walls. So much for the perfect craftsmanship of the Vikings, Colton thought.

"I don't see anything," Alice said, her voice echoing in the chamber.

"We can search for them in the camp. They must've dropped when Forsythe grabbed you."

"Wait." Alice had the lantern placed on the table and was sitting in her chair once again. "Basil left another of his notebooks here. Maybe..." she trailed off, her hands flicking through the book in front of her. "So many insights, Basil. You were a brilliant man."

Colton busied himself with a renewed search for the other books. It was simple work, but it kept the realities of the last few days at bay.

It was the creaking of the scaffolding that brought him around, its echo winding through the caverns like some wounded animal. Colton looked to Alice, who hadn't heard, deep in her studies as she was. He waited, eyes on the main entrance, expecting something or someone, but after a minute of nothing, he went back to his search.

No sooner had he drawn the candlelight across the floor once again than another sound breached the silence. A shifting, a sliding of something over rock. Again, he stared into the darkness of the entryway, the dim moonlight casting weird shadows against the rocks.

"Lee?" Colton moved toward the doorway. The form of a man stood at the entrance, hunched over, one arm supporting itself on the wall, another lost in the darkness at its side wrapped around its guts. "We're almost done here. You should've stayed topside."

"No," the voice buzzed an unpleasant dissonance, the form hastening its pace. Glowing white eyes pierced the darkness as it came forward.

Colton reached for his pistol and found his belt empty at his hip. He made to grab for his knife, but the image of it falling into the pit stuck in Forsythe played across his mind. He cursed.

Lee staggered into the chamber, his face drawn and twisted around elongated fangs into something wild and savage. His hands had transformed into deadly claws, but one of them was still gripping at his stomach where Forsythe had done his best to pull his intestines out.

"Get away from the book," Lee said in the voice he shared with the Viking shaman and made his way towards Alice.

"Keep reading." Colton ran to meet the new creature. Lee saw him coming, his free hand swiping its razor blade claws at Colton. Colton managed to avoid the brunt of the swipe, feeling only the sharp sting of the cut on the far side of his torso before he closed the distance and wrapped his arms around Lee.

The creature was strong, even in Lee's injured body, but Colton had dealt with strong before. He wrapped a leg around the back of Lee's, and with a twist of his own body, he sent Lee to the floor, Colton landing on top of him. He didn't need to kill the creature, he just needed to keep it busy.

"I think I have something," Alice said, thumbing through the book one more time.

At the sound of her voice, the creature thrashed underneath Colton and tried to push him off, but Colton held tight. Pain shot through Colton's shoulder, an intense pressure that dug down to his bones. Lee had sunk those overgrown fangs into him. The sickly warm sensation of blood oozed down his arm. Colton cried out in pain. He wanted to pry Lee free of his shoulder, but his arms were trapped beneath both of their bodies. Colton smashed his head into Lee's. He bit the other man's face and neck. Nothing stopped the creature from biting deeper and harder into his shoulder. The pain overwhelmed him, and he cried out again, cursing. Finally, he loosened his grip.

Lee, the creature, burst forward, pushing Colton across the room. Colton rolled to his knees, his hand covering his injured shoulder. The creature gave Colton a crooked smile and turned back towards Alice.

For her part, Alice was standing back from the table, the notebook in one hand, her other extended above her. She glanced down at the page before her once, twice, gathering her breath. "Stoova, Draugr. Hvila," Alice whispered. Her extended hand fluttered in different positions—signs.

The creature in Lee stopped in its place, its glowing white eyes wide, afraid.

"Stoova, Draugr. Hvila," Alice said again. The white

eyes of the shaman blinked, the light in them dancing like a dying candle flame.

"Stoova, Draugr. Hvila," Alice shouted one last time. A howl went up from the shaman, a shrill wail of anguish and torment. Alice and Colton covered their ears.

When the cry finished, Lee was prone on the ground, unmoving and unbreathing. Colton crawled to his side and put his head to his back. No heartbeat; Lee was dead.

Alice closed the book with a clap, a broad smile on her face, tears flowing from her eyes. She cradled the book in her arms. "It is done," she said.

"Let's hope." Colton stood and cupped his injured shoulder. No sooner than the words were out of his mouth than a low grumbling roared around them.

The earth began to shake and move. Colton could feel the smooth floor of pure rock roll under him like a wave in the ocean. He grabbed Alice's arm and dragged her out of the cavern. They slammed into the walls as they ran, the ground beneath them refusing to stay still. When they burst into the moonlight, the scaffolding was waving back and forth, squeaking and creaking for mercy.

"Hurry!" Colton pushed Alice up the stairs, following her closely. The scaffold rocked and pitched forward toward the Hollow. Colton cried out and tossed Alice towards the campgrounds and watched her roll to safety. He jumped. His hands scrabbled for purchase as he grabbed for the lip of the Hollow. His feet slid along the cavern's walls. With a final effort, Colton flung a leg over the precipice and rolled towards camp. The sounds of the scaffolding falling into the Hollow gave him little comfort.

CHAPTER FOURTEEN

I

Colton didn't know how long they had been lying there, unmoving, shaking in the aftermath of the ground crumbling around them, but when they finally started to come around and get to their feet, the sun was rising over the horizon. Its golden rays warmed his joints and soothed his aches.

They made sure that Bill and the Appaloosa were still where they had left them, and Alice went to work helping Colton wrap his wounds. The shoulder was the worst, with four large punctures that pierced all the way to the bones. With what little supplies they could find, they bandaged it as best they could, hoping that the town of Crimson Hollow had someone who could do better. The slice on his side was nastier than he thought, but it could've been much worse. The creature's claws had been razor-sharp, and he hadn't felt the extent of the damage—a long, thin line that curved from his stomach to his side and ribs. It wasn't deep, but it drew blood. All things said and done, Colton would be stiff and sore for a while, but he'd get better.

He tried not to think about Lee and the others who had fallen because of Forsythe's obsession, but their faces haunted him. Not as they were in life, but as they were after death, with angry spirits riding their bodies to hell. Colton figured it would be a long time before he managed to get those faces out of his mind, if, indeed, he ever could.

Bill stamped impatiently from his mooring, rousing the grazing Appaloosa to do the same.

"Easy, fella," Colton patted the horse's face. "We'll head back to town soon. There's just one more thing I need to do."

Alice was wandering around the camp, her arms half full of notebooks, a makeshift satchel made of burlap crammed with the artifacts pulled from the cavern being dragged behind her. "It's all here," she said as he approached. "All of our notes, all the findings. We may be able to save this dig yet."

"Come over and have a look at this," he said and pointed to the Hollow.

"Do you think that when a museum purchases these items, they'd be willing to name the new exhibit after poor, lost Basil?" Alice said, following him. To speed things up, Colton carried the satchel for her. "I know he made some horrible decisions, that he cost people their lives, but he really was a brilliant man, and without him, none of this would have been possible." She paused to look over the edge. "What am I looking for?"

"The ledge that led to the caves," Colton said and pointed again, "it's gone. It's all gone." Unless a person knew where to look, they would never notice the slightest hint that an opening was in the wall or that a system of caves ran underneath them. With the scaffolding at the bottom of the Hollow and the rocky ledges and stairs gone, it was just another huge hole in the ground. One that Colton was eager to see filled.

"Oh," Alice said. "That is strange. Luckily, I have all the notations needed to find the place again. I even have my maps. No need to worry about that. This dig will continue long into the future. I promise you that."

So caught up in her speech, Alice almost missed Colton kicking the satchel of artifacts over the edge. The sound of metal clanging on rock echoed around them. She stared at Colton in surprise, fear, rage. He could tell she was trying to decide which one to latch onto, but he didn't give her much of a chance—he grabbed Forsythe's notebooks from her arms.

"There won't be any more digs, Ms. Green," Colton said and tossed the notebooks after the artifacts, watching each one flutter down, pages breaking free to continue a solo descent. "This outing you and Forsythe urged onward did nothing but destroy lives. You bring people back here, speak the words in those books, it'll start all over again. I'm not about to let that happen."

Alice watched the books descend into blackness, disappearing from her sight. When they were gone, she turned on Colton, her eyes alight with so much anger that he thought she might spit fire. Just as he was sure she was going to attack him, or at least give him one hell of a talking-to, she deflated. Her cheeks were stained with tears of fury and sadness, but she didn't say a word to him. She wouldn't speak to him for a long time after that.

"Let's get back," Colton said. "See if your words really did help."

II

They made it back to town by midday, the sun beating down on them as they passed through the fort's doors. Alice had decided to ride the Appaloosa back, which didn't surprise or worry Colton much.

The dead were lying in the streets and on the outskirts of town when they arrived. According to Lou, they had just fallen wherever they were standing just before sunrise. It had taken the townspeople most of the morning to build the courage to approach the bodies and make sure they weren't going to get up and walk around again.

The stench was going to become a problem. The town wasn't sure whether they should dig a mass grave or burn all the bodies in a huge bonfire. In the end, they decided that they'd smelled enough burned flesh for their lifetimes and organized shifts so that each person aided the effort to bury the dead. Colton was looked over by a local nurse, the doctor having left a few months back. She rebandaged him in some clean bindings and gave him the go-ahead to help with the rest of the town. He managed to hook up with Lou, helping him sling dirt just outside the old fort walls. Lou was eager to find out what happened to Lee, how they managed to stop the dead. Colton recounted the previous night but left out that Lee had been possessed by the shaman. He didn't know much about Lee and Lou's culture, their religions, so he didn't want to offend Lou much. He wanted him to know that Lee did what he could, that he was a brave man to the very end. Though he didn't say as much, Colton got the feeling Lou was satisfied with the story.

With the help of all the townsfolk and their visitors, it took most of two days to get the dead properly planted and buried. Nothing was said then and there, but Colton could tell by the vacant look in most folks' eyes that this would be the end of their time in Crimson Hollow. They'd be moving on. Colton figured it was about time he did the same.

In a matter of days, the town was packed up and ready to leave. Some had already left in small groups, sneaking out during the night so that no one noticed. The town was fine with that, it had happened enough over the years that they couldn't be bothered. Others left in larger groups, close neighbours who shared the same destination or who offered to share households in the future.

Colton hadn't connected with any of the townsfolk

during his time living beside them in the dusty plains of Colorado, and he didn't have any urge or need to go with them. Instead, he decided to lead the survivors of the camp attack back East. It would be an interesting trek. For one, he'd have to deal with Alice during the journey, and that was something he didn't relish in the slightest. On the other hand, he hadn't been to the East in a long time. Getting reacquainted with the trails and the people would be a challenge on its own. He didn't worry, though. He was with his people; they'd do just fine.

According to Lou, Mack never did make it back to the town with reinforcements. Colton wasn't surprised, but just in case, he left a note for the young man nailed to the fort walls. It wasn't much, just something to let the Mack know they were headed back East, and they'd welcome him back if he managed to find them. Colton wasn't sure the note would ever be read, but it felt good to leave it there.

Colton put the last nail in the wall and affixed the note. He'd told the group to get started without him, and, pulling himself up on Bill's saddle, he watched the group move off, the sun making shadows of them all. He tipped his hat back and let the sun hit him square in the face.

"Come on, Bill," he said, "let's show 'em the way."

Colton rode after the survivors, looking forward to what may come.

THE DEVIL'S WORK

To Dad, this one's for you.

CHAPTER ONE

I

The train flew like a bullet straight to hell, and Jim Colton was along for the ride. Colton had ridden a train once or twice but had made it his business to avoid them as much as he could. Loud, clunky things, they disturbed the natural order—scattered game, drove Indians from their land, and kept him awake at night. Progress, they all said; trains were the future. Colton didn't give a damn about that. How was a body supposed to enjoy the world when they were coasting by it at thirty, forty miles an hour?

They were all the same out East, too busy preparing for the future to enjoy the present. He ended up in New York City, one of the jewels of America's crown, but found it hollow and wrought with people too busy doing and not enough stopping to think if they should. A city, nothing but a pile of too-tall buildings belching their smoke into the sky, hiding the scent of the world under its poisonous fetor.

So, when Colton was approached by his old friend, Alexander Price, about a seat on a Transcontinental steamer to get him back West, he had to sit and really think about it. Price was a good man, a good soldier, but he always had stars in his eyes. Tall, good-looking, blonde with a square jaw and a heavy mustache, Price was a fella who was accustomed to getting his way. Since Colton had last seen him, just after the war, he'd put his particular kind of charm to use in climbing the social and business ladder within the train lines.

"Started from the bottom," Price said in his high-pitched kind of way. "First as a porter, moved quickly into engineering, then conductor. From there, it was all just being invited to the right parties, shaking the right hands." Price laughed at this. Colton tried to laugh along but couldn't commit to it.

The turning point, for Colton, came with two things: the guarantee that he'd be back out West in under ten days and that Bill, his horse, could come along for the ride. Price confirmed both.

Colton sat in a cushioned chair in the dining car, staring out the window at the rapidly passing landscape, thinking all of this over, amongst other things, and praying that those ten days would fly by as quickly as the trees just outside did.

"You don't seem too comfortable, son," an older gentleman said and plunked himself down across from Colton. He was dressed in a full suit and unbuttoned his jacket as he sat, exposing the matching vest with a watch chain crossing it.

"Not my favourite mode of transport, I'm afraid," Colton said.

The older man nodded and motioned for a younger man, a boy, really, with his newsboy cap and short pants, to sit as well. "Name's McCoy, Patrick," the older man said, taking off his old, beaten-up bowler hat, a contrast to his new suit. "This is my son, Bernard."

"Nice to meet you," Bernard said in a nasally tone, his eyes not meeting Colton's.

"Hope you don't mind us joining you," Patrick said. "This is Bernard's first trip on a train, and I figured he'd feel more at ease with someone equally uncomfortable." Patrick laughed and elbowed his son, who sported a shy smile, his eyes still focused on the floor.

Colton smiled and returned to his view of the rapidly passing world.

"What sort of business are you in, Mister…?"

"Colton," he said and turned back to the elder Mc-Coy. "I don't have much of a business. I trade in skins and pelts, or I did."

"Must be damn good at it to afford a trip on this here Express," Patrick guffawed, and gave his son another poke with his elbow.

"The ticket was a gift from a friend."

"Trying your hand out West, eh? Beautiful place out there."

"Returning home," Colton said. "Hoping to reclaim a little bit of what was mine."

"I see." Patrick paused to light his pipe. "The boy and I are heading to California. See if I can get him set up in a business or married off." Another elbow to the boy.

Colton eyed the younger McCoy. Pale, sickly, even, and barely old enough to shave. A woman might do him good—then again, it might do him in. "What do you think of all that, Bernard?"

The sound of his name in a strange voice spooked the boy, and he jumped in his seat. For the first time, he made eye contact with Colton, his jade green eyes trembling before seeking out his father's face. For approval, perhaps. Encouragement, maybe. Permission.

"I…I think that is all just…just fine, sir," he said shakily after a nod from his father.

"He's been coddled by his mother," the elder McCoy said, leaning toward Colton some, his voice low. "Needs some time on his own to man up."

Colton nodded and then turned his attention back to the window at his side. He'd been on the train for a few hours now, the last remnants of city life long behind him.

By the looks of things, they were exiting a forested area and coming into some open space. Might be heading toward a bridge. That was not something he was looking forward to, and he expected he would have to retire to his room for the entirety of that journey.

"Where's the food?" Patrick McCoy called out and twisted in his seat, looking for a waiter or porter. "I paid for meals with my damn ticket, and I expect to have one."

Colton paid no mind to him; his focus was on the outside world, just beyond that little pane of glass, but something was different.

"The train is slowing down," Colton said and stood looking for an employee himself.

"Probably just about to round a corner or some such thing," McCoy said, tapping his pipe against the arm of his chair.

An ear-splitting squeal arose from around them, and the train jerked ahead, sending Colton back into his seat. Gasps and groans rose around him; some shouts of pain and curses followed suit. The train had come to a sudden stop. Colton stood again, dizzy from being shaken about.

"Everybody, hands up! This is a robbery."

II

Whatever peace the passengers had erupted into panic at the gruff voice. The women screamed, the men groaned, and everyone began to chat incessantly, discussing the outrage, the fright. The elder McCoy, wide-eyed, his pipe sticking out of the corner of his mouth, grabbed his son and put his arm over him to keep the boy's face out of sight.

The Transcontinental Express was, for all intents and purposes, a marketing scheme. The story in the papers claimed that passengers could go from New York City to

San Francisco in four days, and that just wasn't true. According to Pierce, while the train could certainly do just that, it would require a much lighter load and breakneck speeds that many travellers would find unappealing. Instead, the Transcontinental Express, as Colton sat upon it now, was a ten-car train with two luxury sleeping coaches and a modified cattle car for the transport of horses. It wasn't going to make the four-day record, but it would certainly attract anyone with enough money to enjoy the novelty. In short, it was a tin can full of rich people—easy pickings for a bold enough thief with a small posse behind him.

Colton chanced another glance around the dining car. No employees were around, but neither were there any outlaws, just dishevelled passengers who were no worse for wear. He tried to look through the doorway into the car beyond but only saw shadows moving. He chanced a look behind him, at the door there, but couldn't get a good angle.

"Only a few of 'em," he said, more to himself than the McCoys. "Can't control the whole train." He pushed himself out of his seat and made for the door behind him, vaguely aware of Patrick McCoy saying something to his back.

He opened the door and stepped out on a car buffer when the first shot went off—a thunderous clap that rang in the open air. He heard another outburst from the passengers he'd left behind, followed by silence. A gunshot meant business, and business required silence.

Colton saw some smoke rise just beyond the car ahead of him, heard another shot, and saw a man collapse into the dirt just beyond the train. Another puff of smoke. He cursed and, instead of moving into the next car as he had planned, grabbed the ladder to the door's left and climbed to the roof.

One bandit stood guard outside the train, still saddled up on his horse and gun in his hand. Two men lay on the ground before him, men who had tried to escape the robbery or stop it. Cowardly or brave, it didn't do them much good. The bandit, black hat and blue bandana pulled over his nose, eyed the train and adjusted himself in the saddle. Colton kept himself close to the car's roof, hoping not to draw attention to himself, and pulled his six-shooter.

He wasn't as good a shot with his revolver as he was with his rifle, but that had been stored special by Price when he boarded. He took aim and fired.

The horseman pulled to the right and fell off his horse, which took off a short distance away, confused and scared.

"Hey, Bart," a voice called from somewhere below. "Ah, shit."

Colton heard the commotion below, the scattering of people, the hurried footfall of boots through the train until they fell on the gravel beside the track. He cursed, holstered his gun, and pulled out his knife.

"Shit!" the voice called out, closer this time. "Boss, Bart's down."

Another voice rose somewhere down the line. "Check on him and kill whoever did it." It was the same gruff voice that had announced the robbery. The voice was tainted by too many cigarettes and too much hard liquor, and it crackled when it spoke, a barking sound that was all too comfortable with giving the order to kill.

Colton peered over the edge of the car; another man stood there, rifle in his hands, his hat moving back and forth, and his long jacket dragging some as he moved slowly toward his fallen compatriot. It was now or never.

Colton launched himself at the new bandit, falling on his back and forcing him into the ground. There was a sickening crunch as the bandit landed with another man's weight bearing him down. Colton heard the crack of bones and a nauseating wet groan. Short of breath himself, Colton rolled away from the bandit, grabbed his shoulder and turned him over, knife to the man's throat. There was no need, he was out. The man's breathing came in harsh whistles, and blood spread around his nose, soaking his blue bandana.

"What the hell was that?" A third voice, high and fluting.

"Never mind," the gruff voice said again. "You and Kurt clean out these folks. I'll check on Jody and Bart."

Colton tossed the rifle out of Jody's reach and made for the train, hoping to keep the outlaws surprised. It wasn't to be. A large man in a dusty black jacket stepped away from the train, a Colt Peacemaker twitching in his hand. A black hat sat askew on his head, and though there was a red bandana covering most of his face, Colton could tell the man was smiling underneath it. A humourless smile that didn't touch the black eyes that stood out under the hat.

"Well," the man said, "what've we got here? Some kind of hero, eh?" He cocked the hammer on his revolver.

Colton gripped his knife hard. "Just keeping myself busy on a long train ride."

The other man laughed. "I can see that," he said, nodding toward the two prone men. "Not much for killing, though." He glanced toward the slowly rising stomachs of each fallen man. "Poor habit, that. Them boys get up, and they won't give you the same courtesy." He pulled down his bandana with one gloved hand, revealing a grave smile surrounded by a short, salt-and-pepper beard. He turned and let go two shots. The folks on the train screamed once more, and the two men Colton had incapacitated were no longer breathing.

Despite himself, Colton's breathing hitched as he renewed his stare at the man with the gruff voice.

"It's for the best, really," the other man said, his smile still in place. "This is a courtesy, boy. If I had some extra time, I'd've taught them what it meant to fail. As it is," he waved toward the train, "I'm on a bit of a schedule." He chuckled and aimed at Colton once more.

"Scratch Maynard." Two men stepped away from the train, rifles in their hands. "Hands up." The first of the men, and the speaker, was tall with broad shoulders and a heavy mustache that eclipsed his upper lip. The second was younger, clean-shaven, with heavy, black eyebrows that curled toward his nose.

Scratch Maynard's face transformed. No longer was he smiling; no, his face became twisted in rage and anger. He turned away from Colton, gun ready to fire. Colton took his chance and surged forward, his knife aimed at the man's lower back.

In that split second, three shots went off, Colton's knife sank home, and three men fell to the ground.

CHAPTER TWO

I

Colton sat up, dazed. He'd plowed into the bandit from behind and followed him to the ground, and as he did, he'd felt something whizz by his ear. A sharp pain ignited at the side of his head, and everything went black for a moment.

Now that he was back in the world, the bandit was in front of him, lying face down on his stomach, Colton's knife sticking out of his side. Not where he was aiming for, but it had done the trick. Standing over Scratch, rifle aimed at him, was the younger of the two lawmen, his gaze flicking back and forth between the bandit and his boss, who was also on the ground and struggling to sit up.

"What do I do, Reeves?" the younger man asked.

"God damn it, Bo, keep your gun on Scratch and help me up." The older man sounded winded, and though his words were harsh, there was little conviction in them.

Colton stood, his fingers probing the side of his head where the pain had begun. "Go check on your partner. I'll keep an eye on Scratch, here." He pulled his gun and pointed it at the bandit's back. Blood oozed from somewhere on his head; a thin row of skin had been dug out just past his temple and all along the side. Nicked by a bullet. He was damn lucky.

Bo's lips twitched to repeat the question to his partner,

his eyes darting quickly between the men before him. Behind him, Reeves cursed around a groan, and Bo's shoulders sank. He backed slowly toward his partner, his rifle trained on the space between Colton and Scratch Maynard.

"About time," Reeves said when Bo helped him to his feet. "The bastard managed to wing me." Blood bloomed out from a small hole in the beige shoulder of his long jacket. His face was pale around his mustache now, and his dark eyes, tired but alert, landed on Colton. "You got him, Mister?"

"Yeah, I got him."

"Good. Bo, plug up my shoulder, would you? I'll get the doc to look at it on the train." Bo shouldered his rifle and began to work on Reeves, his eyes shooting toward Colton any chance he got.

"Hey, pilgrim," Scratch's rough voice came to him. "Roll me over."

"You just get comfortable right there."

"You stuck me good, pilgrim. I can't roll over on my own. Help a poor fella out." Scratch coughed out a wet chuckle.

Colton bent and helped the bandit turn to his back. Blood oozed from the corners of Scratch's humourless smile. Colton could tell he was weak, though. He could barely move, and when he did, it was to finger a bullet hole that had pierced his belly. Colton watched with growing disgust as the man put his finger in the wound and pulled it out again, over and over.

"What's your name, pilgrim?" Scratch asked, his dark eyes drilling into Colton's own.

"Doesn't matter much now, does it?"

"Pilgrim, I'm dying. I have the right to know the name of the man who killed me, to look him in the eyes as I choke out my final breath."

Colton shrugged. "Jim Colton."

"That's a good name, Jimmy. I like that name," he coughed, and more blood erupted from his mouth, but still the smile stayed. "Now, lean close. I got a little secret to tell you," Scratch said and motioned for Colton to get closer. "Close now, I'm awfully weak," he said again as Colton knelt beside him.

"What is it?"

"You're going to pay, Jim Colton. You and those lawmen, Bo Pierce and Jack Reeves. Whoever they got with 'em. You're all going to pay by the end of this," Scratch hissed, his face twisted in a sick delight.

Colton moved away from him. It wasn't the first time that Colton had heard something like that. Men came in two shades: big talkers or big doers. Often, the two didn't cross. Still, something in Scratch's voice gave him pause.

"You hear me, pilgrim? You're all going to pay, you sons of bitches. Before I go, I'm going to make sure that I see you in hell before too long," Scratch said and began to guffaw through blood and coughs.

It was a big boot from Jack Reeves that finally silenced him. The lawman, steady on his feet, crossed the distance and kicked the bandit in the jaw without slowing his momentum. Scratch still wasn't dead; his breathing came in ragged, bubbling breaths, but he wasn't awake either, and that was all right.

The lawmen made their introductions standing over the prone body, Colton and the two of them making a triangle over Scratch's body.

"We've been tracking down ol' Scratch Maynard for months now," Reeves said, favouring his wounded arm. "He's been a menace up and down the trainlines, robbing, raping, killing. Many thanks for the help taking him down."

Colton nodded and hitched a thumb toward the train.

"What about the others?"

"A colleague of ours is watching over them, Marshal Laird Miller. Heard of him?"

"Can't say I have," Colton said and lit a cigarette. Colton didn't take the time to learn the names of most lawmen unless he figured they'd have some impact on his life. There were altogether too many lawmen crawling the streets of the city, an Irishman on every corner swinging his billy club and praying to smash open someone's head with it. No, Colton hoped his return to the west would rid him of all that.

"So, you with the railway?" Colton asked at length. He'd heard that some train companies hired their own law, which helped to keep the passengers comfy and cozy. Alexander hadn't mentioned it, but that didn't mean there wasn't any on board.

"We're Pinkertons, boy." Reeves smirked. "Ol' Scratch and his boys have been harassing trains all up and down this line for months, so the Transcontinental Railroad and the government of the U.S. of A called us in to put a stop to it." Reeves shuddered; his face contorted with pain. "Come on, there's a doctor on board. Let's get him to give us a once-over."

Colton nodded and watched the two lawmen amble toward the train. He kept his eye on Scratch Maynard for a long moment before he tossed his smoke and followed the Pinkertons in.

#It turned out that Scratch and his gang weren't just ruthless but smart about their business. Instead of chasing the train on horseback, they aimed to stop it before boarding it. Scratch had a few different tricks to accomplish this. The first time he did it, he strapped some TNT to a bridge and blew it to kingdom come. It worked well enough for them, and they made away with about $35,000, including cargo and personal possessions. They never did that again, though. Reeves had a theory on that. He said blowing the bridge kept the trains off the line for too long, and Scratch couldn't ply his particular trade without trains running regularly.

The next time a train was stopped, it was because an old wagon was laid across the track, no horses attached to it, and what looked like a woman sitting up front. There was no woman, just one of Scratch's boys dressed that way. Leaving a carriage wasn't a guaranteed stop, though. Reeves heard tell of another carriage laid across the tracks crushed to splinters because the engineer was drunk as a skunk and didn't even see the damned thing. Their next trick was their most consistent, and the same one they used to stop the Transcontinental Express: a large bonfire strewn across the tracks. It took the train workers a few hours to put out the fire and disperse the pile of smouldering wood. In the meantime, Colton and Reeves sat in consultation with the doctor.

The doctor was retired, but he didn't mind helping out when he could. He was an elderly man dressed in an impeccable black suit with a monocle hanging from one eye and a set of wrinkled jowls that hung over his pristine, starched collar.

"I appreciate this, Dr. Walker," Reeves said, stripping to his bare chest so the doctor could get a better look at him. Reeves was a barrel-chested man, thick and muscled from more days on the farm than chasing crooks, Colton wagered. A thin patch of greying chest hair bristled in the air of the doctor's private cabin.

"Not to worry, Agent." The doctor lifted a small black bag with a shake. "I always carry my tools with me." He bent closer to the wound, adjusting his monocle to get a better look. "Won't need many tools for this one. Bullet went right through. Good man," the doctor said and slapped Reeves' good shoulder before he went about bandaging the wound.

"What'll happen to the bandits?" Colton asked. He didn't think Pierce or his company would be too happy about transporting known criminals, and he was sure the likes of McCoy and his boy wouldn't be none too pleased about the prospect.

"It's not a perfect situation," Reeves grunted around the doctor's bandaging, "but we'll likely have to hold the live ones up in a private room. The dead ones, while I'm tempted to leave them where they are, their heads may fetch a bounty. I'd say we put them back there on the cattle cart. I saw some room on it, and it's bound to be cooler out there than in here. Easier for the bodies to keep that way, right, Doc?"

"It'd have to be icier than a witch's tit out there," the doctor said inspecting his work, "but you got the theory right."

"Have you cleared that with the train company?" Colton asked, consciously trying not to touch his bleeding head.

"It's the word of the U.S. of A, son. I don't got to ask nobody nothing. They don't like it, they can take it up with the President."

"Oh, come now, Jack. You Pinkertons have as much to do with the government as I do," Dr. Walker said and turned to Colton. "Your turn, sonny."

Reeves grumbled something under his breath and dressed before muttering something about needing to check on things and was gone.

"Never mind Jack," the doctor said. "He's just proud of his job and line of work. He's a good man underneath it all." He chuckled as he turned Colton's head. The doctor's hands were warm and dry, his thick fingers spoke of manual labour, but the knobby joints indicated that had happened sometime in his distant past.

"What brings you aboard, Doc?" Colton asked.

"I love these little train trips. Enjoy the heat of California even more," he said and bent Colton's head forward.

"I'm hoping to head to California myself."

"That so?" the doctor said, not really listening. Colton let him work in silence and played some things over in his mind. He thought about the West and how he'd left it. Thought about what he saw and heard, of what he did and didn't do. If he could just get back to where he once was, just him and Bill, the world before them, and nothing off-centre to bother them, he'd call that a success. The way this train trip was shaping up, that didn't look possible.

"Well, your brains aren't leaking out, so you're lucky on that account," the doctor said. "Bad news, you were grazed by a bullet. It's bound to leave a scar on the side of your head there, and it looks to have taken a chunk of your ear with it. You won't be as pretty as you once were, son, but you aren't dead."

"There's that, I suppose," Colton said and let the doctor apply some bandages.

II

"Jesus Christ." Price was waiting outside the doctor's room, wringing the rim of his hat between his hands. "What the hell were you thinking?"

"You're welcome," Colton said, holding his hat in his hands, hesitant to place it atop his freshly placed bandages.

"Jim, shit, I knew you were a stupid mountain hillbilly, but I didn't think that meant your head was full of rocks." Price's half smile brought one to Colton's face, couldn't be helped.

Price and Colton had met up during the war. Same platoon, same battles, waist deep in the same mud and blood. They were different people, Pierce, an East Coast city boy with dollar signs for pupils and Colton, a West

Coast mountaineer with a desire to be on his lonesome in the open country. Despite their differences, perhaps even because of them, they struck up a strong friendship that lasted through the years and the distance.

"Glad I had those rocks." Colton pointed to the fresh bandage. "Besides, you'd've done the same, or have you gotten soft?" Colton made a half-hearted jab at Price's gut.

"You wish," Price dodged. "Jim, we had agents, security. They could've handled it." Price's face was sombre under his perpetual grin, his blue eyes darting to the bandages wrapping Colton's forehead and ear.

"Them boys were working too hard, figured I'd give them a break," Colton said and moved to the side. Bo Pierce and a tall, silver-haired man were carrying Scratch on a stretcher. Reeves followed close behind. "You know I can't sit still for too long."

Price and Colton watched as the outlaw was taken to the doctor. Reeves nodded to them as he passed. Scratch, despite everything, was still alive. His belly rose in quick, shaking breaths. His skin had taken on a waxy, pale appearance, and he was unconscious, but he was alive. Colton noticed his knife still lodged in Scratch's side.

"You're my guest, you lummox." Price pushed him onward, "I was hoping you'd enjoy the luxurious life for once. Not take on a gang of train robbers all by yourself."

Colton shrugged. Pierce had good intentions, but he didn't know Colton quite as well as he thought he did. Colton didn't let him.

They made their way to the dining car. Night had fallen since the train had started moving again. Pierce assured Colton that the porters and conductor and engineer didn't need any help moving the debris that had blocked the track, nor did they need help driving the damn train. Moonlight spilled into the cars as they made their way, offset by the orange candlelight in the copper wall sconces that lit the walkways.

A roar erupted from the car as Price pushed Colton through the door. The car was filled with passengers, each with a giddy expression of near laughter, and applause rolled over Colton and his injured head. The room was well lit by candles, and the wood stove in the corner was burning hot. Colton could feel the droplets of sweat forming at the small of his back, and the urge to rip off his jacket was nearly too much to ignore.

Just as Colton entered, the crowd gathered around and began to sing "For He's a Jolly Good Fellow." Colton looked back at Price, who paused mid-clap and shrugged, a devilish smile tugging at the corners of his mouth.

With a sigh, Colton turned back to the room and waved.

III

The prisoners had been tied up and laid down in Reeves' private room, and Reeves himself was taking a rest in Bo's room; Bo decided he could use a break himself. He pulled up a chair just outside of Reeves' room and lit a smoke. Wasn't much to do now anyway.

He could hear the celebration for Colton roaring away. Even over the sound of the train and the wind rushing past, he could hear them just gushing all over that hillbilly. Where was the celebration for the Pinkertons who had been studying ol' Scratch Maynard, huh? Where was the adoration, the booze, the women for them…for him?

Bo snorted out a chuckle and blew a stream of smoke toward the ground. Do-gooders, bystanders, they just got in the way. Hell, on one of his first cases, a porter thought he was man enough to do Bo's job and tried to wrestle a gun away from a bandit. Not only did the poor cocksucker get a gut shot for his trouble, but he blocked Bo's line of sight. Bo couldn't get a shot off, even if he had wanted to.

That didn't happen to Colton, though, did it? Close, but not quite. Bo couldn't say if it was his shot or Reeves's who gave Colton a new part in his hair, but he hoped it was his. Hoped with all that he could hope that it was his bullet that nearly trimmed Colton's brain for him. The thought brought a smile to his face.

"Hey," one of the prisoners said from behind the door. Bo put his ear to it and heard some movement and a loud bang that drove him away from the door.

"Son of a bitch," he whispered and slammed on the door with the bottom of his fist. "Shut it in there."

"Hey," the voice came again, "you better get in here. He's...he's dying."

"Good," Bo said and then, more to himself, "I hope he does."

The noise got louder, the banging, the movement. Bo dismissed it with a wave of his hand and lit another smoke.

"Say, officer," Patrick McCoy said, his head sticking out of the door just down the hallway. Bo jumped from his seat, his hand on his sidearm.

"Jesus, mister," he said. "I'd forgotten these other rooms were occupied."

"Sorry to disturb you, sir," McCoy said, his eyes falling to Bo's six-shooter, "but my son is feeling sick and is trying to get some rest. You mind telling your...prisoners to keep it down?"

Bo stared at McCoy like he was some strange gargoyle that had sprouted from the train's wall. The urge to pull his gun and tell the old fart to shut it himself rose in his throat like bile. Then again, he was sure Reeves would hear of it, and Reeves would give him an earful. It wasn't worth it.

"You go on back to your room, sir. I'll do what I can,"

Bo said with a nod.

He waited for McCoy to shut his door before he made another bang on the door in front of him. "If y'all don't shut up in there, I'm coming in and blowing a hole through each of yer kneecaps, you understand me?"

But they didn't understand, or they didn't hear him, and all Bo could hear was a chorus of unearthly screams.

CHAPTER THREE

I

"What the hell happened here?" Price asked, trying to peer over Reeves' shoulder.

Colton had started to enjoy the little celebration that Price had arranged for him, no doubt in part because of the generous drinks that were being passed his way, when Bo Pierce burst into the room. The young man's face was as pale as a dinner plate, his mouth curled down like he'd just taken a mouthful of curdled milk.

"Mr. Price," he shouted over the party's din, "Agent Reeves needs to see you," and then he spared a venomous glance for Colton, "now." After that, the celebration was done and over. The tiny mutterings of the gathered turned from gleeful to frightened, and they began to shuffle their way back to their beds. Colton and Price shared a knowing look and made to follow Pierce into the bowels of the train.

"Looks like one of our prisoners couldn't take being locked up," Reeves said around a mouthful of cigar. His pouched eyes roamed over Colton, sizing him up and down.

"Didn't you have them tied up?" Price asked then faded away from the sight of the room, and Colton took his place. The room was much like the one that Price had provided Colton: one bed, a small wash basin, and a comfortable-looking armchair. The difference between the two was the lake of blood that darkened the green carpet and slicked the already dark hardwood floor. Two men were tied up and lashed to the bed frame, which was, itself, bolted into the wall and floor. Colton hadn't seen these men before, but he figured them to be what was left of the would-be train robbers: Deacon and Jody Flint. Both men were wide-eyed, a grimace of fear painting their blood-spattered faces. Neither man would look at the armchair. Green to match the carpet, the chair faced away from the door and hanging over one of the arms was a lifeless hand.

"Damn right we did," Reeves said, "two of them boys are still tied up tighter than a preacher's daughter's nethers. It's the other one that's the problem."

"Scratch?" Colton shook his head. "The man was on his deathbed anyway. Why'd you put him in here with the others?"

"Well, Mr. Colton, if I had to know you'd been open to having him bunk up with you, I'd've placed down there." Reeves removed his cigar and spat into the blood. "Since I didn't know about that, well, I just had to make do."

Colton remembered Scratch being carted past him toward the doctor, wounds on his side and chest. "What happened? He split a stitch?"

"Funny thing is," Reeves said and motioned to the silver-haired man Colton had seen carrying Scratch with Bo earlier. He was a short, squat man with hair to his shoulders and a large white hat sitting atop his head. He had a pointed beard on his chin, a slack jaw, and a drunk's nose. He handed something to Reeves. "Thanks, Marshal," Reeves said and held up a knife. It had a six-inch blade, its edge curved along the belly some, but the back was straight all the way to a small, tarnished guard, and a handle made of buck horn. The knife was sharp and deadly, and Colton would know—it was his knife. "Care to explain this, Mr. Colton?"

If Reeves was expecting to shock Colton, it didn't work. Colton returned the man's steely gaze. "Looks like my knife managed to find its way into your hands, Reeves. I think you might need to do the explaining."

Reeves chuckled. "I figured it was yours. Saw that handle sticking out of ol' Scratch's side. I'm just wondering how Mr. Scratch in there got his hands on it again."

"Last I saw, it was still in the son of a bitch."

"Funny," Reeves said, "I'm sure the doctor said he'd returned it to you." He thought it over some and shoved his cigar back into his mouth. "Either way, Scratch somehow managed to keep it in his possession, and he used it to slice his own throat. Wrists, too, if the blood is any indication."

"Jesus," Price said and turned away from the room.

"It ain't a pretty picture, Mr. Price. I'm sure you wouldn't mind getting some of your porters down here to mop this up some."

"Of course." Price moved toward the front of the train.

"Mind if I have a look?" Colton wasn't sure why he said it or why the urge to see the dead man struck, but there it was, and he wasn't going to ignore it.

"Sure," Reeves said with just the slightest raise of his eyebrows. "You take a look, Mr. Colton, but don't touch anything, understand?"

Colton did. He moved into the room, the blood-soaked carpet feeling strange under his boot heels, an unpleasant watery sound rising after each step. The room was thick with the scent of iron, urine, and feces. He cast a quick glance at the two remaining train robbers, noticed that their pants were stained darker colours and nodded to himself. Price might have found this repugnant, might have found his belly turned inside out by the sight or smell, and would've likely added his puke to the mix. Colton, on the other hand, was accustomed to these scents, or as accustomed as a person could get. He hunted and cleaned his prey, skinned it and used it for his clothes and food. As he turned the corner to face Scratch's dead body, he noted that the tang in the air was different than the animals he killed. It had a rotten scent, like sulphur.

Scratch was laid up pretty much as Colton had imagined. Both his wrists had deep slices in them, one of which was nearly cut to the bone, and his throat was open like a horrible second mouth, blubbering red lips wide open in a bloody yawn. Scratch's head was turned at an angle, his open eyes staring at the wall to his right, and he still had that humourless smile plastered on his face. Colton shuddered despite himself.

"Well," Reeves said, coming up behind him, "I suppose we don't have to worry about him getting his revenge." He chuckled.

"Not in this life anyway," Colton said and left.

II

"This is some bullshit, right here," Bo Pierce said to no one in particular. Reeves had set him up on a patrol of the train, all because some lowlife decided to do them a favour and kill himself. Shit, Bo thought, if they all did that it would just make their life easier. It's not like they were bounty hunters, making sure to keep their prey alive to get the best coin for the work. No, they were Pinkertons. Dead or alive, it didn't matter any as long as the job was done. And this job was certainly done. Ol' Scratch Maynard wasn't about to rob any more trains, that's for damn sure.

He stopped in the caboose, an older Pullman car, beds stowed away for the time being, leaving some well-polished wood in their place. Bo popped a cigarette between his lips and watched the ghostly reflection of himself light it in the windows that stared out the back end of the train. He couldn't imagine any of the rich folks spending their kind of money on a lonely car at the back of the train. No, sir, this was likely where the porters and servers went to sleep when they weren't working. He chuckled a bit. That had to be it. This place was colder than the rest of the train by a country mile, no stove to keep the chill away. Rich people, they weren't about to be inconvenienced like that, no, sir.

What about Colton, though? Bo spit on the carpet, his head perked up to see if anyone had noticed. Just him and his reflection. In the clear, he rubbed his boot over the wet spot on the floor and took another drag off his smoke. He had a hard time pinning Colton down. He wasn't rich, that was sure. Not with that crusty blue overcoat and frayed wide-brimmed hat. And certainly not with that long beard he wore, or the quiet way he talked. In Bo's experience, most rich men kept themself clean and presentable, maybe sporting some sort of mustache, but otherwise dressed for business or pleasure. Not Colton, though.

As Bo moved closer to the windows, his reflection got bigger, closer, but also more transparent. He looked out at the tracks that the train was leaving behind, the tracks that seemed to stand in for his reflection's missing legs and chuckled again. Colton might have been a train hopper, or maybe he falsified his ticket somehow, but that'd be giving the man too much credit, and Bo thought he got enough of that as is. Nah, he seemed to be pretty close to that prissy Mr. Price. Maybe that's how he made it. Favours of friends; it's about who you know and not what you know. Maybe, just maybe. Either way, Colton was able to rub elbows with some well-heeled folks, while Bo had to stand at attention in the ass end of the train.

He shivered. It really was colder back in the caboose,

and he had an uncharacteristic moment of pity for the train employees who had to sleep there. Bo took another drag from his smoke, made to toss it to the floor and crush it under his boot, but he remembered the carpet this time. With a smile, he snuffed the cigarette on the wall and put the remnants in his pocket. He wouldn't give Reeves an excuse to dock his pay, not after all the shit jobs he was putting him through. And all because Bo wasn't injured. All because Bo was decent enough at his job not to get shot. Maybe, just maybe, he'd have to chat with their supervisor when they got back to Chicago, see what he thought of it all.

Bo's reflection smiled back at him, an eerie doppelgänger that was made up of shadows and harsh angles. Something behind it moved. It took Bo a moment to translate that movement into something happening behind him and not beyond the train, somewhere in the far distance.

He turned quickly and brought his gun to bear. Nothing but the empty doorway. Bo exhaled and willed away the unsteadiness that gripped his legs, his knees. Jumpy is all, aggravated by everything that had been happening. Still, he was sure he saw something. What was it? A blur of movement, a misshapen face in the haze of the window's reflection? He didn't know. What he did know was that he had to walk back that way or stay in the caboose for the next eight days. He didn't think Reeves or his supervisor in Chicago would be pleased with the latter.

It was simple, Bo said to himself, just take a deep breath and walk to the next car. Nothing could be simpler. *But what if there is something waiting back there?* Easy, we have a gun. A Winchester repeater. *What if they have a gun, too?* They don't. *But what if they do?* Doesn't matter; they don't. *How can you be so sure?* Because there's nothing there. Now, get moving before Reeves comes down here and kicks our ass.

Bo started toward the door. His legs felt like cast-iron stovepipes, rigid and unyielding. His hands gripped the Winchester so hard his fingers turned white, and pain throbbed from his knuckles to his wrists, and still he took slow steps toward the door. His heart beat fast in his chest, he could hear his breathing coming in quick wheezes.

He chanced a look over his shoulder and saw the reflection still there, still transparent over the disappearing train tracks. The face, though, the face wasn't his face. It was twisted, its eyes as red as blood. It wasn't his face at all. It wore a smile that was as humourless as it was chilling, and he recognized it. He recognized the smile and the knife it was holding in its hands.

Then Bo screamed.

CHAPTER FOUR

I

"Major and Mrs. Pickett," Price said with a small bow, "allow me to introduce you to my old friend—Jim Colton." The dining car had been closed for the evening, but Price had insisted on taking Colton to the sitting room. Price had said that it was his favourite car on the train, and Colton could see why. It was a car all to itself that was laid out as if it were some sort of club or lounge. There was a couch, a chaise, and four armchairs all arranged around the focal point of the room: the fireplace. Each chair matched the dark emerald green of the carpet and the accents that played on the walls and wallpaper. Paintings had been hung on the walls, and the sconces were made up of oil lanterns instead of candles. The result allowed for a warm, dim room that smelled of smoke and expensive alcohol and was populated by people who spoke in hushed tones. It made Colton paranoid.

"You're the fella that helped out them Pinkerton boys, eh?" The Major stood to shake Colton's hand. The Major was a tall, thin man with a well-groomed mustache and sagging jowls around a skinny neck. Colton's first impression of the man was to liken him to a turkey, but the piercing blue eyes that stood out underneath the man's bushy eyebrows soon dissolved him of that impression.

"I'm afraid so." Colon returned the firm grip and tried on a smile.

"Bad business, that," the Major said. "Good for you for helping out. Why, if Elizabeth hadn't stayed my sword arm, I might have jumped in the fray myself."

"Believe me, Major," Colton said, watching Mrs. Pickett's eyes widen, "if I had known about the Pinkerton's presence on the train, I would have left it all to them."

II

"Beautiful train, isn't it?" Mrs. Pickett asked, cutting off her husband's reply. The Major's wife, in contrast to her husband, was short and stout. Her cheeks were rosy, her lips thin and pink, and her eyes nearly disappeared in a sea of wrinkles when she smiled. "I love travelling on these trains, just ask Alexander," she pointed to a smiling Price. "I'd sooner live here than in any of our three homes."

"It's true, lad," the Major said. "She won't travel any other way."

"It's truly our pleasure to have you on board," Price said, and Colton nodded his exit to the married couple to sit in an armchair next to the fire, looking toward the car door. He'd been on this train for nearly three days, and he was exhausted. The only break Price had given him from the constant introductions and boring, meaningless conversations was complicated by the train robbery. That, however strange it may sound to Price, was a welcome opportunity for Colton. A way to stretch his legs, so to speak. Perhaps the two remaining robbers would find a way to escape, giving Colton another excuse to let loose, relax.

Colton forced the hope that thought ignited in him to fizzle and die. Not only was it a strange thing to hope for, but those boys were tied up good, and Reeves had set a guard to watch them around the clock. Even if that wasn't the case, Colton doubted that the Flint Brothers would make a move, not after what they saw. Scratch Maynard sliced himself up right in front of them. He didn't even offer to cut them free first, just went to work killing himself. Colton couldn't quite imagine how that might play on a man's mind, but he didn't think it would do anything good. And it was with *his* knife!

Reeves had finally given him back possession of it just as Colton had left the blood-soaked room. Colton patted it for reassurance as he watched Price make a round of small talk.

"Fine thing you did, Mr. Colton," Patrick McCoy said alongside him between puffs on his pipe. Colton stifled the initial impulse to jump at the surprise presence next to him and, instead, levelled a stony glare at McCoy, who was having some trouble keeping his pipe lit. The younger McCoy stood close to the fireplace, warming his hands.

"I'm not afraid to admit," McCoy continued, "that when I first saw you jump up out of your seat, I thought you were one of two things: a coward or stark raving mad." McCoy mustn't have liked how Colton was looking at him and quickly added:. "If you don't mind me saying."

"How are you and your boy enjoying the trip so far?" Colton asked, turning his attention back to the doorway.

"More exciting than we had expected, hey boy?" McCoy smiled and touched the young man's elbow. Bernard McCoy nodded and didn't take his eyes off the fire. "Not only did we have a train robbery," McCoy continued, "prevented, of course, but we found that our private room was situated directly next to the room where they're keeping them boys. In fact, we were even in there when their leader, that Scratch fella, kill…," he shot a nervous glance toward his son, "…did away with himself."

"That so?" Colton shrugged. He hadn't thought about what other folks may have been dealing with having those bandits on board. He guessed it wasn't the most ideal situation for anyone.

"Yes, sir, and hellfire, those boys can wail. Never heard anything like it in my life. Of course, there was the screaming about the fella who—well, you know," he put a finger to his throat and mimicked cutting his throat, "but before that, it was even stranger. If I didn't know better, I'd say them boys were saying their prayers or singing a hymn of some sort. They were all throaty and deep. Damn monastic if you ask me."

"I don't think those boys are the praying type," Colton said.

"You don't have to tell me that," McCoy said around his pipe. "I'm just saying that it sure sounded like they were praying. That's all."

Colton nodded at that. It wouldn't be the first time he'd heard of freshly caught outlaws praying for their freedom and redemption to avoid the hangman's noose, but something about Scratch's crew didn't give him that sort of feeling.

A moment later, a young porter walked in. He was dressed in the uniform of the train, a high-necked, burgundy shirt with a black front and matching black pants with a burgundy stripe running up the leg. The young man was broad at the shoulders, dark skinned, and looked like he might have seen some manual labour not too long ago. He stood by the door, his hands crossed behind his back and said, "Excuse me, Mr. Price, a Mr. Reeves needs to see you in the employee quarters immediately."

Price stood straight, pardoned himself from an elderly couple he had been talking to and made his way to the door. On his way, he nodded to Colton, and Colton followed.

III

Every window of the caboose was covered in blood. But that wasn't quite right, Colton thought; they were mostly covered. In the void, in the absence of blood, there was something drawn or written, but Colton couldn't make out what it was or what it meant.

"Mr. Price," Reeves said. The bullet wound hadn't done the old Agent any favours, and he'd taken to wearing a sling around that arm, but he looked as though he'd aged another ten years since Colton had seen him earlier that day. His face was drawn and sagged around his jaw-line, and his eyes were bloodshot under his hat, which he had taken to wearing high on his forehead. "Mr. Colton," Reeves continued through gritted teeth.

"What the hell..." Price started, his voice filled with something Colton guessed was his managerial anger, but it faded when he saw the body or the blood, likely both. He turned from the scene, the colour flooding from his face.

"That's Bo Pierce in there." Reeves nodded toward the room. Colton could see the silver-haired Marshal staring down at the young man's body, hands on his hips and shaking his head under his large white hat. "Or, what's left of him, anyway."

"What happened?" Colton asked, patting Price on the back and trying to decipher the scene beyond the remaining Pinkerton agent.

"Well, Mr. Colton," Reeves ran his thumb over his chin, "I was hoping you might be able to answer that for me." From his sling, he pulled out a knife with a familiar-looking buckhorn handle.

The icy touch of disbelief ran its fingers over Colton's spine. His mouth hung open, and his thoughts became muddled. He caught a twitch of a grin on Reeves' face, happy that he'd caught Colton off guard for once.

"That can't be..." Colton said and patted around his person, feeling for the knife he knew he still had on him.

"Jim," Price said, "is that your knife?"

"No, damn it." Colton peeled his coat off and let it fall to the floor. Price and Reeves froze, their eyes on his belt where his sheath hung empty.

"We got him, Marshal." Reeves took a step toward Colton, a self-satisfied grin cracking his stony face. The marshal nodded at Bo one last time and hooked out his pistol, quicker than Colton could see.

"Now wait a minute," Price said, stepping between Colton and the lawmen. "Jim Colton didn't kill anyone."

"Really? He seemed more than efficient at it yesterday. Killed two of them banditos without much trouble." Reeves was talking to Price, but his eyes were only on Colton, cold and hard.

"And when would he have had a chance to do it, Agent? The man was with me the whole night. Damn, he's been with me ever since he left the doctor's room." Price was a tall man, his arms outstretched damn near touched both sides of the car. Reeves and Miller weren't about to get past him without forcing the issue. Colton just didn't know how motivated they were to do so.

"Is that so, Mr. Price? Well, maybe you can explain to me how this knife," he brandished Colton's knife in front of Price's face, "this knife that I gave back to him earlier ended up in Agent Pierce's back, hmm?"

"Have you ever been to London, Mr. Reeves?" Price asked, drawing a blank stare from the Reeves and even the marshal, who had his silver gun in his gloved hand. "I have, you see. Managed to take a trip over there to talk to one of their railway magnates, an overly stuffy man, tremendously fat, wore a powdered wig—"

"Is there a point to this, Mr. Price?" Reeves interjected.

"Yes. While I was in London, I took to exploring the city on my own, just to get the feel of the place. Now, you must understand, I didn't carry much on me, but I did have my usual accoutrements: a gold pocket watch gifted to me by my father on his deathbed, my billfold, a silver cigarette case, and a blackjack." Reeves's eyebrows raised at that, but Price paid no mind and continued. "On the particular occasion that I am talking about, I went for a short walk to get a view of the newly completed Big Ben at the north end of Westminster Palace. My stroll was an hour round-trip. Do you know what I found upon returning to my lodgings? Nothing. All the items I mentioned previously had disappeared, including the blackjack." Reeves's eyes recognized the meaning and frowned. "You see, London is notorious for pickpockets."

"So, you're saying that someone aboard your train lifted a knife from Mr. Colton and used it to kill Agent Pierce," the marshal's reedy voice said, lowering his gun.

"No," Price said, lowering his arms, "what I'm saying is that it's not outside the realm of possibilities. What I am saying is that anyone could have murdered Agent Pierce."

IV

Colton bent to examine the windows and the sigils painted there in blood. Reeves and the marshal left to check on the prisoners. They hadn't necessarily been swayed away from suspecting that Colton had committed the murder, but they had some doubt right now, and that was good enough.

"Thank you, Alexander," Colton said. Price, for his part, remained outside the room; his stomach wasn't in for this kind of scene, not anymore.

"Scapegoating is all it is," Price said from behind a handkerchief. "Most of the Pinkerton agents I've worked with on these train lines have been good at their job, but their focus is just that, not the intricacies of it. They were really willing to string you up, even though you were with me the whole time!" The words flew from his mouth, spat in anger and fury.

"They had evidence. Can't fault them for that." Colton returned to Bo Pierce's body. "I'm just glad you had some of your own." Reeves's claim that Bo had been stabbed in the back was a purely symbolic statement, the man hadn't been stabbed at all—he'd been gutted. It wasn't a clean gutting, either. The knife was obviously used to start the process, a straight and precise slice from one side of Bo's belly to the other. The rest of the work was jagged and not at all characteristic of the clean lines of a knife or even someone who knew what they were doing. If Colton had to guess, he'd say that the man's skin had been torn into with someone's bare hands.

"Prisoners are still all tied up," Reeves said, hat dangling from the hand of his wounded shoulder, his other hand preoccupied with pinching the bridge of his nose. "I left the marshal back there to keep an eye on 'em." He rubbed his face and ran a finger over his thick mustache. "Say, what the hell are you doing down there?"

"Checking for bite marks." Colton stood with a sigh. "There aren't any." The events of six months ago came rushing back over him. A wave of nausea followed as he thought of the dead he'd left back West, the dead he was rushing toward, and of the woman he'd left in the city now several days behind him.

"Bite marks?" Reeves placed his hat back on his head. "Jesus, Mary, and Joseph. There ain't no wild dogs loose on the train, Mr. Colton."

"No, apparently not. Something much worse." It was his turn to run a hand over his face. When was the last time he'd gotten any sleep, good sleep that wasn't assisted by whiskey? He couldn't remember, and he felt suddenly exhausted. "Either of you recognize these symbols, here?" Colton pointed toward the windows, the bloody markings outlined by the distant, rising sun.

"Symbols, eh?" Reeves stepped into the room and looked around him. "I didn't think much of these when we first found Bo. Figured it was just a peculiar way the blood had landed." Price didn't venture to follow the Pinkerton, but he managed to step just past the doorway, hand and handkerchief held tight over his mouth and nose.

The three men stood in silence, each trying to make something of what was painted over those windows, the sun casting a bright yellow light on the floor, the dust motes dancing their hedonistic ecstasy in the morning light.

"Is that David's Star?" Reeves pointed to the center window, part of the door that led onto the end bumper of the train. It was a star surrounded by a circle. "We hired a Jewish agent a while back, he wore one around his neck. Looked something like that."

"David's Star has six points, not five," Price said, his attention still on the window to the far left. "Is this here meant to be a snake?"

"Maybe," Colton said, "and I guess this might be a goat's head?" he pointed at the window to the far right.

"And this is a cross," Reeves said, standing to the left of the door he'd been staring at. "Though it looks funny."

"It's upside down," Colton said and frowned.

"Shit, that ain't good," Reeves said and retrieved a smoke from his pocket, lit it.

"Not sure what that last one is," Price said. "A backwards h, maybe?"

"What does this all mean?" Reeves asked, shaking out his match.

"I can't say, Agent," Colton said, "but it's been my

experience that symbols like this can't be good for anything."

"No shit," Reeves pointed his rolled cigarette at Bo Pierce's dead body. "Now, what are we going to do about it?"

"There's no way to know who did this, not yet anyway. Though we can probably count out the prisoners, unless they're some sort of escape artists." Colton moved to the exit but was blocked by Reeves.

"I'm still not convinced you didn't have some hand in this, Mr. Colton."

"And I'm not convinced you didn't, Agent. Nor am I convinced that anyone else aboard didn't do it. But then, we're going about it the wrong way. Why would someone want to kill Agent Pierce?"

"Bo?" Reeves's eyes lit up, an honest reaction of surprise to the question. "Bo could be annoying at times, stubborn as a mule, but he didn't do anything to harm no one."

"What about fugitives, criminals you may have tracked in the past?" Colton stepped around the lawman to stand next to Price. "What we need to do now is get the passengers all together. Not just the passengers, either, but the employees, too. Everyone aboard this train needs to be gathered. Think you can do that, Price?"

Price nodded.

"What do you aim to do once you get them all together?" Reeves asked.

"Well, you'll have a good look at everyone there. See if you recognize anyone you or Pierce may have arrested in the past. In the meantime, myself and Price will keep an eye on anyone who looks suspicious. Anyone we think might have been able to lift my knife from me without knowing."

"Speaking of," Reeves said and drew out the knife

once more. "I think I'm going to keep this on me for a little while. Just for insurance purposes, you understand."

"That's fine, Agent," Colton said. "Just as long as you don't mind me suspecting you of killing someone if another person ends up dead aboard this train."

"Deal, Mr. Colton." Reeves smiled and put away the knife. "Now, if you'll excuse me, I'm going to rest my arm some. Let me know when you have everyone gathered. I can't wait to see the looks on all those rich faces when they get scrutinized by a Pinkerton agent."

Colton and Price watched Reeves walk away. He limped some as he walked, nothing too obvious, but something was giving him some pain.

"You think this is going to work, Jim?" Price asked, finally removing the handkerchief from his mouth.

"I don't know, Price, but it's the only thing I've got to keep the agent from putting me in irons."

CHAPTER FIVE

I

Major Stephen Pickett, veteran of the American Civil War, had never been summoned in such a way. Following a rough knock on the door, two porters stood on the other side, coming just short of ordering him and his wife to attend to the diner car immediately. If he had his youth back, he might have thrashed the two men on bare principle. No one, especially the likes of them, ordered the Major around.

Of course, they must have suspected his irritation, as they went on to explain that they were on orders from Mr. Price and Agent Reeves. He shooed them away and went to tell his wife, Elizabeth.

Lord, how he loathed her. A tiresome nag of a woman, never satisfied with her lot in life, always attempting to climb the social ladder despite his meagre earnings. Just the other night, when deciding on which train to take, she was adamant about taking the Express. Not for any other reason than she had heard that Mary Masterson was planning a trip aboard the same train. Patiently, as patient as a man could ever be, the Major attempted to explain that a trip aboard the Erie and then a quick changeover would only leave them a day or two behind the Express but result in a less extreme price. It was for naught; Elizabeth Pickett had her mind and heart set, and there was little anyone, even her husband, could do.

"Who was that, Stephen?" Elizabeth was already in the process of cleaning herself up for breakfast, her make-up half-done, when she turned to face him.

"Some damned trainmen," the Major said. "That daft Pinkerton fellow is gathering all the passengers for some damned reason."

"Oh," Elizabeth said and turned back to her mirror, "that should be interesting. Perhaps it will add a little flavour to the letter I intend to send home to the children."

The Major smiled, nodded, turned from his wife, and squeezed his ebony lacquered cane between his hands. A squeak rose from the pressure, a groan of the wood that his rough hands continued to squeeze. Sometimes, he wished he could do that to his wife. He dreamed that some night he might grab her fat throat between his still powerful hands and choke the life out of her, watch her tongue, so accustomed to flapping with gossip, wag in her effort to draw a breath that was never to come again. The thought, the wish, the dream gave the Major a deep sense of relief and comfort. Perhaps, with all the death surrounding the train, it would be a good time to live his dream. To practice it to its fullest.

Another, entirely different smile crossed the Major's face as he shrugged himself into his coat.

II

"Oh Jesus, Del, what if they know?" Anne-Marie dabbed at the corners of her eyes with a handkerchief. She was a beautiful woman, her curly, dark hair piled high on her head, her emerald green eyes glittering with tears, her lips plump and kissable, and the curve of her breast just exposed above the neck of her dress. There was no doubt, Delilah Hardin was in love.

"They don't," Delilah said and ran to Anne-Marie's side, taking one small, pale hand into her own. "How

could they? We left it all the way down in Florida."
Delilah pushed a stray hair from Anne-Marie's forehead,
letting her thumb glide softly, quickly over that perfect
forehead.

"Maybe Daddy put the word out. Maybe he sent my
uncles to find us." Anne-Marie sniffled and lay her head
on Delilah's waiting shoulder. Delilah ran a hand over her
beloved's back and squeezed her closer.

"No, Annie, I don't think so." It was more than just in-
tuition or wishful thinking that made her say this. Delilah
knew with a firm certainty that Anne-Marie's father
wouldn't put the word out, couldn't.

"But—"

"You wrote the letter, right?" Delilah asked, raising
Anne-Marie's eyes to her own, a crooked finger on her
chin.

"Yes, but—"

"And you wrote it exactly how I had said?" Delilah
pushed on. "About running off with Joe Everly and that
you'd send money when you could?"

"Yes, you know I did. But—" Anne-Marie said was
hushed with Delilah's finger over her mouth. Delilah did
indeed know about the letter and had read it after Anne-
Marie finished writing it. She also threw it in the fire as
soon as Anne-Marie was asleep. The poor young thing
was right about one thing: her daddy would have sent half
the country, half the world, after his precious little girl.
Especially since she was his last chance to make any kind
of money in his lifetime. Marry upwards and onwards—
the words every little girl wants to hear from her father.
He didn't plan on his daughter falling in love; love didn't
make him any money, and he certainly hadn't planned on
her falling in love with another woman. Let alone a poor,
mousy-haired servant girl with no family to call her own.

Delilah took care of all of it. After the letter burned to

ash, she made sure that Mr. Dubois would never miss his daughter. It was as simple as waiting until the old man had drunk himself asleep. She waited in the bushes out-side his house, waited until the lanterns had been turned out and crept through the house with an axe. It was easy, tremendously easy. Delilah wouldn't have believed how easy it was. The hard part was not telling Anne-Marie. For all the trouble he gave her, Anne-Marie loved her daddy.

"No buts about it, then. We're safe. This meeting is just about all the goings-on aboard the train." She took the other woman's face into her hands and stared straight into her eyes. "We'll make it to California, and then we'll be able to live our lives carefree and in love."

They kissed, neither believing that, not deep down in their souls, and it left a bitter taste in their mouths.

III

Doc Walker smiled at the boys that came to the door to invite him to this impromptu gathering, and he'd smile at them Pinkerton sons of whores, too, but he didn't feel much like smiling. He was a retired man; he'd put up his hands to the sawbones profession and backed away slowly. Oh, he still loved being a doctor, that wasn't it. He loved the science of it. The human body was a miraculous thing.

He'd always enjoyed the intricacies of anatomy. Even as a boy, working the farm with his father, hunting on his off days, he couldn't wait to be the one to kill something. It wasn't just the act of murder, though, no. He didn't care much for that, and he wasn't against it either, but it wasn't exactly his purpose. No, his purpose was to explore. To find out what made things tick. Beating hearts, blood run-ning in the veins, organs helping when they were needed. It was like the cogs of a watch. If everything was in its own place, doing its job, it worked just fine. If anything was askew, well, that was like a watch, too.

Walker grunted. That was all the machinations of life. He'd moved on from that in his retirement. He knew how the body worked, but what he wanted to know more about, what he needed more time to study, was the brain. So much was being learned about the soft, gray flesh that resided under the plate of the skull. All of a man's life was determined by electrical impulses that bounced around the brain. Vision was controlled in the occipital cortical area, while a lesion on the frontal lobe could cause paralysis and loss of speech. The findings were miraculous, and Walker didn't want to miss out.

Of course, there was the God question. Man wasn't made without God, so Walker theorized that maybe those electrical impulses were, in fact, the touch of God, the soul. Imagine being able to find physical proof of the soul, of the afterlife, of God. That's what he hoped to do, hoped to prove.

He looked at the oversized trunk he'd brought aboard, now centred in his room, a new lock hanging from it, the key in the pocket of his vest. All these interruptions by the Pinkertons just delayed his study. He needed peace and quiet, and for no one to look in his trunk. So, he'd smile and smile and smile for as long as he needed, until he could get back to his surgical investigations.

IV

Marshal Laird Miller tilted back his flask, a little metal number his wife had given him years before and made his way to the dining car. When the last of the rum was drained, he cursed and shoved it back in his pocket.

Reeves had lost it. Not only did he manage to get three of his suspects killed, but he managed to get his partner killed, too. Miller felt the burden of helping the Pinkerton on his broad shoulders, and he didn't like it. Never did like them Pinkerton bastards.

Of course, he'd help the Pinkerton out, as long as the Pinkerton kept out of his own business. As long as Reeves didn't find out about Mr. Robert Creed chained up in Miller's room, they'd be just fine. Just fine, indeed.

Oh, Creed wasn't a nice man, no, sir. He cut a swathe over the East Coast, culminating in the death of one Jerimiah Dubois and his family down in Florida way. Axed them to death he did, before he tried to burn the house down. Must've been drunk as a skunk because Miller found him at the scene of the crime the next day, covered in soot and ash and a pile of his own puke.

He likely would've killed him right there or let the neighbours do it. It'd been a long time since he was at a lynching, and he heard they were proficient at it down Florida way. Then again, Creed was worth more money alive than dead. A rapist, a murderer, and an all-around pathetic human being. Waste of space.

So, he made to take Creed back to California, where he was wanted, but Miller was going to have his fun with him on the way. He'd been enjoying the results he was getting from a riding crop before they got aboard the train, but Creed was a screamer, and he couldn't risk anyone else finding Creed. There was no way Miller was sharing that kind of bounty.

Candlewax had been a nice experiment. Creed really cringed at the stuff without making too much noise. Of course, there was always the possibility of getting the flame just a little too close to the man's flesh, burning him up good. The thought of it sent a rush of adrenaline through Miller as he walked, a smile lighting under his big mustache. He'd have to try that but make sure Creed was all bundled up and quiet before he did. No use getting the word out. A knife might do as well. Some small little nicks and cuts in certain places would drive Creed crazy, Miller just knew it would. Not any knife would do; something sharp, something accustomed to that kind of work, would be best. If there was some way he could get his hands on Colton's knife, well, that would just paint the perfect picture, wouldn't it?

"Miller." Reeves' voice cut through his daydream and brought him around. "I'm going to need you to work the crowd some. Walk around the perimeter of the room, keep an eye on them and see if anyone seems out of sorts."

"No problem, agent," Miller said and let the man go on ahead of him. Maybe if they managed to catch this killer, they'd let Miller keep him in his room. Wouldn't that just add something to the picture? Wouldn't that just be a new test to try?

Miller smiled and twisted the ends of his mustache before he waded into the crowded dining car.

CHAPTER SIX

I

"Well, if that wasn't the biggest waste of time, I don't know what it was," Reeves spat and paced around the dining cart.

The passengers had long since left, shooed back to their rooms with the explicit order to stay there if they valued their lives. Colton was surprised at how well they took it. Then again, having their journey start out with an attempted robbery likely set some low expectations for the rest of their trip.

"You see anyone that looked familiar to you, Agent?" Colton asked, rubbing the back of his neck.

"Not one," he said and shook out a cigarette for himself.

"All right, were there any that seemed a little out of sorts?" Colton's patience was running thin. He hadn't been this holed up since the war, and it was playing on his nerves. He had half a mind to take Bill out of the cattle car and ride the rest of the way to California.

"The Major wasn't too pleased about it all," the Marshal said, leaning back in one of the dining chairs.

"I get the feeling that the Major isn't too pleased about much of anything," Price said, "if his wife is to be believed." Reeves and the Marshal raised their eyebrows at that, and Colton sighed. A taste of fresh air and open space was what he needed, but he'd have to stop the train first, and the next stop wasn't likely for another day or two. How many more would be dead by then, and how many of those deaths would be by his knife? Though he didn't wield it, it was being used, nonetheless. Colton had a hard time not taking that personally.

"The doc seemed preoccupied," Reeves said. "A little perturbed, I'd say." He rubbed his chin. "Then there was them two fillies. What's their names?" He snapped his fingers at Price.

"Ms. Delilah Hardin and Ms. Anne-Marie Dubois." Price tapped his temple. "Two friends travelling to see family, if my memory serves."

"Dubois, you say?" Miller said, and something dark crossed his face, his eyes creased, and he pinched his nose.

"We're looking for someone who could take down a young, able-bodied man," Colton said. "I think we can agree that neither the doctor nor the Major would be up for the job."

"Rules out the women, too," Reeves sighed.

"I'm not so sure," Colton said. "A woman sets her mind to something, she's going to see it through." He held up his hand to stop Reeves before he responded. "All the same, I don't like either one of them for it. They came across more shocked than anything else."

"Shocked or relieved?" the Marshal said.

They sat in silence for a moment, the train pushing itself forward, chugging along in the late morning air. Colton hadn't realized how accustomed he'd become to the little noises that made up travel by train: the steel wheels slicing over steel rails, the wind screaming around the engine and cars, the lonely peal of the train whistle echoing around them. Looking out the windows, he could tell that they were going through some previously untouched Indian lands that were beautiful in their desolation, spectacular in their solitude. And white men ruined that with all these new noises that suddenly rushed in around him. He struggled to understand how this, any of this, was better. Colton couldn't bring himself to ask anyone that, not outright. He knew their response—why is this better? It just is.

"So, what's the next step?" Price managed to strangle out, rousing everyone.

"Just because no one seemed out of sorts doesn't mean they didn't do it," Colton said. "And no matter how they looked, we know there is a killer aboard." They all nodded at that, a silent agreement that Colton was hoping for. "I say we each take some suspects and stick close to them. I'd like to have a little chit-chat with the doctor about a few things, so I'll keep close to him. Reeves, why don't you—"

"I'll look after Ms. Hardin and Ms. Dubois," the Marshal said, interrupting. It was Colton's turn to raise an eyebrow, and it brought a flush of red to Marshal Miller's face and neck. "I knew a Dubois family from down south. She may be related, maybe not," he said with a shrug.

"That's just fine, Marshal," Colton said but filed away that reaction for later. "Price, I know you have dealt with the Major and his wife before, so I'd like Agent Reeves to look after them. Get some fresh eyes on how they act and talk."

"Sounds fine by me," Price said, "but what do you want me to do?"

"You will keep an eye on your employees. We haven't discussed them much, but they are as capable of killing as anyone else." Colton looked around the room and was met with a series of nods. It wasn't the perfect plan, but it was something. "We told them to be here at mealtimes, so in the meantime, get some rest. We'll all meet here at lunch and start following our suspects. Price, it might be best if you find a worker you trust more than the others, make them your ally to help you keep an eye."

One final nod and each of the men exited the dining car, heading for their own rooms. Colton eyed each of the men carefully, each member of his little group. He didn't know any of them well, save for Price from the war. But how much had the man changed over the years? And what of the Marshal and Reeves, both law in their own right, but being a lawman didn't make you a good man. Didn't mean you weren't willing to kill. Colton knew he wasn't the killer, but he couldn't say the same for those he had just come into an agreement with. He wasn't sure those men weren't thinking much the same as they filed out towards their rooms, but Colton was sure that he would be keeping a close eye on Price, Reeves, and Miller.

If they were smart, they'd do the same with him.

II

Marshal Miller took Colton's advice to heart and made his way to his room to rest, but there was no way that he was going to wait until after lunchtime to confront those women. Dubois. Could it be the wayward daughter that Creed had supposedly killed? If so, did he set the fire that killed the rest of the family?

Miller shook his head. It was no matter, Creed had done plenty of things to earn his hanging, to earn his special treatment. Still, something stuck in Miller's craw, a feeling of being tricked and misled, that put his back up. He'd have to find out the rights of what happened in Florida, and those girls were going to tell him. If not, well, they'd have to endure some of what Mr. Creed had been going through.

He slid through the door and into the darkness of his room. He'd pulled the blind when he'd first boarded, and he wouldn't open it until all was said and done. There was a harsh tang of human sweat, the kind that grew out of fear and pain, and with it came the soft groans and moans of a man too weak to call for help. Miller smiled.

"Creed," Miller said in his slow drawl, and the groans stopped with a sudden yip of a trap being shut, "what am I going to do with you, hmm?"

"Please," the man croaked, and now Miller could see him, edging toward the bed, trying to stuff himself under there, trying to hide.

"I've got some good news for you, Creed." Miller grabbed the chain that was wrapped around Creed's neck and gave it a yank. "I think we might be able to remove the murder of the Dubois family and their daughter from your list of charges." Miller sat in the comfortable, green armchair and shoved his boot into the man's neck. "What do you think of that, boy?"

Creed uttered a low moan, maybe a sob, and Miller hung his head back and relished it.

"Of course, I'll have to check it out. May even bring you a playmate or two if everything goes the way I think." Miller's face hurt from the smile all of this brought to his face, his cheeks stretched at the sound of Creed's own near pleasurable sounds of relief at the news. He'd crawled out from the bed, now on all fours. It never ceased to amaze Miller just how big Creed had been. A thick man, his chest and arms muscled for pushing around cattle. The man had a tiny head on him, though, something that looked almost comical when you first clapped eyes on him. A tiny little head with just a smattering of greasy, brown hair that horseshoed around the back.

"Now, Creed," Miller said with a mock sort of admonishment that bordered on wild laughter, "don't go getting any ideas in your head, boy. I still got plenty left to do with you, lad. Plenty." He jerked the chain with a little extra strength and pulled Creed to the ground.

"Please," Creed rasped, "please, no more. No more."

"Awfully mannerly now, eh, Creed? I wonder if you were so mannerly with the women and children you raped."

Creed groaned, but there was an edge to it, something that Miller didn't like the sound of. "I meant, please stop talking." Creed's voice was stronger now, different. Miller's smile faded into a grimace, and he pulled at the chain with a savage jerk that should've torn into the skin around Creed's neck.

Creed didn't move, didn't utter a sound. "Not unless you want to talk about what you did," Creed continued, rising to his feet. "C'mon, Marshal, tell your ole pal Creed all of the things you've done."

Miller jumped to his feet and pulled his gun, putting it under Creed's chin. "If you know what's good for you, boy, you'll—"

"I'll what?" Creed's voice was strong now, confident. "I'll slither back under the bed, I'll let you drop hot wax on my stomach? Or maybe you'd rather I let you slice me with a knife. You'd like that, wouldn't you, Marshal?"

Miller's breathing hitched as his eyes widened on the face of his prisoner. How did he know what he was thinking, what he had only thought of hours ago? He clicked back the hammer of his gun. "Shut up."

"Or maybe you'd like to talk about what you did just last night, Marshal. Do you remember that?"

A flash of some memory passed in Miller's mind, but he couldn't quite hold on to it. Images slammed into his mind: a strange symbol, some man's broad back, a knife in someone's hand (was it his?). "I...I didn't...I can't..." Miller said, his free hand rubbing at his eyes, trying to black out those images.

"Of course not, Marshal." Creed took the gun from Miller's hand as easily as if Miller had handed it over.

"You've many deeds to think about, I'm sure it'd all get jumbled in that head of yours." Creed backed the Marshal up against the wall, his hands (different now: so strong, so hot) pushing against Miller's shoulders. "Maybe I can help," Creed said and slid one finger up the side of Miller's face until it reached his temple. Once there, Creed's finger began to press hard into that soft spot above the eye. His fingernail was sharp, jagged, and the pain when he finally pierced the skin, dug through the veins and muscle, was so blinding that Miller couldn't cry out in pain. Instead, he was left gasping for air, his eyes rolling back into his head. "Think, Marshal Miller. Think."

Miller could feel Creed's finger wiggle around under his skin, and for a brief moment, he had a chance to wonder about how this could've happened, lament his failed plans, before images swirled in front of him, ghosts of his past remembering. And he saw everything. Every little thing that he'd ever done, all of the bad and none of the good. Just for him, served up on a platter for him to feed. Amongst those memories was the train itself, and he knew what had happened, what was happening, and he wept.

CHAPTER SEVEN

I

Colton had a bad feeling when he came back to the dining cart. He saw all the passengers, grumbling to themselves around their meals, and made to sit with Doctor Walker, maybe ask him a few questions, but Reeves waved him over. Miller hadn't shown.

Lunch came and went with no sign of Marshal Miller, and their intended suspects went their separate ways once more. Reeves and Price wanted to talk about it, wanted to prepare how they were going to handle Miller and how to deal with the passengers in the meantime. Colton had other plans.

He stormed through the train, his hands curled into tight fists, and headed for Miller's room with Price and Reeves on his tail. The day had taken a turn. The sun that was threatening earlier in the morning had faded from view, and, in its place, rain clouds darkened the sky. The raindrops slapped against the windows like they wanted to smash the glass into shards and do the same to Colton. If he were lucky, thunder might be brewing, and lightning would crack the sky. Maybe the train would be struck, putting an end to all of his problems.

Miller's room, as it turned out, was near enough to the caboose that he didn't have any neighbours, just some prep rooms for train employees and maybe a storage area. Colton slammed his fist against the door and called to the

Marshal. No answer.

"Must've gotten drunk," Reeves said under a scowl.

"I don't care," Colton said and attacked the door again with no more success than before. "Alexander, you have a key to this door?"

Price shook a large key of rings free from his pocket with a sigh and began sifting through them. "I've asked the company for a skeleton key for all these doors, just the one that can get into them all, but they said they can't do it, so I'm stuck with this." He gave the ring another shake, and the keys clattered together. After some hesitation, he handed the key ring to Colton, one key held apart from the rest. "This should be it."

It was the smell that hit them first, the air wet with a sour mixture of sweat and blood and feces. Price immediately gagged and turned to the opposite wall to vomit, Reeves descended into a coughing fit, and Colton's eyes watered so much he had to pull his bandana up around his mouth and nose.

Two men lay prone within the dark room, their bodies just outlined in the light that spilled in from the door. The worst was yet to come.

II

"Bob Creed," Reeves said, holding a cloth over his face. They had managed to enter the room, walking lightly over the splayed bodies to open the blinds and get a better view. Dust motes scattered in the dim daylight, hesitant to land on the dead bodies. The room wasn't different than any other: an armchair, a bed, green carpet. Miller was lying on the far side of the room, an open wound on his skull that still leaked blood and tarnished his silver hair. This new man, Bob Creed, was sitting naked in the armchair, his arms and neck sliced open.

"Creed," Reeves shook his head. "He was a wanted

man, had cut a swath of murder and rape from Nevada to Tennessee. Last I heard, he was in Florida, lying low."

"Not low enough," Colton said. "What was the Marshal doing with him?"

"Bounty, I suppose. The man had racked up a hefty amount, worth more alive than dead. I'd wager that was why he kept him a secret."

Colton nodded, but there was more to keep secret here than just an extra passenger on the Transcontinental Express. Creed's body showed the signs of all kinds of abuse, from lashings to scratches, cuts to fist-sized welts. If Colton wasn't mistaken, there was some candle wax still stuck to the man's face. That and the chain around his neck that ran to the bed. Miller was extracting something from Mr. Creed, but Colton couldn't say if it was revenge or something else.

"Looks like Creed got tired of being chained up." Reeves toed Miller's head to the side. "Jabbed Miller in the temple and then killed himself."

"Maybe," Colton said and knelt in front of Creed. He was a peculiar looking man, small head, small mouth with lips that looked pursed like he'd just sucked on a lemon. "These wounds look familiar to you?"

Reeves nodded. "Scratch," he said and pushed his hat up on his forehead. "All the same, not many ways to slit your own wrists and your own throat."

"True," Colton said, but he wasn't listening, had already anticipated Reeves' response. Instead, he focused on Creed's mouth. Puckered as it was, his cheeks were puffed some under his wide, dead eyes. He'd seen something like that before, in the war. After a small skirmish, he and his men had survived just outside of Missouri, the men took to scrounging from the dead. Most did it to replenish powder or shot, maybe take an extra weapon or knife. Others, more than Colton cared to admit, went looking for treasure. Gold, pocket watches, money—that sort of thing. Colton rarely practiced either. He didn't think it was right to mess with the dead, figured that they'd be found if they needed to be and otherwise, they'd return to the earth, dust to dust and all that nonsense. This time, Colton was persuaded to tag along by a young Alexander Price, who had hopes of finding something shiny to bring home to his fiancée.

They hadn't found much. Some of the others had been scrounging as soon as the guns ceased fire, and Price never did find something good enough for his woman. Colton found something, though, a thin dead man, a boy really, with his mouth shut and dead eyes staring into the sky. When Colton opened the young man's mouth, a gold pocket watch sat there on his tongue. Colton didn't take it, nor did he tell his fellow soldiers what he found. He just shut that man's mouth and hoped whoever he was saving that watch for got it. He later told Price, who pouted about the loss of a potential gift. Colton had laughed, but it was a sad laugh.

"Hey, Price," Colton called now, placing his thumb and forefinger on Creed's chin.

Price stuck his head in the door, a silk handkerchief hanging over his nose and mouth.

"Remember the treasure hunt for your old fiancé," Colton said and watched Price's face screw up in confusion.

"I think I may have found something else for you to write home about." Colton opened the man's mouth, and beetles spilled forth. Colton jumped back, a scream caught around his Adam's apple as the insects poured out, their chittering as loud as gunshots, the scraping of their hard shells over one another like fingernails being dragged across a chalkboard.

"Jesus Christ," Reeves cried and made for the door

that Price had just vacated, going to puke some more, no doubt.

After the beetles were done, the centipedes came hissing, all of them scurrying to find another moist, dark place. Colton kept his distance, trying to flatten himself against the wall. When the insects had finally taken shelter somewhere out of sight, Colton let himself breathe. He wasn't sure how long he had leaned there against a wall, trying to swallow his disgust. A second, a minute, an hour? He couldn't say. All he could do was let his eyes fall on what the insects had dislodged from Creed's throat—a folded piece of paper.

III

It wasn't so much a note as a single name scrawled hastily in printed letters: John Masterson.

Price recognized it immediately. He brought them near the front of the train, another staging area for the crew, for those who worked directly with the running of the train. Those people that shoveled coal, tooted the horn, or whatever was required to keep the damn contraption moving, Colton wasn't sure. What he was sure of was that John Masterson might have been the biggest man he'd ever seen.

Price pointed him out, standing shirtless under overalls, a shovel in one hand, the other wiping sweat from his brow. Masterson stood well over six feet tall, his skin a dark bronze and his eyes a bright gold that saw them coming.

"John Masterson," Reeves shouted and pulled his gun, "drop the shovel and come quietly."

No sooner were the words out of Reeves' mouth than the shovel flew toward them, a working man's javelin, and Masterson was out the side door of the train.

The shovel breezed by them, the sensation of it passing so closely that it caused Colton's head to throb, but he took off after the man without a second thought.

The gust of wind nearly sucked Colton into the air and tossed him to the ground. He groped for purchase; his hand landed on the railing of a ladder, and he looked up to see the heel of a big boot pull itself onto the roof. He followed.

The air and rain attacked him on the wet surface of the train. It was doing the same for John Masterson, and the big man had slowed some. Colton followed. He didn't like Masterson for the murder. No killer worth his salt would leave behind a calling card, but the man took to running—maybe he knew something or had something to hide.

Colton called out to Masterson, his words flying back away from him in the wind. He pulled his gun and fired it into the air. Masterson flinched and looked over his shoulder but pushed onward and hopped to the next car.

Colton cursed and did the same. He made it to the end of the first car just as Masterson was halfway over the next. He was going slow, the wind and his heft working against him, but he had the muscle and the head start to keep out of reach of Colton until the end of the train. He'd get away.

Sliding down the ladder at the end of the car, Colton took to the inside of the train and pushed his way through, knocking over anyone or anything that stood in his way. He found the run much easier, not being hindered by the wind or rain, and he crossed the cars quickly, if not efficiently.

In the caboose again, the symbols still painted in blood on its windows, Colton paused. He had to time it right. If he was too early, Masterson would just run back the way he came; if he was too late, Masterson would escape off the end of the train. In either case, Colton would be forced to shoot the big man, and he didn't want to do that.

He counted a silent ten and plunged out the door marked with an inverted cross, his gun trained on the ladder that led from the roof. John Masterson was there, his eyes wide and scared.

"Come on down, son," Colton said, "I just want to talk to you some."

IV

"I didn't know either man," Masterson said, careful not to maintain eye contact with anyone present.

Price and Reeves had caught up just after Colton had guided the big man into the caboose. Blood still stained the floor, the markings still covered the windows, and Masterson was having a hard time averting his eyes from all of it.

"Well, John," Price said, "how did your name wind up in some dead fella's mouth?" Price knew Masterson in passing, had seen him on a few different occasions when he rode the Express. From what he could remember, John had been an excellent worker and was helpful whenever he could be. Price had never heard of him being violent to anyone, nor did he hear any complaint against the man.

"I don't know, sir," Masterson said, "I never knew them men." He twisted his hands over on themselves and tried his best to keep his eyes there, too.

"That's two white men dead, John," Reeves said. "Two white men dead with your name at the scene, three white men if you include Agent Pierce. Ain't going to be easy on you going down for those crimes." Reeves lit a cigarette, keeping his hand on the handle of his gun.

"I didn't kill no one," Masterson said, his face stony.

"For what it's worth," Colton piped in, "I don't think you did it. I don't think you knew anything about any of this, but that should worry you, John. Someone knows *you*, and that someone is leaving your name in the same room as two dead men. Maybe you argued with someone aboard the train or had a miscommunication with one of the passengers."

"No, sir," Masterson said, but his bright, golden eyes were misty. "But I'm afraid."

"What are you afraid of, John?" Price asked and leaned in close.

"I...I don't know, exactly." Masterson shook with a long sigh. "Something ain't right on this train." Colton put up his hand to signal that Price and Reeves give him a minute and then nodded to Masterson to go ahead when he was ready.

"I've been on this train, doing my job, for over a year now. That's a lot of trips, a lot of time spent away from my family, but I don't mind because I really do enjoy the work, the people. The train has been wonderful too, it is such a beautiful engine. I love riding it. I've been on this train so much that I even have my own little bunk that the others let me claim each time I'm on board. It isn't much, but it is next to a window so I can see the world pass by. I take that bunk with pleasure every trip, but not this time. I switched."

"Why?"

"The voices."

Colton and Reeves shared a brief, meaningful glance, but Price pressed on, bent to his level and put a hand on his shoulder. "Go on, John. You can tell us."

"They didn't start right away, not at the beginning of the trip. At least I didn't notice them right away. At first, the voices sounded like they just might be the wind or a hushed conversation carried on outside the door. Harsh, spitting whispers that made me think someone was going to get in trouble." Masterson took a deep breath and looked to Price. "When they started up in earnest, it was hard to picture them not being there, like they must've been there forever. But they weren't, Mr. Price, they weren't.

"At first, they sounded like a bunch of words jumbled together, and I couldn't make no sense of them. It was like someone, soft," he touched his head and shrugged, "someone crazy trying to tell you a story. That didn't last long, though. Soon, I could hear words coming through the noise, just one or two words at first, calling my name, my wife's name, my brother's. They came mostly at night, so I thought I was dreaming, but then they started in the daytime, anytime that I sat on my bunk. The voices were relentless. It wasn't too long before they started telling me things. Telling me that my wife was unfaithful, that my brother was dead. I would've tried to ignore that, but they had already said some things I knew to be true."

"Like what?" Colton asked, lighting his own smoke and offering one to Masterson. The big man waved off the offer.

"Well, sir, they told me about my past. They knew my pappy died from consumption, that my mother drank more than all her brothers put together, that I had nearly killed my brother with a rock when we were younger. It wasn't just the past, though. No, they told me things about to happen on the train. They knew the agent was going to die, that the Marshal had another man in his room, and… and they said that you were going to kill me," he said, and his eyes settled directly on Colton, those watery globes crisscrossed with red veins dark with fear and something else, something subtler—anger. "They said I had to kill you first, or I wouldn't see my family again."

Colton ran his hand over his head, remembering the shovel pass so close he felt the vibration in his skull.

"Who told you that, boy?" Reeves stepped forward. "What were their names?"

"I don't know, sir. I don't even know if they were people."

"What do you mean, John?" Price stood and gave Colton a quick glance over his shoulder.

"I think it were the devil, Mr. Price. I think the devil is riding this train with us, riding it right to hell."

"Let me ask you something, Masterson." Colton stepped forward. "You said that these voices hadn't started at the beginning of the trip, that it started sometime after we set out proper, right?"

"Yes, sir."

"Could you offer a guess as to when they started?" Masterson started to shrug, but Colton extended his hand to stop him. "Let's say, did the voices start before the robbery attempt or after?"

Masterson took a moment to think. "Well, I still don't think I can say, but when you put it like that, I think it started after the robbery. I remember coming back to my bunk after helping to clear the track and hearing the noises then."

Colton nodded. "Thank you, Mr. Masterson. Why don't you go on back to work. If we need you again, we'll come find you. Just don't throw any more shovels at us, deal?"

Masterson's face flushed with relief, and he stood, towering over the other three men, with a hesitant smile on his broad face. "I'll try not to, sir."

CHAPTER EIGHT

I

"Stephen," Elizabeth Pickett said, prodding her husband's shoulder. "Stephen, it will be supper time soon. I want to get there as early as possible."

Major Pickett grunted something but remained in bed, staring at the wall, trying to listen. The voices had started out like his own thoughts, mirroring them and giving him more to think about. It embarrassed the Major when he realized he was actually conversing with others, many others. He thought he might have been taken aback by the intrusion and push against it, but the truth of the matter was that he enjoyed it. He enjoyed the conversation, enjoyed having his opinions challenged, enjoyed having the monotonous tedium of Elizabeth's talking washed away by the sea of words coming from the voices. They had so much knowledge, so much understanding. Not too much for Major Stephen Pickett, of course, but enough to be a challenge. It was exhilarating.

"Stephen, you still need to get dressed," Elizabeth said from her makeup table.

The Major groaned; she was nagging again. Nagging, nagging, always nagging. The woman couldn't be pleased, she couldn't be satisfied. She was a succubus, draining the life from him one nagging word at a time. The image of his hands wrapped around her fat little neck flashed across his eyelids, and he smiled.

She's a burden, voices echoed in his mind. *She only wants to bring you down, to make you as lifeless and boring as her.*

She wants to spend all your money, said more voices, overlapping with the first.

She wants you dead, said more still.

He frowned, thinking about his life. A poor man's son who worked the fields for some other man to keep his family fed. Life changed for the better during the war. He moved up the ranks and made something of himself. So what if he had to lie about his circumstances from time to time? Who cared if he hadn't made the most tactical decisions? If he somehow managed to get his whole platoon killed. No one knew, and he profited. Was that so bad?

No, the voices hissed in his mind, and he smiled, happy that the voices understood him, accepted him. Unlike Elizabeth.

You were a soldier, the voices said, like their tongue was wet at his ear. *You desire excitement, not a trip on a luxury train. You desire to fight again.*

"Yes," he said and sat up. "Yes, a return to battle."

"If that's what you want to call it, dear." Elizabeth rolled her eyes in her mirror. "Just wear the blue jacket—it looks nicer."

A fighter. A defender of life and liberty.

"Yes," the Major said, feeling a surge of righteousness coursing over him. "Liberty." He approached his wife and clamped his old hands on her shoulders. *Older, yes, but still strong.* Strong enough.

"Not now, Stephen…" she said as he spun her around in her chair. "Stephen?"

She blinked in disbelief when he raised his fist, her mouth shaping the word "Oh," but no sound fell from there. The room was completely silent save for the slap of skin on skin.

II

Doc Walker heard the voices well enough, but they weren't nearly as clever as they thought they were. Slathering his mind with self-doubt, questioning his stability, his theories, his work. Oh, but were they in for something.

At first, the voices were a hum, just low enough to keep his mind alert as he lodged the armchair under the door handle and unpacked the cadaver from his oversized trunk. They rose to a crescendo when he started cutting, using the saw to take off the top of his patient's head.

Careful, old man, they said. *Your hands aren't as steady as they once were.* Of course, Walker had already considered this; that's why he'd retired in the first place. He laughed at the voices' attempt to dissuade him from his work, as pathetic an attempt as it was.

"Tell me something I don't already know," he chuckled, removing the top of the cadaver's head with a sucking, wet plop. What was this man's name? Walker had known him in life, had worked with him in the field. Where was that? Old Barclay in Colorado? Yes, that might've been it. But what was his name?

Caldwell, the voices answered.

Yes, Walker thought, Edgar Caldwell. An old friend and acquaintance, a doctor in his own right. He removed Caldwell's brain in a practiced motion, slicing the stem with little effort and displaying it to the room, to the voices. Steady as ever, bastards.

Caldwell's brain was on par with the others he'd studied. Grey and pink, slick with blood and mucus. A mass of wrinkles divided down the middle in a neat symmetry that practically spoke of divine intervention. Poor Caldwell. Walker thought his brain might be grander, somehow. He was a brilliant man, so shouldn't he have more wrinkles, a larger hemisphere or lobe? Walker shrugged and consulted his notes. How did Caldwell die?

You killed him.

"Did I?" Caldwell said aloud. "I suppose I did." He flipped through his notebook. "Ah, yes. I poisoned him, wanted to keep the brain as healthy as possible."

Opening a dead man's head doesn't take any skill, old man.

"You don't think so?" Walker asked. "Why don't you do it?"

Open a live man's head, the voices taunted, *prove your theory. Show us the—*

"Soul," Walker said. "Yes, the soul has already left a cadaver's brain. The electrical impulses likely stopped within a few minutes of death."

Cut.

Walker dropped Caldwell's brain on the floor with a hideous thud. "I need a live subject," the doctor said, "but where can I find one?"

Slice.

"Maybe someone would volunteer."

Kill.

"But I'm such an old man now. How could I overpower someone?"

Colton. Kill Colton.

"Colton? No, he's much too sturdy, and his skull is already notched by a stray bullet. No, he's no good." Walker was pacing around his room now, unconsciously avoiding Caldwell's brain. He pushed his glasses up to his forehead and rubbed his eyes with one hand. "Who would be worthy of this study?"

Incompetent. Foolish. Old.

"You still believe that, do you?" Walker shouted into the ceiling. "Well, I'll show you. I'll prove it to you." He dropped to his knees, picked up his instruments and gave them a cursory wipe over the leg of his pants. "Watch this, and see who's incompetent," Walker said and began to slice into his own skull.

If anyone were to pass by his room, they'd be hard-pressed to say if the noises emitting from behind that door were screams of pain or satisfied laughter.

III

Anne-Marie sprawled across their bed, the back of her wrist alight on her forehead in a swoon that nearly drove Delilah to a mad passion. Her heart swelled as Anne-Marie pushed herself up to her elbow and smiled across the room at her.

"Watching me sleep?"

"Only a little," Delilah said, her face flushed and hot. "How was your nap?"

"I had strange dreams," Anne-Marie said, and her eyebrows furrowed, casting a shadow over her eyes.

"Nightmares?"

"I believe so," Anne-Marie said and, after a brief hesitation, "What was the last thing you said to my father?"

Delilah felt her stomach drop, a chill threatening to cross her spine and make her shiver. "I'm not sure," Delilah said, forcing herself to smile. "I know that I dropped off your letter and told him that you'd sent me expressly from the edge of town."

"Didn't he find that odd?" Anne-Marie sat up now, her pale features restrained, but Delilah knew Anne-Marie well enough to know that she was keeping something at bay.

"I should say," Delilah cleared her throat, tried to look away from Anne-Marie's probing eyes, to look anywhere in the room but there. "You know how he was with me. He didn't give me much thought, and when he did, it wasn't in the most favourable light."

"Well, you were trying to steal his only daughter away

from him." Anne-Marie smiled, showing her teeth. "Hoping to leave him dowerless and without many options to improve his situation."

"I suppose." Delilah didn't like the way Anne-Marie was speaking, didn't like her questioning. She'd never done this before. Just a young, foolish girl content in the arms of her lover, content being in love. "What got you thinking about all of this again?"

"My dreams." Anne-Marie faltered. "And other things."

"Well, let's not focus on that now. We are so close to our goal, to freedom." Delilah clutched onto that. "Those lawmen out there had no idea who we were, and if they did, they didn't care. Don't you see? We're clear and free." She added extra emphasis on the last word, her smile more genuine now.

"I just...are you sure that's the last thing you said to Father?"

"Yes, Annie," Delilah said and took hold of Anne-Marie's hand. "Of course that was it."

"I remember that night, you know." Anne-Marie pulled her hand away and hugged her knees. "I remember that you were gone for such a long time."

"Oh, it wasn't that long," Delilah said with a wave of her hand. "Besides, I had some errands to run before we left."

"You killed them, didn't you?" Anne-Marie's face was hidden behind her knees. All that was visible were her eyes, dark and cold.

"No...how can you?"

"You never delivered the letter at all. Did you read it before you threw it in the fire?"

"Anne-Marie, please—"

"No. You went to my father's house, my house, and ensured everyone was asleep, slipped out of your clothes, like you did so many nights with me by the river, and walked room to room with an axe. Did you enjoy it, Del? Did you enjoy murdering my family?"

"You don't understand," Delilah fumbled. "I did it for you, so you'd be free."

"You did it for yourself," Anne-Marie said and sprang from the bed. "Don't tell me that you killed *my* family for me."

"I did it for us," Delilah whispered, tears clinging to her eyelashes, her cheeks.

"Keep telling yourself that, Del, keep telling yourself that." Anne-Marie threw open the door.

"Where are you going?"

"I need some fresh air, and maybe I'll go find the Marshal who was giving us eyes, tell him a fine story."

Delilah was up in a second, one hand full of Anne-Marie's hair, the other slamming the door closed. "You will do no such thing," she growled and pushed Anne-Marie back on the bed.

She's betrayed you, the voices came unheeded, a hot breath on Delilah's neck. *She hates you. She'll never stay with you, never love you.*

"You can't keep me in here." Anne-Marie surged forward, trying to get around, find a path to the door. Delilah pushed her back, stood over her, and slapped her hard across the face.

"I can keep you here, my love. I will keep you here," Delilah hissed through gritted teeth. "If you refuse…Well, I have a pretty good record with the Dubois family. I need only to add one more to the tally."

Anne-Marie's face twisted in rage, and Delilah thought it was the prettiest she'd ever been. With a quick movement into her dress, she pulled out a double-barreled derringer and pushed it into Anne-Marie's cheek.

"Now, my dear, we are going to have a short conversation about your view of our relationship, and how sorely wrong it is," Delilah said, and all the while the voices laughed in the back of her mind. They laughed so hard she thought it might be good to join them, so she did.

IV

"Sins," Deacon Flint said, a crooked smile on his bruised face. "We all have 'em, don't you think so, Mr. Colton?"

Colton had tired of waiting around, of being behind on whomever was killing people, and of Price's constant jabbering on about his job. He decided to talk to a few more people. He had passed the elder McCoy on their way to lunch, and it triggered something the man had said about the prisoners, that they had been singing or chanting the night that Bo Pierce had been murdered. Since there was a diminishing number of people to keep guard of the two bandits, Colton volunteered, hoping to clear things up some.

"Well, I guess that depends on your view of God and the Good Book," Colton said and pulled up a chair to sit and smoke. "Pardon me, fellas, but you don't seem much like the reading type, let alone Godfearing."

"God," Deacon spat and smiled at his younger brother, a dough-faced man with a swollen eye and sagging lips. "God has nothing to do with sin. That's the devil's work."

"Is that so?"

"You see, Scratch, he used to talk to us all about this kind of stuff. Never shut up about it. He talked about sin, hell, and the corruption of the good. Shit, Jody and I were damn near priests ourselves when he found us, ain't that right Jody?"

The younger man just nodded and refused to look at Colton.

"That cursed Pinkerton out there." Deacon pointed to the door. "He thinks that Scratch, that we, started high-jacking trains for the money. Well, I got news for him, that wasn't it, no, sir."

"Why don't you tell me the news, and I'll pass it right along," Colton said and leaned forward. He'd already made up his mind that Deacon was as nutty as a bag full of squirrels, but Jody, quiet as he was, might have something productive to add to the conversation if he could ever get Deacon to shut his trap.

"We robbed trains to taste the sin in the air, to breathe in those dark secrets, and give people a chance to live them out. Sure, we stole some money, but it was the people aboard the train who helped us get it. We killed a couple of folks, but the people on the train killed more. You see, Colton? A train is just a tin can filled with worms; you crack it open, and it all comes pouring out."

"Jody, what do you think of all of this?"

"He thinks the same—" Colton levelled a backhand at Deacon that drew some blood from the corner of his mouth.

"I'm not talking to you," Colton said and signalled Jody to go on.

"I...I don't know, mister. I just came along for the money," Jody spoke in hushed tones around a slight lisp, but Colton could picture him at the altar giving rites to folks.

"What about all this talk of sin?"

"Yeah, Scratch did talk about that a lot. Some of the boys believed it, but most were just happy to get their share of the loot."

Colton stared at Jody for a moment, willing him to go on. Jody squirmed under his gaze.

"I did see Scratch talking to some of the passengers one time, and the next thing you know, they're helping us out."

"What did they do?"

"Well, one fella showed us where the train safe was. Another, a woman, killed the man she was riding the train with, and then...then there was the little boy." Jody paused to swallow and used his bound hands to wipe sweat from his eyes. "The little boy killed his parents, used a knife that Scratch had given him and just gutted them. I found him playing in the pool of blood after it was done."

"So, what are you saying?" Colton stood, leaned back, and rubbed his eyes with the heels of his hands so hard that he saw the afterimage. "Scratch could persuade people to give in to their, what, exactly...desires?"

Jody shrugged; a jagged smile crossed Deacon's face.

"Now you understand, Colton. Now you get it." Deacon jumped to the length of his chain, blood still creeping from the corner of his mouth. "Scratch wasn't some bandit for the law to take to jail. He was more than that. A single body couldn't contain him. He was more than you ever thought could be."

"Why don't you enlighten me, Flint?" Colton stood within a hair's width of Deacon's face, doing his best to remain calm.

"He's the devil, Colton," Deacon whispered. "A bastard straight out of the pit, and you pissed him off. Royally pissed him off. How do you think that's going to end for you?"

Colton smirked and took a step back. "'Bout as good as it will for you." He stepped out of the room and closed the door. He had a lot to think about, and he only had a few days to figure it out. Otherwise, there'd be a train full of dead bodies arriving in California.

CHAPTER NINE

I

As supper time came on, porters and waiters escorted the passengers to the dining car and started the food service. Colton watched the crowd carefully from the bar, and Reeves observed from the doorway while Price worked the crowd. There were some noticeable absences, which had him raise an eyebrow.

"Them two girls the Marshal was all hot and bothered for," Reeves said after he sauntered over to the bar.

"Mrs. Pickett, the Major's wife," Price said with a frown and mixed himself a drink.

"And the doctor," Colton finished off, rubbing his chin. "Did you speak to the Major, Alexander? Find out where his wife was?"

"He said she was feeling ill and wanted to get some extra rest."

"You believe him?"

Price shrugged. "I have no reason not to, but it does seem strange. Mrs. Pickett always wanted to be amongst the other passengers, showing off. I'm surprised she hasn't been found scurrying around the train looking for someone to brag to or gossip with."

Colton nodded. "So, what do we know so far?"

"We have two dead lawmen," Reeves said, accepting a drink from Price, "one extra dead body, a criminal, with Miller, and Scratch's suicide to start it all off." He swallowed his drink in one gulp and slammed the glass on the bar top.

"Not many clues to let us know who's been killing folks," Colton said. "We have those symbols painted on the caboose windows, and John Masterson's claim that he's hearing strange whispers. Then there's the word of a couple of prisoners to say that Scratch was the devil and could convince others to act out their darkest desires." He sighed.

"And now we have four missing passengers," Price said and handed a drink to Colton.

"I don't like it," Colton said, "but I think we may need to consider that Scratch isn't dead."

"What are we talking about here?" Reeves whispered. "You think that Scratch survived giving himself a new smile?" He chuckled and shook his head. "Oh, and if Scratch is still alive, who's the body we got resting in the cattle car, huh?"

"I know how it sounds," Colton said, "but think about it. This train hasn't stopped since the robbery attempt, no one has gotten off or on, and we've been stumbling over one another the whole time. If it was a person, we would've caught them by now. There would've been a trail of blood to follow or something to point us in the right direction."

"It's a big train, Mr. Colton," Reeves said. "We three can't be everywhere the whole time, and who's to say that Bo and the marshal didn't stumble upon the killer just to lose the fight. Maybe it's a member of Scratch's gang that we missed, stowed away on board and causing trouble." Reeves finished his drink and slid the glass across the bar.

"What about the whispers, the voices that Masterson heard?" Colton said and realized too late that it sounded desperate, like he was grasping at straws. He frowned.

"The man said himself that he thought it was just a dream." Reeves shook his head. "I know this is a troubling time, Colton, but this isn't my first killer, and I'm sure it won't be my last. Why don't you get some rest, ease your mind a little, and let me and Price here take some time to search the train again and look in on them missing people."

"I can—"

"Listen, if it makes you feel any better, take it as an order and not a suggestion. As a Pinkerton agent working in conjunction with the United States of America, I order one, Jim Colton, to his room for rest," Reeves said with a smile and patted Colton on the shoulder. "We'll let you know if anything comes up in the night." With that, Reeves stood and moved back to his place in the back, keeping an eye on the passengers as he went.

"Maybe he's right," Price said. "You have been pushing a little too hard, and I know you have some funny feelings on all this ghost nonsense, but what's needed here is some detective work, and that's what the Pinkertons do." Price gave Colton a placating smile and returned to mingling with the passengers, his false laughter carrying through the crowd.

Colton turned to leave the room, his head racing with thoughts and his body aching with impulses, but he figured that maybe Reeves was right. It went against his gut, played against his instincts, but it was one thing to face the supernatural when there were no other options and another thing to bring it up as the only option. People were still on the train, and people did horrible things.

II

Colton lay back in his bed, trying his best to ignore the thoughts that whipped through his mind, the theories that were swirling around and building to a tempest that logic soon blew away. Colton, as Price had said, had some funny ideas about the supernatural. He damn sure ought to have, after what he had seen, the ghosts he dealt with.

Wasn't that what you were trying to run from? he asked himself. If he were to say it out loud, he might put a few more words around it, but that was the gist: he was running away from that knowledge, from the people who shared in that knowledge. Running back to his old life, a life not painted by that part of his past—a life made up of just him, Bill, and the solitary life, where no one bothered him, and he bothered nobody. It was a good plan, a good dream, but that was all it was ever going to be—a dream. It was a hope that was built up on a pedestal made by a drunken carpenter and shoddy workmanship. He could see it failing before he climbed atop it, but he went ahead anyway.

What came from his involvement in other people's business? Just blood and misery. Three dead on this train alone, maybe more, and a woman with a broken heart back east. He'd tied so many obligations to those outside of himself that he lost what made him who he was. Perhaps his father was right, strength came from being alone. If so, his strength had been sapped.

Or did it?

Sure, people died, but they would've done so even if he hadn't been around. Others were alive because of him, or at least, he hoped that was the case. Besides, it wasn't as if he had taken his knife and killed folks himself. If he had to take responsibility for what he did, he had to accept that others had a part to play as well. Colton may have sharpened the knife, but it was others who drove it home. They twisted what he put out there, took his intentions and turned them around. Took his knife and cut a slice too close to the bone.

He sat up, ran a hand through his hair, and pulled

the bandage from his head. The blood had stopped, and he was sick of wearing the bandage anyway. He ought to visit the doctor, have him take a look at the wound. While he was at it, he could explain to Colton why he wasn't at supper and why he lied to Reeves about giving the knife to Colton before Bo Pierce was murdered with it.

III

"Walker," Colton said and pounded on the door, "open up." He'd been doing this for five minutes, shouting and banging, and was brewing a headache; his patience was worn thin. "You got one more chance to open up, Doc, then I'm coming in." He quieted down and listened at the door, but the room was silent, as it had been ever since he arrived.

Not a good sign.

His boot landed square on the door, just below the doorknob, and he heard the wood crack and splinter. It opened a sliver, just enough to see a green armchair blocking the entrance. Colton cursed and pushed his way through, damn near taking the door apart as he did. He felt a twinge of guilt for ruining the entryway, but the feeling soon ran dry when the scene stretched before him.

Two more bodies, both missing the tops of their heads, what looked like a brain quivering in the middle of the floor, and a pool of some sort of juice underneath it. Another brain was visible, sticking out of the top of Doc Walker's head where the little patch of grey hair should be. The stink was visceral. A heavy, blood-soaked air with hints of putrescence, spoiled meat and rotten eggs.

"Jesus," Colton said, covering his mouth and nose quickly. The doctor had died recently; Colton could tell by his colour and how his blood flowed. The other man, well, it looked like he'd been dead for a while, likely stuffed into the trunk that was lying on its side next to him. Yellow powder trailed out of the trunk and coated the un-known man's clothes. Sulphur—one way to hide the stink of a dead body.

"Does every damned passenger on this train have a body they're trying to hide?"

"That's a good question, Mr. Colton." The slow drawl of Major Pickett came from behind, his shadow falling across the floor beside Colton's own. "I'd wager that's a yes."

"Major Pickett," Colton turned slowly, "now that supper is over, I believe Agent Reeves requested that you stay in your room."

"You've never been married, have you, boy?" the Major cracked a smile, but it didn't reach his eyes. "A man needs a break from...that, every now and again. I say, what have you found here?"

"None of your concern, Major. Perhaps you should attend to your wife. I heard she wasn't feeling well."

"No, I should say she isn't. Her throat sliced open like the fat pig she was." His smile lightened some at that, and from behind his back, he flashed a familiar knife.

"How did you get that?" Colton dropped his hand to his gun but didn't pull it.

"With the amount you three have been scouring this train, it would've been rather simple to lift this from the agent's room, but I have other ways of doing such things. I'm glad, too. The last time didn't really feel the same without this knife. I think that once my business is done here, I'll keep it. You don't mind, do you, Mr. Colton?"

"So, it was you all along." Colton gripped the handle of his gun and saw the Major's grip on the knife flinch.

"Oh, don't be so daft. If I'm to understand it correctly, I'd say you had it figured out nicely up to this point, pilgrim."

"Scratch," Colton said through gritted teeth. "Your

boys seem to think you're the devil. I think they are a little light in the head, myself."

"Devil adjacent." The Major's smile widened, became too wide. "I believe your pious scholars may call me a demon, but that's their word, not mine. I've lived since before time, have feasted on the souls of creatures more complex and beautiful than any you could imagine, and I've influenced men since they were little more than monkeys afraid of the crash of thunder and flash of lightning."

"And you took over a two-bit thief like Scratch Maynard?" Colton reaffirmed the grip on his gun, felt the grooves slide over his scarred hand.

"For now," the demon sighed. "He was getting quite boring, but this train, oh this train. I must say, I don't think I would've had so much fun if you hadn't forced my hand. If you hadn't interrupted the robbery, I would have missed out on so much…corruption. These people are absolutely filthy with it. Look at your fine doctor here," he pointed to the doctor, hands bloody, mouth slack. "He was so arrogant that he thought he could perform brain surgery on himself! That's on top of his murdering and experimenting in the name of science." He chuckled. "Humans are such foolish creatures, all the better for me, eh?"

The Major moved like a flash, aiming the knife at Colton's stomach.

Colton nearly missed it, the subtle movement of the Major's feet, the small twitch of his eye, and his regrip of the knife. He nearly missed it, but he didn't. He pulled his gun and fired one shot from the hip.

The Major was sent off balance and crashed into the floor to Colton's right. Blood swelled and coursed over the man's starched shirt, but he held on to the knife, and the smile remained.

"You're a hard man to pin down, Colton." The Major's voice cracked, and blood seeped from the corner of his mouth. "Good shot, too. But it's done you no good. I'll just find a new body, a new host. I'll haunt you until the end of your days if need be. But those days will all be bloody. You'll never find happiness with me at your back waiting to stick the knife in." He gripped Colton's knife tightly. "Remember that and see if this has done you any good."

Colton bent over the Major, "I'm the one watching you die, Scratch."

They both heard the car door open, the stampede of footsteps.

"Well, let me help you along," Scratch said and sliced his own throat. A strange gasp left the man's now split throat, and the knife clattered to the floor next to Colton's boot. Colton watched as the Major's eyes went dull, as the breathing stopped, and the blood refused to pump anymore. He watched the man die with a smile on his face.

"What the hell," Reeves said from the doorway, his gun drawn. At his shoulder was Price, a gun of his own in his hand, and on the other side, John Masterson stood, a wrench gripped in his big hands.

"Jim," Price said, his eyes working to take in the entire scene, "what have you done?"

"I caught him," Colton said, "caught him and killed him." He pointed at the Major's body.

"All right, Mr. Colton, I think it's best that you put your gun down and step away from the knife."

Colton dropped his gun, backed away from it and stared at the men crowding the doorway. "It's not what it looks like."

"I should've locked you up with them Flint boys after you killed Bo," Reeves said, picking up the knife and abandoned gun.

"I didn't do this," Colton said, but he knew what they were looking at. The doctor, dead, with a corpse next to him, signs of a scuffle, and the Major, dead with a gut shot and a slice across his neck. He didn't have a photographic memory, but he was willing to bet the neck wound looked pretty damn close to the others. On sight alone, from their perspective, he'd be hard-pressed to believe that anyone did this but Colton himself.

"Jim, it's done." Price eased his way into the room, sliding his gun back into its holster. "You're done. Come along quietly now, I'll make sure the rest of this trip is relaxing for you."

"Might as well, he's going to hang when we get to California. Ain't no judge going to say otherwise," Reeves drawled, an evil smile painting his drawn face. "I'll make sure of that."

"It was Scratch," Colton whispered. "He had possessed the Major. I bet you'll find Mrs. Pickett dead in her room. And he's not done. He said he could come back. We need to—"

"Ghosts again, eh, Colton? I suppose next thing you'll say is that the devil himself crawled up your ass and made you do this." Reeves levelled his gun at Colton. "I ought to just shoot you right here, right now, because I'll tell you something, Mr. Colton, there is no devil, no ghosts. People are evil, they don't need an excuse to act up and do something heinous. We've had it in us all along, and it ain't God nor the devil that pushes us one way or the other. It's us, ourselves. You did this, Colton, and now you're going to pay for it." The hammer of Reeves's gun clicked into place.

Colton didn't want to do it; he had hoped that they might see past the physical and believe what he was saying, but that wasn't how it played out. Reeves had the gun trained on Colton's forehead and was about to kill him, and for a second, Colton welcomed it. It would have made things much easier for him. Then again, nothing was ever worthwhile if you didn't have to work for it, and Colton wanted to see Scratch beaten.

He weaved to the left, got low, and rushed forward. The bullet passed within a hair's width of his head and slammed into the wall behind him, splintering the wood. Rushing forward, Colton managed to shove his shoulder into the soft padding of Reeves's stomach. Reeves's breath rushed out of him, and he groaned as he fell to the floor. With a quick twist of his torso, Colton brought his fist up and caught Price on the chin. Price fell away in a swoon, leaving the massive John Masterson blocking the door.

"I don't want to hurt you, Mr. Colton," Masterson said but raised his heavy wrench over his head just the same. Colton ran forward again and slid between the big man's legs as the wrench came down in what would've been a skull-crushing blow. Colton's feet smashed into the wall on the opposite side of the train car, and he gritted his teeth in pain while he stood. Masterson was regaining his balance and began to turn toward him. Before he could, Colton kicked the big man in the ass. He didn't stick around to find out for sure, but he heard a loud thud and assumed the big man had fallen on his face.

He ran, but as big as the train was, he wouldn't be able to hide from Reeves for long. He needed a place to think and buy himself some time. He needed to figure out how to kill Scratch once and for all.

CHAPTER TEN

I

The horse car was in stark contrast to the luxury of the rest of the train. Its walls were composed of wooden slats spaced enough to let the air come in but not enough to frighten the animals. There were four windows in the car, big enough for horses to stick their heads out to look around, though after being on top of the train while it moved, Colton didn't think that they would enjoy that much. Hay was scattered across the floor, and there were some bigger piles in the corner. A pitchfork and shovel lay against the wall, for whatever train employee was required to come out here and feed the animals or clean up after them. And then there were the corpses. Scratch, Bo, Miller, and Creed were all piled into a corner closest to the door, quieter than they had ever been in life, waiting for the Major and his wife to join them.

Colton entered from the back of the car, closest to the end of the train, and peered through the darkened cart, the only light given off by the dying sun on the horizon. Hulking shadows appeared before Colton. The scent of wild animals, their sweat and excrement, barely overpowered the smell of death that threatened to fill his nostrils. From the opposite side of the car, a familiar whinny carried to him, and he pushed his way toward it.

"Bill," he said and rested a hand on the old Morgan's thick neck, "how've they been treating you?"

The horse stomped his hooves and shook his head. Colton smiled. "That good, eh?" Bill rubbed his big nose into Colton's hand, snorting hot air.

"I've managed to get myself in some trouble this time, Bill," Colton said. "You're lucky I got you set up out here, otherwise, you'd be in it with me." The horse snorted again and nuzzled Colton's arm and shoulder. "I know, I know, but you're too damn big to fit on the rest of the train. Say, you wouldn't know how to kill a demon, would ya?"

Bill stood still; his big brown eyes rolled to his window.

"It's not as easy as it sounds." Colton gathered some hay and fed it to the animal. "He dies in one body then just moves on to another. Who knows how many bodies he's killed just to have an extra meat suit at his disposal."

Colton and the horse sat in silence for some time, just sitting and watching the sun go down from Bill's window. The train track, in the distance, looked to curve around some as it rose to meet a hill and link up with a bridge that was tiny in the distance. The horse stomped one foot on the floor and whinnied. Colton nodded.

"That's a fine idea, Bill. A damned fine idea."

II

Gripping the ladder tightly, Colton wasn't so sure listening to his horse was a good idea. His last experience riding the train on the outside was far from enjoyable, and now it was dark. Climbing atop the slick car, he was sure that he'd fall and break his neck; the train would do Scratch's work for him. At least it wasn't raining.

He'd stayed in the horse car a little while longer, giving Bill extra treats as he could find them, but he couldn't stay long—Reeves would be on the prowl, Scratch too. A plan was forming in his mind, but he had a few more things to figure out first. The biggest question he had to answer was, whose body was Scratch hiding in now?

Scratch's track record was all over the place. First, a train robber and murderer, then, judging by the self-harm inflicted, Creed, a bad hombre who killed the marshal, then the Major, a war hero and possible wife slayer. Colton didn't like the doctor or the corpse for possession. For one, the corpse wasn't living, not for a long time, and secondly, the doctor's self-harm was much different than the others. No slice along the neck or wrists. Not much in common between the three, Colton suspected, except for the fact that they were steeped in death. Creed and Scratch plied their trade in murdering, Pickett too, just in the army, where death was officially sanctioned.

Colton's reasoning was thin, paper-thin, but it was something to go on.

The top of the train was no less windy at night than it was earlier in the day, and Colton was thankful that he wasn't wearing his hat. He gripped the roof, not really in danger of being blown off, but certainly caught up in the idea that he might be rocked off if the train took a sharp turn at speed. He tried to make himself comfortable, he'd be here until Reeves and Price gave up their search, or, at least, until they realized he wasn't in the train, specifically.

Murderers, men who made their way in killing, seemed to be Scratch's preferred candidate for a new body. Colton didn't know many of the people on the train, but of those he did know, most of them had some blood on their hands, even Price, weak stomach and all. The one person he knew Scratch wouldn't go for was himself. Colton was the object of his obsession, the person Scratch wanted to punish and then kill. That meant anyone on the train was a possibility, unless Colton's suspicions were right, and he had to believe they were, or he had nothing.

He pulled himself forward some, trying to keep the

wind from blowing his breath away. He needed to know more about Scratch, needed to understand more about why he did what he did. Reeves might have some idea, as studied as he was on the subject, but Colton didn't think he'd be up to talking at the moment. The only other people on the train with that expertise were the Flint boys, crazy as they both were. Colton shrugged and pulled himself along. It was worth a shot, and he wasn't doing anything else with his time.

III

The room was about the same as the last time he'd checked in on the brothers. A lantern had been lit to cast some light on them, and there were some discarded tin plates with scraps of food left behind. At least someone had remembered that these fellas were down here.

When Colton walked in, a smile grew on Deacon's dull mug, a smirk that Colton wanted to wipe away immediately.

"How's it going, killer?" Deacon asked, his words slurring around his doughy mouth. "I hear you got brave and killed an old man and his wife. I suppose you came here to kill two unarmed, restrained men to add to your yellow-bellied kill list, eh?" Deacon laughed.

"The thought did pass my mind," Colton said and pulled up a chair. "I might be persuaded against it if you answer a couple more questions for me."

"Nah, I don't take orders from a coward like you," Deacon said and spat a wad of phlegm at Colton's feet.

"You know who that old man was, Deacon. So, tell me a little more about him."

"I ain't ever met no Major from the war." Deacon smiled.

"He wasn't the Major, not anymore. It was—"

"Scratch," Jody whispered, his eyes jumping back and

forth, thinking.

"Shut it." Deacon swung a kick at his younger brother, but it missed the mark. "We don't know no Major, do we?"

"So, he was able to do it?" the younger Flint asked, looking to Colton. "He told us that he wouldn't be contained in one body, said that if he was killed, he'd come back in a fresh meat, that's what he called it, I wasn't sure if I believed him, but now...are you sure it was him?" Deacon fumed at his brother's side and cast daggers with his eyes.

Colton nodded. "He spoke like him, tried to kill me like him, threatened to haunt my path for the rest of my life." The room sat in silence for a moment, each man looking at the other, unsure of what to say. "Near as I can tell," Colton started, "he possessed at least three people, likely more, but it was a mixed bag."

"How do you mean?" Jody turned his head like a dog after you say its name. Gotcha, Colton thought.

"Two criminals, right bastards as I can tell, and an Army Major, who seemed on the up and up. Awfully strange, don't you think?"

"Maybe," Jody said. "He always did say that he couldn't come back as an altar boy. Had to be someone with some dark in their past." Colton nodded to the younger Flint, motioned for him to go on. "Listen," Jody said over his brother's curses and threats, "I didn't believe much of what Scratch said. I didn't fall under his trance like my brother here. I was in it for the money, but he said a lot of things. He was crazy and...I guess the only word for it was evil. I'd heard him talking about flaying people alive, about killing women and children and playing with their bones, about raising people from the dead. I thought it was all talk, all of it. I've been around bad men like Scratch before, they made the same claims, maybe not as detailed, but the same. It wasn't unusual, is what I'm saying. The biggest thing about Scratch was that he meant what he said. You could see it in his eyes."

"That's right, he meant what he said." Deacon leaned against his bindings. "He's going to kill you, Colton, but not until he makes you suffer."

Colton stared back into Deacon's hollow green eyes, frowned and bent around him to look at Jody. "I suppose he made sure that he surrounded himself with bad men, like your brother here?"

Jody just nodded, settled back into the corner of the room, giving his chains plenty of slack.

"I hope I get to see him kill you, Colton," Deacon said, backing away. "I hope he lets me help."

"You'll be lucky if he lets you live," Colton said and made his way to the exit. "You've been telling his tales, after all." With a smile, Colton closed the door on Deacon's curses.

The hammer of a gun clicked in his ear as he stepped into the hallway, and he froze. He could feel the cool barrel just a finger's width away from his temple, his uninjured one. "I knew when Mr. McCoy said that the prisoners were making noise again, I was in for a treat," Reeves said, "but little did I know I'd be getting a present."

CHAPTER ELEVEN

I

The train moved on, but Colton was stuck in his tracks, hands raised from his sides and a gun to his head. He'd expected to come upon Reeves or Price at some point, but he didn't think it would be so soon. He still needed time to make his plans.

"You caught him?" It was the elder McCoy, sticking his head out of his room.

"Yes, sir." Reeves hadn't moved much himself, the gun still steady in his hands. "I'll talk to you about it later. For now, why don't you go about busying yourself? I have some work to do."

"Oh, of course." McCoy ducked back into the room. Colton couldn't help but sneer at the other man's presence; McCoy had plagued this entire trip.

"Don't be so hurt, Jim," Reeves said. "Price and I didn't spend so much time looking for you as asking the entire train to help us find you. Smart, eh?"

Colton nodded; it was smart. He hadn't anticipated that Price or Reeves would involve the other passengers in the whole mess. Of course, with Colton now the only suspect, they would let the passengers know and not be so strict about monitoring their movements. After that, it was just a numbers game. Colton cursed himself.

"What to do with you?" Reeves asked. "I suppose we could put you in the room with your good buddies there, have them keep you company 'til California and then see you hanged alongside them. Then again, wasn't I going to kill you earlier?" The gun touched Colton's temple softly, like a kiss.

"Why don't you put that thing down and help me find the real murderer?" Colton said and chanced a quick look at Reeves. The man's skin was pale, and a sheen of sweat swept across his brow. His face was a rictus of pain and agony covered by a humourless smile. Scratch's smile.

"I think we have him, right here," Scratch, as Reeves, said.

Colton stepped away from the gun and turned to face the body of Reeves, the barrel now facing one of his eyes.

"I didn't tell you to move," Reeves said, and Colton could see the struggle that was happening. The man was jittering and shaking all over, everywhere except for his gun arm.

"I figure the gun isn't personal enough, besides, you said you wanted to knife me." Reeves's false smile grew, and, as he dropped the gun to his side, the shaking eased.

"Figured me out? Boy, you are good." Reeves holstered the gun and opened his coat. The knife was sitting diagonally on his belt.

"Seems like ol' Reeves there is giving you some trouble."

"He's a real goody two-shoes, this Reeves, doesn't believe he's done much wrong in his life. No matter, I got him under control."

Colton nodded and took a step backward.

"You think you're going to hide out on the top of the train again?" Reeves stepped forward. "I knew you were there, figured I'd let you get some fresh air," he chuckled.

"Better view." Colton took another step back.

"You're a smart one," Reeves pulled the knife, "maybe

a little too smart." Again, his body started to waver and tremble, but again, his weapon arm was as steady and consistent as his humourless smile.

"What are you planning to do with all these people once I'm out of your hair?" Colton put his hands out in front of him and readied himself for the attack.

"Not much," Reeves said. "I've already worked my mojo on a few of them, and I have a Pinkerton agent's body at my disposal. I bet I can do some real damage in this meat." He paused and looked at the ceiling, reflecting. "If not, I suppose I could have some fun ruining this one's name before I move on to the next."

"What about your two pals in there?" Colton nodded toward the room he'd just left. "Going to just leave them to hang?"

Reeves shrugged. "Yeah. Got to keep up appearances."

Colton knew the lunge was coming, had anticipated Reeves' body lurching forward, the steady arm stabbing out for his gut, but he still couldn't avoid it, not entirely. He jumped to the right, and his own knife cut through the left side of his shirt and sliced into the tender flesh just below his ribs. His whole side was on fire.

"Who knew this body could move so well?" Reeves laughed and lunged again.

Desperation sank its fingers into Colton's brain, panic tried to set in, and his pain pleaded for it to take over, but he wouldn't let it. He pushed it aside just as he did with the knife. Colton's foot came up and slammed Reeves in the stomach, sending him backwards, reeling. It was his chance.

With no weapon of his own, he retreated. Pushing through to the next car, he slammed the door closed behind him, earning him precious seconds to reevaluate and get his bearings. This car was the same as the last, a passenger car with three personal rooms on one side and, at the far end, a door to the next car. Colton fled, his hand pressed against his side, and made it to the next car just as Reeves pushed through the door that had been slammed closed on him.

This is folly, Colton thought, rushing through another passenger car, expecting Reeves to follow any minute. He couldn't keep this up, otherwise, he'd run out of train, and Reeves would have him right where he wanted him—at the sharp end of a knife. He had to do something. Now.

Colton pushed through the next door, yet another passenger car, and closed the heavy oak door behind him. Instead of running ahead, he ducked to the side of the door and waited. Reeves came only a moment later, pushing the door inward. Colton caught it and pushed it back. It didn't do as much damage as Colton had hoped; all it managed to do was catch one of Reeves' feet as he moved through and trip him to the floor.

It was enough. Colton jumped on Reeves's back, pushed him to the floor, and grabbed for the knife. Reeves flailed under Colton and tried to buck him off, but Colton held firm with two hands, isolating the hand holding the knife. He couldn't do it for much longer.

With a burst of energy, Reeves threw Colton to the side, the two men still wrestling over the knife arm. Reeves's face was a bloody mess from being smashed into the floor, but he managed a sneer and tried to pull his arm free. When that didn't work, he drilled Colton's wounded side with his meaty hands. Each strike sent an electric shock of pain through Colton, and a light flashed before his eyes; he felt his grip weakening.

Colton kicked up with one of his legs. It caught Reeves on the shoulder and pushed him to the floor once more. Colton attempted to follow him, mount the possessed man, and minimize any more damage, but his wounded stomach muscles wouldn't cooperate. The most he could do was roll over so that they were both facing each other.

"You're almost too much fun to murder, Mr. Colton." Reeves's mouth twisted into his humourless smile as he pulled out his pistol with his free hand.

Colton acted without thinking. Letting go of Reeves's knife hand, he swung a left haymaker into the other man's head. It must have stunned him because he froze in place, his eyes rolling in his head. Not taking a moment for granted, Colton slammed another fist into Reeves's head and pried the gun from his loosened fingers. By the time Reeves recovered, Colton had rolled away.

"Well played," Reeves said and ran a hand over his face. He got to his knees and made to stand.

"Don't," Colton said and pushed himself up against the far wall. He didn't bother to stand, just leaned there with Reeves's gun aimed and ready.

"Why not?" Reeves leaned on one knee. "This meat doesn't matter to me. You kill it, I'll just find someone else. Pawns, Mr. Colton. You're all just pawns." He stood.

Colton clicked back the hammer of the gun. "Drop the knife."

Reeves raised the knife to eye level and turned it back and forth, studying it. "This knife?" his smile revealed bloody teeth.

The gun fired three times. The sound in the car was deafening, and, for a moment, all Colton could hear was the high-pitched whine of his ears trying to adjust. The car became smoky, and the offensive tang of blood permeated the air. Colton threw the gun away and crawled toward the body.

The shots landed flush in the chest, one to the heart. Reeves's face was still twisted with Scratch's smile, his eyes wide but unseeing.

"I'm sorry." Colton reached across the body to reclaim his knife.

It didn't feel good in his hands, it was soiled. Soiled by what Scratch had been using it for, by the blood spilled in his name. Colton didn't want to hold it, didn't want to sheath it close to his person. He wanted nothing more than to toss it from the train and never see it again, but that wasn't an option.

Scratch, in whatever body he was going to take over next, was going to be looking for the knife. He preferred it now and found some poetic gratification in its use. Scratch was going to come back, and he was going to come looking for the knife.

Colton stood on unsteady legs and thought that the knife would bring Scratch directly back to him. That it might dissuade him from attacking others until the search was over. If there was a chance of that, Colton would take it.

He held his side and moved on; the shots would bring others soon enough.

CHAPTER TWELVE

I

Colton didn't waste time convalescing. Instead, he took Reeves's gun and went to work.

He imagined that gathering the entire population of the train around him would be an issue, but it wasn't as hard as he'd thought. He started with the engineer, Cornelius, the man driving the train. He was a round man, his stomach leading him wherever he went, and had an equally round face with ruddy cheeks and a red nose. Cornelius's arms underneath his striped shirt were strung with thick muscle that bulged as they moved. Colton kept him out of arm's reach.

Once he had the engineer, the rest was easy. He'd set them up in the dining cart, ordering porters to push back tables where they were able and make room for passengers to sit on the floor. Once all that was done, he had them bring Price to him. Poor, weak-stomached Price entered the room with Colton's own revolver drawn, holding it like he was trained, but with none of the conviction that was needed to use it.

"Put it down, Alexander," Colton said from behind the rotund engineer. "Put it down and slide it to me." It was with an audible sigh that Price followed through.

"Why are you doing this, Jim? What made you into a murderer?" Price moved to the centre of the room at the direction of a waving gun.

Colton pushed the engineer forward and made him sit, picked up his gun and held it in his other hand. "I'm no murderer, Alexander. You'll see."

He ordered the porters to gather the other passengers, to force them out of their rooms if they had to and had Price reinforce the order. They went about their work with slumped shoulders and resigned faces but returned successfully, nonetheless. Their work done, the porters were asked to sit with the passengers, and soon the entire train was sitting in front of Jim Colton.

"Ladies and gentlemen," Colton said, moving around the perimeter of the group, elbow tucked close to his damaged side, "there is someone amongst you who is not what they appear to be." He paused. He recognized most of them but focused on those he'd interacted with most: John Masterson, looking downtrodden with his large, sulking shoulders; Delilah Hardin and Anne-Marie Dubois sitting further away from each other than expected (Anne-Marie with a fresh bruise under one eye), and Alexander Price looking forlorn and anxious. "Someone here is an impostor."

Some heads moved, scanning the rest of the passengers. There was some low chatter and some renewed hatred in the eyes of those watching Colton pace around them with two guns in his hands. Of all that, he noticed the quick head turn of one person in particular and pounced on it.

"Ms. Dubois," he said. "Can you think of anyone who might not be who they say they are?"

Anne-Marie nodded. "Delilah Hardin," she said, pointing to her travelling companion.

"No, Annie," Delilah said, getting to her feet, but whatever else she was going to say was halted in her throat by the clicking of a gun's hammer in place.

"She has a gun," Anne-Marie said with a sour smile. "In her dress."

Colton raised his eyebrows and let his guns fall on the accused young woman. Her face paled, and her mouth shrank to a tight line. "Hand over the gun, miss, nice and slow."

Derringer in his possession, Colton said, "Sit near the front, Ms. Hardin. Sit and be quiet, I'll be with you in a moment," and motioned with his gun. For her part, Anne-Marie Dubois looked relieved, like a weight had been lifted from her shoulders. Colton nodded.

"Anyone else?"

"Jim, please," Price said, "end this. Give yourself up. Let the authorities handle all of this. If you're truly innocent, it'll come out in the wash. Right?"

"No, Alexander, that's not how it works." Colton panned his guns over the crowd.

"Well, at least let Cornelius go back to the engine room. For God's sake, he's supposed to be driving the train." Another rumble of conversation went up, more harried than before. Colton took aim and fired. One of the sconces exploded on the far wall, the candle within scattered about in waxy chunks.

"I'll get him back up there as soon as I can, but I need to figure something out first," Colton said to the renewed silence. "Anyone else acting strangely?"

The young McCoy raised his hand.

"Yes, son," Colton said, keeping an eye on the boy's father. "Anything you'd like to share?"

The boy nodded, his eyes looking sidelong at his father, whose face took on a fierce scowl.

"Out with it, boy," Colton said.

"Bernard, no," the elder McCoy said and reached for his son. The boy flinched away.

"Come on up, Bernard," Colton said. "Come up and tell me what's been going on." Colton trained on gun on Patrick McCoy as Bernard weaved his way through the group to reach Colton.

Colton waited for the boy to speak, but he just stood in front of him, his head down and hands entwined in front of him. He remembered the young McCoy from their first meeting, a shy young man who was nervous about his first time on a train. "It's okay, Bernard. Tell me when you're ready."

The young man nodded, kept his head down. It was another moment before he started mumbling something to himself, something that Colton couldn't quite understand. He bent lower to hear what the boy was saying, his eyes flashing toward those gathered.

"...He said that I needed to do this...he said that if I did, I'd feel better..." Bernard spoke barely above a whisper.

"Bernard," Colton said and felt a sharp sting in his neck. He reared back to see young Bernard, his face masked by anger, the blade of a small penknife poking out from his fist.

"Jesus," Colton said as Bernard lunged forward again, the blade flashing. Colton was aware of the shared gasp that went up from the crowd, and he saw some of the men standing, including the boy's father. He couldn't let this get out of hand, not now.

The boy slashed at him, quick little slices that wouldn't do much more than scratch him, but if he got in close, he might be able to do some real damage. Bernard was quicker than the dead Major, but not nearly so efficient and not as effective as Reeves. Still, he was motivated. Colton had a few options ahead of him, but most involved hurting the child, and he didn't think he had that in him. With a curse, he leaned into the boy, taking several slashes across the belly with the effort, and wrapped one big arm around the young McCoy, pinning the boy's arms to his body and stopping the attack. As quickly as he could, he turned toward the rising passengers and fired a shot right down the center of them, striking a wall at the back of the room. They froze in their place.

"John," Colton said and nodded toward Masterson. "Come and take this boy for me and then keep him restrained. Sit up here next to Ms. Hardin, if you please."

"You bastard." The boy's father stood. "Leave my son alone."

Colton carefully handed the boy to Masterson, who wrapped him in his large arms, a grimace on the man's soft face. Colton pried the penknife from Bernard's hands and held it up to the boy's father. "Nasty piece of work," he said and flicked off the drop of blood that clung to the small blade. He pointed his gun at the elder McCoy and motioned for him to sit.

"Here's the plan. You're all going to go back to your rooms, you too, porters," Colton said and chanced a look at his stomach. Just deep enough to be bad scratches, but if the boy had some more strength behind him, Colton would be trying to hold his guts in about now. "Mr. Masterson, Mr. Price, and I will escort Ms. Hardin and the young McCoy to the roof—" Another murmur went up through those gathered. A strained groan from Patrick McCoy drowned them all out. Colton made sure to keep his gun trained on him.

"Cornelius, I want you to keep the train going but slow it down some to make it easier to climb atop." Colton peered out the window. "I want us back at full speed by the time we hit that bridge, you understand?" Cornelius nodded. "Good, porters, lead these people back to their quarters. Price, kindly escort Ms. Hardin, if you don't mind."

"Jim, what the hell is wrong with you?" Price said, coming forward to stand next to Ms. Hardin, "This won't end well for anyone."

"I'm sure of that, Alexander, but it needs to be done." Colton motioned for Ms. Hardin to stand with the barrel of his gun. "It'll be all over soon."

II

It wasn't easy guiding four people by gunpoint to climb atop a moving train, but Colton managed. John Masterson had the easiest time, wrapping the young McCoy up in one huge arm and climbing with the other. Hardin was another story, and she fought Price every inch of the way, spitting and scratching like a feral cat. She only calmed when Colton flashed a gun in front of her face.

"Give me a gun, Jim," Price said. "This would go a lot quicker if I had one. Ms. Hardin might pipe down some if she knew I was as serious as you."

Colton shook his head and pressed them to begin the climb.

"At least give me your knife," Price whined. "Anything to keep her moving."

"She's moving just fine, Alexander. Worry about yourself."

The engineer had taken Colton seriously, and the train started to slow by degrees. The wind atop the train was persistent but not as bad as Colton had just recently lived through. He gathered the small group of people in a semicircle on one side of the train and set himself up on the opposite side, his guns trained on them.

"You may think I'm crazy, but there is a devil onboard this train," Colton said, watching each person in turn. "He came aboard during the failed robbery attempt, and he's been killing people ever since." They all kept good poker faces, though Masterson blessed himself and Price shook his head.

"Give this up, Jim, before it's too late," Price said.

"He's been jumping from body to body since he came

aboard, possessing people he believes have more than a few sins in their past. I figure this devil, or demon, or ghost, or whatever it is, can jump into anyone he wants, though it's easier to control people with some dark already in them. Jumping out, well, that's another story. He can't just do that on a whim, and I think it's because the body, his host, needs to die before he can move on." Colton looked to Price.

"That's why Scratch killed himself. The Major and Creed did the same thing. I killed Reeves, so he's made some moves. This demon doesn't seem to be a layabout, and I figure he jumped a body as quickly as he could. I figure it's one of these two." Colton pointed to Bernard McCoy and Delilah Hardin.

"Okay, Jim. Okay. Let's just say I was to believe you; you're missing out on a couple of things here. What about Agent Pierce, Mrs. Pickett, and Marshal Miller? They all died since the robbery; how do you account for them?"

"Pierce and Miller were on Scratch's list. He swore vengeance after I stabbed him in the back and put him down. Mrs. Pickett is harder to pinpoint, but I think she was just a victim of convenience. Scratch wanted into the Major's body, and killing his wife was just a bonus."

"The voices," Masterson mumbled, "they came to me, telling me all the bad things I did, taunting me. Maybe they did it to the others as well." At the mention of voices, both Bernard and Delilah turned their heads to Masterson, their eyes wide with recognition.

"Scratch did say he had other ways of getting things that he wanted," Colton said. "Maybe he could force people to do things they wouldn't normally do. Maybe he was able to coerce people into helping him."

"Oh, come now," Price said, "this is becoming too much. A demon that can not only possess people's bodies but, with a word, can convince them to murder someone?

You must see that it is too much to believe, Jim. Just too much."

"Can't convince everyone," Colton said and nodded to John Masterson. "I think you're good here, Mr. Masterson. Why don't you take a step or two back and give me some room?"

"Masterson? You're letting Masterson go? But he was the only one to admit to hearing voices! You can't be serious!"

"I heard voices, too." Bernard raised his hand, his head down. "They told me that Mr. Colton was going to kill my daddy, that he wanted to kill me. Told me that if I killed him first, I would be a hero."

"They put doubt in my head," Ms. Hardin said. "Made me believe in my worst fears. Made me act out in anger toward someone I care deeply about."

Colton nodded.

"So, what is your plan here, Jim? Why are we all out on top of the train?" Price asked with a frown.

"The way I figure it, Scratch needs to be close to possess someone. Maybe not face-to-face, but in the same area. I figure out which one of you is possessed, I'll wait until the train is over the bridge and throw you over the side." Masterson put an arm around Bernard, putting himself between Colton and the boy. "Scratch won't die until he hits the water, and any train worth its salt will be long gone by then. He'll have no one to possess, and unless he can deal in animals, I'd say he'll be shit out of luck."

"And who are you thinking of?" Price waved a hand toward the others. "The young boy or the defenceless woman?"

"That woman," Colton nodded to Hardin, "is far from defenceless. You got the scratch marks to prove that. The kid, well," Colton motioned to his stomach, blood seeping from his shallow wounds. "As to how we pick, well, I figured I'd let you choose, Alexander."

"Why me?" Price grimaced and swallowed.

"You've always been a good judge of character, and I trust you."

Price considered that for a moment, stroked his chin. "It's the boy," he said. Hardin gasped and covered her mouth while Masterson guided the child behind him and moved back toward the ladder.

"What makes you say that?" Colton trained a gun on Masterson.

"Hardin here hasn't done much but defend herself. Says she hurt someone she cared for. That doesn't sound like Scratch. The boy, on the other hand, well, he set a trap—a ruse—and suckered you into it, getting a few clean shots in too. That's more like Scratch, right there."

"I got to admit, you make a good point." Colton waved for Ms. Hardin to move away from Masterson and the young McCoy.

"Give me a gun, Jim," Price said and turned his gaze on the boy and his impromptu defender. "Give me a gun, and I'll make sure Masterson is out of your way when we reach the bridge."

"Change of mind, Alexander?"

"I guess. I just had to think about it, is all. You may be a little crazy, but it all fits. Come on, Jim, I want to help you with this. I want to help my friend one last time."

"You're not my friend," Colton said and pulled the trigger. Fire exploded from the barrel of his gun, and blood exploded from Price's shoulder. The impact spun him around so that he faced Colton once more. Despite the obvious damage, Price didn't cry out in pain, nor did his face betray any emotion whatsoever. In its place was Scratch's humourless smile.

"John, take them back inside," Colton said, aiming both guns at Price.

"So soon, Jimmy? I think we could've had some fun with them." Price's voice was rasping, like rock grinding on rock. Price bent to the side, his wounded arm dangling from his body, his fingers dancing a rhythm that Colton couldn't hear.

"Shut it." Colton cocked the hammers of both guns.

"What gave me away, Jimmy? I thought I had the tortured conscience thing just right."

"Price wouldn't have chosen," Colton said.

Price rolled his eyes. "It's always the little details with you, Colton. You should've been a lawyer, then we would've gotten along just fine."

"Why don't you keep your mouth shut, huh?"

"You mean, be a good little boy and wait for the train to cross over the bridge? Do you want me to bend over so you can kick me in the ass along the way?" Price chuckled and stuck a finger into the bullet wound. "Speaking of which, for someone whose entire plan was to keep me alive so I couldn't jump meat, pumping me full of leaks just seems counterproductive."

Colton shrugged. "I was hoping you'd learn your lesson with the first one." He fired again. His aim was lower this time, directed at the kneecaps. He could maim the demon and still keep him alive long enough to toss him off the train. The bullets put holes in the roof of the train, a scream rose up from the car below.

"Over here," Price said with a wave. He was on the opposite side of the train car. "Be careful there, Jimmy. Poor old Price won't be much of a dance partner if you keep up that kind of malarky."

Colton fired again, but all he struck was the open air.

"Nope," Price said, standing in his first position and lighting a cigarette. "May want to check those shooters, boy. Their action seems a mite off."

Colton pulled the guns around to fire again, but the

strong hands of Price gripped his wrists and stopped him. With that same smile and a cigarette poking from the corner of his mouth, Price managed to shake the guns free of Colton's hands. A thunderous pain thumped in Colton's forearms and his injured side, and he collapsed to his knees when Price finally let him go. The two guns had slid off the train and had fallen into shadow.

"You know what pleases me the most about this?" Price crossed his arms. "The fact that you thought you had all of this figured out. You thought I was bound to the meat I was hiding out in." He barked a false laugh. "Boy, I can do whatever I want." He bent over and grabbed Colton's face in one hand. "You want to see me change Mr. Price here into some gibbering, tentacled monster? I can do that. You want me to sprout wings and horns just so I look the part more? I can do that, too."

"Then why didn't you do it before?"

"No sport," Price said behind a widening smile. "Do you actually think that lording my power over you monkeys is entertaining? It's boring. It's much more fun to beat you at your own game."

The train started to pick up speed. Colton and Price looked toward the front of the train—the bridge was in sight.

"Oh, but to give you a chance to win and then just pluck victory away at the last second, that is the best."

CHAPTER THIRTEEN

I

"So, this is what you wanted?" Scratch said through Price's mouth. "You wanted me on top of the train about to go over a bridge?" He chuckled. "Price knows things about you, Colton. He knows you're afraid of heights. Is that why you're doing this? Are you so arrogant to believe that because the almighty Colton is afraid of high places, others must as well?"

"No," Colton said, rubbing his forearms.

"But you are arrogant, aren't you? Price thinks so, oh yes. He thinks that you are the most arrogant man he knows, and he works with rich businessmen. Imagine a mountain man daring to be more arrogant than the rich and powerful."

Colton reached into his jacket and felt for the handle of his knife, the buckhorn rigid under his fingertips. The train was picking up speed, but the bridge was still ahead of them. He had time. "Price didn't think like that," he said.

"No? Perhaps you'd like me to regale you with some of his more interesting thoughts. For instance, he once considered murdering you. Oh yes, it was during the war, and loyal Mr. Price had lost the stomach for it. You and he were in a forest, he doesn't remember which one, and he saw a chance to escape. A chance to leave the war behind him. The only thing in the way was you. He thought about bashing your head in with a rock, maybe slicing your throat. He wanted to do it, too; he could feel it in the twitch of his hand over his knife."

"But he didn't act on it." Colton managed to get to his feet.

"He didn't, but the thought was there. Then of course was the time that he had planned to rape a passenger. This was back when he was just a humble conductor, working his way up in the company. He saw a woman, not too unlike Ms. Hardin, in fact, that really turned his crank. He had spoken about this with a few of the porters and he made plans to rape her and blame it on them. Naughty boy, was our Mr. Price."

"And he didn't rape her." Colton gripped the handle of the blade under his jacket.

"No, not that woman. Not that time." Scratch smiled with his too-large, humourless grin. "This boy's mind is filled with so much delicious sin. So many thoughts, so many plans. If the robbery had gone any other way, I could have helped Price become the man he'd always wanted to be."

"Men and women, people, have their dark sides," Colton said. They have thoughts that might bring them shame, or they might bring them some secret excitement. Those thoughts aren't important, it's their actions that are important. That's what makes us different than the animals, than you. We have negative thoughts but can act against them and work against them. We have a choice, and it's the choice that matters." Colton pulled his knife.

"Choice?" Scratch laughed. "I'll tell you a little bit about choice. It's an illusion you people use to make yourselves feel better. Do you think the Major would have murdered his wife if he had a choice? Do you think Doctor Walker would have cut his own skull open if he had a choice? All it took was a word or two, and they acted on their instincts. Just one little push and they began to spiral."

"A push from you," Colton said and flipped his knife so that the blade was facing up.

"A push from me," Scratch said and bent to match Colton's stance. "But, since you are so interested in choice, let me give you one. You can choose to carry on with your plan, attack me, and attempt to throw me from the train and die trying, or you can give up now and join me. We'll start up a new gang, and maybe you'll have a little fun along the way."

"No chance," Colton said and slashed at Scratch in a wide arc. The demon moved in a blink, dipping far enough backwards to avoid the blade completely.

"Death it is," Scratch said and lunged forward, his hands contorted like claws. Colton felt the talons bite into his chest, tearing his skin, and he fell backwards and away from them. Fresh blood dribbled on his chest and stomach.

Colton cursed and lunged forward, driving the knife toward Scratch's stomach, but again, the demon moved too quickly for him to see and was behind him.

"Push," Scratch said, and Colton was sent sprawling face-first. His instinct to survive, to find a good grip, nearly caused him to lose his knife, but he held on tight. He swung himself around, and his two feet caught the lip of the roof, halting his fall. His breathing was coming hard and fast.

Scratch, who was momentarily in the middle of the roof, was now standing in front of him, bending over to grab Colton's wrist and reel him back in. Once Colton's feet were safely in the middle of the car, Scratch tossed him, one-handed, to the other edge. Despite the obvious discomfort, Colton managed to keep his composure and pulled himself up once more to face the smiling Scratch.

"This is pointless," Scratch said, his smile faltering

some. "I should be in there." He pointed to the train below him. "I should be down there, influencing, sinning, murdering. Imagine the tales they would tell if a train rolled on down with no survivors. 'The Ghost Train of the Transcontinental Express.' Yes, I think that's what I'll do when I'm done with you. That's a lot of souls to collect in one day, but I feel up to the challenge."

"Stay still, you froggy bastard." Colton slashed at Scratch's legs, coming up short once again. "Quit jumping around and act like a man."

"I thought you wanted a display of my power, Mr. Colton. I'm very disappointed in you." Scratch shook his head.

Colton jumped to his feet and ran at Scratch, who welcomed him with open arms. Colton's shoulder slammed into Scratch's stomach, and he reached around with both hands behind the other man's knees and dumped him on his ass. Colton fell atop of him, keeping close, smothering Scratch so he couldn't get a chance to move or break. He tried to stab the knife into Scratch's side and ribs, but all he managed to do was cut into the demon's arm. Scratch laughed in response.

"Is this more to your liking, Colton?" Scratch pushed him off like a man tossing aside a toddler and followed him, laying one knee across Colton's chest to keep him in place, like a bug pinned to display.

"You have been fun, Colton, but I think it's time that I end this. I will say, you have been quite the distraction for the last few days. Something to while away the time as the train approaches its final destination. But, as I said, if I'm going to leave this train with no survivors, I still have some work to do."

Scratch grabbed Colton's knife hand and began to pry his fingers away from the handle. Colton's fingers cracked as pain ran up his arm and screamed in his mind. He thrashed under Scratch's knee, but it held him tight. He looked to the engine, where smoke rose steadily from the stack, blowing back in the growing wind and speed. The bridge was just in front of them.

"Damn it," Colton said and swung his free hand into Scratch's stomach. It struck home, and the thud resonated through Scratch's body, but he stood fast, still smirking. It wasn't his smirk that Colton was watching; it was the tremors that ran up Scratch's free arm.

"Alex," Colton said, "you're still in there."

"No, Mr. Price is no longer with—"

"Alex, fight him. Don't give him what he wants."

Scratch sneered at Colton and raised a shuddering hand to backhand him.

"Reeves fought him the whole time," Colton said, "you can too."

Instead of the backhanded strike, the weight lifted from Colton's chest. He rolled away from Scratch, his knife already lost, his hand already mangled, but he was away, and he had a chance.

"Clever," Scratch said, standing. "Foolish, but clever. I wonder if your old friend Alex realizes that for your plan to work, he'll have to die as well. We'd both have to die together. How do you think he'd feel about that?" Scratch tossed the knife and caught it.

"Let's find out." Colton rushed the demon, his good hand letting a haymaker fly as he closed. It landed on Scratch's cheek, a small abrasion opening that sent the demon back a step. His smile transformed into a grimace.

The demon moved to meet Colton, slashing the knife wildly as he came. Colton backed away but was caught in the forearm with a slice. He reared back in pain, and Scratch stabbed at his stomach. Colton saw it coming and twisted to his right, avoiding the blade. Scratch was left open and off balance, his eyes moving quickly to keep track of his opponent. Colton landed another punch to the head, just behind the ear, that buckled Scratch's knees.

From the roof, Scratch slashed out with the knife and glanced Colton's thigh. A thin line of blood cascaded through the air, and Colton fell again just as the train bumped over the tracks that led to the bridge. It was now or never.

Both men rose and locked eyes on one another, waiting.

"I'm sorry, Alexander," Colton said. Scratch grunted, his lifeless smile stretching the face of one of Colton's oldest friends, and he ran forward, knife leading the charge. Colton knew this was coming, knew the demon couldn't resist throwing that apology in Colton's face. As Scratch came, Colton widened his stance and timed the demon's approach.

The knife found its way into Colton's side, and another piercing stream of pain exploded in his mind like a red haze. Still, he followed through. Grabbing Scratch's coat lapels, Colton fell backwards, bringing the demon with him. He placed one foot on Scratch's midsection and, with the momentum they built up, kicked the demon up and over him.

Scratch snarled but was already airborne, his face a mask of anger and terror. There was something else there, too. Colton liked to think there was some relief there, that Price had felt at peace in the decision they'd made.

In days hence, Colton could remember what happened next in cold, slow motion. The demon, imprisoned in Price's body, flew over the train and fell, screaming into the creek below, that humourless smile no longer etched on his face.

"I'm sorry," Colton said as tentacles of darkness began to bleed into his vision. "I'm sorry, Alexander," he said again and let the darkness take over.

CHAPTER FOURTEEN

I

The train wasn't too far from California when it stopped. The sun, just rising in the east, promised to keep the rain and cloud away, allowing a small hope that it was going to be a beautiful, warm day. They were in the middle of nowhere, land that the railway company had stolen from the Native peoples, who had learned to keep their distance but not give up their watch. The ground was dusty and hard, and there were mountains in sight.

Colton took in a deep breath of open air, the familiar scent rushing to his head, and nodded. With the help of John Masterson, he stepped off the train. His entire body was stiff and sore, particularly his side. There were so many bandages draped across his chest that he couldn't button his shirt all the way closed. Still, the air felt good on his skin.

"We figured it would be best to leave you here, Mr. Colton," Masterson said. "There's no stops for some distance, but there is a small town just to the south, toward those mountains." Masterson pointed with one big finger.

"Much obliged." Colton tipped his hat to him. It still hurt his head to wear his old wide-brim, but he couldn't bear to be without it any longer.

A loud snort echoed from not far off, and Weston saw one of the porters bring Bill toward him. Colton smiled at the sight of the old horse waving its head back and forth despite himself.

"There's some of us that don't quite know what to make of what all happened on the train," Masterson said. "Many of us are scared and confused. Some were against the idea of letting you go." He turned to join Colton in looking out at the horizon. "They figure it might make more sense to keep you around to explain a few things."

"You mean to blame some things on," Colton said, taking Bill's reins from the porter, patting the horse on the nose.

"There are a few who used those words," Masterson said.

"I thought of that too," Colton looked toward the big man, "so why didn't you do that?"

"Just because you can't explain things right, don't mean they didn't happen." Masterson smiled. It was a big, handsome smile. A smile that made you want to grin along with him. "God works in mysterious ways, after all."

"Have you thought about what you'll say once you reach the last stop in California?"

"We still have two thieves on board, I suspect we'll lay a lot of the blame on them and their dead friends."

"They may have something else to say about that," Colton said.

"What will they say? That the devil was aboard the train, that he possessed passengers and made them kill themselves. Sounds absurd, don't you think?"

"I do indeed," Colton said with a smile of his own.

"What do you intend to do, Mr. Colton?"

"I don't know," Colton said and looked up at his horse. "I took this trip because I wanted to return to my old way of life, to live in the purity of the past. Let me tell you, John. If I've learned anything, there's no purity in that. It's only a longing for something lost, it's grief. As easy as it is to fall into that, to hold on to it, it ain't no way to live."

Masterson nodded. "That ain't a bad way of looking at things."

"I can't say if it is good or bad, but it's the way it has to be." Colton swung himself into Bill's saddle with great effort and a lot of pain. "What I do know is that there is a lot in this world that we don't know about, a lot that we don't understand. I aim to look for that."

Masterson climbed back onto the train. "And what if whatever you find ends up being like old Mr. Scratch?"

"Well, let's hope there is a bridge nearby so I can toss it off again."

Colton flicked his reins and rode south, the echo of John Masterson's laughter following him on the way.

THE STONE OF THE UNDER GOD

This one's for you, Mom.

CHAPTER ONE

I

Icy cold tendrils lashed out at Jim Colton and his big Morgan, Bill, stinging their flesh. Collar pulled up around his ears, bandana over his mouth, the ferocious wind stole Colton's breath while the sleet restricted his vision. Poor Bill, the snow up to his knees, trudged onward, his big head down and body shivering. Truth be told, Colton couldn't tell if it was the horse or his own legs that quivered more as they pushed through the sudden storm.

He had passed through the last town just days hence. Freevale, a lonely little rut of dirt that had grown from a solitary whorehouse that itself had been on the tail of lonely miners who'd setup nearby. The miners and the whores didn't last, the town did.

The old man, what was his name? Albrecht. He'd tried to warn him. Albrecht had been passing through Freevale as well. Came in with the wind just a day after Colton, decked out in well-worn furs and hunched over a grey Mustang that looked about to shatter. The old man had shared Colton's drink at least one night and, in return, shared stories of his time in the wild.

"Path you're going," he said, "you'll come within a hair's breadth of the old castle. Stay clear of there, boy. Nothing good ever came out of that castle. Nothing good ever went in either."

Colton laughed. The old man with his cocked eyebrow and toothless grin didn't fit the mold of a soothsaying crone, but he was close enough.

"Besides, there'll be weather," Albrecht said. "I feel it in my bones, boy. There's a storm brewing. Might not let up for days. If you were smart, you'd set up here with a bottle of whiskey; keep your toes warm."

Colton didn't listen. He sought out the high country, the last remnants of fond memories driving him back to the rocky, mountainous land of his boyhood. A last-ditch effort to recapture some of those old feelings of comfort and assurance, a final farewell to the life he used to know, a life lost to him.

He'd forgotten about the mountain weather. It was strange how his memories, limited and biased, pushed the harsh winters in the mountains out of his mind. Colton never actively remembered the near starvation that came with a poorly prepared harvest or the intense cold that crept deep into the bones, aching every part of the body. No, his memories were of the sights, the sounds, of childhood laughter and the warmth of a fire, or his mother's hand on his face. Memories, it seemed, were as treacherous and deceptive as anything else.

The blizzard was heinous and constant. The wind moaned in his ear; it screamed in the distance. The path he was on had disappeared, replaced by snow that would only get higher, making Bill struggle more. Even if Colton were to unsaddle and walk the horse, it would be a slow trek and one that he didn't believe either would live through. He rubbed a gloved fist over his eyes, clearing the icy buildup that threatened his vision.

At first, the dim, orange light he spotted through the snow squall appeared to be a miniature sun, beckoning to him. A lighthouse in the fog. It hung in the air, wavering and blinking, and Colton halted Bill to get a better look. His mother had warned him of strange lights in the wild, of things that seemed too good to be true. They say that of deserts, of wide-open spaces with far too much dust and far too little water, but it's the same for thick forests and tall mountains. You might hear the hollering of a girl late at night, the howling of a wounded friend, a light in the dark—none were to be trusted.

"There are things in the trees that want you, Jimmy. Don't matter what they want you for, but it ain't for anything good." It was his mother's words, but Albrecht's voice that echoed in Colton's head as he sat there staring at that lonely light.

Bill's whinny brought him around. The horse shook his head furiously and stomped his hooves. Colton cleared his eyes once more, squinted into the distance and got them moving.

They got closer, and the lamp became clearer, its single flame fighting valiantly against the weather in the confines of its glass container. With each step forward, a shadow grew from behind the lamp, a monstrous shape of sharp rises and dangerous drop-offs. Jagged growths crept out of its back, and its eyes were both plentiful and dull.

"Hey there," a voice came out of the storm, followed by the figure of a man, his arm raised to protect his face from the storm's assault. "This way." The stranger took hold of Bill's bridle and guided them towards the lamp and its hideous shadow. Colton tried to tell the man to leave him be, to get away from his horse. All that he managed was a shuddering whimper of chattering teeth that didn't have enough energy to rise above the howling wind.

Another man emerged from under the lamp and helped Colton out of his saddle. The first man came to Colton's side, arm around his shoulders. He pushed them both toward the lamp, the heat of the flame barely registering as Colton passed underneath it.

Colton looked back once, saw the second man leading Bill back into the storm, and Colton wanted to cry out again but couldn't find his voice. He pushed against this first stranger, pulled away from the man's grip and plunged into the snow after his horse. He didn't get far. His shaking knees betrayed him, and he fell to his stomach.

Hands were around his arms and shoulders, and he was lifted to his feet once more. Bill had disappeared in the storm. Not even a trace of his shadow remained in the white sheet of the world.

Colton was dragged backwards, the lantern still overhead, and the heat of the monster's breath was on his neck, his back. The hands were going to feed him to the beast, and there was nothing he could do about it.

II

Colton sat upright in the dark. He was in a small room, stone floors and walls, with a window that was little more than a slit in the stone. Glass sat there, somehow, but it didn't let in any light. Wind howled all around him, outside the walls, eager to get inside and bite into his skin once more.

He shivered.

He was shirtless and in bed. Heavy blankets pooled around his waist and crept towards the floor. His eyes adjusted quickly to the dark. Shapes stood out in the room: an armoire, a desk, a chair. There was a door directly ahead of him, wooden and rounded at the top. Custom and expensive. He had a vague memory of hands gripping his arms and legs, pulling and dragging him towards…something.

The room was small, and the stone floor had a strange warmth that welcomed his bare feet. But they weren't bare, not completely. Bandages were wrapped around them. One foot was covered mostly from heel to toe, the other just the toes. Standing out of bed, Colton realized he was fully nude save for more bandages on his hands and arms, his face. What had they done to him?

Colton resisted the urge to tear off the dressing and searched the room for his belongings. He could find none, not his clothes, not his hat, not his gun. His mind slipped to Bill and wondered if he had been stowed away somewhere warm. Were those hands he remembered also grabbing at Bill's reins?

Some clothes were folded on the desk. A shirt and pants, loose fitting and cotton, both in the same sickly yellow. Colton shrugged them on; they'd have to do for now. He returned to the bed and wrapped one of the blankets around his shoulders. Even with the warm stone under his feet, Colton still felt the chill of the outside, could feel it right down to his bones. He huddled in his makeshift cloak and wondered what would come next.

A noise echoed from the hallway. A strange squeaking sound rose and fell in volume. Colton had heard the nighttime sounds of every animal in Colorado, the soft noise of a mouse searching for food, the swift flap of an owl taking flight, the night screams of foxes in the distance, but he could not place this sound, the one he heard from beyond his room.

He moved to the door, his blanket discarded on the floor next to the bed and placed his ear against the wood. The same noise came again, not far away, by the sounds of it. Squeaking—no, that wasn't right—more of a chittering sound like an insect or a bird. Something was out there.

Precious little light came from the space between the bottom of the door and the floor. What light did shine was the flickering orange of fire or candlelight. Colton pushed open the door and moved into the hallway.

The stone walls and stone floors continued from his

room. Torches were held upon the walls by blackened steel sconces on either side of the doors, of which there were no less than five, excluding Colton's own. Only every third torch was lit by Colton's count, and it did little to illuminate the hall. The darkness was thick and only gave up small patches of itself to the torchlight.

The chittering came again, and Colton moved towards it. He went slowly, unsure of where he was or who had brought him here. He bent to the floor and took shuffling steps to reduce the noise he made; Colton knew how to be quiet. A life in the wilds of Colorado, in its mountains, hunting for survival, had taught him well. Silence was an old acquaintance of his, and it greeted him eagerly.

Sweat ran into his eyes, and a heat came over him as he moved towards the sound. He rubbed his brow with one arm and did little more than displace the bandages that were wrapped around his face. He wondered about the noise. It sounded familiar, as though he should be able to place it, but the noise itself rebuked classification. It was stranded somewhere between insect and bird, or was it the clicking sounds of a lizard or feral cat? Whatever it was, it stood out to Colton. He knew it.

By the time he reached the end of the hallway, his shirt was damp under his arms and at his lower back. He could feel the bandages on his forehead loosening, could feel his perspiration soaking his hair and the back of his neck. Despite this, his body had become wracked with shivers that made his progress arduous.

The hallway led to another. Like the first, it was spotted with rooms at even intervals, but it was much darker, less travelled. Only one torch was lit at the end of this hallway, and, though it did little to reveal the secrets of the hallway itself, in its glow, the torch did unveil stairs that looked to lead down.

Colton hesitated. His body quaking, he attempted to

silence it by hugging himself tightly. He cursed and leaned against the nearest wall, but the stone was no comfort. He shook, and with him, the room shook. Colton slid to the floor and saw this new hallway twist upon itself, turn upside down and back again. His head throbbed, and the urge to vomit fluttered in his stomach and throat.

The noise sounded again. It was closer than before, not a mere echo anymore, but somewhere close. Colton tried to get his feet underneath him but couldn't; the hallway spun. Placing a hand on the smooth stone floor, he was able to ground himself and slow the twisting room down some. At the end of the hall, just before the staircase, a door opened. It was just a crack, but a thin ray of light slashed across the shadowy floors.

Crawling, Colton moved to it. His stealth had been forgotten as he slapped his hands on the floor to drag himself along the gloomy hallway. The world spun around him, but he focused on the door, on that sliver of light. He pulled himself toward it.

The chittering was louder than ever, and with its volume, Colton swore he knew it. He had heard that noise somewhere before. Was it in the barren plains near Crimson Hollow or in the high country in the caves where his family made a home? A home he had been heading toward before being caught in the storm. It didn't matter, and even though the world turned over and over, he scoured his mind for some answer. For something familiar. And it all fell away at the touch of a hand on his back.

III

"Easy there," a honey-sweet voice said soothingly. "You're safe."

Colton tried his eyes. They opened after a few blinks. A few more and his surroundings came into focus. Back in the room again, a torch lit in the sconce next to his door.

To his left, an oil lamp tossed shards of light across the desk. A man sat there watching him.

The stranger sat in the dark, his broad shoulders and the outline of a square jaw protruding from the shadow. Otherwise, the man was insubstantial; his clothes were loose, and where they ended, skeletal limbs protruded, and what little skin was there was cascaded by blue veins. Knobby hands joined over one knee that crossed the other leg, a black leather shoe that needed a shine dangled there.

"You're one lucky son of a bitch, Mister," the honeyed voice continued. "In this storm, if you hadn't strayed from the path, we wouldn't have seen you."

"Where am I?" Colton said, his voice hoarse. The effort to talk, to think, put a strain on him. The nausea he felt in the hallway came flooding back. His head throbbed, and he feared the room would turn on its head.

"Ahh…yes. You weren't in a good state of mind when you first arrived," the man chuckled. "You're in Chtharian Castle, home of the Order of Chthar."

"What's that mean?"

"Oh, I'm sure you've heard of the Free Masons, the Pythian Order, perhaps." The man paused and allowed Colton to nod. "Well, we're very much the same."

"So, why not just join one of them?" Colton said and worked himself up to his elbow.

"Well, there are many reasons, I suppose. The biggest difference between our order and the others, and it is indeed shocking to some, is that we allow women to become members of our society."

Colton swallowed his urge to vomit. What was it Albrecht had said about castles in the woods? "I never heard of an honest-to-goodness castle taking root in Colorado," Colton said after a time. "I don't suppose there are many around."

"In Colorado? No. We're the only castle in the state, likely in several states."

Nodding, Colton pushed himself up to sitting. It was a mistake. His stomach churned, bile burned at his throat, and he retched. The man rushed to his side, his hands on his shoulder and back. Colton pushed him away, wiped the saliva from his mouth and got a good look at the man who had just stepped into the light. He wasn't an ugly man, nor was he as old as Colton had figured, but his features were small. Clenched brown eyes that wrinkled his temples, a thin, pointed nose, and a pinched mouth. More interesting still was the bright square of white that stood out over his throat, his collar.

"You're a priest?" Colton said.

"Father Samuel Wallace," the priest said around a thin smile. "And you?"

"Jim Colton."

IV

The priest answered as many of Colton's questions as he could. He said that Bill had been taken to a barn they had on the property where he would be sufficiently comfortable while waiting out the storm. He apologized for removing all of Colton's belongings, but his clothes had been frozen with the cold and snow, so they put them up to dry in the kitchen. His gun, well, Father Wallace said that they hadn't found a gun on him, only a rifle on his horse that they had left there.

"Come," the priest said, helping Colton out of bed, "it'll be supper time soon, most of the others will be in the sitting room. Let's go meet them, shall we?"

The hall was as Colton had remembered, though with all the torches lit, the darkness had been banished to the corners and crevices between stones, where it waited. In the light, Colton could make out more of the details that surrounded him. Old paintings hung high on the walls, covered in dust, the paint dulled by the sun, he thought. If so, Colton couldn't tell how; there were no obvious windows in the hallway that would expose the paintings to light. Father Wallace laughed when Colton pointed out the paintings and claimed they were of the original members of the Order. Six men, four women. Not that Colton could tell which was which with his unsteady sight.

The priest guided him in the opposite direction from which he had gone in search of the noises. Colton played with the idea of mentioning it to him but ultimately decided against it. Though the priest seemed like a good enough man, kind, Colton had only known him for what amounted to a few minutes. He couldn't say what kind of man he really was, not until he saw him in his element. Of that, Colton firmly believed. Man could be deceiving, could play act damn near anything they wanted or what they thought others wanted. The true measure of a man was to see them where they felt most comfortable, where they felt at home. Some men were great speakers, some were great writers, and others could farm. Others still were only good at killing. Colton wondered where Father Wallace fell.

"Why am I wearing these damn bandages?" Colton asked after the fifth time he nearly tripped over his own feet.

"You came in out of the cold, Mr. Colton," the priest said. "Maybe you don't remember, but you had been exposed out there for some time. One of our members, Joe Crane, is a doctor. He was afraid you might have frostbite. We wrapped you up just in case."

Colton had seen frostbite up close, and it wasn't pretty. People lost their fingers and toes to the cold more often than he'd like to think about. If the priest was trying to comfort him, it didn't do any good. All Colton wanted to do now was rip off his bandages to see if his hands or feet were covered in black flesh. Whether he wanted to or not, he knew it wasn't a good idea. Colton pushed it out of his mind, but he'd have a few questions for the doctor when he met him.

"Guess I have a fever too," he said, a cold shiver crossing his spine and drawing his arms around his torso. "Must be a pretty bad one, had me out walking around the halls in the dark."

Father Wallace gave him a strange look. "You've been walking the halls?"

"Yes, weren't you the one who found me there on the floor? Next hallway over from my room?"

"I'm sorry, Mr. Colton. I don't know what you're talking about," Wallace said. "I've been sitting with you for hours."

CHAPTER TWO

I

"That is some fever you got there," Joe Crane said as he removed his hand from Colton's forehead. The old doctor padded his pipe with tobacco and puffed on it. Crane was as bland as water, his features were middling, and Colton figured that if the man just wanted to get lost, he only had to step into a crowd, and it'd be done. The only feature that stood out was his thick moustache. It started as auburn brown, but years and deeds peppered it with white and grey. It grew from his top lip, spilled over his cheeks, and died at his chin.

"Rest is what you need," Crane said, fanning off his hand. "Plenty of it." Wallace had taken him to the castle's sitting room, but Colton had seen entire houses that could fit in this one room. Stone and chain made up the room's foundations, leather chairs and rugs its furnishings. The scent of the fire and its smoke was an acrid but welcome smell, and it helped to put his jagged nerves at ease, even as he was stranded and surrounded by strangers.

"Really?" The whining voice of Abigail Parsons rose over the low hum of subtle conversation. "Does that mean he has to stay with us for another night?" Abigail was a statuesque woman with blonde hair tied tall to her head, a face full of makeup, and wrapped in several furs. Her mouth puckered like she'd been sucking on a lemon, and the creases and wrinkles around her lips told a tale of a lifetime of lemon sucking.

"Yes, dear, I think that is what Dr. Crane is saying." Jesse Parsons, her husband, was a hefty man. Broad about the shoulders, the man's large stomach pulled his buttoned shirt tight around his torso as he stepped beside his wife and gave her a pat on the hand. From what Wallace had told Colton, Jesse was the person taking care of Bill. That made him all right, even if his wife was a pain.

"I think that is something that the *doctor* should answer, don't you, *darling*?" Abigail rolled her eyes.

"Now, Mrs. Parsons." Wallace stepped into the center of the sitting room. He was a powerful speaker, likely from years spent behind the pulpit, and the others in the room turned just to drink in his presence at the utterance of those three short words. "I don't think any of us here would be inclined to throw Mr. Colton back out in the storm. The snow is still pelting down, the wind is still furious, and he is ill. What kind of people, nay, what kind of Christians would we be if we sent him back out there in this condition?" He panned the room, the hint of a smile on his lips until his gaze fell upon Crane. "The final decision, of course, is up to the good doctor."

Crane collapsed into a leather chair opposite Colton and made some loud puffing noises with his pipe. His dark eyes roamed over Colton, a frown growing on his mouth. "Well, we can't let him out in this," he said, waving his hand at the room. "He'd die before he took two steps."

"Are you quite sure, doc?" Colton asked. "I feel all right." He didn't, though. There was something that felt incredibly off. It could indeed be the fever or even his exposure to the cold, but Colton felt something more. His thoughts kept going back to the dream he'd awoken from. He could hear the chittering even now, its ticks and taps playing on the last nerve of his hearing.

"Yes, well, that as it may be," Crane said, "you are not. Bed rest, that's the only thing for it."

Colton tried to stand but fell back onto the couch with little success. "Damn it," he said. "I can still ride my horse. Storm can't last that long."

"It doesn't look like it's about to stop anytime soon," Clem Burns said. He was another of the Order of Chthar. A shorter man, blocky, with red hair that hung in a horseshoe wrapped around his head. His nose was large but flattened, and he had a permanent sneer. "Only a fool would venture out in that. Are you a fool, Mr. Colton?"

Colton tried to stand again, but it went about as well as the first attempt.

"Why don't you keep out of it, Clem Burns," Abigail said. "The man wants to go, he should go. It's too important a season for an outsider to ruin for us."

"Of course, Abigail," Wallace said. "Everyone here knows that. However, this man won't interfere with anything. He'll be holed up in his room, resting until the storm subsides. Once that happens, he'll be on his way."

"With a song in my heart," Colton said.

"Very well," Crane said. "It's settled. Now, why don't we see about having some supper?

II

"Friends, with this feast begins the season of Chthar. Let us say a silent thanks to the Master for this meal and for the coming days of joy, celebration, and new beginnings." Crane returned to his seat at the head of the long table. More people had arrived after the dinner bell had rung, and food had been laid out ready for the diners to serve themselves.

"Joseph," Wallace said in his smooth, easy voice and stood. "Perhaps we could say a more traditional prayer. Grace would be nice, seeing the occasion."

A low murmur encircled the table, none of the Order able to conceal their disquiet at the priest's suggestion. Colton, too, was confused. Hadn't they just done something of that sort? Wallace smiled widely, testing his stare with everyone else at the table. None challenged it.

"Very well, Samuel," Crane said with a long sigh. "However, in keeping with the coming days, please keep it to yourselves." The priest clasped his hands together and muttered to himself, but the others didn't join him.

The meal was tasty and fulfilling. Colton had spent the better part of a month on the trail, and aside from some stringy rabbit and jerky and his reprieve in Freevale, he hadn't had anything substantial in a long time. He salivated over the food before him, its enchanting scent, but, try as he might, he couldn't eat much. He succeeded only in taking a few bites from what he'd piled on his plate, his stomach clenching even at that. After supper, the Order retreated to the sitting room where they served tea and coffee, or brandy and whiskey if that was preferred. Colton gladly took a whiskey to sip on. The opulence of it all, the sheer grandeur that the Order of Chthar took part in, would have baffled Colton had he not taken part as well. He wasn't sure if even the richest train barons could afford such extravagance. Though he appreciated being able to experience it, even in his sickness, he was glad that he wouldn't take part again.

The members of the order remained dour. Perhaps that was what happened when you experience such luxury regularly—indifference. At the same time, Colton did not doubt that if the meal had not been what it was, the members assembled wouldn't just be dour; they'd be inconsolable, perhaps even angry. He figured that when something becomes normal, anything less than that could be seen as a deficiency, a hindrance to basic needs, as ridiculous as that was. No, Colton didn't want to fall into that habit.

Conversations carried on around him, hushed and whispered, kept away from his ears. Even as the fever came on again, as he began to feel light-headed, he was aware of their eyes on him. Their gazes crept over him like a predator its prey, licking the saliva from their chins in anticipation. Like a predator, they had patience, they would wait, but not forever. No, they would leap, gnash their teeth, and clack their jaws as they tore into him. It was up to Colton to decide if he would let them do it. Prey had power, too.

"Well," Wallace said with a clap of his hands. "I think that we have sufficiently bored our guest for the night." It aroused a few chuckles from the other members of the order. "I think it's best that I get him back to his room. He needs his rest, no?"

Wallace was at his side, one hand on his shoulder, the other on his back, guiding Colton out of his seat.

"One moment, Father," Crane said. He went to a small bar at the back of the room, his hands fluttering over a small box that reminded Colton of a jewelry box his mother once had. There were several small drawers that Crane pulled open, muttering to himself, before he came to what he was looking for. He took out a small glass vial with white powder in it. "Meadowsweet," he said and handed it to Wallace. "Mix it in with his tea, and it will help with the fever."

"Thank you, Doctor," Wallace said and pocketed the vial. "Off we go, Mr. Colton. Adieu, my friends, until the morning."

Colton stumbled along beside the priest, who had linked their arms together to keep him steady. His gaze went back to his surroundings, an urgency to remember the path welling up in his mind. Paintings and stone seemed to be the only things that kept this castle together. The stones were identical, and the paintings were obscured by shadow and dust, cruelly denied and overlooked for many years. Colton wouldn't be able to mark his path, not yet.

"Don't judge the Order too harshly," Father Wallace said. "Our members are terribly spoiled and quite used to a certain way of life. An introduction of something that may interrupt that is seen as a threat more than an opportunity."

"I'm an opportunity?" Colton asked, his words slurred.

"I believe so, yes. An opportunity to learn more about those outside of the Order. An opportunity to see someone outside their class up close. An opportunity for most of our members to remember why they joined the Order in the first place."

"And why is that?

"To create a fraternity, no, a community, of all men and women. To work towards equality for all people."

"That's not a bad goal." Colton's eyes rolled in his head, and he stumbled over a loose stone.

"It's the only goal worth following," the priest said.

"How did you get involved in all of this, Father?" Colton's legs faltered as they made their way up the stairs. Despite his small frame, Wallace muscled them both up the last few steps with little more than a grunt of exertion.

"My brother, Theodore, was a member for many years. My father was a member long before that. I suppose, you could say, it's in my blood."

Colton rolled his head around to look at Wallace. The man's face was twisted in a grimace, his eyes hard under a furrowed brow. "Where is your brother?"

"Theodore," the priest sighed, "died some time ago. His death assured my place in the Order."

"I'm sorry to hear," Colton said, and he was sincere. The priest had treated him with nothing but respect since he had awoken. Kindness, even. The only priests Colton had known were just as likely to take a swipe at you as they were to give you some encouraging word. He didn't mind the change. "Are all the members of the Order chosen in that way, by death and inheritance?"

"As far as I know. Inheritance and marriage. Jesse Parsons, husband of the charming Abigail Parsons, had not been a member of this order before marrying into it. Abigail's father was a member of the order, giving her the direct bloodline."

"I'm not sure the Free Masons are that strict on their membership policy," Colton said.

"Perhaps not," the priest smiled. "Yet another reason that we have little in common with them."

It was only a moment later when the priest led Colton through the door to his room. The lantern remained on the table, still lit, and Wallace placed the glass vial next to it after depositing Colton on the cot.

"I'll send a servant up with some tea for you to mix that in to," he said.

"Thanks, preacher." Colton lay on the bed, his eyes heavy and drooping.

"I'll be going, then. Good night."

"Father, wait," Colton said and rose to his elbow to see the priest's shadow outlined in the door. "I have one more question to ask you."

"Go ahead." The priest's shadow crossed its arms.

"At supper, Crane said that a celebration was beginning tonight. What kind of celebration?"

The priest offered a quiet chuckle. "I suppose we are both going to have to wait and see. Good night."

As the door closed and the light flickered in the lamp, Colton whispered, "Good night," before closing his eyes and falling into a fitful sleep.

CHAPTER THREE

I

The room echoed with the chittering noise. It quaked with the harsh breath of the beast that Colton knew was bent over his bed, staring into his face, waiting for him to look upon it. As soon as he opened his eyes, it would strike, lancing him with some serrated claw.

Colton kept his eyes shut tight, the pressure from doing so giving him a headache, the pain telling him to open his eyes. He wouldn't, though. His imagination conjured the image of a large spider straddling his bed, venom dripping from its sharp pincers, a mantis turning its head at unnatural angles, ready to bash him to death with its claws, a man with a bowie knife and a slanted smile.

"Jim." A soft voice broke through the eager, bestial noises, a familiar voice. "Jim, help me. I need your help."

"Alice?"

"They have me, Jim. Stop them." Her voice trailed off, and the sound of a struggle rose in its place.

Colton opened his eyes.

He wasn't in bed; he was in the storm. Great snow drifts surrounded him, ominous in the dark, like giant creatures waiting with eager anticipation. Waiting for him. The cold bit into his exposed flesh. He had no coat, no boots, not even the bandages he so loathed, just the sickly yellow outfit the Order had provided him. He wrapped his arms around his chest and walked into the snow.

The wind howled past his ears, the wet scent of snow assailed his nostrils, but there was more. The distant echo of a woman's voice and the rotting stench of swamp moss that just grazed the surface of Colton's mind pushed him onward.

Hands came out of the storm, dozens of them, grabbing and scratching at Colton's bare arms, his neck. He tried to fight, but they had no body, had nothing to feel his retaliation and rage. They dragged him onward, the snow and wind stronger, stealing his breath and blinding him until...

He opened his eyes upon a large foyer. Snow littered the floor around the door, and torches were lit in their black metal sconces, exposing the stone walls. The hands had receded and left him with nothing except...

The castle.

Colton didn't remember this part of it, but he had seen enough to know he was in the Order's headquarters. Except something was amiss. The snow didn't just spill in from the door to the foyer, it crawled through the entire building. It crowded the corners, floor and ceiling, running along the seams of the walls and floors, piling on the furniture in each room Colton passed. It wasn't fresh snow, either. No, it was old snow, hard and aged, dirty. It latched on to the castle and wouldn't let go, strange barnacles feasting on what was underneath.

Colton moved through the castle. He didn't want to do it. The sight of the snow disturbed him, his stomach rolled, and his heart fled to his throat, but he was drawn onwards anyway. Most rooms he didn't know, he had never seen before, but when he passed the dining room, he felt a brief hope that he might find his way back to his room. Eager to get his bearings, he managed to turn himself towards the sitting room.

It was how he remembered: couch and chairs surrounding the fireplace, a small bar near the back of the room where they'd kept the whiskey. And yet, it was all wrong. The snow, crystallized with age, sat upon the chairs and couch, dusted the tables and bar. Snow fell from the mouth of the fireplace, piling into the room as though it had choked on the stuff, had been suffocated by it.

Colton made for the stairs that led to his room. The castle was silent; even the sound of the blowing wind died the further he moved into the castle. He padded up the stairs, eyes darting all around, his stomach clenched. The paintings remained high upon the walls, if not more askew than before, and in place of dust and dirt, snow marred the features of each. Colton shuddered and shuffled forward.

The door to his room was in sight, just a few steps would lead him there, but snow drifted out from beneath the door. Not piled up as it had been in other parts of the castle, but there all the same. As he stood, watching the snow roll beneath his door, a low buzz started behind him. The sound of insects flying passed his ear. He waved his hand, but the sound didn't stop; it only got louder, more frenzied. Instead of one or two insects, there were now dozens.

Colton moved to his door. Snow or not, he needed to get away from the buzzing. His hand moved to the latch, but he drew it away quickly. It was cold. Freezing. The buzzing sound grew, and Colton turned to face it.

There were no insects, only the shapes of men and women. They surrounded him, shadows with no body. Colton backed into his door, and it flew open; he spilled to the floor. The shadows reached for him. He slammed the door closed.

The room was full of snow. It was pouring in from a small window that was now without glass, creeping out of the crevices in the stone floor, seeping from the walls. It wasn't the old snow that plagued the rest of the castle, but fresh and akin to powder. The bed was covered in snow, but Colton wanted to lie down. Without pushing the snow out of the way, he got into the bed. The snow melted into cold water against his hot skin. He could feel it soak into his clothes, but he didn't care; he sighed with relief. He'd found his room, his bed, he could sleep now and forget about the snow, the castle, everything outside his door.

Colton closed his eyes, and the chittering started again. Something large sat beside him, the bed creaking with its weight. Without opening his eyes, Colton jumped from the bed, ran to his door, and pulled it open.

II

"Mr. Colton," Father Wallace said, his arm raised as though he were just about to knock.

Colton turned back to his room. There was no snow, though the storm continued to blow outside the small window. There was no one and nothing else in the room. Colton moved back into the room and fell into the chair beside the desk, his breathing was quick and sharp.

"You're completely soaked," Wallace said and followed him into the room. "Your bed is as well." He rubbed his chin absently, examining the rest of the room.

The priest was right. Colton could feel his shirt sticking to him, it was as though he had actually taken a dip in a pond instead of having a fitful sleep. The bed, too. He could see his impression in the sweat covering the sheets.

"Are you all right?" Wallace knelt beside him, looking into his eyes.

"I don't know," Colton managed and bent forward, elbows on his legs.

"I'll go get Dr. Crane and arrange for a change of clothes and bedding. Don't move." The priest fled the room in a hurry, his footsteps echoing out into the hallway. It was brighter out there with the torches lit. Any natural light would've been blocked by the still raging storm that clouded the sky and blocked the sun. He wondered what time it was, morning or night. Did he sleep at all, or was it interrupted by feverish dreams?

He leaned into the chair, threw his head back and closed his eyes. His body ached, his skin crawled at the slightest touch, and his eyes throbbed behind their lids. Colton was tired. Will I ever leave this castle? he thought.

CHAPTER FOUR

I

Dr. Crane came in short order and examined him. He did little to help Colton other than provide him more tea with crushed meadowsweet mixed in. Father Wallace stood outside the room during the examination, and when the doctor left, he brought another set of yellow clothes for Colton to change into and an extra pair besides.

"You have many of these outfits lying around?" Colton said, switching his wet clothes for the dry ones.

"It's practically the only thing we have on hand. We all have a set, though women members are provided with a dress in lieu of pants. Would you prefer the dress?" the priest asked with a smile.

Colton laughed. "No thanks, preacher. I wouldn't mind some of my own duds. Might make me feel a little more myself."

"I'll see what I can do about that," the priest said and leaned against the desk. "In the meantime, are you feeling up to a tour of the castle?"

"It'd be nice to stretch my legs," Colton said. Though his body would have appreciated more rest, Colton didn't want to chance any more dreams. His body would just have to deal with it.

"Excellent," Wallace said with a clap of his hands and led the way out of the room.

II

Father Wallace was a good tour guide. He took Colton on a winding trip through the labyrinthine halls of Chthian Castle, making sure to point out landmarks as they passed them. Here was the painting of Lord William Crane, great-grandfather of Dr. Crane; there was the painting of Sir Christopher Shelby, grandfather of Abigail Parsons; and a dozen more paintings of distant ancestors of members Colton had no recollection of meeting. Each picture was from a different time, some part of the deep history of the Order of Chthar. Their clothes reflected their period, some even going back as far as the Mayflower, maybe before. The one thing each picture had in common was a fist-sized ruby, blood red, sitting before each and every person depicted upon the wall.

"That's some chunk of jewelry." Colton pointed at the gem in the picture of an elderly man with a small, sour mouth and sagging brown eyes.

"Yes, it's an heirloom, of sorts. It has been with the Order since its humble beginnings."

"You still have it? That's impressive. Times such as they are, I would have wagered that someone would have run off with it by now."

"As I'm sure you've noticed, none of the Order are of the needy sort. Besides, the gem represents our ceremonies, our beliefs. None of us would look at it in a monetary sense, it had never represented that."

"Fair enough," Colton said and followed Wallace further into the castle, taking note of the ruby in every picture they crossed.

As they passed rooms, the priest might point out who was staying there or who may have stayed there at some point or another. At the end of one particular hallway, a door stood open. The room looked exactly like Colton's own, a small space with small pieces of furniture, including a bed, desk, and armoire. In this room, Dr. Crane was hunched over the desk writing furiously, a glass of amber liquid clutched in his free hand. The doctor didn't acknowledge or even look up at them as Colton and the priest passed by, he just continued to scribble, his hand and pen pressing hard on the paper. So hard, in fact, that Colton could still hear the pen's scratches as he wandered further into the castle.

"You'll have to excuse Dr. Crane," Wallace said once they were at a distance where their conversation might not carry back to the other man. "He doesn't mean to be rude."

"Perhaps he doesn't see me as an opportunity like you do?" Colton shrugged.

"That is almost certain." The priest frowned. "Joseph is our de facto leader. Most of the coming celebrations will fall on him and his planning."

"Sounds stressful."

"It's not a job I'd take on voluntarily," Wallace said. "There's also the needs and demands of the other members to contend with and being the only doctor on hand. I'm sure he feels overwhelmed."

"Perhaps I should leave?"

"No," Wallace said and laid a hand on Colton's shoulder. "Not in your state, not in this weather. As I said, don't worry about Dr. Crane. Let's finish off this tour so you can rest before lunch."

Despite his initial excitement at leading Colton through the castle, Father Wallace's tour became much more diminished after their talk about Dr. Crane. Even the castle became more desolate as they moved through it. Hallways that were closed off due to damage or disuse, stairs that were no longer safe to use, and other places that were strictly forbidden.

"Forbidden?" Colton asked, peering down a dark hall-way marked with a strange crest he couldn't quite make out.

"I'm afraid so. Order members only," Wallace sighed.

"Something to do with the coming celebrations?"

"In some respects, yes. In truth, it is where we keep our Order's documents, our artifacts. To have someone outside the order look upon those is considered disre-spectful and strictly forbidden."

"That word again," Colton said, staring into the shad-ow of the hallway.

"It's the only word for it," the priest said and led on-ward.

"We are nearly at the end of our tour," Wallace contin-ued. "I hope it will help you feel more comfortable here while you recover."

"I'm sure it will," Colton said. He was having a hard time getting his breath; the walking tour had taken a lot out of him. More than it should. Perhaps he really was sick.

"Here is our final stop," Wallace said. "The beginning. This is where all of our guests arrive, such as you did just a few nights hence—the grand foyer."

Colton stopped in his tracks; his breathing hitched in his throat. The foyer was exactly like the one he'd dreamt of: its high stone walls, its black metal sconces with their torches, the large, dark oak double doors. There was even snow scattered on the floor around the doorway as if he had just been dragged in by the disembodied hands of his dream.

"Mr. Colton," Wallace said, approaching him. "Are you all right?"

Colton stepped back. His eyes, seeking escape, found the stairwell that would lead to his room. Despite his aching limbs and wheezing lungs, Colton dashed up the stairs as quickly as he could, taking two at a time when he was able.

"Mr. Colton," someone called to him, but he wouldn't look back. Images of the shadow people at his door flashed in his mind.

"Not this time," Colton said and pushed into his room, closing the door with a slam. Even that was like his dream. The edges of Colton's reality seemed to slip. The world turned upside down, and he did all he could to hold on. With more strength than he thought he was capable of, he pushed the armoire and desk in front of the door. With that done, the knocking started, a loud, angry banging on the wooden door. They shouted his name. Whoever they were, they shouted his name over and over. They pushed and shoved and banged.

Colton lay on his bed, his body unable to stand any more. His eyes fluttered as he watched the door heave, the furniture piled against it move. He closed his eyes.

They were going to get in.

III

Colton woke, a sheen of sweat still coating his brow, to a dark room. A candle had been left burning on the desk. Wax dripped from its golden holder, hardening on the surface below. The flame flickered; it was nearly at the end of its life, but it still cast twisting shadows throughout the room. There, covered in the webs of discarded wax, was a small envelope.

Colton stood and, for the first time, noticed that the furniture he had shoved against the door had been moved. Not back to their original places but moved just enough to allow entry into the room. The armoire had been shoved to the side, its doors facing the opposite wall, and the desk with the candle was closer to the middle of the room than it had been, on a slight angle away from the bed. They'd come in. It hadn't been a dream.

He picked up the envelope, his name was scrawled there under the fat tears of wax that had fallen upon it, the candle shedding its skin like a snake. Within the envelope was a note from Father Wallace:

Dear Mr. Colton,

It is obvious that you are in the throes of a deep sickness. Dr. Crane is very worried. Truth be told, we are all concerned about your well-being. Dr. Crane believes that you may have had some sort of hallucination in the foyer, brought on by your high fever, which caused panic and subsequent flight to your room. He has prescribed more meadowsweet tea, I'm afraid, and you should find it on a tray just outside your bedroom door.

I'm sorry that we had to force our way into the room. After your panicked escape, we were afraid you might do yourself some harm. Upon entering, however, we realized you just needed your rest. I do hope that you are feeling better, and if you are reading this, I can only assume that you are. Please take some more time to rest, imbibe on some of Dr. Crane's tea and try to relax.

The celebration and rituals begin tonight, so I'm afraid you'll have to keep to your room. I'll arrange for your supper to be delivered with your tea and endeavour to have someone waiting outside your room. Not as a guard, mind you, but to ensure your safety.

I'll come visit you in the morning.

Sincerely,
Father Samuel Wallace

Colton rubbed the bridge of his nose. The bandages that covered his face and hands scratched him. With a curse, he tore them off. His hands and feet looked fine, no sign of frostbite, if there truly had been a danger of that. The room had no mirror, but he assumed his face had fared much the same. He ran his fingers through his long beard.

As Wallace's note had said, there was a tray with tea and some food waiting for him outside his door, but there was no guard. Colton tried to judge the time of day, but his window was dark, and the snow and wind still crashed against it. It could be morning or night or any time of day. He cursed.

The tea was cold and bitter, but he drank as much of it as he could. He was more lucid than he had been before, the hazy feeling of being in a dream within a dream having finally abandoned him. If Dr. Crane were to pay him another visit now, would he declare that his temperature had finally broken? Colton assumed as much.

It came all at once, as if it had been lingering in the background, unnoticed or waiting until the perfect moment to return, the chittering. Colton's ears twitched at the sound, and he jumped from his seat to ensure he was the only person there.

It varied in speed and tone. At one moment, it would be frantic and high-pitched, and the next, it might be the meandering bass drum of a large beast breathing. It tittered and squeaked, groaned and bellowed. It wasn't in his room, but it was close.

Colton stepped out into the hallway, careful not to make any noise. Once again, he peered around corners and into shadows, ensuring that the wayward guard Wallace had promised wasn't stumbling back to their post. Nothing. The castle was as still as a grave and nearly as silent. It was a pregnant silence that sent a shiver up Colton's spine.

Someone had come by to douse the torches and, as before, only kept every third torch alight. Whoever had done it had made sure that the light was evenly spaced. Colton gave himself time to let his eyes adjust to the bleak hallway before he moved on. He thought he might be able to figure out his way back to the sitting room, but he wasn't sure if that was the best way to go. For all he knew, some of the Order may be celebrating there.

A faint shuffle of cloth on stone brought Colton around, his eyes straining to see in the gloom. The noise came from the opposite direction of the sitting room, further down the hallway and deeper into the castle. A familiar path, the same he had taken his first night in the care of the Order. The idea of night and day, with the storm raging outside, was muddied. It was so dark, perhaps he had only been in the castle for one night. Perhaps this had all just been one extended day. Colton took a deep breath and quieted his thoughts. He'd find the rights to it in the end, but for now, he had another plan in mind.

The hallway stretched before him, each door a possibility of discovery, but the sounds were ever further on. Colton hesitated to stop at any door and try the latch, he didn't want to arouse anyone who would halt his exploration or coax him back to bed. Instead, he shuffled quietly along, ears cocked to the side to better hear, and avoided the doors at all costs.

Colton came to the short hallway that he remembered from that first night. He hadn't been sure if it was a figment of his imagination, some image brewed up in his feverish mind. How had that dream ended? With a hand on his shoulder.

It was as dark as he remembered, with no torches lit. There was a pale halo of light sliding its craggy fingers to their limit on the downward-facing stairs at the end of the short hall, but he couldn't see the source. It wasn't a torch, nor a candle, it looked as though it were moonlight, ethereal, weak.

Colton couldn't remember if Wallace had shown him this hallway during his tour or if he had mentioned whether it was off limits or not. Colton didn't care. He needed to find the source of the noises, end this and perhaps regain some semblance of his sanity.

As the stairs wound downward, the light got brighter, but the source still hadn't shown itself. As with the light source, the noises also continued to be a mystery. At one moment, the sound was so close, Colton thought he might round a corner and bump into whatever was making the godawful noise. The next moment, it would be further away, deep within the castle's bowels. Colton kept his pace slow; every step was feather-light, his bare feet never making a sound. The air became muskier the further he went, the scent of earth freshly dug, of wetland moss, and even the hint of fresh air, not cold but warm. A spring breeze. Goosebumps covered Colton's arms, and the hair prickled at the nape of his neck.

The light source came into view as Colton made it to the bottom of the stairs: an arc lamp. Not the casual electric lightbulb that had been popping up in the east, the arc lamp was bright, the white light hard to look at. Colton hadn't seen one this small. He'd seen them being used to Indiana; large suckers set atop a courthouse over that way. And he had heard Detroit had more than a few towers that stood exceptionally tall to light up a good chunk of their city.

Squinting his eyes, Colton could see the tiny arcs of electricity bouncing between electrodes. He bent closer, but the heat coming from the glass bulb pushed him back again. Rubbing away the ghostly remnants of the lamplight in his eyes, Colton stared into the newest hallway he'd come across. Certainly not a part of Wallace's tour, Colton assumed this may have been one of the areas that was off-limits to those not within the Order.

There were several more arc lamps set up to light the way, which was in opposition to the torches and candlelight used in the rest of the castle. Equally as strange was that the floor was made of dirt. It was tightly packed earth that had remained dry despite the storm outside and the many tracks that had been stomped through it. From where he stood at the bottom of the stairs, Colton counted at least a dozen different boot tracks, coming and going. He wagered he'd see more if he was to look for them, but that wasn't why he skulked his way down the stairs.

The sound was lower now, calmer, but still it drew him onward. The walls, hastily strung with wires that ran power to the lamps, were of an older stone, cobblestone by the looks of the sandy mortar used to keep it all together. Colton ran a hand along the smooth stones, letting his fingers follow the bumps and grooves. The walls were warm. Heat had been saved up within them, but it wasn't pleasant to touch. It felt like he was touching the innards of a living, breathing creature, slick with mucus or saliva or blood. He drew his hand away quickly and wiped it off on his pant leg.

It wasn't a long hallway, and it ended with the wide maw of a cavern. The hole had been carved with a precision that Colton had rarely seen. Even still, a craftsman of that skill would need years and an unyielding desire to work tireless hours to complete it. As he moved into the cave's mouth, he was tempted to run a hand over the tool work, but he had learned his lesson from the cobblestone and resisted.

There were no lights in the cavern, only the promise of light at its completion. The darkness shrouded him with a blanket of shadow as he stumbled toward the exit. Colton was preternaturally aware of his unprotected feet as they scraped over the carved stone passageway. Most people took their feet and their hands for granted. They lived with them their entire lives, and the idea of losing them just simply didn't occur to them. Colton knew differently. His father beat that particular drum more times than Colton could count. Living in the mountains, as they did, if a snowstorm hit you the wrong way and caught you unprepared, you were in for a world of hurt. Extremities go first—fingers, toes, nose—followed by the hands and feet. If you were really unlucky, the cold would turn your skin to ashen paper. Only course of action once that set in was amputation, and he'd seen enough of that in the war to know it wasn't as pleasant as the doctor's made it out to be. Aside from all that, Colton had a way of life to maintain. He spent his time alone and made his own way. If anything happened to his feet or hands, that would change the way he lived life. Sure, he'd make adjustments. He'd be able to return to his way of life, but not for some time. And not without the help of someone else while he adjusted. Colton wouldn't do that.

The tunnel ended as suddenly as it had started and opened into a sprawling forested area. Trees and shrubs and bushes and flowers sprouted out of the fertile earth, their heady scents of growth and life nearly knocking Colton back. And still, there was something not quite right about the things that grew around him.

He looked up, beyond the tallest reaches of the trees before him, at a stone ceiling, and then looked around him to see stone walls with no windows. These plants were growing without sunlight or rainwater. Colton tried to find the source of the light that was promised from within the cave, but even though the room was lit and clear, he couldn't tell where it came from. It was as though the light came from everything and nothing all at once. The branches of the trees, the dirt at his feet, the flowers at his sides—all glowed without producing light. Colton's head began to hurt, and he wondered if he was living this or if he was still in his bed suffering through another nightmare.

Colton pushed through the brush, his hands sliding through the thick leaves and branches, and made his way into a clearing void of vegetation. His hands and arms came away wet, a clear viscous slime dangling between his fingers. His borrowed clothes were covered with the thick substance, and he had to slough it off with the edge of his hand. It landed with a soft plop that made Colton shudder.

The clearing was almost a perfect circle of short grass, excluding the other vegetation from the area entirely. The trees, unwilling to yield to the clearing's wishes, leaned into the circle as though they were drawn inwards, intruding on what had attempted to seclude them. Their branches made a hasty canopy that would've done a fair job of blocking the sun had it been able to crack the stone walls. Flat rocks made a pathway through the clearing, a single, straight line that led from where Colton stood to the far side and an altar.

Stairs of polished stone led from the pathway to a flat surface that served as the altar's predella. This was, in turn, surrounded by five stone pillars, each about three meters high. Three banners hung between the pillars, one on either side and another in the center. Those to the left and right shared an emblem that looked familiar, though Colton couldn't place it, a large black bat. The banner in the middle was also familiar, a red ruby. Just like the ruby he'd seen in the paintings on his tour with Wallace.

The table at the center of the altar was large and draped in a long red sheet that fell over the front to form an antependium of sorts. There, too, was the symbol of the ruby, but behind it was the black bat from the other banners. On the table were some of those things Colton had always associated with a religious altar: a candelabra, candlesticks, and a large open book. Among it all, however, was some sort of container covered in a black cloth. It was small, about the size of a bucket, and had a golden stand that stood out from underneath its covering. This must be where the Order of Chthar did their rituals. He now understood why Wallace had forbidden him from seeing any of this, it was downright blasphemous.

Colton moved to the altar.

Instead of following the path as it was laid out, Colton kept to the cover of the trees, suffering through the return to the slimy plants to ensure he wasn't seen. He allowed himself to move a little faster. The branches and leaves, laden with the thick substance as they were, didn't yield much sound when he pushed through them, and he didn't fear drawing attention to himself. Still, he kept his head on a swivel, ensuring that nothing or no one emerged that might see the jagged path he made through the brush.

The sound of water greeted him as he neared the altar. Not the gentle bubble of a stream or the thunderous lapping waves of an ocean, but the dozy rhythm of a pool or pond in the breeze, its water sloshing against its boundaries. The scent of the water, fresh and clean, came with the sounds of lively bubbling; it called to Colton. He was thirsty, the bitter taste of meadowsweet tea still on his tongue. With a shake of his head, Colton made it to the edge of the altar, and he ascended.

Colton shivered as he stepped foot upon the predella, as though a cool breeze blew over his wet clothes. It forced him to be still, to take stock, but there was no breeze, only the humid air that pushed against him. Still, there was no sun, and yet the plants grew. Would it be so far-fetched to think that a breeze could be manufactured in such a way, as well?

The table was larger than he had thought, and it was hard not to picture Jesus and his twelve disciples crowding one side of it for the final meal together as in the painting. He pushed the thought away as if he were spitting something sour from his mouth. Colton wasn't a religious man, but he'd been raised Christian, and whatever the Order of Chthar did on this altar was not to be likened to Christianity, or any religion for that matter. This was sacrilege through and through. Colton didn't know how he knew that, but the thought was there in his mind, shouting at him. Despite these misgivings, Colton approached the table and the black clad container. If he were going to do one thing at the altar, it would be to discover what the Order had so reverently covered.

As he approached, the soft sounds of water became more aggressive, more tempestuous. The water slapped the ground of its confines in such quick succession that it sounded like laughter, or a cruel imitation of it. Colton spun on one heel, drawn to the noise, and found it directly behind him. The pool surrounded the backside of the altar in a half-moon shape that pushed back the trees another eight to ten feet. The water itself, though it smelled fresh, was murky; Colton couldn't see into its depths and couldn't judge how deep it went. Looking over it now, Colton didn't want to find out.

And still, his eyes were drawn to it, his eyes jumping at any small thing that was stuck in water or floated on its surface. A twig here, a leaf there, it didn't matter—Colton's eyes locked onto anything, thinking it might be some kind of sign. That's what people did, after all, put together patterns, find them where they couldn't be. It was how the brain worked, helping to keep people comfortable by keeping everything around them predictable in some way. Colton's fever could be playing tricks with his mind, forcing him to come up with a story that had no place in reality, that turned predictability on its head. Colton sighed. If that was the case, he'd had this fever for many of the last few years. He wondered if he had any solid grip of what had been happening to him, on what he had been doing.

The water bubbled, a slight ripple of the surface as

Colton stared down into it, his arm reaching out as though he were hoping to shake someone's hand. The chittering brought Colton back around, his eyes narrowing toward the cavern he had come through. No shapes appeared in the distance, not in the clearing or the small forest. The chittering got louder, got closer. Colton managed one last look at the altar before he disappeared into the trees once more.

The slime crept over him again, giving him a shiver of recognition as it smeared itself across his entire body. He looked toward the pond, and the urge to sneak through the trees and catch another glimpse of its steady, gentle movement nearly overtook him. He had to stop himself from physically reaching out to the pool as if it were some past lover he'd missed. The chittering grew louder, and he again turned toward it, though his eyes yearned to look to the water again.

A stomping sound came with the chittering, loud and rough, echoing their entrance. It wasn't until something breached the tree line at the opposite edge of the clearing that Colton's body forgot its urge to witness the pond once more. Something large and black emerged from the trees, a creature that Colton had never dreamed of, let alone seen before. It stood over six feet, though its posture was little more than a crouch that appeared to fold the beast into itself. Leaning forward at such an extreme angle, its thin arms bent before it, its hands limp on its wrists. From those wrists, and crawling all the way to the creature's back, were leathery wings like the wings of a bat, all stretched flesh and cartilage. Though the beast had some human features, its face couldn't be counted among them. Certainly, it had a nose, a mouth, and eyes, but whatever it had there wasn't normal, not like how Colton thought of as manlike or even sane. It had long ears that bent and twitched as the creature turned from side to side.

Its nose, if it was indeed such a thing, stretched back over its forehead, its nostrils visible even at Colton's distance. Its mouth was a crude slash of red, with jagged yellow teeth and a lolling pink tongue that darted out to caress its gray lips. Perhaps worst of all were the creature's eyes. It had four, two where one would assume a human to have it, and two more just above them. The whole symmetry of that ugly face was ruined by those eyes, and trying to look upon them caused Colton's head to spin. Colton counted the eyes several times before he would believe that his mind wasn't playing tricks on him, and still, when he tried to stare into that face, his vision blurred, and his head hurt.

The creature's mouth moved rapidly, and the chittering sound echoed through the clearing. Colton had found the source of his torment. The creature stalked forward. It would bend forward, its face nearly touching the ground, before it would right itself and, with a lightning-quick jerk of its body, face the ceiling. It did this from side to side as well, scanning the entire area for something.

Colton's heart raced, beating against his chest. Was it looking for him? He had no gun, nothing to help defend himself. Not that he was certain that a gun would work on the bat-like creature, but it would've made Colton more comfortable.

When the creature got to the center of the clearing, it leaned back, straightening its hunched shoulders and unfurled its wings. They were massive, like the sails of a ship, with ragged edges at the bottom. Was that age? Could such a thing get older? The wings, open, were a deep ebony, a black that gorged itself on the light around it, never letting it win. But that wasn't quite true either; in those wings, there was a light of their own. Small pinpricks of light that reminded Colton of a starry night sky. Even at his distance, Colton thought he might be able to see constellations, shooting stars, and other worlds. It was only when the creature reared back its bizarre head and released a piercing shriek that Colton was able to turn away from the beast once more, his brow sweating, his eyes tired.

Leave, his mind whispered, and Colton nodded. It was time to go. Even though the slime dampened the noise of his progress, he took his time circling around the clearing. He had no idea how sensitive that creature's hearing was, and he had no desire to deal with the beast without even the simplest weapon to help. It took more than twice as long for Colton to reach the cavern entrance to the strange, forested room. Before he had extricated himself from the area, he chanced a quick look back at the beast: it stood upon the altar, staring into the pool below.

CHAPTER FIVE

I

"Mr. Colton," Father Wallace said, descending the stone stairs that led to the sitting room. "I just stopped by your room and found you missing. It gave me quite a start."

Colton managed a smile and waved the priest over. The truth of it was, he had only returned to his room an hour before, his experience in the basement and the sunken altar still fresh on his nerves. He'd barely managed to change out of his soiled outfit before he heard footsteps outside his door. Heavy, thumping steps that set his heart to racing; his mind still agitated by the appearance of the creature he'd seen. When he'd built up enough courage to open the door a crack, the only ugly face he saw was that of Clem Burns, the sour man Wallace had introduced him to, his horseshoe smattering of hair disheveled, his eyes bloodshot.

"I persuaded Mr. Burns to let me leave my room a little early. Hungry," Colton said and rubbed his stomach.

"I see." It was Wallace's turn to try on a smile. "And where is ole Clem? Did he persuade you to remove your bandages as well?" The priest made a show of looking around the room.

"I got rid of those. Nothing but a nuisance, you ask me. As for Burns, I sent him off to bed. Your celebrations must really be something. Poor fella was more asleep than awake. His eyes were like two piss holes in the snow."

Wallace chuckled, rubbing at his own eyes. "They do take a toll," he said and sat in one of the leather armchairs across from Colton. "I'm glad to see you are feeling better," Wallace said innocently enough, but Colton read between the words—a question, not a statement.

"The miracle of meadowsweet tea." Colton raised a cup in salute. "Your good doctor knows his remedies."

"Dr. Crane is worth his weight in gold."

They fell into a short silence, not something Colton had been prepared for. His interactions with Wallace had always been filled with conversation, the priest yammering on about something. Perhaps that never was the case; perhaps Colton's fever had played another trick on him.

"Storm is still blowing," Colton said after a time.

"It's the longest blizzard I've been witness to," Wallace said, brightening. "They can last a day or two up this way, but this one has just stretched on. It may be some kind of record."

"I reckon you have the rights of it," Colton said and placed his cup on the table between the two men. "All the same, I think it might be time for me to take my leave of your hospitality, Father."

Colton watched Wallace carefully, saw the slow blink that lasted a two-count, saw the priest's left hand clench for a moment on the chair's arm, saw the frown.

"Are you sure?" Wallace said, fixing his face to neutral. "We wouldn't want to send you out in the weather if you were ill-prepared, or, God forbid, still sick."

"I think you'll find I'm fit as a fiddle." Colton bent forward and smiled.

"Perhaps," Wallace rubbed his chin. "I'll make you a deal," he said. "Let's have Dr. Crane examine you one more time. If he gives you the free and clear, then we'll make arrangements to see you on your way. Fair?"

"It does. Though I'm in no hurry to wake Dr. Crane up from his well-earned rest. In the meantime, perhaps you could direct me to the person taking care of my horse."

II

"Well, Mr. Colton," Parsons said, his mouth still full of his breakfast, "I gave the horses a load of feed and hay the day you arrived. I'd wager they're doing just fine."

Wallace had sent Colton to Jesse Parsons and made his way to find Joe Crane. Parsons, as it turned out, had made his start as a livery owner. All the members of the order trusted him with their steeds, and he was more than happy to take care of the animals, despite outgrowing the hands-on work he'd started doing.

"All the same," Colton said, "I'd like to check on my horse. Make sure he's all right. I can't even remember the last time I'd seen him, as sick as I was."

Parsons nodded along to Colton and forced the last of his toast into his face. "I suppose it would be good to get out to the barn and see how all the horses are doing. Might need to clean out the barn some, maybe replenish their feed."

Colton smiled. "I'd be glad to help."

"I'd be glad to have some," Parsons said, then bent toward Colton, his voice low. "I'm not sure any of these stuffy Order members have had to even brush their horse by themselves, let alone clean up after one." They both shared a laugh. "So, when do you want to head out there?" Parsons said and buttered another piece of bread.

"Now."

"What's the rush?"

"I'm aiming to head out before too long. Just want to make sure everything is good to go."

"I see," Parsons said around a mouthful of bread. "Well, I don't see any reason why we can't go right now.

Let me finish my breakfast, and we'll go have a look."

III

"Stuck," Parsons said and put another shoulder into the front door. "Snowed in."

Colton gave the door a try himself, but all they could manage was a wedge of open space between the door and the snow.

"There got to be some way out," Colton said, then added, "wouldn't be much good to have a door no one could use. What if there was a fire?"

Parsons sighed and pulled the heavy oak door closed. He scratched his head and looked around. "Well, depending on the height of the snow, and I'd say it's pretty high right now, we might be able to climb out a window."

Colton pictured the small window in his room, barely more than a pane of glass. "I didn't think the castle had any windows that opened."

"Most windows are stuck in place, that's true," Parsons said and started walking. "But there are a couple on the second floor that open well enough, you put some muscle behind it."

They found another stairwell, one that hadn't been included in Wallace's tour, and ran up the small stairs. They came out into a large, square room about the size of the sitting room, and Colton figured this was the room that sat just above where he'd had his tea early that morning. Unlike the sitting room, this room was filled with windows. Glass almost outnumbered the stone in building materials here; it was likely designed as a sunroom or a sick room.

"Come on," Parsons said and made for the middle section of windows that stood just ahead of them. "Let's see if we can do this." Parsons lay his face flat against the window and looked down, while Colton found a window with a latch and started to open it.

"There might be enough snow down there," Parsons said, but it was a whisper. Colton ignored him, he just needed to get out of the castle, to see Bill, to escape. "Wait there," Parsons said and ran off.

Colton pushed the window fully open. Snow spattered onto the floor as the icy wind blew a gale and pushed him back a step. He could feel the cold rush over him, goose-bumps prickling up all over his body, and he fought the urge to cross his arms to block out the freezing air. When Parsons hadn't returned, Colton peered out into the storm. He was greeted with a vast, snow-laden wasteland, everything covered in layers of the white stuff; trees sagged with its weight, paths disappeared under its assault, and the sun paled against the swirling clouds and snow. The world was in a permanent state of dawn or dusk, light just trying desperately to break through the darkness but not having the strength to do so.

The ride out would be rough, Colton thought, his eyes wandering across the front of the castle where drifts of snow had fallen upon the doors like waves in the ocean, frozen in place. If he could get Bill out of the barn, they'd be riding in hip-deep snow, maybe higher. Wouldn't be as easy to put the distance he'd hoped for between him and the castle, but it was better than nothing. The best scenario he could hope for was to come upon a cave, take a night or two there and see if the storm died down some. It didn't matter, as long as he was finished with the Order of Chthar.

"Here," Parsons said, jogging up the stairs. He tossed Colton a jacket and threw a pair of old boots to the floor. "Put those on, you'll need 'em." He shrugged into a coat of his own and tossed a shovel out the window, looking after it to mark where it landed. "There's another shovel in the barn. When we get down there, I'll get started on the main entrance, you check out the barn. If you need to shovel in, just come get me."

Colton nodded. With a smile, Parsons shoved one leg out the window, then the other and slid down the bank from the window, disappearing into the storm. Colton hauled on the boots and beige jacket, feeling the warm fur lining as he buttoned it closed. He took another look into the storm and saw the figure of Parsons already at the front doors, digging away with his recovered shovel.

He tried to slip out the window as easily as Parsons, but it turned into a graceless fall before it was all done. Colton rolled most of the way down, the wet snow soaking through the yellow cotton pants that drew the cold to his legs and rear.

"Shit," he said and pushed himself to his feet.

Colton struggled to make it to the barn. The wind blew against him, and his legs were stuck deep in the snow, threatening to slip out from under him with every step. He looked to Parsons, still engrossed in digging out the doorway, his broad shoulders bowing with the weight of snow before tossing it over his head.

The barn was another victim of snow drifts, the white stuff having swirled and pooled around the entrance and sides of the building. Unlike the castle, however, the barn doors weren't fully submerged. Colton dug at the snow with his hands, clawing handfuls away from the door as best he could before his hands became too cold to continue, and he made them retreat into the pockets of his jacket. He did this a few more times, digging with his hands then giving them a reprieve in the warmth of his jacket pockets before he managed to make the headway he was hoping for.

The door still wouldn't open, not all the way. Colton pulled on the door with all his strength and managed to create a big enough opening to slip inside and out of the storm. He collapsed to the floor, his back hitting dry hay, before he curled into a ball to regain some of his heat. The barn was warm, filled with the heat of the horses that had taken to whinnying in his presence. He expected the barn to be dark, but an oil lantern was hanging next to the doorway, lit and ready.

"Jesus," Colton said and shut the door against the storm. If what Parsons said was right, and the last time anyone was in here was when Colton arrived, the lantern had been lit for days. The horses could've easily knocked it over and started a fire. The whole place would've gone up. Then again, maybe Parsons wasn't right. Maybe someone had been out here since.

Colton forced those thoughts away, gathered himself up and made a few shivering steps into the barn. It was a large building, built with an open dirt floor, and to the side, there was a stairway that led to a balcony. There were at least ten horses milling around, and the stench of them was overpowering. Colton was accustomed to horses, but it was surely more than a few days since Parsons had cleaned the place up. Of the horses, only a few had been tied up, the rest roamed free. Amongst those tethered to the barn, Bill stood out, alone, in the far corner of the room.

Colton ran his hand over the old horse's snout. "How're you doing, boy?"

The horse nudged him in response, grunting.

"Been sick, buddy. I couldn't come see you, this was my first chance." Colton rooted around in his saddlebags. "Glad to see you're okay."

He pulled out a change of clothes, nothing fancy, just a pair of jeans and a flannel button-up, and ditched the yellow duds the Order had given him. Wallace had mentioned that he had no gun on him when they pulled him out of the storm, which was fair. A man in his condition might have dropped his gun, or maybe it fell from his holster as they dragged him into the castle. The problem was, Colton knew that he had other guns on Bill, a Winchester repeater and a sawed-off double-barrel shotgun, neither of which was on the horse now. Didn't Wallace mention finding a rifle on Bill, as well? Colton rummaged through the saddlebags and found nothing more than some jerky and his slicker.

"Be right back," Colton said and patted Bill on the nose. He made his way through the barn, searching any little nook or cranny that might hide or hold the missing firearms, but he found nothing except for some more hay and the extra shovel Parsons had promised. On the balcony, he crawled around on the dusty floor, his hands groping along edges and corners to see if anything gave way. But no, there were no hidden drawers concealing his belongings, none that he could find anyway.

A sound brought Colton around.

The sudden movement was difficult to pinpoint. The horses that were free moved about at their leisure, and even those tied up stomped their feet or nickered and snorted. Still, Colton picked up on something that hadn't been there just a few minutes ago. The hairs on the back of his neck stood, and the rush of foul air hinted that something wasn't right.

The off-beat staccato of something scuttling through the barn got Colton to his feet. Each movement brought a scratching sound. Colton bent his ear to listen. It could be the sound of a horse dragging its hooves over a waylaid board, Colton supposed, but his mind kept thinking back to the creature from the basement oasis and how long talons hung from its fingertips.

The sound stopped.

A stillness fell over the barn. Colton cocked his head to the side and listened. He closed his eyes to force himself to focus only on the sounds around him: his slow breaths, the stomping of the horses, the creak of wood underfoot. Nothing.

Chittering sounded below him, a clacking of something sharp against something hard, a guttural breath hiding just beneath the surface.

Colton stood at the balcony's railing, his eyes scanning the barn, still dark despite the lantern lit at the entrance. Horses, it was only the horses. Colton sighed and went to work, slapping the dust from his jeans and shirt.

"Mr. Colton?" Parsons said, pulling the barn door wide open.

"Up here," Colton said as he made his way down the balcony stairs.

"Nice duds," Parsons said with a nod. "What were you doing up there?"

"Looking for some of my belongings. Haven't seen them, have you?"

"No, sir, I left your horse the way he was, saddle and saddle bags included."

Colton nodded and picked up the extra shovel. "Let's get to work." He nodded to the mess the horses had left on the floor, and both men bent to their work.

IV

Back sore from cleaning the barn, Colton said his goodbyes to Bill, promised him he'd be back soon, and followed Parsons back to the Castle. He'd done a fair job clearing the door, but it was a singular entrance, a tunnel of snow dug through the drift leading to the door. Colton looked back at the barn, already fading into obscurity as the storm surged on. And still, even as the snow folded the barn into its clutches, Colton was sure he saw something large exit the barn doors. Something large and black.

CHAPTER SIX

I

The castle returned to a contemplative quiet after Parsons and Colton stomped into the foyer. The members of the Order were still sleeping off their celebration, Colton assumed, but he was hesitant to think of what sort of ritual might have been started or ended in that sunken altar.

After a shot of whiskey, Parsons excused himself and left Colton alone in the sitting room. Drinking his own glass of whiskey, Colton took in the silence but didn't enjoy it. All he could picture were beasts gnawing away under the stone, creatures submerged and ready to pounce. He turned to look into the foyer and was only able to see the edge of the entryway and the snow that he and Parsons had kicked off upon entering.

He thought of his dream, the hardened snow creeping about the floor like lesions on the sick. He thought of being pulled into the foyer by disembodied hands. Was that a dream, or was it real? How did the members of the Order get him inside?

Colton couldn't remember much before waking in the strange bed aside from hazy images, fuzzy with fever. The snow, that's what he remembered the most, the snow pelting him, sticking to him. The snow and the cold, how he huddled into the cold, bent forward to be closer to Bill and sap some extra heat from the horse. He remembered something large in the distance. Something with burning orange eyes.

"Mr. Colton," Wallace said, giving Colton a start. "Did Jesse manage to take you to see your horse?" Wallace was followed by Dr. Crane and Clem Burns.

"He did," Colton said and raised his glass. "I appreciate you setting that up."

"I see you found a new set of clothes?" Wallace smiled and sat across from him once more.

"I'm not the only one," Colton said, nodding to Crane and Burns. While Wallace maintained his usual priestly garb, black jacket, shirt, pants, and white collar, his companions had changed drastically. Both men wore robes that covered their entire bodies from neck to ankle, and hoods were draped over the top of their heads. On the chest of each robe was a red ruby, light lines stabbing out from every side. The robes were the same pale yellow as Colton's borrowed clothes. Neither man wore a smile.

Wallace shrugged. "These are our ceremonial robes. You'll see more of us wear them over the coming days as the final date of celebration approaches."

"Father Wallace informed me that you would like to leave." Crane sat next to Colton, leaning towards him.

"I would. I hope to leave tomorrow morning, now that I know my horse is healthy and up to moving."

"I see," Crane said and took hold of Colton's wrist, his two forefingers placed just under Colton's palm. "This all depends on my giving you a clean bill of health, of course."

"Of course," Colton said and met Wallace's gaze. The priest's eyes were half-lidded, like he was bored or tired, but he smiled at Colton. Burns stood behind the priest's chair, staring toward the booze cabinet.

The doctor did his examination, poking and prodding Colton from face to stomach, his dry hands pushing Colton where he needed him. While the doctor went to work, no one spoke. Wallace and Burns would sometimes let their gaze roam over towards Colton and Dr. Crane, but they would rarely stay longer than a moment before finding something else to focus on. Abigail Parsons was another story.

Abigail sauntered into the room shortly after the doctor had begun his examination. Face fully dressed in makeup, she was still wrapped in her furs instead of the ceremonial robes worn by Crane and Burns. Abigail poured herself a drink and watched Colton intently.

"I hear you dragged my husband out in the cold," Mrs. Parsons said, swallowing her drink loudly. "Pour fellow had to wrap himself in blankets just to warm up."

"Your husband did help me tend to my horse," Colton said just as Crane pushed his chin to the left, shifting his eyes away from the woman.

"So, it's true," she said, "he's finally leaving us?"

"Abby, Mr. Colton is our guest," Father Wallace said. From the periphery of his eye, Colton could see the frown take over the priest's face.

"And a guest surely knows when they've overstayed their welcome."

"That's enough," said Crane, releasing Colton from his grip. "Guest or not, this man is my patient, and I have the say over whether he can leave or not."

"And what's your verdict, Doctor?" Wallace asked. Colton turned his attention back to Dr. Crane, the short man's blue eyes intent on him.

"He must stay," the doctor said with a sigh.

"Why?" Colton and Mrs. Parsons said at the same time, drawing their eyes to each other for an instant before she rolled hers at him.

"He is still much too sick to travel, let alone in this storm."

"I'm fine, Doc. Ask that one's husband." He pointed

to Mrs. Parsons, who huffed at the mention, "I just helped him clean the barn, for Christ's sake. If I can do that, I can ride a damn horse."

"Are you sure, Doctor?" Wallace's voice rose over the din, silencing the budding argument.

"Yes," Crane said, his face set in a grimace. "I damn well ought to be. The fever has passed, but this man is only one day removed from having a serious hallucination. Who knows what is going on inside that thick head?"

The room fell silent, but Colton's ears exploded with his own heartbeat, with the blood streaming through his veins. "I appreciate your concern, Dr. Crane. How many days do you think I'll be held up?" Colton drank the last of his whiskey in one pull, hoping to calm his inner workings.

"I'd say," Crane said and made a show of rubbing a hand over his chin, "at least another two days. After that, we'll have to perform another examination. If you're in the clear, then…" he trailed off and waved his hand.

"What do you think, Mr. Colton?" Wallace spoke up, his eyes boring into Colton.

"Not much I can say or think," Colton said. "I suppose I am stuck here for another day or two. And before you ask, no, I'm not happy about it. At the same time, Dr. Crane has been nothing but professional, so I respect his opinion." At that Abigail Parsons stormed from the room in a huff, Clem Burns's gaze following her out.

"I suppose that's that then," Wallace said and settled back into his chair.

"Indeed." Colton rose from the chair with a grunt. "If you'll excuse me, gentlemen. I think I'd like to rest now." He could feel their eyes on his back, digging holes there. He just hoped they took him at face value. Doctor's approval or not, he was taking Bill and leaving.

II

Colton was tired, his eyes heavy. He wanted nothing more than to lie back on his bed and sleep, but he couldn't do that. He'd told Wallace and Crane that he'd be staying, though he wasn't sure what kind of torment awaited him if he did. He had to leave and not while the Order were up and active. Instead, he'd leave in the middle of the night, when they were all in their celebrations or asleep.

It wasn't easy judging the time. The storm still blocked the light of both the sun and moon, so he watched the space beneath his door.

The last two times he had wandered into the castle in the middle of the night, the torches had been doused, leaving only sporadic light to brighten the hallway. He waited for the change in the light that crept underneath his door. He hoped to put his plans into action before he nodded off. It was a struggle. Colton's eyes stung, his limbs were heavy, and he was plagued by an overall tiredness. Perhaps Dr. Crane was right, perhaps he was still sick.

"Not sick enough," Colton said and pinched his own arm, hoping the pain would wake him up some. It was true, his only remaining symptom was tiredness, but that was a sign of illness and fever. Perhaps the doctor was right to err on the side of caution, but Colton couldn't afford that, nor did he believe it, not with that creature roaming around in the depths of the castle. Besides, if he could get away from the castle, he would feel much better. He was sure of it.

As soon as he noticed the light underneath the door had diminished, he jumped from the bed and bolted to the doorway, his hand outstretched to push it open. He stopped himself before he could do so. He didn't know how long the lights had been dimmed or what time of night it was. It would be better to wait a few more minutes before heading outside.

Colton paced his room. He'd removed his boots again and let his bare feet slide over the stone. It'd be quieter that way. He didn't care much about leaving footprints or any other marks for that matter, as long as he didn't wake any of the Order members. Or draw the attention of the beast.

Opening the door was an obstacle all on its own. Its old hinges creaked, though they showed no signs of rust. He hadn't noticed it before, but there was an audible sound of age and use, the jagged laugh of an old woman, the wheezing cough of an old man. It practically announced his departure to the entire castle.

With a silent curse, Colton poked his head into the hallway, his eyes searching for any indication of discovery. There was nothing, and the halls were dim with only every third torch lit. Colton slid an extinguished torch from its sconce and gave it a practice swing. Without a gun, it'd have to do.

Makeshift club in one hand, boots in his other, Colton made his way through the castle. The stone floor was cold, as though the storm had finally broken through the outer wall, slipped through the cracks and taken hold. He remembered the humid air of the basement oasis, an unnatural heat in Northern Colorado, and couldn't help but wonder if that had something to do with the strange atmosphere in the castle. If so, what was causing the sudden change? What ritual were the Order of Chthar taking part in to draw that weather to it?

Colton crept down the stairs that led to the sitting room, where darkness pervaded. He chanced a look into the room as he passed, a cursory glance to ensure he was still alone. The fireplace was alight, but the flames were low, the orange hue barely fighting back the shadows around the hearth. Even in the dim light, Colton saw someone. A hand, curled in upon itself, lay on the armrest of a chair that was turned to the fireplace, its back to Colton and the rest of the room.

As quietly as he could, Colton kept himself low to the ground and passed the entrance. There was no movement from the room, no voice calling to him or asking him what he was doing, it was just the thick, palpable silence. Colton slid his back against the wall, curious to know who was up so late and if they were supposed to be standing sentinel to ensure he wouldn't attempt an early escape.

Taking as much care as he could, Colton edged his head around the corner of the entrance, his eyes darting around the room before settling on the chair. From this angle, he could partially see the front side of the chair, just a small corner of the cushion, more of the armrest, and a slight view of the headrest, where his eyes fell, hoping to identify who the Order had set for guard duty.

The chair was empty.

With a sharp intake of breath, Colton girded himself and looked further into the room. No one. Even the fire appeared to have dimmed more in just those few moments. Colton ran the back of his hand over his forehead, wishing he wasn't so encumbered that he'd be able to rub his temples, his eyes. A wave of surreality fell over him, and he leaned hard into the wall behind him so that he wouldn't fall over. Fear plucked at the hair on his arms, the nape of his neck. Was this a dream? he almost said aloud. It wasn't. It couldn't be. He'd had strange dreams before, but this wasn't one of them. At least, that's what he hoped.

Attempting to shake off this strange feeling, Colton pushed onward, his stealthy progress now plagued by his trouble seeing straight. The world twisted around as he ambled into the foyer. A single torch was lit next to the doorway. The sound of the storm battering against the wooden doors finally broke the silence and made Colton feel at ease. The foyer was bitterly cold, and Colton's feet stung with its bite. He hastened to put on his boots.

"Mr. Colton," Wallace said. His voice was still honey sweet, marble smooth, but it was tinged by something. Disgust. "Now, now. It is awfully rude to leave without saying goodbye."

Colton turned to Wallace and came face to face with all the members of the order. He could hardly tell who was who from the bunch as they all wore the ceremonial robes that he had seen Crane and Burns wear earlier in the day. All of them sneered from behind their hooded faces, save for Wallace, whose hood was still dangling about his back. The priest's white collar stood out under the man's darkened features as he bent his head.

"I was never one to cause a fuss," Colton said and finished pushing his feet into his boots. "Figured if I ducked out early enough, you folks could go on about your celebrations, and I wouldn't be cause for disturbing them."

"That was mighty kind of you, Mr. Colton, but I'm afraid I may have led you astray. You see, I said you were forbidden from witnessing any of our rituals, but the truth is quite the opposite. As it turns out, we need you to complete them."

"I'm afraid I'll have to refuse the offer," Colton said and raised his makeshift club.

"I figured you'd say as much," Wallace said. "But really, as it stands, you simply can't refuse. It would be a terrible chore trying to replace you this late in our preparations. You are, as the French say, the pièce de résistance."

Feinting with his club, Colton set the entire room into action. Some of the Order members scattered, while others surged forward, hands out to grab and subdue him. Father Wallace, for his part, didn't move a muscle, instead, he continued to smirk, his blue eyes boring into Colton.

Taking a wild swing with the torch, Colton ran to the door and burst through it into the storm. The wind immediately tore his breath away, and even in the small tunnel Parsons had dug, the snow stung as it pelted down on him. It hadn't been a full day, but the work that Parsons had done on the snow was barely noticeable. The storm had already begun to refill the trenches dug and had started to retake the land that had so recently been freed.

Heedless of the shin-deep snow, Colton aimed himself for the barn. It was a gamble. The order knew that he meant to ride out of there on his horse, that he had even endeavoured to check on him just that day. They would make to cut him off. It might've made good sense to run in the opposite direction, use the storm as his cover, find a nook or cranny to hide in until their search ended, then double back for Bill. Colton didn't care. He wanted to leave the castle behind and never return.

Running, his knees high to avoid the sucking, grabbing snow that endeavored to slow him, Colton cast a glance over his shoulder. He couldn't see any of the Order; the storm kept his vision limited, but none were near him. There were no hands ready to grasp his shirt and pull him down, no hooded figure ready to tackle him from behind, just the snow driven mad by the wind.

He made it to the barn, his breath coming in large gulps, his chest and lungs burning. Colton fell against one of the doors, his eyes toward the castle, his grip on the torch still strong. Nothing. He cocked his ear, hoping to push past the noise of the storm to hear the telltale signs of men crashing through snow just as he did, to hear the crushing and crunching noise as they struggled against the grip of the fallen snow. Nothing.

Colton stared into the storm for another minute, his breath coming in shorter gasps, his chest burning less and less. From behind him, he heard a horse neigh and the stomping of hooves on frozen earth. Hesitantly, Colton turned to open the barn door, but then he heard it. Not the sound of men crashing after him in the storm, but of something he'd become far too familiar with, a chittering.

He backed away from the barn, his eyes drawn to the clicking and inhuman noise that came from above him. There, on the apex of the barn's roof, the black mass of the creature sat, its four red eyes staring down upon Colton.

The urge to run back towards the castle nagged at Colton's mind, but, as much as he would like to be as far away from the beast as possible, he knew that the castle would provide him no more sanctuary than the open field. Instead, Colton brandished his makeshift club and made to open the barn doors.

The high-pitched scream that rose from the beast nearly pushed Colton to his knees. Instead, he dropped his torch and cupped both of his hands over his ears. It was so loud that Colton's eyes bulged from his head, his heart thudded in his chest, and his teeth were set on edge.

In one fluid movement, the creature brought its arms up to the sky, unfurling its long wings and stretching them to the side. Colton's gaze froze on the wings. They weren't just the stretched flesh of the beast's body, but they contained something else inside of them. Like his first sight of them, he saw that the wings contained the stars. Each wing was the night sky, dark and unknown, but spotted with the stars that seared holes in the sheet of night, providing reprieve against its unbearable darkness.

The stars moved and twisted; a shooting star here, another there. Constellations appeared and disappeared. Colton knew most of them and had a good guess for those he thought looked familiar, but there were others that just didn't seem right. They didn't line up with any other constellation Colton had studied and may have been something new or maybe something extremely old. It didn't matter to Colton either way, he supposed. Here were the stars. Those tiny dots of light that had been scrubbed from the sky by the unending storm they'd finally returned.

A heavy pressure weighed on Colton's shoulders as he tried to connect those motes of light, make a tangible image from them. It would help him along on his future journeys, make them easier to navigate if he happened upon this stretch of sky again.

"Ow," Colton said. Something bit into his shoulder and drew his gaze from the stars. A large claw pierced the skin around his shoulder, a small, thin hand gripping him there and squeezing.

Colton shook his head and looked to the source of the arm, only to find the large, batlike face of the creature snarling just inches from his own. Colton tried to rear back and away, but the creature had a tight grip, and it wasn't letting go. Other hands came out of the storm as the Order finally emerged, their hands grabbing Colton wherever they could.

Wallace's voice rose over the wind. "I told you, Mr. Colton." He stepped alongside the creature, almost shoulder to shoulder with it. "You are a part of this ritual now. You have nowhere else to go."

CHAPTER SEVEN

I

They took Colton to the basement and placed him in a cage. He leaned against the cool bars at the back of the cell, his hands hanging from his knees. There was no chair or bed, desk or armoire, only the steel bars to keep him company.

The Order had set a guard, a younger man with a neatly trimmed goatee and harsh grey eyes. He, too, was wearing the pale-yellow ceremony robes, and he would not remove his gaze from Colton. Colton sighed; it was a far cry from Clem Burns being hungover just outside his door.

"Hey," Colton said, rapping his knuckles on the iron bars of his cell. "What is Wallace planning on doing with me?"

The guard said nothing, just uncrossed and recrossed his arms.

"What about that thing out there, that beast? What is that?"

"We've been told to call it the Disciple," Wallace said, turning the corner into the room. The young member of the Order jumped from his seat and bowed at the priest's entrance. "He isn't like anything else, is he? A unique animal, though I'd be loath to call him that. He is quite intelligent."

"Didn't seem to need much intelligence to hunt me

down like that." Colton rubbed at his shoulder where the creature had jabbed him with its talons.

"He is the guardian of this order and of our Master Chthar. So, as I'm sure you can imagine, it pained me to use him as a bird dog to catch you when you scampered away. All the same, it was quite effective."

"His wings…"

"Ah, yes. The Disciple is a true gift from Chthar. In his very form, you can see the miracles of the world, the inner workings of the universe, perhaps even reality itself." Wallace stepped close to the cell, giving Colton a quick look over. "You know, some would consider you lucky, being in this position."

"And what position is that?"

"Being a sacrifice for Chthar. Not only a sacrifice—we've done our fair share of that over the years—but *the* sacrifice. You are the last piece of a large puzzle that has taken hundreds of years to put together. You, Mr. Colton, will be the end and the beginning. The alpha and the omega. Your death will bring forth Chthar, our master, and with him, the world will begin anew."

"And what would you have done if I hadn't stumbled by in the storm? Abduct someone from the nearest town?" Colton stepped up to the bars, his hands clenched into fists. He was in arm's reach of Wallace, could easily thrust out his hand and wrap it around the priest's neck, but it would solve nothing. Colton would still be in a cell at the mercy of the Order, even if their strength had dwindled by one.

"As I told you, Dr. Crane had to make some tough decisions." Wallace stepped closer to the bars, as if he were able to read Colton's thoughts, call his bluff.

"Who?"

Wallace stepped back and made a quick flourish and a bow.

"Jesus," Colton said, a mirthless smile crossing his mouth. "No wonder you didn't want me to leave. And here I thought you were defending me, keeping me safe, because you were a good person. Are you even a priest?"

"'Do not fear what you are about to suffer. Behold, the devil is about to throw some of you into prison, that you may be tested.' Revelations. Seems awfully fitting, don't you think?"

"'The devil can cite Scripture for his purpose,' Shakespeare, I think."

Wallace let out a genuine, whole-hearted laugh. The kind that made Colton want to join in, even if he didn't get the joke or much feel like laughing.

"Here I thought I was dealing with some dull mountain man," Wallace said through subsiding giggles. "You are interesting, Mr. Colton. I am genuinely sorry that I will not get to have any more conversations with you. I think we might have gotten along quite well if circumstances weren't what they were."

"Give me a gun, you'll find me plenty interesting."

"No, I think not. That does remind me." Wallace reached into his robe and pulled out a leather bag tied tight with a piece of twine. "This is a gift, Mr. Colton. Few people have seen something like this, though many would lay down their lives for just a glimpse." He untied the bag and slipped a large red gem into his hand. It was shaped like a diamond, sharp to a point at one end and flat and wide on the other. "This is the last of its kind. Opposed to what I had previously told you, hundreds of these have passed through this order, but this is the last, just like you, Mr. Colton. The end, the beginning."

Colton turned his head to look at the gem; he'd seen it before. "The paintings," he said.

"Yes, good eye, Mr. Colton. Those portraits are of order members who sacrificed themselves to Chthar. Who gave themselves up for a new beginning in the wake of the master. This will be yours."

Colton reached his hand out for it.

"Oh no, Mr. Colton, we can't trust you with it, not with its sharp edges," Wallace said and tutted. "Instead, we'll keep it close by." From behind Wallace, Colton's guard brought a wooden stand, similar to an easel or a podium, but with a flat top. He laid it just outside of Colton's reach and placed a pink cushion on its surface. Wallace placed the gem atop.

"There, that should be close enough. The gem and the sacrifice must link. Don't worry, Mr. Colton. It is effortless on your part. In fact, you've likely felt the effects of the gem already. We've had it stored close to you since your arrival."

The dreams, his sickness, the sounds in the dark. Perhaps all of it, or none of it, Colton couldn't say, and he was done entertaining Wallace. He turned away and sat in the corner of his cell, the bars digging into his back.

"It won't be long now, Mr. Colton," Wallace said. "The last of our rituals starts at midday. By midnight, we will be ready for you. It is an exciting time, and you play a crucial role. Please, take some time to rest. If you have any regrets in your life, now would be the time to deal with them. I think you'll find that, in a situation such as yours, past slights and missed opportunities will seem small, trivial. It might be good to have that kind of perspective as you are brought before Chthar. I hear that the sacrifice ritual brings you into communication with him. He will know your every secret, Mr. Colton. It is best to meet him with a clear conscience. Oh, but what a lucky man you are."

Wallace shuffled away as quickly and as quietly as he had arrived. The guard remained, surly and unspeaking, but for when his eyes wandered toward the gem. There was awe there, reverence, but above it all was a stone-cold sense of fear. Colton could sympathize.

II

The chittering call of the Disciple roused Colton. He wiped away his bleary vision and expected to find the creature baring its wings, hypnotizing him so he wouldn't cause trouble on his way to the sacrifice. The creature wasn't there, nor was his stalwart guard, or his cage for that matter. Colton was back in his room, his desk and armoire resting at odd angles around his bed. He'd made a maze for himself.

Colton bolted to his feet. A breathless feeling of relief made his stomach sink. His capture had been a dream, another vision brought on by whatever sickness plagued him. He smiled so hard that it hurt his face.

The chittering stopped him cold. The beast was still out there, roaming the halls. He'd have to be quick. Removing his boots, Colton exited into the hall. It was dark, most torches doused save every third. Colton wavered for a moment as he removed a flameless torch from its sconce; the feeling of having done this before twisted his stomach.

The castle was dark without the torchlight, and the endless storm provided no reprieve from the sun or the moon. Instead, there was a red hue that fell over the castle. It brightened the dark shadows, darkened those areas already exposed to light, and made everything look as though it were coated in a viscous layer of blood.

Colton tried to shake off the strange feeling and focus on his plan of escape, but it nagged at the back of his mind. He slowed his pace, his eyes wandering in the strange light. The paintings that Father Wallace had pointed out to him previously had changed. Once stately pictures of former members of the Order of Chthar, they now showed corpses. If they were the same people, Colton couldn't say, but each painting was a deathbed, the manner of death singular. Each corpse had a red gem lodged in its body, though it was never in the same place for two people. One corpse had the sharp end jabbed into its chest, perhaps piercing the heart. Another had the gem implanted in its forehead, its skeletal mouth hanging open in a silent scream of agony and fear.

Chittering sounded ahead of him, not distant, but not close. Images of the dark beast bearing its wings forced Colton to retreat in the opposite direction. He moved as quietly as he could, bent low to the floor, the same way he had that first night he spent in the castle, and again another night where he discovered the basement altar. The gloom wasn't an issue this time, the red light provided enough illumination to see his path. Colton moved fast, avoiding doors as much as he could, the soft patter of his bare feet barely loud enough to rouse a mouse.

The path didn't lead him to the basement, instead, it led him to the sitting room. Colton found himself sitting on the couch, facing the fireplace and the back of an armchair. A hand dangled from the chair's side. It was a thin arm attached to the limp hand. Colton, brandishing his doused torch, spun the chair to face him. It was Dr. Crane, his face slack, blood leaking from the corner of his mouth, a red gem jammed between his jaws.

Colton backed out of the sitting room into the barn. Lit by the same red hue, Colton spun around to get his bearings. It was cold and quiet; even the horses didn't make any noise at his sudden presence. Nothing moved. A sour smell brought his hand to his mouth and nose. It was the smell of rot and death. The horses, all of them, were dead. Their huge carcasses surrounded him, their stomachs bloated with death, bearing down and ready to explode in a shower of gore. Each and every horse had a red gem embedded in them.

"No," Colton said, his voice a cracked whisper, as he frantically searched for his horse, Bill. The horse was tied where Colton had remembered but was on its side. Bill's stomach had bloated like the rest, had somehow grown around the saddle that Colton had left strapped to him. Bill had two gems stabbed into him, one for each eye. Colton cried out, a scream soured by sorrow and anger. Tears streaming over his cheeks, he stormed through the barn doors, intent on taking the castle apart even if he had to do it brick by brick with his bare hands.

He walked into the foyer. The front door at his back, already closed, Colton stared around in confusion. Snow had accumulated across the floor, old, hard snow that resisted the melt. Puddles of water dotted the foyer, and wet footprints dotted the stone floor. Most were boot and shoe marks, but there was one large print that Colton couldn't place. It wasn't made by any boot he'd ever seen, nor was it a bare foot of any human or animal. It stretched too long, the indentation too heavy and awkward.

The chittering sounded ahead of him, echoing from somewhere deeper within the castle. Renewing his grip on his makeshift club, Colton followed the sound.

The beast's call led Colton onward. He followed the old paths he had become used to, past his room and into the basement. He followed the chittering into the secret oasis, the humidity of it draping him immediately in sweat. The noise brought him through the slime-covered brush and trees and led him to the open clearing. Colton's feet cautiously touched the stone walking path that ended with the stairs ascending to the altar.

The Order of Chthar were already there. They surrounded the sacrificial table, their voices low in a chant. Colton tried to make out the words of the chant as he got closer, but it was in no language he had ever heard before, nor did he want to hear it again. The words hurt his ears, made him want to cover them, tell the Order to shut their mouths. He didn't, though. Instead, he continued toward them, hoping to get a glimpse of what was on the table.

He elbowed his way through the Order, no one giving him any resistance as he made his way to the front of the line. Colton broke through to the altar, familiar faces stood apart from the rest of the group, Wallace, Crane, Abigail and Jesse Parsons, Clem Burns. The five of them surrounded the altar, their hoods pulled back, their faces serene, as they chanted those horrible words.

On the stone table, Colton saw himself. His arms were tied to his sides, his legs were tied to the table, and more ropes secured his neck. He could hear the garble of angry grunts and moans that the other him was making, and he finally noticed that his mouth was being held open by some metal contraption. Colton saw his own eyes wide with terror as they bounced between the prominent members of the Order, pleading his case, begging for his freedom.

Colton wanted to turn away, to avoid the scene playing before him. No one deserved to see their death before they were going to have to live through it. In that case, Colton would rather be surprised than prepared. As he shielded his eyes, the Disciple uttered its chittering call, a clicking that drew Colton's eyes back to the center of the altar. The beast wasn't there, not in the center of the room partaking in the torture of Colton, but he was near the pool that stood just behind the altar. Colton could see the large black figure, the red glow of its eyes staring at him.

He pushed past the ceremony that was taking place and moved to the creature. Ripples caressed its black surface as bubbles gathered at the pool's limits. The Disciple was squatting on the opposite side of the pool, its legs ready to spring forward should if need be, but its arms were thankfully held at its sides, one long finger and claw dangled into the water, swirling back and forth.

"What are you?" Colton asked, but his voice was a distant echo, a memory.

The creature's mouth shook with the chittering noise, its eyes intent on Colton and what was happening behind it. *I am the servant of the Under God.* A guttural voice rose in Colton's head, matching the head movements of the Disciple.

"And what is the Under God?"

Chthar the Infernal, the Forebearer, the Many-Armed, the Glutton, the Master. Chthar comes from blood and will gorge upon all.

Another ripple crossed the pool, bubbles popping at the surface.

"Why the gems?"

The stones are the blood of the Master. Only when they have taken a life will they feed Chthar, and only then will the blood sacrifice be complete.

"And what if a person didn't die?"

Blood without death will not suffice. The Master is hungry.

A rumble shook Colton's feet, nearly knocking him into the pool. As he leaned over, his reflection staring back at him in the murky water, the pool exploded into tentacles. Large and grey, they slapped at the ground around the pool, trying to find purchase.

The Master rises, the Disciple said and stood away from the pool.

A muffled scream came from behind Colton. He turned to see Crane forcing the red gem into the other Colton's mouth. The corners of his mouth split at the lips, and jagged lines ran up his cheeks, but still, Crane pushed, and still that Colton screamed.

He ran back to the altar, determined to stop Crane, but even before he passed through the Order members, he heard a loud crack and pop, almost like a melon being crushed. He pushed into the inner circle to see Crane and Wallace shaking hands, congratulating themselves, their faces giddy with self-righteousness. The Parsons were celebrating as well, enjoying a long, passionate kiss, even as Colton's fresh corpse lay there, bleeding.

Colton made his way to his own dead body, bent close to it to make sure it was, in fact, dead. But the emotionless eyes, the jaw open too wide, and the gem shoved nearly all the way down his throat said that death was certain, and it had been painful.

The floor shook again, a thunderous sound of earth clapping against itself, and members of the Order were flung to the ground. Colton turned back to the pool. The tentacles had grown taller and were no longer concealed. It looked like they had found purchase, and they were trying to push themselves out of the water.

Instead of fleeing in terror, of realizing their mistake, the Order celebrated more. Their shouts were not of those screaming as they ran for their lives, instead, they were overjoyed.

"The Master comes," Colton heard one of the Order members say, followed by a stream of hysterical laughter.

Another quake shook the room, but Colton focused on the gem lodged in his throat. He wrapped his fingers around the edges and tried to remove it, tried to pry it from his own gaping mouth and throat, but it had been driven so deep, lodged so completely.

A hand on his shoulder spun him in place, the gem forgotten about. Wallace stood before him, a frenzied smile on his face. "He rises," the priest said. "He rises, and it's all thanks to you."

Colton pushed the man away and gripped the gem one last time, his fingers cramped even in the unnaturally wide mouth. It wouldn't come.

Bow before Chthar, the Disciple's voice rang in his head. *Bow and accept your fate as lambs for the slaughter.*

He was spun around again. This time, Wallace was a corpse, his pale skin torn asunder, leaving little but muscles and bone, but no blood. One half of Wallace's face was missing, his skull crushed and skin flayed, his one eye bounced in his head, never stopping to focus on anything. It was as if the eye were attempting to roll back in his skull, but the priest wouldn't allow it.

"You got a good eye on you," Wallace said and grabbed Colton by the back of the head. Another gem in his free hand, Wallace angled it towards Colton's mouth and pushed.

CHAPTER EIGHT

I

Jerking out of his haze, Colton slammed his head against the bars of his cage. Wincing, he cursed and rubbed his head. There was no blood, at least. Staring at him, straight on, was the red gem. A sudden gleam cast over its surface like the reflection of a passing light. The only light was the harsh bulbs of the arc lamps that hung along the wall.

His guard was asleep. A chair had been afforded him, and he slouched with his legs splayed to the center of the room, his head back, and a stream of nasal snores rose from his mouth. Colton had fallen asleep on the cold bars of his enclosed cell, but even he couldn't understand how his lone guard had managed it in that position.

Quietly, Colton got to his feet and checked his surroundings. The cell was like something he might've seen in a sheriff's office, sturdy and good at its job, but not the best in the business. That honour went to the honest-to-goodness prisons where the cells were built into thick concrete walls. This cell, like others he'd been in, was built on its own, an afterthought. Colton would've expected the castle to have a dungeon, but it didn't seem the Order were too interested in that aspect of recreation. Instead, they spent their time on altars and an underground oasis. Priorities.

He managed to give the door to his cell a slight jiggle

without making too much noise. It was loose, but it was locked and in place. He scoured the rest of the cell, top to bottom, but couldn't find any obvious weaknesses, nothing that he could exploit anyway. They hadn't left him much to fashion a makeshift weapon with, not even a bedroll or even some hay to make his stay more comfortable.

"Shit," Colton said under his breath and rubbed his bumped head. He caught a glimpse of the red gem out of the corner of his eye and turned from it completely. The only thing he could use was the guard.

The Order of Chthar were confident in their purpose, which was likely the reason he hadn't seen any real weapons while he was exploring the castle and why they had hidden or destroyed his guns. Just because he hadn't seen them didn't mean that they weren't there. Colton examined the sleeping guard. Though he was wearing the flowing robes of the Order, Colton could see the faint outline of something at the man's hip. It wasn't so obvious that Colton could tell if it were a gun or a knife (hell, it could've even been a flask of booze), but there was something there. Something was better than nothing.

"Hey," Colton said and jostled the cage door in its frame. "Hey, shit head."

The guard woke with a snort and gathered himself together in a quick, clumsy effort to look as though he'd been awake the whole time. Bleary-eyed, the guard looked at Colton with mild annoyance and confusion before he scrunched his face into something a little more serious.

"What?" he barked, straightening his robes.

"I need to take a piss," Colton said.

"So, take a piss." The guard sat in the chair and closed his eyes.

"You want me to piss on the floor? Or maybe you'd like me to piss on your boots?"

"That'll be the last thing you ever do."

"We'll see," Colton said and started to unbutton his jeans.

"Mister, you piss anywhere in my general direction, and you'll regret it." The guard stood and jabbed a finger at Colton.

"Yeah, yeah. What are you going to do? Give me another of your stern looks?"

"I'll do more than that." The guard reached to his hip and, after a moment of playing with the robe, pulled a six-shooter. A smile grew on his face.

"Okay, okay," Colton said and buttoned up. "You're a big man with a gun. I won't piss on your boots." The guard nodded and put the gun back in its holster. "Though, say I did. How would you explain the bullet in my head to Dr. Crane and Father Wallace?" Colton asked and nodded to the gem.

The guard's eyes widened some, and his mouth trembled.

"I got a feeling I could piss on your face, and you wouldn't do a god damn thing about it. What do you think?" Colton said and slid into the corner of his cage, a smile of his own cresting under his beard.

"There are other things…" the guard stammered.

"Save it, kid. I'm not going to piss on you or your boots. I'm just glad to know that someone around here knows the value of a good shooter in dire situations."

They settled into an uneasy silence. Colton could tell the guard had some more things he wanted to say, maybe get a threat or two out in the air to make himself feel better, but he didn't say anything. That was more wisdom than Colton had given him credit for.

In the silence, the presence of the gem grew. Colton didn't want to stare at it, didn't want to give it any attention. It was a strange thought, but that's the feeling he had. If he looked at the gem as it sat there on its little podium, he'd be giving it attention, giving it what it wanted. Wallace said that there had to be a connection made between the gem and the sacrifice. Could it be that Colton's dreams were the realization of that connection?

The gem was like a nightmare all to itself. It was like the fears children had. Fears that you didn't give in to, or they grew. There's no monster under the bed unless you look, and there it is, ready to devour you. There's no madman on the other side of the door, unless you look, and there he is, killing axe held high. Colton didn't want to look at the gem; the fear of it being something more than a shiny rock took root in his mind and began to grow. He noticed that the guard was doing the same, trying his best not to look at the gem, looking anywhere in the room but at the gem. Was it affecting him, too?

Colton tried his best, but in the end, the curiosity was too much. He tossed a quick glance at the stone and confirmed that it was still what it had always been, just a shiny rock sitting in its cradle, waiting. Still, even as Colton turned his gaze away, the image of Wallace shoving the gem into his mouth flashed in his mind.

The time was nearly at hand.

II

Colton had managed to fall into another fitful sleep, his back and behind aching because of it, but his mind was clearer. He had to ask himself how much sleep he had really been getting during his time as a guest of the Order of Chthar. His nights and days had seemed plagued by dreams and terrors, by feverish stumbling throughout the castle, whether he had been accompanied or not. At least this short nap wasn't interrupted by nightmares or, perhaps, premonitions.

His guard eyed him warily. The young man had taken to placing his hand on his gun whenever Colton had stirred. Colton had figured that opening the young fellow's eyes to the dangers of damaging the main course for Chthar might have dissuaded him from such action. Colton shrugged; it wasn't to be. Some people took the opposite meaning when you told them plain enough; you prepared for the worst.

"Mr. Colton," Wallace's honeyed voice broke through the shadowed hallway first, bringing the man along behind it. "It is almost time. How are you feeling?" Wallace was accompanied by three other men, Crane, Burns, and Parsons. Aside from the priest, none of them came across as chipper.

"I could use a bath, I suppose," Colton said and put his arms through the bars, leaning on them. "Otherwise, I'd say I'm doing tip top. You might even say that the fog has cleared. "

"I'm glad to hear it," the priest said with a smile. "Now, about this next part. We're here to take you to the preparation room and get you all sorted before the ritual begins. Are you going to come along with us, civil like, or…" Wallace trailed off and waved his hand at the men in the room.

"Now, that is a question," Colton said. "Will I go along to my own doom in a civil manner or not? Why don't you open the cage door and find out?"

Wallace frowned but nodded to the guard. The young man came forward, nervous. His hand held the butt of his revolver tight and only released it when he had to fish the keys from his robes. Colton backed into the cage and rolled up his sleeves.

The door popped open, and they came in. Colton was ready. Only one man could manage to get through the door at a time. The hefty Parsons came first, his shoulders dipping to the side to fit through. Colton rushed the man and knocked him back into the doorway, blocking the path of the others. For a minute or two, Colton held his own against the Order. Parsons was battered from both sides, Colton punching and kicking to keep him in place, and the Order members pushing against him to force their way in. It couldn't last, though, and Colton knew as much. All it took was a wild swing from Parsons. His ham-sized fist caught Colton on the temple and pushed him back into the cage. It was only a moment before Colton's legs stopped wobbling, but it was enough for the others to get in. From there, it took no time at all to sort Colton out and drag him from his cage.

Colton smiled and could feel the blood in his mouth coat his teeth. "Made you boys work for it though," he said and attempted a laugh that came out as a series of coughs.

"Someone shut him up," Crane said, holding his forehead.

Colton didn't see it, but he felt something hard bounce off the top of his head. Darkness swirled in front of his eyes, and he feared he might pass out. Before he did, he managed to shove what he had stolen from the ailing Parsons into his pocket.

"That all you got, junior?" Colton slurred.

"Jesus Christ, give me that thing," Burns said, and another blow landed on Colton's head. This time, he didn't have the time to think or pause. Colton fell into the darkness like a man dunked in water, all at once.

III

"Hurry up," a distant voice said, bringing Colton around. "The ceremony is due to start anytime now."

Colton's head hurt, a searing pain that tore across the crown of his head all the way to his eyes. He'd have more than a bump if he managed to survive any of this. His first instinct was to place his hand on his head, check for blood, and see what he needed to do to get himself fixed up. He managed to stop himself, keeping his eyes closed and remaining still.

"I know that, Gregory," Abigail Parsons said, followed by the sound of splashing water and her incredulous sigh. "I just haven't had to do this before. We've always had volunteers; they've just done this themselves."

"Dr. Crane was adamant. The body must be clean. This time more than the others,"

Gregory, who sounded like Colton's guard, said.

"'He's the final enticement to bring the Master unto us,' I know, I know," Abigail whined. "I just don't think I can do it."

"Goddamnit, Abby," Gregory said, and Colton could hear him pace along the stone floor. "All right, I'll undress him, and you wash him down. Deal?"

"But…"

"I'll be doing all the heavy lifting; you just have to give him a scrub."

"Fine," Abigail said in a huff. "If Jesse was thinking straight after your scuffle with *him*, he'd never have allowed his wife to wash down another man. Imagine."

"Yes, well, be that as it may, you were the first woman here. Aren't you all supposed to be motherly and matronly?"

"Just get him undressed," Abigail said.

The pacing stopped, and the footsteps moved toward Colton.

He wasn't sure of where he was or what he was lying on. Perhaps he was already in the garden, being prepped for the ceremony so that they wouldn't have to chance moving him again. He didn't think so, not by the stale smell that surrounded him. He was still inside the castle and not in the humid growth of the underground oasis.

"Come here, you bastard," Gregory said as he reached

Colton's side. The young guard grabbed two handfuls of Colton's shirt, twisted his torso to the side and began to unbutton it. Colton took the opportunity to let his free arm drop behind his back, his hand moving in quick but subtle movements to see if they'd found what he'd stolen.

"Jesus," Gregory said and undid the buttons on Colton's pants. "You owe me for this," he said under his breath.

Colton fought off a smile and let one of his eyes open a fraction. The room was blurred by his eyelashes, but the quick view he got was more than enough to prove his initial theory: he was still in the castle, and there was no one else in the room.

"Abby!" Gregory called across the room, "I'm going to need your help pulling off the pants."

"That's not part of the deal," Abigail said.

Colton sat up quickly. His free hand grabbed Gregory around the back of his neck while the other hand flicked open the pocketknife and brought the sharp edge to the man's jugular. "Deal or not," Colton said, "I think it would be in Greg's best interest if you made your way over here."

The room wasn't as large as Colton had imagined. It was smaller than the room he'd been given in the castle and only slightly larger than the cage he'd just been removed from. Colton sat on a wooden table, and there was a washbasin with a water pump in the corner of the room near where Abigail now stood, frozen. There was one window, not as small as the one in his previous room but still showing signs that the storm raged on outside. The room was lit by four torches, one in each corner.

"Kill him then," Abigail said after a pause. She drew her mouth up into a hesitant smile, but her eyes weren't going to hold up to that lie.

Colton tried to return the smile, but his head was spinning. The pain from his headache had worsened when he leapt into action, the speedy ascent sending everything askew. His mind, unsure of what was happening, played against him and set his stomach to doing backflips. Bile threatened to fill his throat and mouth.

"Abby," Gregory started but held fast when Colton pressed the blade into his neck.

"Listen, girl," Colton said. "Me and Greg here go way back. I know that he has a gun riding on his hip; it's probably what was used to knock me out. I can kill him, sure. You might think that would give you enough time to run away and go get help. Well, you might outrun me, but you won't outrun a bullet. So, it's up to you. I kill him, then I kill you, or you come here, and we'll have a little discussion about what happens next."

Guiding Gregory with the knife, Colton made room and managed to slide off the table. His legs weren't steady, but if he leaned his hip against the table, he could fake it. Abigail watched, her eyes flitting back and forth between them and the door just to her side. She was going to make a run for it.

"Goddamnit," Colton said through gritted teeth, and before she could move, he brought his elbow to Gregory's nose and threw the knife at the door. It wasn't a throwing knife, and it wasn't good for much of anything, if Colton was to be honest, save for whittling a stick or cutting up soft food. Still, the sight of a knife coming at you often stops you in your tracks. Colton figured it was the shock of it all. Anyone who'd regularly had bullets or arrows shot at them wouldn't have stopped so quickly, but Abigail Parsons, with her vast array of furs and skins, her meticulously done makeup, and aversion to any manual labor, was not accustomed to that and she froze not two steps from where she'd started.

The knife proved to be as useless as Colton had anticipated, and it struck a wall with a thud before it fell to the floor and out of consequence. Or perhaps it was Colton's addled mind that made the knife throw useless, it didn't matter. Colton had used the opportunity to slip Gregory's gun from his hip as he fell to the floor, grabbing his nose. Colton had it pointed at Abigail, her eyes wide with surprise and more than a little fear.

"Now," Colton said, trying to rub the bleariness from his eyes with one hand. "If you'd be so kind as to join young Gregory over here, we won't need to engage in any more unpleasantness."

Abigail dropped her chin, defeated, and nodded her assent before she took slow steps toward Colton. Once there, she followed his directions in helping Gregory to take Colton's place on the table, his nose running freely with blood, his eyes already swelling shut.

"I think he broke my nose," Gregory said through cupped hands. Abigail didn't respond, she only flashed a quick glance at Colton.

"What do you want?" she said.

Colton leaned against the table and closed his eyes tightly for a moment. The afterimage of the light in the room danced across his eyelids in the darkness, but it danced in red. "I want to get out of this castle, get away from you people."

"You can't."

"I can try." Colton held up the gun and gave it a shake.

"No, you can't. It won't let you." Abigail said slowly, as if she were talking to a child.

"I get out of this castle, get my horse, and we'll make it through the storm. We've seen worse."

Abigail laughed a horrible, mocking laughter that felt like nails running over a chalkboard. "You still don't get it. There is no storm. Hasn't been since the first night you arrived. It's the gem. It won't let you leave."

CHAPTER NINE

I

"The gems, all of them, have been a part of the Order of Chthar since its creation," Abigail said. She hadn't been eager to tell the story, but Colton had persuaded her. It was remarkable what holding a gun in front of a person's face would encourage them to do.

"Our founder, Louis Cardinal, found them embedded in stone in the depths of a mountain. The same mountain that would eventually become the base for this castle."

"Embedded?" Colton said. "Like veins of gold? Silver?"

"No. The story goes that old Louis found them embedded like a gem in the socket of a ring. It seemed too good to be true, but Louis wasn't a man to turn his nose up at the opportunity. It was only after he removed the first stone that he realized what he had found.

"Once he came in contact with the gem, it started to change him, giving him visions. If the stories are correct, he envisioned everything that we have here: the castle, the people, the wealth. He foresaw success and with it the rise of Chthar, our master. Some would say that he even had a vision of you, Colton."

"Crane? Wallace?"

"Maybe," Abigail said and applied a damp cloth to Gregory's nose. "It wasn't long before Louis gathered others, helped them see the power contained within the gems, the strength of Chthar and what he offered. My great-great-grandfather was one of those founding members, and the reason why I'm here."

"How did Cardinal escape the influence of the gem?"

Abigail smiled. "And here I thought you just wanted to know more about Chthar."

"Fine, tell me about Chthar and then tell me how Cardinal escaped."

Abigail's smile soured. "We don't know what Chthar is besides a god and our master. Some of our scholars have thought of him as the antithesis to the Christian God. Instead of a creator, a destroyer. Instead of a shepherd, a wolf. Others have postulated that he may not be of this world. Those people, as smart as they are, believe that Chthar fell to earth riding on a star, and what Cardinal found was the remnants of that star still surging with the power of the master."

Colton shook his head. His eyes darted towards the window where snow slapped the glass and wind howled. If Abigail was right, how long had he been under the spell of the gem? Had the gem already drawn him into it before he ever arrived? Had there ever been a storm he had to ride through? The thoughts made his palms itch, and the urge to put the gun to good use rose like bile at the back of his throat.

Abigail's false smile faced him when he turned his attention back to her. "As for Cardinal, he wrote or dictated the specific rites over the coming days and weeks. Some claim he lived for years, but no one can say for sure. The visions he suffered from guided his hand and words, and he managed to encase all our rituals in a single book. Did he escape the hold of the gemstone? I'm sorry to tell you, Colton, but he didn't," she said with a feigned sadness. "You see, after having just about all the traditions copied down, he said that there was one more that needed to be witnessed before it could be written. He was our first sacrifice, Colton. He gave himself up, gemstone embedded in his heart."

Colton tried not to give any indication of his emotions to Abigail Parsons, so he stood there and blinked at her, the gun trained on her guts. If she were telling the truth, was he really damned to die by the will of some sparkling rock?

Abigail must have misread his expression for interest and sputtered onward. "They say that with Louis Cardinal's death, the first sacrifice of Chthar, the Disciple sprang forth. The records say that he dragged his way up through the gem itself, like it was some sort of red doorway from another world. I know the rights of it, though. It was my kin that was there when Cardinal died, and he said that the Disciple tore itself out of Cardinal's body. It stood above the Order members, covered in strings of gore and dripping with blood. One body for another. The Order of Chthar is based on this sort of dreadful symmetry. It's how Cardinal saw it, and it was how it was written. You know what that means, right?"

Colton squinted his eyes and cocked the hammer of the pistol. "It means that when I die, Chthar is going to rise up from me, tear me asunder and come into the world bloody."

"Alpha and omega," Abigail said with a smile.

"The beginning and the end," Gregory added, his voice muffled by the damp rag.

"As it was prophesied, so shall it be," Abigail removed Gregory's rag and dumped it in the wash basin again, ringing it out, freshening it up.

"No," Colton said after a moment. "I don't believe in an inescapable fate, in some preordained life set down by creatures with too much power and not enough sense."

"Louis Cardinal's records would disagree with you,"

Abigail shrugged.

"Tell me, Mrs. Parsons, do you believe in the prophecy?"

"I do."

"Have you read any of Cardinal's records?

"Some, yes. His predictions for the future are remarkable."

"And did it say anywhere in those records that two members of Chthar were going to be captured on the day of the final ritual?" Colton jabbed the gun in the air.

"N-no, but he didn't need to be so specific..."

"And what about a premonition about the final sacrifice, murdering those same two members? Was that in there anywhere?"

Abigail stared at Colton with wide eyes. "Please," she said, handing the rag back to Gregory, whose swollen eyes were also drawn to Colton but more readily to his former weapon.

"Well then," Colton said, "I guess that Mr. Cardinal didn't have all the answers after all. Why don't we three have some fun and really spoil his plans for the rest of the day, shall we?"

II

Abigail led them through the basement towards the underground altar. Colton could smell the sweet scent of death and rot getting stronger as they approached, and though he could already feel the growing humidity, a shiver ran down his spine.

Before they left the preparation room, Colton donned a set of the Order's pale-yellow robes and pulled up his hood. He made sure that Gregory followed suit.

"Just know," he said, pointing the gun barrel at them both, "that if we do this correctly, if there are no problems at all, I won't kill you." He let his eyes fall on Abigail's thin face. "If you do anything to give me away, I won't hesitate to kill you first. You understand?"

They did.

There were no guards posted anywhere, no members of the Order ambling around the castle in last-minute haste to make final preparations. It was just Colton and his two hostages, their footsteps echoing in the empty castle. Even though they were in the basement, Colton could still hear the storm. The wind roared the snow into a swirling cyclone of rage, flailing against the stone walls. He had no reason to trust the word of Abigail Parsons about the effects of the gem, and he was sure that even if he wasn't in a situation such as this, a person like Abigail would surely twist her words to cause him as much pain as possible. That being as it was, Wallace had said that the gem had been bonding with him, feeding off him like a parasite.

Colton didn't know much about parasites, but he knew a bit about rabies. When an animal was rabid, its entire personality might change. A calm, obedient dog might turn into an angry son of a bitch that tried to bite anything and everything. Maybe that's what the gem was doing to Colton. Instead of making him angry, it was making him see things that weren't there. Protecting itself and its motivations by causing hallucinations, just like a rabid animal was apt to bite to pass along the disease.

He shook his head. The machinations of what was happening around him were more than Colton could figure out. What he did know was that if the gem were really causing him to see things that weren't there, then destroying the damn thing would put a stop to it. Or at least that's what he hoped. There was only one way to test out that theory.

They ducked into the tunnel and broke through into the underground garden. A cold, eerie green light hung over everything, and the plants and trees swayed despite there being no wind. Voices carried from behind the trees, a deep chant of words Colton couldn't quite understand. What he could hear sounded like a bastardized version of the Latin he'd learned as a child, but it was more guttural. It was a cruel imitation of his last dream. Perhaps the gem did offer up visions of the future.

Colton had arranged them in a line, Abigail and Colton on either side, with Gregory in the middle pretending to be the sacrifice. Abigail was a step ahead of them and led them to the stone path and into the clearing. He sighed in relief when he saw a path that didn't require him to come in contact with the sludge that hung from the vegetation that grew here. The memory of the gelatinous gray matter still twisted up his stomach.

At the end of the path, surrounding the altar, was the Order. There were more than Colton had expected, and from his count, at least two more women joined the ranks alongside Abigail. Wallace had been telling the truth about the membership after all.

Colton could feel Gregory tense under his grip. He made sure to click the gun's hammer in place to keep him quiet and shot a murderous glance towards Abigail. She didn't return the gaze.

"It's about damn time," Crane said from behind the altar, and made a show of closing his pocket watch. "The ritual is supposed to start in just five minutes."

Colton turned another hooded gaze to Abigail.

"He still has some spirit left in him. I expect you boys didn't get him as good as you thought," she said with a coy smile. A gruff chuckle came from beside Colton, and Jesse Parsons stepped forward, his eyes blackened, his nose crooked, and scratches along his face and arms.

"Spirit is one way to put it," the big man said and made to step toward Gregory, the false Colton.

"Mr. Parsons," Wallace said with unnerving calmness.

"I think enough damage has been done to the Master's prize, don't you?" He stepped from behind Crane and waved the three of them forward. Parsons cracked his knuckles and stood there for another moment before stepping back with a scowl.

Abigail took Gregory's other arm, and the three of them made their way onto the altar. Just as Colton's foot landed on it, a chittering sounded above them. Colton froze and fought the urge to look up lest he reveal his face or knock his hood off. The chittering petered off into a slow clicking and a thunderous clap of wings as the Disciple landed on one of the stone pillars at the back of the altar. It squatted there on its thick legs, its red eyes surveying the Order until it spread its wings in a flourish.

"Come, Gregory," Abigail grunted and pulled the young guard ahead with her, which, in turn, pulled Colton. It jostled him enough to turn his eyes away from the lights he saw within the Disciple's wings and move ahead with the others.

"Has he made a decision about placement?" Crane asked, stepping back to allow them closer to the altar. Once he moved, Colton caught a glimpse of the red gem, displayed on a pillar of stone, cupped in the black box he'd seen on his first visit to the garden. Colton heard the raging storm, but he didn't dare turn away from the stone. Instead, he had the feeling that the stone itself was staring back at him.

"He refused," Abigail said. "But I think we should just jam it into his big, stupid skull. Really make sure the Master is getting his money's worth." This brought on some chuckles from the crowd. Colton moved in time with the two others, never taking his eyes from the jewel. It called out to him, a desperate yearning, but not of love nor lust. It was something deeper, more primal than anything Colton had ever felt. It was like a pleasure-laced hunger. Colton's head became light, his heart and breathing slowed, and he felt as though he were going to swoon like ladies did in plays and novels. And yet, his body clenched, his muscles tightened as though in preparation for a fight.

"Gregory?" a voice said, but Colton couldn't place it, didn't care. He moved to the gem.

More voices assailed him, but Colton ignored them. He was vaguely aware that he had released the real Gregory, that his free hand was reaching for the gemstone. He could feel hands grabbing him, trying to hold him back. He felt the gun jump in his other hand, something hot and wet dousing it and his face. His hood had been removed at some point, but none of that mattered. It didn't matter because the jewel was finally in his hand. Its sharp edges and smooth surfaces were warm against his skin, as if it were welcoming home a long-lost lover; it embraced him.

The storm raged.

CHAPTER TEN

I

The sitting room was dark. The torches had been lit, but they emitted a strange light that did little to brighten and instead covered everything in a red hue.

Colton sat on the sofa, a glass of whiskey in his hand. The gun was gone, so were the robes. Instead, he sat upon the couch completely naked. He didn't feel exposed, nor did he feel the anxiety of finding yourself in such a situation. He was calm, comfortable.

Across from him, in the two armchairs that stood before the fireplace, were Abigail Parsons and Samuel Wallace. They each had a cup of tea, coupled with a matching saucer, and neither of them was naked. In fact, they were dressed in elegant evening wear, the priest in a tuxedo complete with a bowtie, and Abigail in a long red dress that exposed her shoulders and cleavage.

"Mr. Colton," Wallace said with a slight bow of his head. "Welcome."

Colton raised his glass. "Father Wallace, you've shed your priestly attire."

"Not much need of it, anymore." The priest smiled and took a sip of his tea. From somewhere in the distance, Colton could hear the ticking of a clock.

"What am I doing here?" Colton asked. "I thought we were supposed to be attending the ceremony."

"All in due time," Wallace said.

"It's time you made some decisions, Colton," Abigail said.

"What kind of decisions?" The clock continued to tick in the background, joining the rush of the storm. "Do you hear that?" Colton asked, looking over his shoulder.

"Don't worry about that," Abigail said. "Worry about your choices."

"Such as," Wallace broke in, "do you accept our Lord and Master into your heart?"

The ticking echoed in the halls, magnifying its noise, making it deeper. "I've been baptized if that's what you mean."

"Will you serve him in the Never? Be his source of life?"

Wind smashed against the stone walls surrounding him, and the torchlight danced and flickered. The ticking crashed around him. "The Never?" Colton turned in his seat and stared out into the dark maw that was the castle. There was nothing there, only a long and empty space—a void.

"Will you rejoice in the torment of his will? Suffer in his pleasure?" Abigail and Wallace spoke together now, their voices as one. The ticking pressed onward, shaking the stone at Colton's feet. The cold of the storm clawed at his bare skin. A door had been opened.

Colton fell back in his seat. "Don't you hear that? Feel it?"

Before him, Abigail and Wallace were gone along with their chairs. In their place sat a bulbous, sagging creature, its glutinous mouth hanging open in a slack grimace. Its face was at once Abigail and Wallace, their features muddled and mixed together in frightening and grotesque movements and undulations.

"Will you be the feces for his engorgement? The lather for his deceptions?" the creature growled, not in Abigail or Wallace's voice but in both at the same time.

Colton tried to push himself back, but the void had reached him, the ticking clock thunderous now while snow began crawling up his legs, gripping at his knees.

"Will you die so that he can live?" the creature shouted and pushed itself toward Colton, crawling with four mismatched hands.

The room around him had fallen darker, a deeper crimson. Colton looked into the void once more and saw that it was a swirling pit of blood that frothed in its intensity. Within it, he could see writhing tentacles slashing out, reaching for him.

The creature that had been Abigail and Wallace latched onto Colton, grabbing his legs and arms. He could feel its oozing flesh wrap around him, suck him into it, and crawl up his body.

"Do you accept him?" they groaned.

Colton fought against the creature's grip, attempting to pull away from it and break free, but it was impossible. It was like he was sinking in mud, drowning in shallow water. The more he fought, the quicker it climbed his body, tendrils of its flesh reaching for his mouth, his eyes.

"Will you…"

"No!" Colton yelled and tore at the viscous flesh that threatened to invade his mouth. It was no use; the creature had already claimed him. It drew him down into it, drowning him, suffocating him. In his final moments, within the creature, the flesh attacking him and digesting him, he opened his eyes, and all he saw was red.

CHAPTER ELEVEN

I

"Quick, get the stone," Crane said, and hands fell upon Colton, pulling and tugging.

Colton was lying face down on the stone predella, a dull ache running along the left side of his face, the familiar taste of blood in his mouth. He rose with the grabbing hands, his vision spinning with the sudden movement, his head rolling to his shoulders.

"Get him on the altar," Wallace said. "Time is running out."

He was pulled forward, the altar just a few feet away. Just beyond it, members of the Order of Chthar started to move in close, wanting to get a better look at their faith coming to fruition. They started to chant in their obscene language.

"No," Colton said and raged out at the arms that held him, that dragged him forward. He still had the jewel in his hand and could feel its sharp edges digging into his palm. It was warm, comfortable. In his other hand, something cold, but familiar. He pointed the gun at the nearest person on his side and fired.

With a howl, someone dropped. The rest of the hands receded. He swayed but managed to catch himself on the altar. Colton turned and stared at his assailants. Crane, Wallace, Parsons and his wife, Abigail, Burns. They all stared at him with a mixture of fear and hatred.

"Put it down, Colton," Wallace said with only a twinge of fear souring his voice. "This is a foregone conclusion, it's been written."

"No, it hasn't. Just up to a few days ago, it was you who was supposed to you standing in my shoes," Colton said and steadied himself. "Besides, did your prophecy say anything about the final sacrifice shooting up your ritual, your Order?"

"Shooting dear Gregory is unfortunate, but it won't stop what is going to happen tonight. Right now, nothing you say or do will stop the Master from rising."

"What about this?" Colton said and threw the red gem onto the hard stone floor. A gallery of moans rose over the clearing, and from above, the Disciple cried out a horrendous bellow of pain and frustration. Even through all of that, Colton could hear the splashing of water from the pool that stood behind the altar. In his peripheral vision, he could see things writhing in the darkness above where the pool had been.

For all of his strength and bravado, the gem did not break. Colton had hoped it would but hadn't counted on it. What he had intended was to distract the Order. He had four bullets left, and before him stood five people. Sure, there were more Order members, but they hadn't tortured him. Hadn't played with his mind. A smile cracked his beard.

Colton pointed the gun at Wallace, his finger squeezing the trigger, when he felt thick limbs wrap around his waist and toss him toward the back of the predella. His shot went off, but he didn't see if it landed. Another terrible screech shouted overhead, and the Disciple took flight, its wings thunderous in the underground Altar.

Colton slid under a tall column, the water sloshing just over the edge he'd landed next to. He rolled to his stomach in time to see Parsons throw a kick with murderous intent. It landed at his side and sent air fleeing from his lungs. Colton aimed the gun, but Parsons slapped it away from him with a meaty hand before he grabbed two hand-fuls of Colton's shirt. The gun tumbled close to the edge of the predella, the water behind it even more restless.

With a knee to Parson's groin, Colton scurried to-wards the gun. His fingertips just on the handle, Parsons grabbed it away from him. A smile now on the big man's mangled face, he aimed.

Colton saw the tentacles rise from the water be-low, but Parsons was blissfully unaware until they had wrapped themselves around his thick body. They were oily, greasy-looking things, each wriggling like a snake. Parsons dropped the gun and screamed a strange, high-pitched scream before the tentacles dragged him into the water, tearing at him as it did.

Grabbing the gun once more, Colton turned back to the Order. They were in disarray. The Disciple was amongst them, tossing whomever or whatever passed in front of him. Searching for the gem, Colton thought. He was pleased to see that many of the Order had begun to flee the scene, shedding their yellow robes as they went. Those who remained were bent forward, scrambling around the altar, attempting to find the missing jewel, Wallace among them.

It was Burns who first noticed him coming, the stout man stepping forward with his fists clenched. Colton re-membered Burns sitting outside his door, guiding him to the sitting room, all the while ensuring Colton's mind and body were poisoned by the gem, the castle. The gun bucked in his hand.

Crane's head popped up at the sound, his spectacles bouncing on his nose. He backed away from Colton and stumbled over the stone floor. Colton remembered his prescription of meadowsweet, all to keep Colton calm and exposed to the gem and its effects. The gun fired again.

Abigail stopped her searching and stood tall. Her eyes festered with hatred towards Colton, her lips pursed in a scowl. She didn't flee, nor did she intend to. She simply stared Colton down, daring him to shoot her next. Colton's hand squeezed around the gun, and he thought of Abigail preparing him for his death. Still, he hesitated, and then it was too late.

Brandishing the gem in one of its hooked feet, the Disciple landed between Colton and his prey, its wings spread wide. They encompassed the whole room, their utter blackness, the complete void of light, until spots of brightness began to appear upon the surface, stars in an endless night sky.

Everything became muted, the colours of the trees greyed, the ache in Colton's side numbed, and the screams of the Order faded away. All that mattered was there in front of him, the night sky with its alien constellations. Colton focused on the little motes of light, his eyes guiding him past the darkness through a swirling purple energy, an endless rainbow of rocks and stars that merely floated over the dark. The purple swirls slashed across star and sky, twisted amongst rock and light, swallowing them whole in their magnificence. Like tendrils of energy, tentacles of some great beast, they engulfed everything they touched, destroying whatever was in their wake. They were beautiful and horrible, and they twisted toward Colton.

One last shot rang out in the under garden. A screech rose from the Disciple as it fell away with a fresh hole in its wing. Colton staggered back, the gun falling to the ground with a clatter. On the ground before him was the gem, still in pristine condition, light gleaming off its surface like an eye that stared straight into Colton's soul.

"Get the jewel," Wallace called out, and his arms

wrapped around Colton's body, dragging him to the ground. The priest put all of his weight atop Colton, held him in place, and kept him still.

Colton, still stunned, thrashed under Wallace, bucked his hips to knock the other man off balance and throw him to the floor.

"Got it," Abigail shouted and ran forward. The gem gleaming in her hand, she knelt next to Colton, her eyes wide and frightened, tears running down her cheeks.

"Jab it into his skull," Wallace grunted. "We need to finish this now." Somewhere behind him, Colton could hear the sloshing of water, could hear something heavy and fleshy slapping against stone.

Abigail crawled closer to Colton and, with two hands on the gem, raised it into the air above her head. Colton still fought with Wallace, but the priest held on tight, hands locked behind Colton's back.

As Abigail brought the stone down toward Colton's face, he bucked his hips one more time and used his arms to push the priest further up on his chest. There was a scream of pain and a sudden gasp. The priest's grip relaxed enough for Colton to shimmy away. The gem was in the priest's shoulder, blood oozing from where it had pierced the skin. It didn't go deep, though. The shoulder blade had blocked it from doing that. Abigail screamed and raised her hands to her face.

Without thinking, Colton pulled the gem from Wallace's shoulder. With a quick snap, he brought the flat part of the stone down upon Wallace's head in a glancing blow that stopped his moving about.

"I didn't give anything away," Abigail whispered.

Colton looked at the woman, his tired, stinging eyes questioning her.

"You said that if I didn't tell anyone about your switching with Gregory, you wouldn't kill us. I didn't give anything away. It was you, not me."

Colton looked down at the rock in his hand, and a familiar thrum of energy ran through it and into the rest of his body. It was comforting, and Colton almost smiled. But there was blood on this stone, more than what Wallace had just painted it with. It had been responsible for so much pain and agony, almost two hundred years' worth. Abigail and her family, her ilk, had been using this stone and its kin to serve their own purposes, to gain power, respect, and money. In return, they provided it with death and ceremony, a life everlasting.

"Run," Colton said and sat back on his heels. "Run and don't come back." Abigail sat for a moment longer, looking between Colton and the jewel, tears still flooding her eyes. Maybe the gem drew in everyone, Colton thought. Or maybe, the bastard knew its final preparations were not to come to fruition, and it wanted to give itself another option.

She must have seen some change come over Colton's features, because Abigail took a sharp inhalation of breath and ran back towards the castle. Colton slumped to the ground, his breath coming heavy and laboured. The overwhelming feeling to close his eyes and go to sleep assailed him, but he managed to stave it off for the time being. Soon, he said to himself.

The chittering sounded to his right and gave him an idea of what was about to happen, even if he did have the energy to get up and run. The Disciple climbed upon the altar one more time. It tried to spread both of its wings, but shimmering black blood oozed from the bullet hole, and it was forced to stop with just one. With an undulated clicking, the beast moved forward, stalking Colton and the gem.

His limbs tired, his mind weary, Colton pulled himself away from the creature. Even while holding the gem, his hands did most of the work. The Disciple saw this, turned its head, and followed.

The sound of flesh slamming against rock got closer, and Colton risked a quick look over his shoulder. Blood spattered the stone podiums, tiny remnants of skin and muscle crunched under his hands. The altar was being destroyed, and Colton would soon have to choose between the Disciple and the tentacled fiend to compose his end.

The Disciple shrieked and ran forward, eager to be done with all of this.

Colton moved to the edge of the predella, could hear the rise in tenacity of the tentacles that flailed in the water. One of the tentacles smashed the ground next to Colton, sensing the presence of something warm, perhaps, or even the jewel itself.

He twitched away from the tentacle, but the large, clawed foot of the Disciple drove down upon his chest. Colton tried to bring his free hand up to push the foot away, but before he could, a heavy tentacle wrapped itself around his arm and pulled.

More tentacles rose from the water, slapping along the surface all around Colton and the Disciple. Colton's head was filled with the thuds of the tentacles lashing out, the triumphant screaming of the Disciple, but something else sounded below all that. A deep, thunderous bellow; a cry of rage and agony and hatred. Chthar roared.

The Disciple turned its head and let its red eyes land on the gem in Colton's hand. Its inhuman face relaxed into what Colton figured was the closest thing the creature could manage as a smile. It hooked one of its wings toward the jewel, chittering all the while. The tentacles weren't satisfied with only Colton's arm, however, and they slashed up and over the precipice, catching hold of the Disciple. The creature's eyes went wide as tentacles wrapped around its wings, neck and body, and it screamed its opposition even as it was dragged down into the depths of the pool.

Without the Disciple's weight keeping him in place, the tentacle that had latched onto Colton twisted and squeezed Colton's arm, readying for one final pull to drag him down after the Disciple. With only one recourse left to him, Colton brought the jewel down upon the tentacle, stabbing it with the sharp end over and over. Chthar's pained bellow rose over the under garden, shaking the trees and bushes, knocking over the altar and anything else that wasn't firmly rooted. The pillars that stood at the edge of the pool, above Colton, began to sway and topple.

Hurt, the tentacle retracted from Colton's arm, and he managed to roll away from the debris that fell all around him. More roars echoed in the underground oasis as more tentacles were trapped under stone pillars and archways. Rock from the ceiling fell, splashing into the pool and crashing into trees. The eerie luminescence of the garden darkened, threatening to die out.

"You must finish the ritual," Wallace said in a breathy, halted voice. Colton looked to his left and saw Wallace lying under the altar, the heavy stone it had been made of pressing down on his torso.

"It's done," Colton said and waved his hand at the wreckage that continued to fall all around them.

"No." Wallace smiled, blood leaking from the corner of his mouth. "The ritual, the gem, it requires blood. Chthar requires death. You will never have peace."

"Why don't you take it then?" Colton shoved the jewel into Wallace's face.

"Look at your hand shake, even now, presented with an easy way out, you can't bear to part with the gem. No, Colton, it must be you. It was always you." Wallace tried to move, but all he managed was to cry out in more pain.

"The gem requires blood," Colton whispered and turned the gem over in his hand. "Chthar requires death." Could he live his life with the jewel on his back? With that temptation following him, with hallucinations plaguing his every living moment, awake or asleep. He could end it, kill himself with the gem and not have to worry anymore. Not about the gem, not about anything. He would release Chthar upon the world, and others would have to suffer the torment he'd suffered with the Order of Chthar. Worse.

Colton sighed. He remembered the paintings of former sacrifices, their gems penetrating their vital organs. The image of one in particular came to mind as he rolled the jewel around in his hands, his fingers.

With the under garden falling around him, Colton brought the gem to his right eye and slowly inserted it. The pain was excruciating. He couldn't remember if he screamed or cried or both. The only thing that was certain was the pain. The hurt.

When he was done, he fell to the predella and faded into a red-tinged darkness, Wallace's laughter plaguing his ears.

CHAPTER TWELVE

I

When he woke, the garden was silent. The groans of the Under God had quieted, the splashing water sat still, and no rocks fell from above. Everything was calm.

Colton's pain remained. He couldn't see out of his right eye, not that he expected that he would. All the same, the magic gem could've had magic healing powers. He shook his head. It hurt.

Wallace was dead. The altar had done the job, squeezing the air out of him, likely crushing his spine and ribs in the process. A small pool of blood had formed around his mouth, his eyes wide open and terrified. He remembered Wallace's laughter as the gem slid into Colton's eye socket. Perhaps the fear came soon after when Wallace realized that Colton wasn't dead. That he had given his blood to the jewel, but not his life to Chthar.

Colton wiped at his cheek, and his hand came away bloody. The gem didn't want all his blood.

II

Escaping the garden was slow going. The debris that had fallen during Chthar's rage made for an obstacle course that Colton, in his condition, wasn't up for. Even walking with only one good eye was a challenge, hurdling boulders and fallen trees was something that would take time. Besides, Colton knew more than one soldier who had returned from the war with one less eye, arm, leg, what-have-you, and they managed to adjust to their condition. It would take time, but Colton had plenty of that.

The castle was brighter than he remembered. Windows were bright with sunlight, and the sky appeared to be clear. Some torches were lit, and they helped, too. As for the remaining members of the Order, there was no sign of them. That was a good thing. Colton didn't think he could fight. He'd just give up and die.

Death: That was an interesting subject now. The gem required blood; Chthar required death. Well, he gave the gem blood, and it seemed to work out, but every man dies. Sure, Colton might make it for a few more years, but he'd die all the same. Would that be all Chthar needed? Even by natural causes? Colton sighed and let his fingers probe his cheek and eye around the jewel. He was too tired to think about it right now. All he could do was hope that he did the right thing.

There was a path of snow beaten down in front of the castle, a stampede of Order members reeling for escape. Colton looked to the window that he and Parsons had jumped from, had slid down from. The snow wasn't that tall. If they had jumped, they would've likely been injured in some heinous way. Was it all a hallucination?

The doors to the barn were left open, addled hoofprints were scattered in all directions, seeking escape. The barn was as he remembered, even though he wasn't so sure that he had visited it during his stay, but it was empty. The silence was hollow, full of echoes and little else. The scent of horse lingered in the air, and it drew Colton inside.

It was dark in there; the sun couldn't breach the dusty windows except in thin rays that spotlighted the dirt floor randomly. It was enough, and the dark soothed his head anyway. He made his way around the barn, looking for anything useful. He managed to find an old saddle, and with the switchblade he'd stolen from Parsons, went to work cutting off a strip of leather. That done, he wrapped his head with a makeshift eyepatch. It wouldn't do to bring that much attention to himself. Besides, he didn't want any half-witted thief planning on gouging out the gem while he slept.

There wasn't much else of use in the barn, though he did find a small fur blanket. Probably bear or wolf, though he didn't take the time to study it, and didn't much care. He slipped it over his shoulders and left.

Colton hadn't walked more than a mile when he heard the pounding of hooves on snow. It came from behind, the direction of the castle. He ducked into the woods, huddled behind a bush, and waited. A familiar black horse rode past at a trot, riderless.

He let out a loud whistle that stopped Bill in his tracks. The horse turned and walked back with a series of neighs and whinnies. Colton met the beast on the road and embraced its massive head. Bill nuzzled into the man's chest, stomped its hoof, and snorted.

"Sorry, Bill. I had some things to work out," Colton said and rubbed the horse's neck. "'Bout time for us to get a move on though, what do you say?" Colton pulled himself up into the saddle.

They rode down the trail, the horse almost giddy in his trot and speed. Colton smiled despite himself and pulled the blanket tighter around his shoulders, the jewel in his eye little more than an itch. One that he wanted to scratch.

ACKNOWLEDGEMENTS

As always, many thanks to my wife, Ashlee, who has always and will always be my alpha reader. Her support and encouragement have been a draft of cold water in a hot desert. You are the reason I continue to do what I do. Another special thank you to my mother and father for their unyielding support of my writing from an early age.

I would also like to thank my closest friends, Steve Power, Jon Mercer, and Kevin Woolridge, for reading what I give them and helping me pick it apart for what it's worth. Without their input and patience, I'm not sure I'd be writing today.

Thanks to Brad Dunne and Paul Carberry, Matthew LeDrew and Ellen Curtis, Peter Foote, The Dead South, Graham Plowman, and a long list of many others who have helped me along the way.

Cheers,
Jon Dobbin

Jon Dobbin is an award winning author living in the St. John's, Newfoundland metro region.

He is a father of three, the husband to an amazing wife, an educator, and a tattoo and beard enthusiast.

Dobbin's work has appeared in the all four *Terror Nova* novels, *Chillers from the Rock*, *Dystopia from the Rock*, *Pulp Science-Fiction from the Rock*, *From the Rock Stars*, and, *Kit Sora: The Artobiography* collections. In 2019 he released his first novel, *The Starving*.

The Hallowed is his fourth novel with Engen Books.

www.ingramcontent.com/pod-product-compliance
Lightning Source LLC
Chambersburg PA
CBHW011420010726
47494CB00011B/2422